Seek and Destroy

Seek and Destroy

Alan Evans

Walker and Company
New York

All the characters in this book are fictitious and any resemblance to a real person is purely coincidental. But *Seahorse* and *Flying-Fish* are based on real craft that carried out operations in the First World War similar to those described in this book. And an Austrian torpedo-boat, No 11, deserted to Italy on 5th October 1917 after the mutiny of her Slavonic crew.

oz edition

First published in the United States of America in 1986 by the Walker Publishing Company, Inc.

Published simultaneously in Canada by John Wiley & Sons Canada, Limited, Rexdale, Ontario.

Library of Congress Cataloging-in-Publication Data

Evans, Alan, 1930–
  Seek and destroy!

  Reprint. Originally published: Seek out and destroy!
London : Hodder and Stoughton, 1982.
  1. World War, 1914-1918--Fiction.   1. Title.
PR6055.V1354   1986   823'.914   86-15739
ISBN 0-8027-0928-1

Printed in the United States of America

10 9 8 7 6 5 4 3 2 1

My thanks to the staffs of the National Maritime Museum, Imperial War Museum, Public Records Office, and Walton-on-Thames Library.

- Admiral Massimiliano Marandino, Commander C.F.E. Cocchi and staff of Ufficio Storico Marina Militare, Rome.
- Museo Sacrario della Bandiere della Marina Militare, Rome, who hold Rizzo's MAS boat 15.
- Admiral Gottardi, Signor Ramelli and Chief Petty Officer Gottardo of the Museo Storico Navale, Venice.
- The Marciana Museum, Venice.
- Dott. Ing. Artu Chiggiato and Aldo Fraccaroli.
- The Naval Attaché at the British Embassy, Rome, and the British Consul, Venice.
- Dorde Mirkovic and the staff of the library at Pola now Pula.
- Gianna Marchesi.

But, as always, any mistakes are mine!

Contents

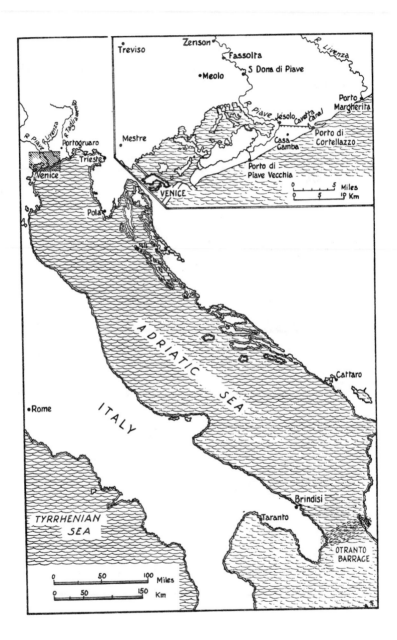

8

Prologue

In 1915 Italy joined the Allies and was plunged into war against Austria. They fought on the mountain frontier where the Alpine peaks rose ten thousand feet. After more than two years and eleven battles the Italians had gained little at a large cost and halted on the defensive.

In the autumn of 1917 the Austrians were ready to attack. The Austrian build-up took a month and 2400 trainloads of supplies and ammunition, and the German High Command sent the Fourteenth Army of six divisions under General von Below to spearhead their attack. They looked with hungry eyes beyond the mountains to Venice and the Venetian Plain, but the real prize could be the defeat of Italy itself. Then the Austrian army would be free to hammer at the French back door, a France already drained and weakened by the bloodbath of Verdun and the mutiny in the army in 1917.

1 Seek and Destroy!

HM Light Cruiser *Dauntless* eased her battered frame through the night at a cautious ten knots. Her captain, Commander David Cochrane Smith, stood on her torn bridge and thought the November darkness was kind to her, hiding the ravages of her recent action, but she could wear he⁀ scars with pride because she had fought her fight and won.

He was thirty years old, a middle-sized, lean man, seeming frail, but that was deceptive. His thin face was drawn with tiredness now, the pale blue eyes narrowed by continual strain. But that night *Dauntless* was bound for the dockyard at Alexandria, only hours away, and the survivors of her crew were looking forward to leave in Cairo. Smith shared this anticipation, and there was a girl in Cairo who would share his leave ...

The signal yeoman broke into Smith's reverie: "Escort's signalling, sir! Making the challenge to somebody ahead!"

Smith saw the winking light off the starboard bow where a destroyer patrolled, a black shape under her smoke. A second cruised to port, the pair of them shepherding *Dauntless*. Another light flickered in the darkness ahead and the yeoman read the signal: "It's the destroyer *Harrier*, sir."

Harrier was expected. Only hours before Rear Admiral Braddock had sent a wireless signal that he was sailing from his shore command in Alexandria to meet *Dauntless*. That had surprised Smith: Braddock was a grim, taciturn near-seventy and not the man to come bustling out to offer congratulations. A growled "well done" from Braddock counted as fulsome praise.

Smith paced across the bridge, halted to watch *Harrier* appear out of the night, slender and swift. No plodding ten knots for her. She ripped towards *Dauntless* at better than twenty knots with her big bow-wave a silver flame in the darkness, tore past her to port then turned neatly, reducing speed, to slide into station off the starboard beam. Again the light winked from her bridge and the yeoman reported, "Admiral's coming aboard, sir."

11

"Very good. Stop both." That last to the men at the engine-room telegraphs. The destroyer's motor-boat was already dropping down to the sea as the way came off *Dauntless*. Smith left the bridge to Ackroyd, the First Lieutenant, and went to meet Braddock as he came aboard, broad-chested, his black beard streaked with grey. He saw the Admiral's sweeping glance along the upper deck where the entire superstructure was twisted wreckage and not a gun survived, saw Braddock scowl. *Dauntless* had been a lovely ship and Braddock remembered her so. But then he turned on Smith and said abruptly, "I've got orders for you."

"Orders?" Smith could not believe it. "Sir, with respect, *Dauntless* is in no condition –"

"Not for *Dauntless*. For you. Ackroyd assumes command of this ship now. Tell somebody to pack your kit and he's only got ten minutes. Where can we talk?"

Smith wondered numbly if he had misheard or misunderstood. He was tired out – could his mind or his ears be playing tricks? Leave *Dauntless* in ten minutes? Why?

Braddock grumbled, "Come on, man! We haven't got all night. Is that Buckley?"

It was Leading-Seaman Buckley, hovering discreetly close by, a big shadow in the gloom. Smith told him, "Pack my kit. All you can find. You've got ten minutes."

"Aye, aye, sir!"

Smith turned to Braddock. "We can talk in the sea-cabin, sir."

It was at the back of the bridge, a small steel cubicle holding a desk, a chair and a bunk, Braddock hung up his cap, took the chair and Smith sat on the bunk. Braddock dug a fat envelope out of his pocket and tossed it on to the desk. "Your orders are in there, but I'll tell you what they are. Admiral Winter commands the British cruiser squadron in the Adriatic. The operation's his idea and he's asked for you."

The Adriatic. Italy was Britain's ally there and she faced the Austrians across the Adriatic, fought them in the Alps in the north. This was the beginning of November. Smith tried to remember what he knew of weather in the northern Adriatic. There would be snow in the mountains, of course, a cold wind, plenty of fog –

Braddock said, "You probably know the Austrian fleet is not

as strong as the Italian so since the start of the war they've followed a policy of maintaining a fleet-in-being, staying in their bases either at Trieste or at Pola, just across the northern Adriatic from Venice, knowing that that ties up the Italians who have to keep a similar fleet-in-being in Brindisi and Taranto in the south just in case the Austrians come out. Obviously the Italians can't blockade Pola any more than we could mount a blockade of the German High Seas Fleet. Any attempt at that would leave the blockading ships wide open to attack by U-boats. So, stalemate. But now –" He paused, then asked, "Have you heard of a Kapitän-zur-See Erwin Voss?"

Heard of him? More than that, Smith had met the man. But what had Voss to do with him now? "He has the reputation of a daring and aggressive officer."

The admiral nodded his grizzled head. "The Germans have sent him to the Austrians as an 'adviser'. Winter believes that's eye-wash and Voss is there to instil dash and aggression into the Austrians, to set the Adriatic alight. We've had several attacks of jitters over the years when it looked like the German battle-cruiser *Goeben* might break out of the Dardanelles into the Mediterranean, and that was just one battlecruiser. The Austrians have half a dozen battleships, three of them newish dread-noughts. If they start rampaging up and down the Adriatic and that long Italian coastline, then the fat will be in the fire! The Italians should settle them but God knows what damage they might do first."

Smith could imagine it. A force of capital ships like that could sink whole convoys and be back in port before any pursuing battle squadron could come up with them.

Braddock said grimly, "You take the point. The Austrians have a battlecruiser, too. *Salzburg*. She's big, new and fast. Voss is aboard her and, Winter believes, effectively commanding her. He's also convinced that Voss, in *Salzburg*, will give a lead in aggressive action."

Smith thought that sounded more than likely. *Salzburg* was a fine ship and Voss was a fighter. But where was this leading?

Braddock went on, "Catching Voss at sea will not be easy and beating him something else again. That's where you come in." He paused a moment, then finished: "Your orders are to seek out and destroy *Salzburg* – in harbour."

Smith stared at him. "In harbour?"

Braddock nodded. "Don't ask me how. I don't know. But something's planned, I'm sure. Your orders come from Admiralty and you have an independent command. That was at Winter's insistence, oddly enough." It was very unusual for a senior officer to insist on a junior being given an independent role in waters where he commanded. Braddock continued, "The operation is most secret and the senior officer, that's Winter, of course, is instructed to give you all assistance possible in his judgment. In other words, whatever command you get will come from him. There's a letter from Winter with the orders, promising his support. He doesn't say how the job is to be done but I'm sure he has ideas. Any questions? Though I warn you, I've told you all I know."

There was one. "You said he asked for me, sir. Why?"

Braddock shrugged heavy shoulders. "I've known Jack Winter for donkey's years. We keep in touch. He knows my opinion of you."

Smith said incautiously, "I've heard one or two of your comments myself."

Braddock scowled. "That's right. You'll hear more of the same, if necessary. I told him about some of the scrapes you've got into and been damn lucky to get away with. At sea – and ashore."

He was talking about the women. There had been affairs, one of them scandalous, but that was in the past. Smith started angrily, "Sir!" But he stopped there, Braddock's eye on him. Few men argued with Rear Admiral Braddock.

Braddock sniffed, then grinned. It made him look younger. "Cheer up! He's a good man, one of the best and you'll have a command." He reached for his cap. "I'm looking to have a sea command myself before long. I've set up an organisation in Alexandria for convoys that's virtually running on its own under my second-in-command. Fact is, he can probably do the job better than I can. So I'm making urgent requests to their Lordships for a sea appointment. Jack Winter has that squadron and I'm only five years older – and a sight fitter; I hear he's in poor health. There was a time a sea appointment would have been out of the question at my age but the longer the war goes on the more men they need."

He stood up. "You'll transfer to *Harrier* now and she'll take you to Venice. That's at Winter's order. His squadron is based at Brindisi but for some reason he wants you in Venice – and quick. You'll take Buckley, I suppose?"

Smith was surprised by the question. He had unthinkingly assumed that the big leading hand would go with him. "Yes, sir."

A startled Ackroyd was told he now commanded *Dauntless* and Braddock would go with him to Alexandria. The motor-boat took Smith to *Harrier*, Buckley with him, carrying Smith's valise and his own kit-bag. Buckley had packed that on his own initiative. Where Smith went . . .

Harrier spun away and hastened north-westward, bound for the Adriatic and Venice. Smith stood on her bridge beside Lieutenant-Commander Bennett, her captain, and watched *Dauntless* fade into the night astern. He was leaving a ship and men he knew for an unknown command. He had lost his leave in Cairo. He was sorry about the girl and felt a twinge of conscience then. He was fond of her and he told himself she deserved better than himself and this treatment. But soon the thought of his orders and what lay ahead drove her from his mind.

Seek out and destroy . . .

2 "Attacking!"

At the start of the passage Smith slept a great deal aboard *Harrier*, the weariness of weeks soaking out of him, but the second day found him poring over the charts and the silhouette book in his box of a cabin. In the late afternoon he became restless, knowing the short journey was nearly over; *Harrier* would lie at Venice that night.

He got up from the table and the chart and began to pace the cabin, the silhouette book in his hands, head bent over it. There was just room for two strides one way, two strides back. He was not studying something new but refreshing his memory. *Salzburg* was a carbon copy of the German battlecruiser *Seydlitz* and Smith had studied her silhouette and the notes on her many a time when he served with the Grand Fleet in the North Sea. *Salzburg* was the spit and image of *Seydlitz* and there was no other ship like her in the Adriatic, no Italian or Austrian battleship had the long, lean, greyhound look of this battlecruiser.

Kapitän-zur-See Erwin Voss, because he had served in *Seydlitz*, would have little to learn about his new command. Smith could recall him, too, saw the man in his mind's eye as he stared at the silhouette of the ship. He had met Voss at Kiel before the war when Smith was serving in a visiting ship, and the man impressed him then. Voss was tall and darkly handsome with a lean strength about his face and a piercing glance, but a man ready to smile and mean it. He was good company. He would be a good man to serve with and under; men would follow him. And Voss would lead, no doubt about that. He was no man to sit in his cabin and wait for orders while his ship swung around her anchor. He would look for action.

Seek out and destroy . . . The orders might refer to *Salzburg* but implicit in them was the destruction of Voss as well. Smith was not being sent head-hunting, but the Austrians had given Voss the pride of their navy and if he lost *Salzburg* he would be so discredited that his mission would fail before it started. That was how Voss was to be destroyed – if it could be done.

Seek out . . . That was the first part. *Salzburg* had to be found and that should be possible. Destruction was another matter. Aircraft would help him to find *Salzburg* but they could not destroy her. Bombsights were inaccurate and bombloads small: in the course of a hundred attacks aircraft would be lucky to score a single hit and then the damage would be minor. Whether *Salzburg*'s base was Pola or Trieste it would be well defended and Voss would leave nothing to chance. Smith would have to find some way to break into the harbour and then – what? He did not know the answer to those questions and the letter from Winter promised support and demanded haste but that was all. Nevertheless he was certain, like Braddock, that Winter could enlighten him when he reached Venice.

He stopped at the desk and stared down at the chart spread on it. Pola and Trieste were strong, well defended bases but both were in the north of the Adriatic. If he were Voss and he wanted the Austrians to attack he would – his finger traced down the chart, stopped – he would move the Fleet to Cattaro, three hundred miles to the south with a deep, landlocked harbour, far stronger even than the others and that much nearer to the Mediterranean. Voss could raid out from there all along the Italian coast and into the Mediterranean . . .

The deck tilted beneath his feet and he staggered, then snatched his cap, threw the book on his bunk and dived for the door as the klaxons blared, ran for the bridge.

Lieutenant-Commander Bennett, captain of *Harrier*, turned as Smith came up the ladder. He was a cheerful young man given to a casual attitude but fearsomely efficient. Now he said laconically, "Masthead's sighted a force to eastward of us, sir. Their course is due north and they're steaming twenty-five knots or better. We've no report of friendlies around here so I thought I'd turn and take a look-see. Thirty on the bow."

Smith nodded, tried to control his panting breathing as he set the glasses to his eyes and looked out over the starboard bow.

Bennett went on, "We can only see smoke at the moment but the masthead claims he can see three destroyers and more smoke further east."

Smith lowered the glasses. Like Bennett he could see only smoke on that distant horizon but the man high above them at the masthead would see further and better. Also *Harrier* was working up to her full speed of twenty-eight knots and headed

17

on a course to intercept the other ships. In a minute or two they would know more. He saw Buckley standing at the back of the bridge, gave him a quick grin.

Bennett said, "I've wirelessed a sighting report, of course."

Smith grunted acknowledgment, waited, once glancing astern where there was only the empty sea, the coast of Italy out of sight over the western horizon. Forward the crew of the four-inch on the fo'c'sle were bringing the gun into action, the barrel training around to point like a finger at the distant ships, the shouted orders coming faintly up to the bridge. The men staggered as they worked about the gun because *Harrier* was leaping and pitching now through the lumpy seas. Clouds scudded on the wind across a leaden sky and rain mixed with spray that drove over the bow.

"Masthead reports three four-funnel destroyers an' a big ship!"

"Thank you." Bennett glanced at Smith. "That clinches it. The Italians don't have any four-funnel destroyers but the Austrians do. Tatra class; bigger than us and faster, better than thirty knots. Yeoman! Wireless: 'Three enemy destroyers and one possible capital ship bearing due east ten miles course due north speed twenty-five knots. My position –' Get that from the pilot. '– In pursuit.'"

Smith lifted the glasses to his eyes again. Now he could see the specks that were ships under the smoke. Minutes later he tried again and this time the four funnels of each destroyer were visible. The ships were steaming in line ahead, obviously a screen for the bigger ship they were escorting. So an Austrian patrol in strength, making a sweep and steaming at surprisingly high speed. *Harrier*'s navigator had estimated at least twenty-five knots, yet the Austrian battleships could not approach that speed.

As if to confound him the report came down from the masthead: "Destroyers are screening a battleship! And more smoke to eastward of her!"

That smoke would be more destroyers, of course, the other side of the screen. But Bennett was voicing Smith's thoughts: "She *can't* be a battleship, steaming like that!"

A signalman came running from the wireless office and thrust the flimsy at Bennett. He read it, passed it to Smith. "Admiral

18

Winter and his squadron are thirty miles east of us. He orders us to shadow and report." He paused, then added, "He'll have his work cut out to catch them."

Smith said, "I'm going to the masthead." He climbed the ladder and squeezed in beside the look-out in his cramped circular steel perch that gyrated widly as *Harrier*'s mast swept forward and back. He steadied himself and peered through the glasses, finally managed to hold them on that reeling horizon and the ships there. He took one long look, rested his eyes then looked again. He lowered the glasses, grunted non-committally and climbed down, returned to the bridge.

He said, "*Salzburg.*"

Bennett's mouth opened. He checked the question before it was uttered but Smith answered it anyway. "I'm positive. And there are another three destroyers."

Bennett stood still for a moment, staring out over the bow at the destroyers that were hull-up now, and close behind them the smoke that marked *Salzburg*. He said slowly, "That – has torn it. We can't shadow her; she's two or three knots faster and she'll just steam away from us. Besides –" He paused. This was his ship and his decision. Smith was only a passenger. Bennett threw at the signal yeoman, "Wireless: 'Enemy squadron is *Salzburg* and six destroyers. Attacking.'"

Smith thought it was the right decision; on her present course *Salzburg* intended turning towards Trieste at the end of her sweep, was too far north to be bound for Pola. There was a chance that Winter's squadron might intercept her but only a slim one. If *Harrier* could make a successful attack, score with just one torpedo, she might at least so cripple *Salzburg* that Winter would be certain of catching her.

If.

Bennett was stooped over the voice-pipe, talking to the torpedo gunner aft. "– don't know which side but most likely we'll engage to starboard." He lifted his head to smile wryly at Smith, "May as well be ready, sir."

Smith returned the grin. "That's right."

A look-out yelled, "Enemy's opened fire, sir!"

Smoke wisped away from the three destroyers. Each of them mounted a pair of four-inch guns and they were within range. Bennett ordered, still laconic, "Open fire. Leading destroyer."

Seconds later the four-inch on the fo'c'sle barked and the smoke whipped acrid across the bridge. It caught at Smith's throat and he coughed, swore under his breath, wiped at watering eyes. *Harrier*'s ensign cracked on the wind above him. He stared up at it then turned his gaze forward. Water-spouts lifted from the sea ahead, one barely fifty yards away, the rest just beyond in a close group. That was good shooting. *Harrier* tore through the churned patch of sea, still on a course to intercept the destroyer screen and put her in position for a torpedo shot at *Salzburg*. The range was closing only slowly because the other ships were steaming almost as fast as *Harrier*. If Bennett turned directly towards them he would not close the range more quickly; they would simply steam on northwards and leave him to cross their wake.

So the range closed slowly, too slowly. The four-inch banged away as fast as its crew could load and lay it but *Harrier* was seriously outgunned. The salvos shrieked in, two shells at a time, every few seconds and always creeping closer. Bennett could not take evasive action – swerving would lose him precious distance he could not afford if he wanted a shot at *Salzburg* – so *Harrier* steered a course like a ruled line.

The crash and the shudder through the ship told them they were hit amidships and smoke poured up and laid out in a long, flat black trail astern of them. Flames roared from the hole in the deck and a damage control party scrambled towards it dragging the hoses. Bennett chewed his lip and dug his hands deep in his pockets, squinted ahead at the destroyers where muzzle-flashes winked and the gunsmoke sprouted then trailed on the wind.

Smith wanted to pace the deck, chafed at his own enforced inaction yet knew there was nothing he could do. Bennett was doing all that could be done and now he yelled triumphantly as he saw the shell from the four-inch burst in a flash of yellow flame on the leading destroyer. Smith stared beyond her, glasses to his eyes. *Salzburg* was barely four miles away now and clear in the lenses. The silhouette in the book had come to life and she steamed lean and swift and deadly, a fearsome beauty. Voss would be on her bridge. *Salzburg*'s turrets were trained round, the guns pointing at Smith. He saw the long, yellow tongues lick out from them, the smoke that balled up and

20

almost hid the great ship for a second.

The crash of the hit and the shudder seemed more distant this time, but immediately *Harrier* swerved to port and Smith could feel her slowing. Her head came around again as Bennett snapped at the coxswain at the wheel but still her speed fell away. Then the salvo from *Salzburg* roared in with the sound of a train and plunged into the sea a cable's length ahead. The water-spouts lifted higher than *Harrier*'s masthead and hung there for seconds before falling in a jewelled, green-white curtain of spray.

Bennett lifted his head from the engine-room voice-pipe, looked at Smith and said flatly, "Chief thinks the port side shaft has gone. Reckons he can give us ten knots." He turned to stare out over the bow at the destroyers and *Salzburg* still racing away towards the north. "Yeoman. Wireless: 'Hit. My speed ten knots. Enemy in sight four miles –' Wait." He stared after the ships.

Smith said, "They're changing course." A signal had broken out on *Salzburg*'s yard, was now hauled down, and the destroyers and *Salzburg* were turning.

Bennett continued: "'Course north-east. Speed twenty-five knots.'"

Smith said, "They know Winter's out there somewhere, so they're heading for home." And cutting the corner to Trieste on that course. *Salzburg* or one of the destroyers must have picked up the wireless traffic between *Harrier* and Winter's squadron. It was in code but the exchange itself would tell them there was another warship or warships in touch with *Harrier*. Or the fact that *Harrier* had attacked rather than shadowed them would tell Voss there was a supporting squadron close at hand. Voss would guess at once the reasoning behind *Harrier*'s neck-or-nothing, suicidal charge.

Bennett nodded gloomily. The Austrian squadron was slipping away from him. *Harrier* plugged slowly along after the receding ships but they became small with distance and then were gone over the horizon. For some minutes their smoke still marked them but then that, too, was gone.

Bennett swore bitterly, then told the yeoman, "Send: 'Lost contact with the enemy. Request permission to resume course for Venice to make repairs.'"

Within minutes they received Winter's affirmative and his endorsement: 'Well done.' Bennett said heavily, "Good of him to say that. Well, we tried, anyway."

They had. Smith thought Bennett had done all he could and had got off lightly. By now *Harrier* might have been a shattered wreck, shot to pieces, lying on the bottom of the Adriatic. Even as it was the young medical student shipped as doctor had reported three dead and a score of wounded below.

Salzburg had escaped without a scratch. As *Harrier*'s head turned towards Venice Smith still looked out at the distant horizon where the battlecruiser had disappeared. He had met *Salzburg* and Voss sooner than he expected and been dealt with and dismissed. Voss had wasted no time in making his presence felt and this was only a beginning — if he was going to Trieste then it was for a reason, so Smith's time was short.

The battered *Harrier* came limping into Venice in the dusk, through the low-lying littoral that was no more than wide sand-spits enclosing the lagoon on which the city lay, its spires and domes lifting ahead, the tall tower of the Campanile of San Marco standing above them all. *Harrier* entered by the Porto di Lido, the way into the lagoon, passing between the long arms that stretched out to sea. The torpedo-boat on guard there challenged and *Harrier*'s lamp blinked in answer. A puttering launch led them to a mooring off a long stretch of quay. The tall tower of San Marco was close now, looming high above them. Only one dim light burned on the quay opposite where *Harrier* lay. A picket boat stood off until she was moored then closed the ship.

Bennett said gloomily, "Welcoming committee."

Smith forced himself out of his brooding and managed an encouraging grin. "Cheer up. I agree with Winter. I think you did your whole duty and if I'm called to make a report that's what I'll say."

Bennett smiled in return. "Thank you, sir." He went aft to meet the party from the boat but Smith stayed on the bridge. The city showed no lights and the lagoon was a flat, smooth black in the night but he noticed a staging to one side of the channel and on it rested, lowered for the night, a huge spherical balloon. That would be part of the city's defences against aircraft attacks. Venice was well within range of the Austrian Air Force bases.

A messenger came to him on the bridge. "Cap'n's respects, sir" – that was Bennett – "but there's a Cap'n Devereux asking for you, sir. Liaison officer here, sir. He came aboard with the dockyard man."

Smith dropped down the ladder from the bridge and walked aft past one of the ragged shell-holes in the deck. The timber patch clapped on it by the carpenter had been moved away and a tubby little man was investigating the damage, torch in one hand, note-book in the other. He would be the agent from the dockyard.

Captain Devereux strolled on the quarter-deck of *Harrier* where a small police light glowed. He was tall, his uniform immaculate, the four gold rings on his sleeve and the gold on his cap gleaming brightly in the light. His shoes were highly polished and he carried a walking-stick that showed the glint of more gold on its handle. He halted to lean on this and said briskly, "Ah, Smith. You had a little trouble I see. However, as soon as I got Bennett's signal I set about making arrangements. *Harrier* should be in the dockyard some time tomorrow and on her way back to Braddock in Alexandria in a day or two."

Another officer, a big man, stood back in the shadows. Smith could not see his face or his rank but there was something foreign about his cap and uniform. Italian? Devereux did not mention him. Smith said, "Any news from the squadron, sir?"

"One signal from Winter saying they were engaging the enemy but nothing since. Let us hope that no news is good news. We need some. There are rumours of unrest among the Austrians." Smith had heard them. The Austro-Hungarian empire was a mixture of races and the Slavs were calling for independence. But Devereux went on, "They're only rumours – the Austrians seem to be fighting as well as ever. The Italians have been beaten in a battle at Caporetto in the mountains to the north and are falling back. Venice itself has suffered a number of air raids and they've done some damage. Hopefully the weather will soon curtail that activity."

Now Devereux's voice took on a tone of emphasis. "With regard to the Italians, Smith, everything is arranged with them through me. I am the liaison officer, the senior British officer here – and liaison is *my* responsibility. Without boasting I can say I speak the language well. I have an office at Naval Head-quarters in the dockyard and over these last two years I've built up excellent relations with them. These must not be damaged by people barging in. Understood?"

"Yes, sir." If those were the rules, then Smith was bound by them.

"Good." Devereux relaxed slightly. "I know about your orders, the secrecy and so forth. Winter told me what he wanted. I acted on his orders" – Devereux managed to suggest he disapproved of them, which sounded a warning note to Smith – "and persuaded the Italians to co-operate. Some things I'd rather leave to Winter to explain, but for now I can say you've been lent a small flotilla of MAS boats and no questions asked. All the Italians have been told is that the boats are wanted for an experimental mission. They are under your command unless or until the demands of the service necessitate their recall."

MAS were motor-torpedo-boats and Smith thought that to be lent them for some unknown and experimental mission was generous. Devereux must have been very persuasive. Or possibly the Italians had great faith in Winter ...

Devereux went on, "I've brought along the senior captain to meet you, Lieutenant Pietro Zacco." He lowered his voice: "He seems a surly type but I'm told he knows a little English. God knows how little. However –" Devereux turned and called, "Tenente!"

The big man moved forward and Devereux performed the introductions: "Tenente Pietro Zacco – Commander David Smith."

The dockyard agent came bustling aft then and engaged Devereux in rapid conversation. Smith held out his hand to Zacco who gripped it and said, "Signore." He was about thirty years old and clean-shaven, but for a thick black moustache. That looked odd to Smith after the all-or-nothing, full beard or completely clean-shaven rule of the Royal Navy. It was a strong face, impassive in the light, dark eyes watchful. Devereux had said Zacco was surly but maybe the Italian had been given reason. Smith would have to find out later.

He groped for words but did not find a single one of Italian

24

except: "Tenente."

An uneasy pause, then Devereux returned: "Smith! I have to go back to the dockyard with this chap. I'll send a boat and an interpreter along in the morning about ten to take you over to the Giudecca, that's where the MAS lie. And as *Harrier*'s going to the dockyard you'd better have your kit packed. We'll have to find you some quarters." He strolled to the side and his waiting boat. He had a strutting walk, head back and looking down his nose.

Smith went with him. "I'd like to start before then, sir."

Devereux smiled. "Don't be in such a hurry. *Salzburg* isn't going to fly away!"

Smith realised that Devereux did not take seriously either the threat from *Salzburg* or Smith's orders. He said, "She won't lie idle, either, sir."

Devereux's smile became a frown. "That's as may be – but my interpreter doesn't report for duty till ten and that's when I'll send a boat to take you to the Giudecca."

He turned away and went down to his boat.

Smith decided he did not like Devereux nor the way things were going. The liaison officer might be carrying out his orders but it was clear that he personally had no faith in Smith's secret mission.

He returned to Pietro Zacco, the big lieutenant waiting by the light. But the watch-keeping officer and his quartermaster also stood there so Smith moved on to the rail, beckoned to Zacco to follow him, stood staring out at the dark city, the long stretch of quay. Smith pointed to it. "This place?"

"Riva degli Schiavoni, signore."

"Are you regular navy?"

"No, signore. Merchant ships. Reserve. Most MAS officers are reserve."

"What is the Giudecca?"

Zacco turned to point across the lagoon. "Big mooring. Six hundred metres."

"Do many MAS boats lie there?"

"Yes, signore. All. Many."

Smith thought, many curious eyes too, and gossip, in a crowded mooring. That was inevitable but – he leaned forward over the rail. A dark-haired girl had walked along the quay and halted under the small light there. She wore a cape but the hood of it was thrown back and Smith saw her face in the light, turned towards the ship.

Zacco said, "Ecco – La Contessa. That is what we call her, but she is an English lady, Signorina Helen Blair. She is also called Angel of Mercy. She is much loved, much respected lady."

Smith was certain she was lovely. He could barely make out her features across the gap of black water but he was certain of that and sorry when she walked on, out of the light and into the darkness, lost in it. Only the tap of her heels came back to him and then even that was gone.

He stirred, tried to pick up the thread of the conversation. "If the Giudecca is crowded I would like a more secluded place." He explained, "A place with few people."

Zacco said slowly, "There are many places out in the marshes. But here – there is only San Elena. It is an island. The dockyard is close. It is only two kilometres from here." He pointed towards the sea. "Near the Porto di Lido. Only the church is there – and *il Professore Eccentrico*."

Smith glanced at him, startled. "The – what?"

Zacco smiled apologetically. "The Mad Professor. He is an officer who works in a shed there. He sings all the time. Everyone says he is a little – you know?" He tapped his forehead.

Mad? Smith was curious, but he said, "San Elena sounds good. I will meet the MAS boats there tomorrow morning. Thank you, Tenente. Good night."

"Good night, signore." The big man left, impassive still, crossed the deck and climbed down to the boat that waited for him. He was reserved, certainly, but hardly surly. Evidently Devereux's 'excellent relations' with the Italians had somehow left out Lieutenant Pietro Zacco.

Smith went to his bunk and lay awake, restless, seeing again the lean, wicked beauty of *Salzburg* and the flickering flame of her guns.

He could not count on Devereux; had to see Winter as soon as possible.

Seek out and destroy. With three MAS boats? How?

3 The Boats

Morning found Smith impatiently pacing the deck of *Harrier*. The sky was grey and mist drifted on the surface of the lagoon. The city seemed to float on the water, rising spectral out of the mist. Close by was the long stretch of the quay leading to the Piazza San Marco and the Doge's Palace with its exquisitely colonnaded front. That and the faces of the houses lining the quay were piled with sandbags, protection against air raids. Gondolas clustered before the palace.

An hour to wait for the boat sent by Devereux. Smith chafed at the delay. He had not taken to Devereux and hated the idea of dragging an interpreter around with him. He wished that he knew Italian, but he had hardly a word of it. He wished he knew how to start to carry out his orders but he did not. He swore bad-temperedly, scowled down at *Harrier*'s boat lying at the foot of the accommodation ladder and at the steward in his best number one dress crossing the deck to go down into her, probably on his way ashore to buy some fresh food for the wardroom.

Smith's eyes lifted to the quay, the Riva degli Schiavoni, swept it as he turned, then checked. There was the girl of the night before, more than a hundred yards away but he was certain it was the same girl, the same straight back, the swinging walk, the tilt of the head. The quay was almost empty but for her. Helen Blair. La Contessa.

He remembered the name when he was halfway down the ladder. He dropped into the sternsheets of the boat beside the startled steward and said with forced casualness, "I think I'll stretch my legs ashore." The crew tugged at the oars and the boat shot across the narrow neck of water. Smith was first out of it and on to the quay. The girl walked a score of yards away, young, slender, with dark hair piled shining under a small hat. She wore a dress that was simple, silken and expensive even to Smith's untutored eye. Her head turned at his sudden appearance.

That was when a warning yell came from above them and

further along the quay to seaward where a machine-gun was mounted on a platform on the roof of a hotel. An instant later the machine-gun opened fire. Smith's head jerked round and he saw the biplane banking round a balloon and coming in low over the lagoon, wings rocking, heading straight for him. He sprinted across the quay. The girl stood frozen, a hand to her face and lips parted in shock, staring at the aircraft. Smith grabbed her round the waist and dragged her along with him to the nearest building, into a gap in the stacked sandbags. The engines of the bomber roared over their heads and there came the *crump!* of an exploding bomb. The ground bucked under them and the girl shook in Smith's arms. Then the engines were droning away. The machine-gun hammered on briefly, then stopped. In the silence voices were lifted, nervous, excited.

Smith took a deep breath, trying to steady his breathing. Christ! That was close. The girl still clung, her eyes wide and staring out at the empty sky. They were squashed together in the narrow space between the sandbags that smelt of damp earth. Smith pushed out of it and away from her. "Wait here", he said.

He trotted across the quay. There was a crater about fifty yards away, people appearing along the quay and heading for the crater, curious. He stood on the edge of the quay and looked down into the boat, its crew still at their oars, the steward in the sternsheets. Blown dust from the explosion lay on all of them and the steward was blaspheming with rage at the filth on his best suit.

Smith asked, "Anyone hurt?"

Silence, then the boat's coxswain answered, "No, sir. There was a lot o' stuff flying but we all had our heads down."

The steward grumbled, "Sod this for a lark. First yesterday and now this morning. Never a minute's bloody peace."

A voice murmured in the boat, "If you can't take a joke you shouldn't ha' joined."

That raised a laugh and Smith grinned, left them and returned to the girl. She was out in the open on the quay now, patting her dark hair casually back into place. She and Smith had escaped the flying dust that covered the boat's crew. And he had been right the previous night when he had glimpsed her and guessed she was lovely. Hers was a cool, elegant beauty but he suspected

28

passion might lie close beneath its surface.

He said, "I had to see to the men. You're all right?"

She seemed calm though pale. "Quite, thank you. And your sailors?"

"They're swearing a bit but not hurt. They were down below the level of the quay." He gestured at the ragged stones that carpeted it now, hurled there by the bomb.

The girl looked round at them and at those beneath her feet, and said quietly, "Yes. I see. I believe I must have been standing just about here."

Smith changed the subject. "Didn't I see you here last night?"

"I walked this way, yes. I have a house not far from here. But today I came in my launch."

"Miss Helen Blair?"

Her brows lifted. "That's right."

He explained, "An Italian officer was with me and recognised you. He said you are much respected." He held out his hand. "David Smith."

She shook the hand, released it quickly. "You're on the destroyer?"

"In her but not of her — I'm just a passenger. Now I'm waiting to go to San Elena. I have to join some MAS boats there."

"San Elena?" Helen Blair hesitated a moment, then: "I'll take you there, if you like." She glanced once more at the rubble around her. "I owe you that, at least."

Smith did not hesitate. "That's good of you. Thanks." He could do without Devereux's boat, suspected he would manage very well without Devereux's interpreter. Zacco clearly spoke more than just a 'little' English.

The girl set off along the quay away from the Piazza San Marco and *Harrier*, the heels of her buckled kid shoes tapping briskly, Smith walking at her side. They swung out to pass the crater and the crowd now gathered round it. Further on a flight of steps led down from the quay and at the foot of them lay a small motor-launch, smart with white paint and gleaming brasswork. Helen Blair said, "This is mine."

Smith moved to hand her aboard but she was too quick for him and led the way down the steps, sure-footed on the weed that covered them. She cranked the engine into life with the dexterity born of long practice, cast off, took the wheel and steered the launch out into the lagoon.

Smith stood beside her, leaning on the coaming of the cabin as she eased the launch around to port and they ran along close inshore. They passed a narrow canal that cut under a bridge in the quay and wound away between tall pink and terracotta houses standing out of the water. The girl nodded. "The canal Ca' di Dio – that means house of God. I suppose because it leads to the Church of San Martino. My house is the one on the left and just inside." It was narrow, four-storeyed, its flaking stucco decorated with painted scrolls and panels. The tall windows of the top two floors had little iron balconies and looked out over the lagoon towards the Porto di Lido and the sea.

Smith was very conscious of the girl beside him, and that she was keeping a cool distance between them. The conversation she made was merely polite but it was better than no conversation at all and he wanted to know more of her. "You look after your boat well. She's very smart."

She smiled faintly. "Thank you. But my crew see to that. I have a yacht." She took one hand from the wheel to point a slim finger. "*Sybil*. There she is."

The cutter, a trim, grey-painted little craft, was moored out in the lagoon. She had a single mast forward, the lift of a cabin in the waist, and a well in the stern where two blue-jerseyed figures worked at some task.

Helen Blair said, "I bought her two years ago in the south and sailed her up here. She used to be owned by a Swiss businessman who sailed her when he could get a few weeks away from his office in Switzerland, but the war made that difficult for him so he sold her. The two sailors came with her. They're Swiss, German-speaking and I don't have a word of it. They only know a few phrases of English but I'm fluent in Italian and we get on in that. There isn't much room aboard but we only potter up and down the coast a few miles."

Mention of the seamen reminded Smith of Buckley, aboard *Harrier* and wondering where the hell his hare-brained officer had got to. Smith grinned at the thought, then asked, "Does the navy mind you – pottering?"

"Oh, no. They all know me and what I'm doing. They even warn me where mines are laid though that isn't really necessary

30

– we draw so little water it's unlikely we'd touch a mine anyway."

They were passing another canal that led inland and Smith glimpsed two towers. Helen Blair said, "You'll find the Italian Naval Headquarters up there." Smith only nodded. Devereux had made it clear that any dealing with the Italians would be done by him. As if mention of the navy had reminded her, the girl went on gravely, "The news of the war is not good. There is a big battle in the north and rumours of a retreat." She finished bitterly, "This bloody war!"

The strength of her bitterness startled him. He remembered Devereux had said the Italians were falling back but – a retreat? He did not like the sound of that.

Helen Blair glanced across at him. "Your ship has been in action. I heard there were several wounded and dead. I'm sorry."

Smith said grimly, "So am I." He stared out across the water. "I hope to do something about it."

The girl said with distaste, "An eye for an eye?"

"No. Vengeance is no good." He saw her flinch at his words and he wondered why. He went on, "It's meaningless. Voss was doing his duty as I shall try to do mine." That sounded pompous but it was true.

Surprise made her ask, "Voss? You know the other captain's name?"

He nodded. But he did not want to talk about Voss or *Salzburg* – this girl intrigued him. His eyes kept turning to her but he sensed she was keeping distance between them still. He said, "You hate the war."

"Don't most people hate the war and want it ended?"

He knew that was true. "You have a special reason?"

"Not special." Her tone was cool. "Personal." And there she was telling him to mind his own business.

The launch slipped inshore of a line of destroyers and came up past a boatyard, the slipways running down into the lagoon. The girl said, "That is the SVAN yard where they build the MAS boats."

Smith saw the hulls of two on the slips, men working on them. Then the boatyard slid astern and the launch went on, passed a long stretch of parkland, a deep fringing of green to the

31

wintry grey-blue water of the lagoon. Helen Blair said, "There is the island of San Elena – and your MAS boats."

She pointed ahead. The island was a low-lying, bare expanse of grass and reeds separated from the parkland and the rest of Venice by a narrow canal like a ditch, spanned by a single wooden bridge. The girl said, "And the tower is that of the Church of San Elena."

The tower on the church stood solitary above the flat green of the island, about a quarter-mile away. The MAS boats were moored at the furthest point of the island and before the launch came to them it passed a small inlet with a wooden building, a shed or workshop, on its shore. On a slip inside this building lay a craft like a barge but they were past before Smith could make out its details. He guessed that must be the workshop of the Mad Professor whom Zacco had mentioned, then returned his gaze to the MAS boats now close ahead, moored bows on to the shore and side by side.

MAS stood for *Motobarca Anti-Sommergibile* or Anti Submarine Motorboat. They were long, low little craft with slender lines, built of wood. Men were clambering about them. They had to climb because there was no real deck to tread. Right aft was a counter a yard or so long, then the stern cockpit. Forward of that was the housing of the engine-room, then the forward cockpit and the foredeck which was rounded, giving the boats a cigar shape. This much Smith already knew from photographs and descriptions. Now he saw that movement aboard them was complicated still further by their torpedoes, two of them, each eighteen inches in diameter and fifteen feet long. There were no torpedo tubes. The 'fish' were carried on the narrow side decks, one either side of the forward cockpit, and held in clamps, further obstacles to movement.

Aboard the boats they had now seen him, his arms deliberately laid on the top of the cabin coaming so that the three gold rings of his rank were clearly visible on the cuffs. A tall figure in the after cockpit of the nearest boat straightened his cap and men climbed out of the cockpits on to the foredecks to balance there in line and at attention. The launch slowed and Helen Blair turned her, laid her neatly alongside the nearest boat. Smith said, "I hope we will meet again."

She did not look at him. "It's possible. But I am very busy and

32

I'm sure you have your duties, Commander."

That was a polite dusting-off and Smith grinned wryly. "Thank you for bringing me." He raised his hand in salute, then turned and clambered up on to the counter of the MAS and saluted again in the traditional act of respect when boarding. Out of the corner of his eye he saw the launch curve away across the ruffled surface of the lagoon, the slim figure of the girl at the wheel. Then he gave his attention to the boats and their men.

The tall officer returning Smith's salute was Pietro Zacco, still impassive and watchful. Smith could understand that: he was watchful himself. This was his command – with these men and their boats he had to go after *Salzburg*, and on them would depend his career and his life. His gaze went beyond Zacco to the men standing at attention, to the other two boats and their rigid captains and crews. He said, slowly and clearly, "The men can carry on. I would like to see over the boats and meet the other officers, but first I want to talk to you."

Si, signore." Zacco seemed to understand. He shouted an order over his shoulder and the rigid figures relaxed, dispersed about the boats. He turned back to Smith. "Signore?"

Smith said, "I have a lot to learn about the Royal Italian Navy, these boats and the men in them and very little time. I need your help. Captain Devereux said you spoke a little English. Last night I watched you listening to him and when I talked you understood me. So – how good is your English?"

Zacco answered evenly, "It is good. I studied it and before the war I talked with many people in England. My ship went there many times." He paused. "Captain Devereux did not ask me about my English."

Smith nodded, unsurprised, but made no comment. "And the other two captains?"

"Pagani speaks well. Gallina a little but he understands a lot."

Smith said from the heart, "Thank God for that." He was rid of Devereux's interpreter. "Now I'll see them."

"Yes, signore." Zacco shouted, the officers clambered over from the other two boats and were introduced. Both were reserve officers like Zacco but he was the senior of the three. Tenente Gallina was bearded, short, broad and stolid while Tenente Pagani was lean, dark and raffish with a long sweep of moustache and the look of a pirate about him.

Smith said, "I am sure we will get on well together, gentle-men." Pagani looked sceptical. The others showed nothing at all, reserving judgment. Smith went on, "And now – the boats."

He was conducted over each boat by its captain. He might as well have gone over the same boat three times because they were identical, but at least this gave him three opportunities to study the boats and a chance to look at all the men and exchange a word or two with some of them, Zacco interpreting. Each after cockpit was six feet long by five feet wide and a Colt machine-gun was mounted on a post there. Here also was the wheel and the entrance to the engine-room beneath its low housing. Smith peered in at the big petrol engines and the electric motors crammed into the restricted space. From there he worked along the narrow strip of deck that ran either side of the engine-room, past the torpedoes to a forward cockpit hardly more than four feet square. Here was mounted another machine-gun and stretched across the deck forward and aft were the tackles for hoisting the torpedoes.

That was all. There was no cabin since the range of the boats was limited by their restricted fuel capacity and their crews were not expected to be long enough at sea to need one. There was no wireless either, because no such apparatus small enough had yet been designed to fit into their crammed hulls.

He returned to stand on the counter of Zacco's boat, Gallina, Pagani and Zacco in the cockpit. They watched him, warily silent. He heard, faintly, the sound of singing. It seemed to come from the shed farther down the shore. He asked absently, preoccupied with other problems, "What is that?"

Zacco supplied, "That is Tenente Balestra. He is in the workshop. Nobody knows what he does there, but all the time he sings. He is the one called the Mad Professor. He is an engineer. That song is *Le ragazze di Trieste* – all about the girls of Trieste."

Balestra sang well and he sounded happy. The three captains were clearly not and Smith needed to know the reason. He probed, "You are volunteers?"

They glanced at each other and shook their heads. Smith had gathered that much. Zacco said diffidently, "We were told that Captain Devereux wanted volunteers for an experimental mission. But we also heard that the captain thought it was a waste of time and would soon finish, that he was simply acting under orders. You understand?"

Smith did, all too well. 'Going through the motions' was one phrase. Devereux had made it clear to Smith he considered his mission a waste of time. Apparently he had also made that clear to the Italians. Smith said, "So?"

Pagani said stiffly, "We did not join the navy for that. There were no volunteers. So they put all the names in a bag and ours came out." He finished cynically, "We won."

Smith took off his cap and ran his fingers through his hair. He looked at Zacco and asked, "The boats are ready for sea?"

"Yes, signore."

"Very good." Smith clapped his cap smartly back on his head. "Let us go to sea."

The other two captains returned to their own boats, bellowing orders. Smith stayed with Zacco and stood with him in the after cockpit as the engines fired and roared, settled down to a steady rumbling. Zacco stooped, reached into the engine-room and pulled out oilskins and sou-westers, one set for himself and another for Smith. He dragged on the oilskins and Zacco hung Smith's cap in the engine-room. The moorings were slipped.

Pagani shouted across, "Signore! If you please – what is this experimental mission?"

Zacco's boat was sidling astern out into the lagoon and Smith shouted back over the widening gap, "My orders are to sink *Salzburg* . . . at her moorings . . . in harbour!" He saw Pagani's incredulous stare, Gallina's jaw drop, was aware of Zacco's sharp turn of the head. He summoned one of his few words of Italian. "Avanti!"

At that Zacco's startled look became a grin. He acted on the order and the boat moved ahead, the other two falling in astern. In line ahead the three boats cruised at half-speed across the lagoon, following the buoyed channel towards the sea. They turned to port past the ammunition stores on the islands of La Certosa and then Le Vignole where lay the seaplane base of San Andrea. A turn to starboard then and they entered the Porto di Lido, passed through its long arms, and began to pitch to the open sea.

It was a cold steel-blue winter's sea made grey by banks of mist that limited visibility sometimes to a mile, often to only a few hundred yards. They exercised for an hour, every manoeuvre that Smith could think of. The boats tore through the sea at their full speed of twenty-five knots, their straight stems lifted and sterns tucked down in their boiling wakes. They turned as one from line ahead into line abreast, then back into line ahead, scattered to play hide-and-seek through the coiling grey banks of fog, reformed. For a time the petrol engines were stopped and they slipped along at four knots under the electric motors. Smith found that eerie at first, the boats' slow, almost silent forward motion, as if they were drawn across the surface of the sea by an unseen hand. There was only the low hum of the motors and mostly the lapping of sea hid that. He realised that this slow but silent cruising might well prove useful in the future.

They practised signalling and night signalling, the lamps blinking and flickering, and they demonstrated the operation of the torpedoes. A man hauled on each of the two tackles attached to a torpedo, swinging it up and outboard until it hung in the clamps, like pincers, above the sea. They did not fire the torpedo, too expensive to waste on a practice. Zacco explained how the torpedoman would yank back the lever on the system of rods linking the clamps, opening them so that the torpedo dropped into the sea, where its engine would start automatically.

So Smith put the captains and their crews through the hoop, testing them, and soon saw more than enough to convince him of their seamanship and efficiency. He was testing himself too, for their benefit, demonstrating that he knew what he was about, had experience of small craft and their handling. A lot of the time he was also learning from Zacco the Italian helm orders and a host of others. And at the end he stripped off his oilskins and burrowed into the engine-room, saw the *motorista* and the *meccanico,* the engineer and the stoker, clambered with them around their throbbing oily charges and collected a deal of the oil on himself.

Zacco's engineer was a young man, broad and deep-chested, a mat of black hair showing on his chest above the oil-smeared singlet he wore. He spoke English with an American drawl. "These are the main engines – those babies are the electric motors. Know anythin' about engines?"

"Not much," Smith answered frankly. "Just basics. These are good?"

"Sure they are. I make 'em that way." That was not boasting, just huge self-confidence. There was no deference in this man, to Smith or his rank. He went on, "They ain't powerful enough. Top speed is only around twenty-five knots. But what the hell – if you put in bigger engines, you have to take out somethin' else, like the electric motors, an' they're a useful trick."

Smith nodded. Every ship was a compromise and he had already decided on the worth of the electric motors. He asked, "Are you an American?"

"Hell, no! I'm Italian. My folks went to the States when I was two, three years old, but they kept their nationality and when I finished school I came back here to learn engineering." He rubbed his big hands on a lump of cotton waste and said thoughtfully, "Kinda like it over here, though. I might stick around."

"So you didn't come back to fight?"

He stared at Smith. "Are you kidding? This is a job. I only joined the reserve because I have to eat." He jerked his head at the cockpit. "Lieutenant Zacco runs a taut ship up there. I run a taut ship down here."

"What's your name?"

"Angelo Lombardo."

"Angelo?" He was unruly, aggressive, a long way from angelic, but Zacco had said he was an excellent engineer. Smith stored that knowledge away along with everything else he had learned in the last few hours.

He returned to the cockpit and told Zacco, "Heave to and signal the other boats to come alongside. I want to talk to them."

And when the three boats lay rocking together on the sea he said clearly so all aboard them could hear, "Good. I am pleased with the exercise."

Zacco smiled. Gallina still showed no emotion at all. Winning him over would not be easy. Pagani called, "Signore, if you please, why are you chosen for this command?"

Smith answered seriously, "They put the names in a bag. I lost."

There was a moment of silence then Zacco and Pagani roared

37

with laughter. Gallina stared at Smith's solemn face, then his lips twitched and he was laughing with the others.

Smith relaxed slightly. He had made a start.

But only a start. He said, "We return to Venice. Refuel and be lying off San Elena, ready to sail, by nightfall."

There was silence for a moment, then Zacco said, "We know the orders are secret. We will not talk. Can we know where we go?"

"Trieste," Smith answered. "That's where *Salzburg* was headed when I saw her last night."

"You saw her!" The captains edged closer as Smith briefly recounted the action.

At the end Pagani said fiercely, "You had much bad luck! A great attack! That is the way – straight in and fire the fish at close range!"

Smith thought, 'If only we get the chance ...'

The boats returned to Venice in line ahead, Zacco leading. Smith stood lost in thought. The fog had turned to rain now, pattering on the engine-room housing and mixing with the salt spray on his face. He needed up-to-date intelligence of Trieste and for that, unfortunately, he had to go to Devereux. As they passed through the arms of the Porto di Lido and entered the lagoon he broke his silence: "Put me ashore by the dockyard – Naval Headquarters."

"Signore." Then Zacco asked, "Can I make a suggestion?"

"Of course."

"The booms at Trieste are affairs of hawsers and buoys, I think. Perhaps we could mount hydraulic shears in the bows of the boats, big cutters, and cut our way in."

It sounded simple, easy. Smith knew, as must Zacco, that it would *not* be easy. But simple ideas were often the best, and he thought this one might work. "That's fine! We'll look into it."

Zacco smiled. "I will ask at the dockyard."

They ran in past San Elena, then the long green stretch of parkland and the SVAN yard. The other two boats turned towards the Giudecca but Zacco held on for the canal leading to Naval Headquarters. He pointed again. "That is the house of La Contessa." Smith nodded, his eyes already on the narrow house with the tall windows and the little balconies. But the girl was nowhere to be seen. Zacco asked. "You are friends?"

38

"We only met this morning. She is very reserved, I think."

"Reserved? You mean – not friendly?" Zacco shook his head in disbelief. "Always she smiles, talks, laughs. Always very friendly, very" – he groped for the word – "hospitable? Many officers go to her house for dinner. I go there two times. Very happy times."

Then her reserve only extended to Smith. He could do nothing about that, knew he was no great charmer. He told himself he didn't care, but he did. Anyway, he was on his way to see Devereux. Also he must somehow get in touch with Winter. He had a hell of a job to do and still no idea how to start except with Zacco's cutters.

Zacco said, "She is a brave lady. She has a sad story –"

He was steering the boat towards Naval Headquarters. Smith could see *Harrier* lying two hundred yards further on and beyond her there now lay another destroyer. But closer was Buckley, standing on the quay cap in hand, waving furiously.

Smith told Zacco, "Put me ashore here!"

Zacco swung the boat away from the entrance to the canal and ran her in alongside the quay while Smith pulled off his oilskins and grabbed his cap from the engine-room. The two seamen at bow and stern held the MAS by the steps and Smith climbed quickly up to the quay. Buckley came running towards him, his urgency and the set look on his face telling Smith that something had gone badly wrong.

Buckley halted in front of him, panting, and came straight to the point. "Admiral Winter is dead, sir!"

4 *Hercules*

Smith halted, trying to take it in, staring at the two ships lying under the rain, the damaged *Harrier* and the newly-arrived destroyer beyond her. She had also been in a fight: the muzzles of her guns were smoke-blackened. "Dead? How?"

"There was an action. The Admiral's cruiser was hit. They came up with *Salzburg* but she got away."

Salzburg. Voss again. And Winter was dead. Smith started to walk towards the ships, mechanically. It was bad news, the worst. This had been Winter's scheme and he the prime mover. Without his leadership and support –

Buckley, striding alongside, said, "The squadron's patrolling outside to the north but that destroyer's come in to bring the Admiral's body ashore. His Flag Captain, Pickett, he's aboard an' he had the Admiral's corpse off on the quay and away as soon as they secured." Buckley was scowling at the indecent haste of it. He added warningly, "He's waiting to see you, sir."

Smith quickened his stride. "How long?"

"Near an hour, sir."

A Flag Captain left kicking his heels for an hour. Smith knew he would need Pickett's help now, and this was a bad start. A boat carried Buckley and himself out to the destroyer and he boarded her as he was, wet and grimy from the exercises with the MAS boats. He was immediately conducted below to the captain's cabin, but not before he had sensed an edginess in the officer on watch and the side-party. If that was because of Pickett's presence aboard then the prospects weren't encouraging.

It was indeed a considerable presence. The destroyer's cabin was small and Pickett seemed to fill it. He was bluff and bearded, sat broad at the little desk and greeted Smith in a bellow. "Ah! Smith!"

"Yes, sir."

Devereux sat on the bunk, a hand smoothing his hair, cap and walking-stick beside him, a folder of papers and signals open on his knee.

Pickett had been reading a signal, now handed it back to Devereux and said to Smith, "I've heard a few tales about you!" He did not seem favourably impressed. His lips moved in a smile but his eyes stayed fixed coldly on Smith. "You soon wangled yourself a run ashore, I gather."

"I was at sea with the MAS boats, sir."

"You were seen going off with a young woman!"

"The lady offered to take me to the boats."

Devereux put in, "My boat and interpreter came to *Harrier* and you were already gone. They also went to the Giudecca to look for you and the boats had gone from there. If you want my assistance then I will expect some co-operation!"

"Of course." Smith made a neutral answer. "I saw the chance to join my command a little earlier and I took it."

"And the young woman." Pickett scowled under heavy brows. "Officers under my command find life more real and earnest. And they appear before me as an officer should." He looked Smith up and down where he stood in his grimy suit.

Smith felt the first real stirring of anger, but he replied evenly, "As I said, sir, I was at sea. When I learned you wanted to see me I came at once."

"Um." Pickett did not seem impressed by that, either. He changed the subject. "*Harrier*'s in a mess."

"Bennett did all any man could, sir. He was unlucky not to get a shot at *Salzburg* and very lucky to be alive to tell the tale."

Pickett waved a hand dismissively. "I had him aboard while I was waiting for you and he told me the whole story. Sounds as though you got a bloody nose for nothing."

"There was a chance we might disable *Salzburg* and give the Admiral a chance to come up . . ."

But Pickett was waving the hand again. "Anyway, she's not one of my ships." So he had finished with *Harrier*, her wounded and her dead. He said pointedly, "You realise Admiral Winter is no longer with us?"

"What happened, sir?"

Pickett looked up at Smith, frowning. "What? Oh, – we came up with *Salzburg* twenty miles south of Trieste but she ran for it. There was a short action at extreme range. I doubt if we hit her and she only landed one on us. Not much damage but a splinter killed the Admiral. Damn bad luck." The words

41

sounded hardly more than a formality. Pickett was impatient to get on.

"Then *Salzburg* tucked her tail between her legs and ran into Trieste. We did what we could, patrolled out of sight of land and kept wireless silence through the night and into the forenoon in case they worked up enough courage to come out but, of course, they didn't."

Smith asked, "What force did the Admiral have, sir? The whole squadron?" That was four cruisers and ten destroyers.

"Certainly." The Flag Captain drummed his fingers restlessly.

"And *Salzburg* only had a screen of six destroyers." Smith was silent a moment. No single one of the cruisers would have a hope against *Salzburg*, but four was another matter. Winter had seen his chance and tried to take it but Voss had seen it, too. Smith said, "I'm sorry, sir."

"Yes. Pity." But Pickett ran on without pause, "Now I command and I tell you frankly, because I always speak frankly, I should have had the squadron long ago and I did not always see eye-to-eye with Winter. Nor did Captain Devereux. We did not question Winter's orders or his ideas because he was the Admiral. But there'll be some changes made now." He exchanged glances with Devereux and both were smiling broadly. Smith saw that Pickett was enjoying his new command and expected to keep it. And that Devereux was clearly in favour, delighted at Pickett assuming command. He understood now the edginess of the men he had seen on the quarter-deck.

Pickett turned back to Smith. "Those orders of yours, for instance. Winter's business of *gatecrashing* the booms to sink *Salzburg*. A hare-brained idea if ever I heard one."

Smith put in quickly, "That's why I was with the MAS. I like what I've seen of the boats and the men and one of the officers, Lieutenant Zacco, has suggested a way we might cut through the booms. Now we know *Salzburg* is in Trieste I propose to carry out a reconnaissance –"

Pickett's hand slapped the desk impatiently. His beard jutted and he boomed, "There's only one way to settle *Salzburg* and that's bring her to action at sea and sink her!"

Anger had been building in Smith since he met Pickett and now it broke. "Admiral Winter thought of this 'seek out and destroy' mission because he saw the difficulty in bringing *Salzburg* to action. First we have to catch her. Voss didn't run from this squadron because he's afraid: he's proved his courage before now and he won't throw away his ship and his men in pointless heroics. He refused action because he has his own ideas of where, when and how he fights. He means to *win* – and whenever he sees his chance you'll –"

A rap came at the door. Pickett bellowed, "What is it?"

"Signal from Italian HQ, sir. The Admiral would like to see you and Captain Devereux if convenient, sir."

"I'll leave in five minutes!" The messenger retired abruptly. Pickett's eyes, narrow with rage, had never left Smith. Now he said menacingly, "Admiral Winter is dead. Officers in *my* command do not argue with me!"

Smith knew he should keep his mouth shut but anger still drove him. "I was merely offering my opinion, sir. And as I understand it, I am not in your command."

Pickett leaned forward over the desk, hands splayed on it, glaring at Smith. "True. You are not in my command. Frankly I'm glad. You're under orders from Admiralty and I suppose you must make some show of obeying them, though I think –" But he stopped short of criticising those orders and instead went on: "Mine are to render all assistance possible – in *my* judgment. And the war is going badly here. The German Fourteenth Army has broken through the line at Caporetto. The Italians have been defeated. In four days they've lost all they gained in more than two years and they're retreating still. There's talk of a stand on the line of the Tagliamento river but I'll believe that when I see it."

Smith stared at him, shocked. The Tagliamento was deep inside Italy, far behind the frontier at the start of the war.

Pickett nodded with grim satisfaction. "So at this time I can't spare a ship or anything else." He waited but Smith said nothing. Pickett shifted in the chair, sighed. "I suppose you could have *Hercules*. I understand she's just come in with her captain wounded and they've taken him to hospital. I'll write you orders for her. And there's a midshipman – name of Menzies ..." Pickett scowled. "He already has orders to join you and should be on the quay by now. You're welcome to him. Anything else?" His bushy brows lifted.

43

"No, sir." Smith would go to hell before he asked Pickett for anything.

"I'll prepare your orders for *Hercules* before I leave." Pickett pointed a thick finger at Smith. "But just remember this! You may have an independent command, but *anything* you command in these waters comes from myself or the Italians. So before you attempt any action you will clear it with the Italians through Captain Devereux. Over the time he has been here he has worked very hard to achieve excellent working relations with the Italians and we can't afford to have them destroyed. Is that understood?"

'Excellent relations.' He was using Devereux's words, had obviously been primed by him. They were two of a kind. Smith answered shortly, "Yes, sir."

Pickett said, "Captain Devereux will clear this reconnaissance of yours with them."

He glanced at Devereux who nodded his sleek head, then added coldly, "I'll send the latest intelligence I have of Trieste down to you in *Hercules*. The Italians make reconnaissance flights every day but they haven't seen much lately because of fog over Trieste. Still, nothing of importance will have changed in a few·days."

"Thank you, sir."

Smith, fuming with rage and frustration, climbed to the quarter-deck of the destroyer. He saw Buckley lurking in the background and told him curtly: "We've got orders for a ship."

"What – now, sir?"

"In five minutes. Fetch your kit and mine."

Buckley looked at Smith's set face and said only, "Aye, aye, sir." He saluted and hurried away to explain his errand to the officer of watch, went down the ladder to be rowed across to *Harrier*.

Smith found a space where he could stand alone at the quarter-deck rail without meeting curious eyes and stared out over the lagoon, breathing deeply, the wind and rain on his face. For a minute he swore softly, at Pickett, at Devereux, at himself because his temper had made a bad situation worse. Pickett and Devereux were thick as thieves. He should have played them diplomatically, agreed with them all along the line, criticised Winter's plans and laughed at Zacco's idea – then pleaded his orders so as to wheedle some help from them. But then came revulsion. He knew he could not have done that. He should have avoided a row but now it had happened, and he would not take back a single word. He would have to go on from here.

He remembered Pickett's news of the war, that the German Fourteenth Army had broken through the line at Caporetto and the Italians were in retreat. But surely they would be able to stand – Pickett's pessimism was simply the result of his own bile and his anger with Smith.

Already Voss had scored a victory over him. He would not know it but when *Salzburg*'s shells had killed Winter so Smith had lost the only man he could turn to for help. He had expected an independent command but this was – isolation. Even the girl, the Contessa, who according to Zacco talked and laughed with everyone, had made it plain that he was not welcome.

"Beg pardon, sir." Smith looked round and saw a boy at his side, offering an envelope. "From Captain Pickett, sir."

"Thank you." Smith's orders for *Hercules*. He did not know what kind of ship she was but he took the envelope and thrust it into his pocket unopened because the side-party was scurrying into place. It became a white-gloved, rigid line as Pickett appeared, bull-like and confident, scowling about him as men working on the quarter-deck jumped out of his way. He was enjoying every moment of this, his new command, but he gave Smith a frigid glare in passing. Devereux, following a pace behind with walking-stick in his gloved hand, ignored Smith completely.

Smith stood at the salute as the pipes of the side-party shrilled and Pickett went down into his boat with Devereux. Then he set out to look for his own new command.

She took some finding.

The destroyer's signal yeoman could tell him roughly where she lay and pointed to the crowded shipping shrouded in the rain. "'Course, sir, you can't actually pick her out from here." He finished tactfully, "She's not very big, sir."

Smith was rowed to the quay, found Buckley waiting there and somehow he had procured a barrow. It held Smith's valise, Buckley's kit-bag and a box on which was painted: *Midshipman E.F. Menzies*. Menzies stood by the barrow, hand at the salute. He was small, snub-nosed, wide-mouthed, and his ears stuck

45

out from under the cap. He stared patiently to his front. Smith thought he looked like a monkey with a philosophical turn of mind. He returned the salute and grunted, "Come on!"

He started off along the quay, Menzies hurrying one pace behind and Buckley bringing up the rear, pushing the barrow. Smith was curious to know why Menzies had been sent to *Hercules*, and asked him point blank.

The midshipman hesitated. "Captain Pickett's orders, sir."

"Don't waste my time with evasive or stupid answers. He could have chosen any of a dozen midshipmen. Why you? I doubt that you were the biggest or the most senior, so – why?"

"I . . . I think it was because I got into a bit of trouble, sir." Smith looked at him coldly and Menzies hurried on: "I mean, I was giving an impersonation for some of the chaps – midshipmen, sir – and Captain Pickett saw me."

"Impersonation?" Smith saw light. But: "You mean a comic song? Marie Lloyd, perhaps?"

Menzies was looking straight ahead and confessed, "No, sir. An impersonation of Captain Pickett."

"Ah! And the – chaps – thought it was funny."

Menzies said sadly, "They laughed a lot. I suppose the captain heard them."

"Giving funny impersonations of a Flag Captain! You were lucky he didn't have you shot!"

"Yes sir," Menzies answered meekly but his monkey face was stubborn.

"You don't take it too hardly."

Menzies explained simply, "I'll be leaving the navy when the war finishes anyway, sir."

"You don't like the Service? Why?"

Menzies frowned. "It's fine sometimes, but a lot of the time it's just patrols or sweeps or exercising in harbour, just – boring." Then Menzies added quickly: "Sir!" He was startled to realise he had been betrayed into talking to this senior officer as if to an equal.

Smith grunted. He could understand how Menzies felt, knew only too well the long periods of waiting, the deadening routine. But leave the Service? To Smith it was unthinkable, but he could not put his feelings into words and said only, "I'll try to see you're not too bored, Mr Menzies." He lapsed into silence.

Buckley, shoving at the barrow, grinned to himself. Let the lad just wait a while!

Smith strode on along the quay, eyes searching for his ship. Far across the lagoon he could see above the other shipping the masts of the *Saint Bon* and the two other old Italian battleships stationed at Venice. *Salzburg* could annihilate them. With no other deep water base in all the long Adriatic coast, the bulk and the best and newest of Italy's capital ships were far to the south at Brindisi and Taranto. The Austrians were in Pola and Trieste in the north and the days when a blockading squadron could cruise off a port were long past: any attempt to blockade Pola and Trieste would invite attack by U-boats – and disaster. So the Italians sowed mines before the enemy ports which the Austrians swept up – then laid their own mines outside Venice, to be swept in their turn.

There was a trot of three minesweepers lying here off the quay and beyond them a pair of Italian destroyers. Rain swept in from the sea, a fine drizzle that set him blinking against it.

He halted so suddenly that Buckley had to throw his weight back to stop the barrow and still it nudged Smith. "Sorry, sir."

But Smith had not noticed the bump. They had almost missed *Hercules* where she lay tucked in between the minesweepers and destroyers. Her name was lettered on her stern and below it her port of registration: Yarmouth. In days of peace she had sailed out of there to fish round the coast of Britain. Now she was in the northern Adriatic. She had come a long way.

Hercules was a drifter, a little wooden ship, black-painted. She measured just ninety feet from stubby bow to stern and twenty across her fat waist where stood the wheelhouse and narrow funnel. Aft of them was a single mast and right forward in the bow a six-pounder gun.

Smith asked, "Well, what do you think of her?"

He spoke to Buckley, who peered out at the drifter, then at Smith, thinking this must be a joke. He saw Smith was in earnest and answered morosely, "Well, they say any ship's better than no ship, but I'm not sure about this one." He stepped to the edge of the quay and bellowed, "*Hercules!*"

A man appeared at the door of the wheelhouse and looked across at the three of them on the quay. His grizzled hair was cut short above a square, leathery face with a fringe of grey beard. "'Ullo!"

Buckley shouted, "Send a boat for the captain!"

"What captain?"

Buckley said disgustedly, "Jesus wept!" He bawled, "*Your* captain! Your *new* captain!"

"Bloody 'ell! A *Commander?*" The greybeard shoved out of the wheelhouse, turned forward and shouted, "Ginger! ... *Ginger!*"

A red head appeared on the drifter's foredeck, poking out of a hatch. The old man rasped, "Get yer cap an' into the boat an' fetch the new skipper aboard!"

"Aye!" The red head vanished to reappear seconds later with a bluejacket's cap clapped on it. Their owner trotted aft to where a boat trailed by its painter from the stern, hauled it alongside and climbed down, unshipped the oars and pulled across to the quay.

Buckley passed down the kit and followed them. His mutter came up to Smith and Menzies, "Put your hat on straight, son. You're supposed to be under it, not in front of it." The young sailor's cap was hastily crammed forward in the regulation fashion above the eyes but it still had an irregular list to starboard.

Smith, last to enter the boat, sat in the sternsheets by Menzies. Buckley shoved off and the seaman bent to the oars. Smith asked him, "What's your name?"

"Gates, sir."

"You're not regular navy."

"Nossir. I'm one o' the old hands. Fred Archbold, he's the mate but he was her skipper afore the war, he's my uncle."

Many of these drifters had been hired by the Admiralty for the duration of the war and their peacetime crews stayed in them. Ginger Gates, 'one of the old hands', was possibly twenty, but Smith reflected that he had probably been to sea since he left school at the age of thirteen or fourteen. He told Menzies, "We'll have some fine seamen, that's one good thing."

He climbed aboard *Hercules* and found her crew drawn up on her deck forward. He saluted and it was returned by the greybeard, now dressed in blue jacket and cap. Smith said, "I am Commander Smith."

"Fred Archbold, sir. Mate." He was around sixty years of age but straight in the back, set solidly on his feet in shiny black leather boots. His grey eyes were clear and if he had been startled by Smith's sudden arrival he didn't show it now. Smith decided that after a lifetime at sea Fred Archbold would neither be easily upset nor for very long.

He walked forward and Fred Archbold followed, the shiny boots creaking. Smith read out the orders that gave him command of *Hercules* then looked at her ship's company, seventeen including Archbold. They had all turned out in a hurry and were dressed haphazardly, only their caps being uniform. But Smith remembered they had only entered harbour a few hours ago and before that had been in action – their former captain was in the hospital now. They would have been short of sleep and snatched the chance of it. More faces and names to learn – and quickly.

He asked, "Engineer?"

Fred Archbold answered, "Geordie Hogg, sir."

The engineer stepped forward, fat and filling out his boiler-suit, pale and sweating.

Smith said, "Raise steam."

"Right y'are –" Geordie Hogg corrected himself: "Aye, aye, sir! C'mon you!" He waddled away, his stoker trudging after him.

Smith looked at the rest of the ship's company. "More than I expected."

"The five to starboard are the hands, sir," Archbold explained. "T'other nine are the crew o' the six-inch gun."

One of the nine wore the badge of a leading seaman gunner on the sleeve of his jumper and Smith asked him, "Name?"

"Davies, sir." He was a squat, bull-terrier of a man with a hard eye and a hoarse voice.

"Where's this gun?" It was obviously not aboard. A six-inch gun weighed six tons and fired a hundred-pound shell.

"Dockyard, sir. It's an Italian gun but they were short of crews so they loaned it to us. It's mounted on a pontoon. We towed it up the coast to give supporting fire for the Eyeties – Italian Army, sir. This last trip we came under fire and the captain was wounded. The pontoon was holed and we only just got it back, so it's gone to the dockyard for repair."

Smith looked at the gunners and asked, "Are they a good crew?"

"Not bad, sir," answered Davies. "And they'll get better." That sounded both promise and threat; they would get better, or else –

Smith spoke to every man, briefly but assessing, putting names to faces and committing them to memory. Then he inspected the ship with Archbold and Davies. It did not take long. She was not smart, a work-horse, but she was clean and showed the signs of care. He saw the little six-pounder gun forward that was Davies' charge, the wheelhouse and the cramped and steamy galley. He descended a companion aft to the mess-deck where a dozen of the crew lived, and Buckley would bunk, then down another companion forward that led to the quarters of the rest. Here he also found the cabin shared by Fred Archbold and Geordie Hogg, the engineer – and the tiny cabin that was his own.

A strapped valise lay on the deck of the cabin, the kit of the last captain of *Hercules*, waiting to be taken ashore. Fred Archbold picked it up. "I'll see to this, sir. It's a mortal shame. He's a real man, a good skipper. I just hope he'll be all right."

"So do I." Smith looked around the cabin, crowded already with its small table, bunk and one sagging, old easy chair. He would have to squeeze his kit in here, but where would Menzies go?

The mate said hesitantly, "She's a good little boat, sir, though not what you were used to in your last ship, I suppose?"

"She was a light cruiser." Smith recalled the spacious cabin aboard *Dauntless* but as he had last seen it, blasted into tangled wreckage by an eight-inch shell, the torn bodies of a gun's crew amongst it. He sighed. "I'll be more comfortable here."

He pushed past Archbold and Davies where they stood outside the cabin and left them exchanging puzzled glances as he went on deck. He was satisfied with *Hercules* and that she was ready for sea, ready for what he planned. She would do, had to because Pickett would give him nothing else and Smith would not ask. He knew he had only got *Hercules* so that Pickett could claim he had given 'all assistance possible'.

Smith found a strip of deck aft on the port side, away from the thickening smoke that poured from *Hercules'* funnel as Geordie

Hogg raised steam. Here he could pace up and down between the steel covers hiding the coal-chutes to the bunkers below, and the bitts in the stern to which the drifter's little boat was secured alongside. Eight long, quick strides forward, eight strides aft, his face set and expressionless but inside him the frustration boiling. He was worried by the news of the German advance and an Italian retreat. His task was daunting enough but Winter who had set him that task was now dead. His orders came from Admiralty but Pickett and Devereux were against him, and he was alone here. Winter must have had some plan in mind when he asked for Smith, surely? More than just to lend him three MAS boats and leave him to get on with it.

He turned again and strode aft, eyes shooting swift glances about the ship, taking in the details of her while his mind worked. He was aware of Menzies standing stiffly right aft, saw the youngster's eyes flick away; he had been watching Smith covertly. Menzies' cap was crammed down onto his stuck-out ears. He was a funny, stocky little lad, standing there so straight. Pickett had sent him to Smith as a punishment and Smith suspected the boy felt it, despite his attitude of not caring. And the MAS captains had lost the draw – but he thought he was lucky getting them. Then the face of Helen Blair rose in his mind, his memory of it when they first exchanged glances –

A boat was coming alongside and the rating sitting in the sternsheets had the gold star of a Writer on his sleeve: probably one of the clerks from Devereux's office. He called up to Menzies, "Signal for the captain, sir!"

He stood up and held out a package. Menzies took it, signed a receipt and brought the package to Smith as the boat pulled away. Smith ripped open the seal. As he had expected, the package was sent by Devereux, and contained the intelligence information on Trieste.

He strode forward to the companion and climbed down to his cabin. There he spread the papers out on his desk and found the information was dated four days before. He remembered that Devereux had said fog had hidden Trieste these last few days. Besides a map there was an aerial photograph, and a damned good one, he thought, showing the ships that had been in the harbour four days ago, one of them neatly lettered:

51

SALZBURG. The length of her made her stand out from the others. It seemed Trieste was her base – so far. The photograph also showed the booms stretched between the moles. A sheaf of typed papers clipped together, a brief, described the three moles spaced across the mouth of the harbour as breakwaters of stone, high, thick and solid. The booms connecting them were affairs of buoys joined together by wire hawsers and supporting anti-submarine nets. In the photograph they looked fragile, lines stretched like thread between the moles. That was deceptive; they were probably an inch thick and would certainly stop a ship trying to force an entrance. But if they could be cut as Zacco suggested, then –

He had to see for himself. And he had to see Zacco about those cutters. He looked at his watch. There was time enough and he could not waste it. Voss would not.

He swung away from the desk, his anger and frustration forgotten, eager now. He climbed the ladder but paused with his head still inside the companion. Menzies appeared from behind the superstructure, pacing the deck on the port side with ludicrously long, restless strides. His hands were clasped behind him and his head thrust forward. He halted, paused to scowl from under his brows at some distant part of the ship and then turned and strode aft, was lost behind the superstructure.

Smith recognised himself. It was for an act like this that Pickett had banished Menzies to *Hercules*, but Smith was not Pickett. He grinned and stepped out on deck to stand in the shadow of the superstructure. Menzies came striding, halted to peer again, his back to Smith, then turned and stiffened to attention as he met Smith's glare, awaited the blasting. But Smith only growled, "Don't keep looking for trouble, Mr Menzies. You'll find it'll come of its own and fast enough. Now call Mr Archbold. We're going out to the MAS boats and we need a meal first."

HM Drifter *Hercules* sailed at dusk. Old Fred Archbold took his place at the wheel, pipe in mouth, then caught Smith's eye on him and tamped it with a plug of old newspaper, put it away in his pocket. He said placidly, "Some o' these regular navy ways I keep forgettin', sir. Like not smoking at the wheel."

Smith looked ahead, straight-faced. "I can understand you forgetting when there's no regular officer to remind you."

Fred Archbold understood too; the bargain had been struck and he was content.

Hercules steamed slowly across the lagoon to the island of San Elena and there she anchored. The crews of the three MAS boats watched her and at Smith's hail they started their engines and crept out to lie alongside her. As the engines stopped Smith heard in the silence the sound of singing. The captains came aboard in the gathering dusk and found him with Fred Archbold staring towards the big shed some two hundred yards away. Pietro Zacco saluted and said, "Balestra again, sir. I told you about him."

"The Mad Professor you called him."

"Yes."

"Why?"

Zacco shrugged. "So people call him. He looks wild sometimes. He has funny ideas."

"What ideas?"

"Well . . . he says one day aircraft will control the seas like they control the air." Zacco smiled apologetically.

Smith remembered a young naval pilot called Pearce who said that one day aircraft would sink capital ships. He had not done that but he had crippled a cruiser with one big bomb. But Pearce was dead, killed in the attack.*

Zacco said, "He plays all the time with engines. He has a car, American. He keeps it on the mainland in Mestre, and they say he takes it apart and puts it together. Crazy . . . If Pagani here had a car he would drive it and look for girls."

They laughed at that, Pagani included. Smith grinned but then got down to business. "If you'll come below, gentlemen." And to Buckley standing nearby, "See if the cook can make us some coffee, please."

He paused at the head of the companion and shouted, "Mr Menzies!" And as Menzies came running from aft, "You'd better be in on this. Come on."

They all crowded into the tiny cabin, Smith by the desk where he unrolled the chart and spread out the intelligence information on Trieste. The three captains and Archbold sat on the bunk and Menzies stood wedged just inside the door. Smith made the introductions then Buckley arrived bearing a tray

* *Dauntless*: Hodder and Stoughton, 1980.

holding a collection of thick china mugs and a battered coffee pot. He filled the mugs and passed them round. Smith said drily, "There seems to be a spare. You might as well have it."

"Thank you, sir." Buckley filled the mug he had brought for himself and stood outside the door, looking over Menzies' head into the cabin.

The captains sipped at the mugs. Pagani peered into his and said, "English coffee?"

"That's right." Smith said solemnly, "I bet you don't get coffee like this in Italy."

They looked at him and then grinned.

Smith put down his mug, serious now. "Tonight we reconnoitre Trieste. I want to see those boom defences, all of them." He took them through the planned operation step by step, using the chart and the intelligence information. Then he asked, "Any questions? Suggestions?"

Zacco said, "After I refuelled I went to the dockyard and saw the metal cutters we talked about. I saw them used on hawsers like this" – his finger tapped the intelligence sheets – "and they work. I asked if they could be fitted tomorrow. Was that right?" Smith nodded and Zacco added, "You will have to go to the dockyard, sir. They are very busy. To get the work done will need an order of priority."

"We will get that." Smith paused, then: "If all goes well tonight then tomorrow night we go for *Salzburg*."

There was silence for a moment. Events were moving quickly. The captains had only met Smith a few hours before and already they were embarked on one operation with another to follow in twenty-four hours. And that one to cut a way into an enemy harbour at night and attack a capital ship, in the teeth of the defences of the port, the guns of the ship herself and her escorts.

Zacco broke the tension. "This squadron of ours – what is its title? We have a number – a name?"

Smith shook his head. "Not yet. Any ideas?" And when none were forthcoming he remembered Pickett's phrase. "How about *The Gatecrashers*?"

Pagani said slowly, "It means someone who crashes at a gate. Yes?"

"It means someone who goes to a party when he hasn't been invited."

Pagani roared with laughter. "That is good! *The Gate-crashers!*"

The conference broke up in a cheerful mood but as Buckley collected up the mugs he thought grimly, 'Here we bloody go again!'

The engines of the MAS boats coughed one by one, roared, subsided to a low rumbling. They eased away from *Hercules* and left her at anchor as they fell into line ahead, Zacco's boat leading. Smith was in the cockpit with Zacco, Buckley sitting behind him on the counter. Menzies, in borrowed oilskins that hung to his ankles, was with Gallina in the boat astern. Last of the line came Pagani.

Smith looked astern. It was night now. The rain had briefly stopped but there was the threat of more to come in the overcast sky. That was good, the kind of weather that would cover them. The city was a series of humped shadows in the darkness but he could still make out the long sweep of the quay of the Riva degli Schiavoni. Helen Blair was there, in the house on the Ca' di Dio. He asked Zacco, "You said the –" he paused because her title, applied to this English girl, was still incongruous to him "– the Contessa had a sad story?"

The big lieutenant nodded. "I do not know the details but she was living in the south and her man, she was to marry him, he was an officer of the British Army in the Dardanelles. He was killed and so she came here. On the mainland she has a car, like Balestra, and she goes up to the line and gives chocolate and cigarettes to the soldiers. She has a yacht and sails up and down the coast on the same work. It is her duty but her own duty. You see?"

Smith said, "A task she's set herself."

"That is so."

That was not odd, there were plenty of women doing the same thing in England and France, only here in Italy was it a rarity. Smith had already heard criticism of the Italian army for providing little or nothing in the way of comforts or recreation for their men when out of the line.

Her story was not uncommon, either. Far from it. This war made more widows every day. That did not make it commonplace, grief was no less for being shared with millions. The girl had courage and was going on living. Smith was glad that he had no ties, that no heart would break over him. He did not give a thought to the women he had met and left on the way.

Now his thoughts were on Trieste as the little flotilla of MAS boats slipped past the guard-boat, and out of the harbour by the Porto di Lido.

Salzburg. Voss. Seek out and destroy.

The note of the engines changed, grew to a snarl as the boats worked up to twenty knots, their sterns dug in and bows lifted and spray came flying back at him where he stood in the cockpit.

5 Night Action

Trieste lay before them.

A dark, chill night and the sea flat calm under low-hanging clouds but a white line showed where small waves broke against the mole ahead of them. Smith stood by Zacco. He could just make out close astern the low, narrow silhouette of Gallina's boat and further astern that of Pagani's. The boats were running on their electric motors. As the mole was sighted Zacco reduced speed further, to a bare couple of knots. They slipped on in with the only sound the low hum of the motors, and that almost lost under the mutter of the sea as it washed the base of the mole. The boats made hardly a ripple. No lamp flashed a challenge, no gun blazed at them out of the darkness. Yet. The machine-guns in the three boats were manned and ready. One Colt machine-gun was mounted before the forward cockpit, one on the port side of the after cockpit. In the forward cockpit of Zacco's boat, beside the gunner, were the two seamen and the torpedoman. The after cockpit was no less crowded with Zacco, Smith, the machine-gunner and Buckley. All of them aboard the boats were tense. One of the seamen climbed out of the forward cockpit and crept forward over the curved deck to the bow.

This was the most southerly of the three moles, breakwaters, built across the mile and a half wide entrance to the harbour. Booms closed the openings between each of them and between them and the shore. Smith could make out the loom of Punta Ronco, the headland at the south of the harbour's mouth. There would be a boom between it and the mole. Smith pointed and Zacco nodded, the boat's head turned south and they crept along close to the mole, the other boats following.

The end of the mole was close, a square-cut black shape against the darkness of the night when the searchlight's beam snapped out from somewhere on Punta Ronco, wavered, then slowly traversed across the sea between shore and mole. Smith ordered, "Stop engines!" The hum of the motors ceased and the three boats rocked gently. Smith watched the long thin cone of the searchlight's beam drift hesitantly across the sea, following the line of the boom and Smith could see the path it was taking and became uneasy. But the beam slid on, washed over the mole, leaving the boats hidden in the shadow close alongside. Moved on along the length of the mole. Went out.

All of them blinked against the sudden return of the darkness. Smith waited until he could see to the end of the mole, then ordered: "Slow ahead." The motors hummed and the boats slowly closed the boom. Zacco was watching the seaman sprawled in the bow, saw the lift of his hand and stopped the motors again. The boat slipped on with the last of the way on her, bumped gently, was still but for a gentle rolling as the sea pushed at her.

Smith climbed from the cockpit and went quickly foward along the narrow strip of deck beside the engine-room, passed between the port side torpedo resting in its clamps on the deck, and the forward cockpit. The men in there glanced at him, dark faces watching him pass, a glint of eyes. He lay down by the seaman in the bow who held on to the boom with a boat hook. He had hooked on to a link in the six-foot length of chain that, where the photographs had shown wire hawsers and buoys, joined two baulks of timber, each baulk two feet in diameter and the chain itself massive. Smith eased over the bow and down to kneel on one of the baulks of timber with the sea washing over it, running around him. He lay flat and reached down under the surface, searching with fumbling fingers, and found two more chains. So the timbers were joined by at least three of those huge chains, and there might well be a fourth deeper and out of his reach.

The log rolled gently to the push of the sea and he clung on with hooked fingers and clawing boots, involuntarily took a mouthful of seawater and spat it out as the log recovered. He rose to his knees and grabbed the bow of the boat, dragged himself aboard and clambered aft to the cockpit to stand dripping by Zacco. He said quietly, "Big timbers and big chains." Somebody had been busy since the aerial photos were taken. He saw the dismay on the lieutenant's face but only said softly, "Move north."

The motors hummed and the MAS turned and nosed back along the mole, the other two turning and following.

58

They stopped as the searchlight's beam searched again but once more were hidden in the shadow of the mole, moved on when the beam was snuffed out.

Another boom. The same construction of huge baulks of timber and chains.

The three boats crept on along the central mole to its end and a third boom.

The same.

To the third mole, and on to the fourth and last boom that ran to the northern shore. Here lay the city of Trieste, in darkness, but the lift of the buildings to the medieval castle on its hill was clear. The fourth boom followed the pattern of the other three, identical in its solid strength of timber and chains.

They lay in the shadow of the mole but not for long. What they had found was bad enough, but Smith wanted to know if there was an inner boom to cut off any direct approach once the outer line was breached. So they returned to the centre mole and stopped at the southern end of it where began the shortest boom of the four and that furthest from either shore. In the pitchy blackness close under the mole Smith started to strip down to his vest and drawers. Buckley followed his example.

Smith was under no illusions as to his prowess as a swimmer. He had to go himself, see for himself, but – He whispered to Zacco, "I need another good swimmer."

Zacco nodded. "Lombardo is the best, best of all I know."

"Can you spare him?"

"The *meccanico* can do his job. He is not a *motorista* like Lombardo but good enough. I'll call Lombardo."

Smith said, "Ask him. I want a volunteer." And besides, Lombardo was – well, Lombardo.

He came crouching out of the engine-room at Zacco's quiet call, straightened as he stood in the cockpit.

Smith said, "I'm a rotten swimmer but I want to take a look at the boom. I need another good one with me. What about it?"

Lombardo looked over the side. "Christ! It'll freeze the balls off – "

Smith broke in impatiently, "I know that! I'm freezing *now*! Make your bloody mind up! Do you know anybody better for the job?"

For answer Lombardo stripped off his vest, muttering

59

obscenities under his breath, unbuckled his belt.

Smith shivered despite himself as he whispered his orders to Zacco. "Time us. If we're not back by first light, get out. And if a patrol sees you, run for it."

Zacco nodded, whispered, "Have luck."

Smith lowered himself on to the boom and from there into the water on the inshore side, gasped as the cold of it took his breath, then struck out as the other two followed him. Together they swam slowly forward into the harbour, Smith thinking that he was a fool, he could have sent Buckley and Lombardo because their reports would be absolutely reliable. But he needed to see.

He counted to himself, trying to measure their progress. He had told Zacco to get out if they weren't back by first light but if they did not return to the boats in half an hour they would not return at all. He knew he could not last long in this bitterly cold sea.

If a patrol chased the boats away then at best he would live out the war as a prisoner. Devereux and Pickett would laugh and shake their heads smugly.

He remembered the elegant beauty of the Contessa, and his belief that there could be the heat of passion behind that cool exterior.

Christ! It was cold!

Buckley said softly, "Summat ahead, sir." He and Lombardo were swimming easily, only Smith, the poorest swimmer, was splashing and blowing. But now he could see what Buckley spoke of, a darker shadow stretching across the water before them. They reached it and found yet another boom of timbers and chains.

Smith hauled himself onto the boom and rested there a moment with Buckley one side of him, Lombardo the other. But the wind froze him. He had to go on. There might be a third line of defence. He had to know. He groaned inside then gritted his teeth and lowered himself over the boom, shoved away from it, struck out again.

He had counted to a hundred and seventy-six on the first leg. He counted again on this one. At two hundred and fifty they had encountered nothing, only the ruffled surface of the harbour faded into the darkness. He gasped, "See anything?"

"No, sir." That was Buckley.

Lombardo growled, "Not a goddam thing!"

Smith turned and led them back, to rest again on the inner boom, then swim on. He was tired and bitterly cold, certain that on his own he would have panicked now at the certainty of drowning. He cursed his weakness but blessed his foresight in bringing Buckley and Lombardo who could drag him back if he collapsed. But he would not return towed ignominiously between them. He would keep on. Keep on. Keep on . . .

"Here y'are, sir." That was Buckley's whispered warning.

Smith blinked water from his eyes and realised they were in deeper darkness and the mole towered above them. He reached out and gripped its rough stone surface slimed with weed and clung to it. All three of them hung there, heads just clear of the water. Smith peered to left and right. Was this the mole against which lay the boats? Or had some current carried them north or south and this was another mole? Should they go left or right? It was a desperately important decision for him. He could not go much further.

He thought the current might have set them to the north, took a breath and pushed away from the mole, swam southward. The searchlight's beam fingered out from Punta Ronco to the south and they edged into the mole again, clung on. They watched the beam trace the line of the southernmost boom, the first mole, the second boom – Smith took a gasping breath. Now he could see where he and his party were, near the southern end of the correct mole and around that end the boats would be waiting.

The searchlight went out and left them in seeming deeper darkness. Smith did not wait for his night vision to return but struck out again. The square end of the mole was clear enough when they reached it. He banged his knuckles on the timber of the boom as it rose out of the sea before him, swore weakly, clambered up on to the timber. Seconds later a MAS nosed out from the shadow of the mole and its bow nudged against the timber. The seaman sprawled in the bow hooked on and Smith pushed at Lombardo and Buckley, urging them to climb aboard. He followed them, was dragged in by them, skinning his knees, and stayed on hands and knees in the bottom of the boat, head hanging, gasping as the boat retreated again into the shadow of the mole.

61

Zacco crouched beside him and Smith could see concern on the big man's face but told him, "All right. We'll get out now."

They had been here long enough, every second on edge as they listened and watched for a patrolling boat or a sentry on the mole, tensed for discovery at any moment, for the challenge and the hail of fire out of the night.

The motors hummed and the MAS turned away from the mole and headed seaward, the other boats following. Smith towelled himself dry and dragged on his clothes and boots. Lombardo, cursing steadily in American, had dressed and gone back to his engine-room. Now he appeared with a thermos and two enamel mugs, poured into them, slopped in something from a flask he took from his pocket and handed them to Smith and Buckley.

Smith gulped at the steamy mug of coffee laced thickly with grappa and said, "Thanks."

Lombardo grunted, asked, "See what you wanted?"

Smith said, "Not what I wanted. But I saw."

Buckley was smacking his lips over his own big mug of coffee and grappa. Smith said, "Well done, both of you. Thank you." Lombardo only grunted, went back to his engines. That had to be said because they had earned it, but Smith's thoughts about what he had seen were bitter.

He was not left to brood on them.

A hail came from the machine-gunner in the forward cockpit, his arm outstretched, pointing out on the starboard beam. Smith stared in that direction and saw the silhouette of a ship under its trailing plume of funnel smoke – a near shapeless hump in the darkness bracketed by the white water of bow-wave and wash. He thought it was less than a mile away and did not look big enough for a destroyer, was more likely one of the old torpedo-boats the Austrians used on coastal patrols. She would be nearly as fast as the MAS boats when she worked up to full speed but that would take her some time. She was broadside on, her course nearly parallel to their own. A light flickered out from the ship. The challenge. She had seen them!

Smith swung on Zacco but the lieutenant had already given the order. The hum of the motors ceased, the petrol engines roared into life and the boat surged forward. Smith glanced astern and saw Gallina's boat following suit. But Pagani? The third boat lay still in the sea and was being rapidly left astern.

Smith shouted, "Pagani's engines haven't fired!"

Zacco glanced astern and as he did so a searchlight's beam flashed out from the Austrian ship and settled on Pagani's boat. Smith swore. The torpedoes of the MAS boats were not swung out for a torpedo attack and by the time they were Pagani's boat would be shot to pieces.

He shouted, "Tell Gallina to tow Pagani!" He waited as Zacco yelled the order at the forward cockpit. A seaman stood up with the lamp and as it began to flicker the signal, Smith ordered, "Hard astarboard! Open fire!" The boat heeled, turning tightly, stern skidding. "Midships!" Zacco had anticipated that and now the bow pointed at the torpedo-boat and the MAS raced in at her, accelerating with every second. A gun flashed aboard the Austrian ship and Smith saw the shell burst short of Pagani's boat and Gallina's. He had turned and was running down to Pagani, as ordered. The machine-guns hammered and tracer curved out in lazy arcs towards the torpedo-boat, arcs that wavered as the MAS bucked at near full speed now. The gun mounted on the port side of the cockpit was close by Smith and Zacco, deafening.

Zacco was bellowing above the din and at his order the torpedoman and the seamen climbed out of the forward cockpit. They balanced spread-legged on the leaping deck, hauling on the tackles to swing the starboard torpedo out into its firing position. Smith looked beyond them. The boat was closing fast on the Austrian. Despite the darkness and the driving spray he could see that she was an old torpedo-boat, a little like one of the old thirty-knot destroyers with her turtleback bow. Old she might be, but she was three times the size of the MAS, nearly ten times her tonnage and she carried two 4.7cm guns. They were both in action and firing rapidly. A direct hit or two from those guns could put an end to an MAS boat with its fragile wooden hull.

Now the searchlight's beam slid away from Pagani's boat and jerked across the surface of the sea seeking Zacco's boat, seeing her as a threat. The guns also shifted their aim. So Smith's tactic had worked to that extent; he had bought Pagani and Gallina a brief breathing space. But what would it cost?

The searchlight's beam fastened on the boat and lit all aboard her. He heard the rip of shells overhead, turned and saw them burst astern in the frothing wake. He faced forward as the starboard torpedo settled into its firing position with a solid *clunk!* It hung over the sea held only by its pincer-like clamps. He squinted against the light, one hand held up against it, and saw the torpedo-boat had turned away, the silhouette foreshortening, the two funnels blending into a single stack as she showed her stern. She was clear now, barely a quarter mile away and she had swerved away from a threatened torpedo attack. Stern on like that she showed no target to shoot at.

Smith ordered, "Starboard ten!"

Zacco turned the wheel, the boat's head swung and she went racing out wide of the torpedo-boat but still gaining on her rapidly till they were abeam of her. And all the time the machine-guns hammered at the limit of their range, and the searchlight held them, the Austrian guns flashing and shells falling astern but creeping closer. Forward in the boat they were hauling on the tackles of the port-side torpedo. Smith shouted, "Fire at the searchlight!" He heard Zacco's bellow, passing on the order, heard also the yelled answers, guessed from their frustration that the machine-gunners were already trying to put out the light that harassed them. He ordered, "Hard aport!"

The boat's head swung in again, stern skidding, to point once more at the torpedo-boat and go charging down at her. There was a *crash!* forward and the boat shook through her length. Something droned past Smith's head. They had been hit, there was a ragged hole in the curved foredeck but somehow the boat held on. Again the torpedo-boat turned away to show her stern and at Smith's order the MAS swerved away, went bucking across the churned water of the torpedo-boat's wake then turned to race up on her port side, trying again for a torpedo attack.

The searchlight went out and the machine-gunners yelled and cheered – then resumed firing. The MAS went charging in once more and the torpedo-boat turned away. A shell fell close alongside the MAS and hurled seawater into the cockpit, flying into their faces as if hurled from a bucket. Buckley was at Smith's shoulder as he wiped at his streaming face, shouting and pointing. "They're under way, sir!"

Smith turned and saw the blaze of white water, the two little low shapes of Gallina's boat with Pagani's hauled up close astern in tow. They were moving at speed. He faced forward, shouted, "Hard aport!" The boat turned tightly. "Midships!" They headed away from the torpedo-boat on a course to meet Gallina and Pagani. He turned to look astern at the torpedo-boat but she was almost out of range of the machine-guns and had not turned to follow, her own torpedoes virtually useless against the darting MAS boats. "Cease fire!"

He did not intend to chase. Her captain was obviously not going to give him the chance of a torpedo shot and in a gunfight the MAS was hopelessly out-matched. As it was they had been lucky. They had been hit once but without serious damage. If that near miss by the after cockpit had been six feet to the right then the cockpit and all in it would have gone. Besides, there was the lame duck to think of, Pagani's boat.

The deep snarl of the engines was comparative silence after the ear-ripping rattling of the machine-guns. His ears still rang from the din but he could hear the cheering of the boat's crew. Zacco was grinning widely, delighted. They came up on Gallina's boat, towing Pagani, and slipped into station ahead of them. Their crews cheered too. Smith realised he had been sweating from excitement and felt it chilling on his body now. He was cold and drained of emotion, saw the turn of Zacco's head and managed to return the smile, but his face felt stiff. Reaction had him now, as always when the danger past, and as always he found no cause for self congratulation. They had shot-up the torpedo-boat and its crew would not forget it for a long time. But he had survived by bluff and luck; all three of the boats could have been blown to pieces by the Austrian guns.

He asked, "Any casualties?"

The signal lamps flickered between the boats and the answer came to him from Zacco. "No casualties."

He was glad of that, anyway. "Tell them, 'Well done'." That was no more than the truth. They were pleased with their night's work; to survive an encounter with a bigger and more heavily gunned boat, give as good as they got and send her running for home, that was reason to be pleased.

He was not. The boom defences at Trieste would not be broken by hydraulic shears. He knew no way to penetrate them and was certain it was no coincidence that they had been thus strengthened since the arrival of Voss. Their sudden installation carried the stamp of his energy, drive and foresight. Smith's joke about gatecrashers had recoiled upon him and he told himself bitterly that he still had to learn to hold his tongue.

Forward they had hauled on the tackles and swung the torpedoes inboard again to rest in their clamps on the deck. He shifted away from Zacco, managed to stand apart from all of them in that small well, silent and brooding. He merely grunted acknowledgment when it was reported that Pagani's *motorista* had got the boat's engines firing and she had dropped the tow, was proceeding under her own power. Only when they came to Venice and entered the lagoon, the three boats slipping slowly across its glassy surface, engines muttering, did Zacco ask, "The booms. They are bad, yes?"

Smith replied flatly, "They are bloody awful. We can't break through or slip under. The only thing that would pass those booms is a flying-fish."

Smith and Buckley climbed aboard *Hercules* and only then he remembered there was no bunk aboard for Menzies. They would have to arrange something –

But Menzies called up from where he stood in the cockpit of Gallina's boat, "If you please, sir, Mr Gallina can fix me up with a berth for the night." Menzies was obviously getting on well with the men of the MAS. Now he went on excitedly, "That was some scrap, sir!"

Some scrap! The boy still talked as if it was a game when he might well have died this night. Smith answered drily, "I'm glad you weren't bored, Mr Menzies. Good night to you all."

The night was turning grey, it would be light soon. The three boats went away across the lagoon with a low rumble of engines, headed for the island of the Giudecca and their crews' quarters. Smith looked around at Venice, the city seeming in that first light as soft-edged and insubstantial as the mist that furred the water. There was an atmosphere of mystery about it now, as there was about that girl. He was curious to know more about her but doubted that he would ever learn much.

He went down to his cabin, stripped off his clothes and fell on the bunk, dragged the blankets around him. The face of the girl floated before his eyes, then the heaving timber baulks and massive chains of the boom. He jerked briefly awake as the Austrian torpedo-boat roared down on him, guns blazing. He groaned and turned over.

'The only thing that would pass those booms is a flying-fish.'

Seek out and destroy.

His objective was as far away as ever.

6 "What the hell is that?"

In the house on the Riva Ca' di Dio the old housekeeper woke Helen Blair before it was light. She breakfasted on coffee and rolls then bathed quickly and dressed in the clothes laid out for her. The dress was pale blue silk, as were the stockings that clothed the slender legs showing under the hem of the skirt. She made up her face carefully, pinned up her dark hair and set atop of it a wide-brimmed hat that tied with ribbons in a bow under her chin. Her map went in a pocket of her cloak and she checked that the small note-book with its pencil was in her bag, snapped it shut. She was ready.

She stood at the window for a minute looking out over the lagoon as the sky paled in the east. It was clear. For once it would be a fine day. Each morning she treasured this moment of quiet because going to the front was dangerous, became more dangerous with every passing day of the war. From the window she could not see San Elena where the three MAS boats lay. The face of the young English naval officer was clear in her mind. He, too, was alone. She did not want to go but knew that she must, turned from the window and went down and out of the house.

From the quay she took one of the *vaporetti*, the little steam-boats that plied up and down the Grand Canal. The *vaporetto*, crowded with people on their way to work, carried her up the winding course of the canal. She got off at the railway station and took a train to Mestre. The engine puffed along the causeway joining Venice to the mainland, the smoke from its chimney coiling back along the train and over the still waters of the lagoon and marshes.

Mestre was busy. She saw a hospital train in the station that was headed south and another loaded with troops, reinforcements, bound for the north. The soldiers were mainly *bersaglieri*, light infantrymen. They stood by the open doors of the train, their hats rakish with the plumes of green cock's feathers. They were young, handsome men and their eyes followed her admiringly as she walked by. She smiled at them. There was a full battalion or more, close on a thousand men.

The house she sought in Mestre was close to the station, shabby but standing in its own little plot of land. There was a shed, a lean-to built on to the side of the house and its doors were open to show the car. Luigi waited there. He was short and fat, too old for military service. He was a mechanic and he owned the house that had been his mother's but the car belonged to Helen Blair. He told her that it was all ready; he had checked it himself. He also showed her the two baskets on the back seat of the car, one packed with chocolate bars and the other with packets of cigarettes. She paid him from her purse and thanked him. He swung the handle of the car and as its engine started he said as he always did, "Take care. It is dangerous."

She knew that, thanked him again then left him looking worriedly after her as she drove out of Mestre on the road to San Dona di Piave.

She crossed the Piave river at San Dona and drove on northwards. Twice she passed columns of soldiers and several times troops of field-guns drawn by teams of plodding horses, the drivers sitting slackly in their saddles. The road had dried under the sun and the cold wind from the mountains so dust rose around the marching men and lay finely on the polished coach-work of the car. Before noon she crossed the Livenza river, roaring in spate. Far away to her left lifted the mountains, snow-capped. This was the road to Portogruaro.

The road was very busy now, crowded with supply wagons and more bodies of troops moving north-eastward towards the front. There were also empty wagons returning and a lot of civilian traffic, carts loaded high with sticks of furniture, the women sitting in front dressed in black and their heads covered with shawls, a man plodding along at the head of the donkey hauling each cart. There were peasants shoving wheelbarrows and a wizened woman had an old perambulator with a big blanket-wrapped bundle squeezed into it.

Just south of Portogruaro, Helen Blair was forced to stop at the tail of a convoy of supply trucks, the road ahead of them blocked. A regiment of *bersaglieri* had pulled off the road to let the convoy pass and now they lounged under the spread branches of the trees that lined the road. Further up the column the whips of the drivers of the horse-drawn wagons cracked and the engines of the trucks roared then subsided into a frustrated grumble. The light infantrymen waited patiently and stared up at the black branches of the trees. Despite the sun the day was cold with the wind from the mountains but their faces were sweat-streaked from the marching.

The convoy moved slowly on and Helen Blair engaged low gear and slowly followed. She smiled and waved at the *bersaglieri* as she passed and they sat up, startled at the sight of her, then smiled back. There was hunger in the eyes of many of them but only once did she detect lust that forced her gaze away. She thought there must be close on two thousand of them.

A minute or so later the convoy halted, to roll forward a few yards and halt again. The rumble of gunfire was loud now, a constant thunder that over-rode the muttering engines of the creeping column. She conformed to its stop-start progress for some minutes before it dawned on her that there was no civilian traffic on the road here, that the trucks and wagons coming down on the other side were still fully loaded like those she followed. She heard the drivers of the two columns shouting across at each other as they passed. She opened the door and stood up, leaning out and holding on to the leather roof of the car. Now she could just see over the wagons ahead to a field a quarter-mile up the road where trucks ground around in a circle, churning up the soft earth. She frowned, puzzled, then realised the convoy was being directed into the field, turned around and sent back. She sat down and carefully marked her position on the map then edged the car forward again as the convoy moved.

She came to a house that stood back from the road, its courtyard crowded with troops and these were not fresh replacements like the *bersaglieri* she had seen. Dried mud coated their uniforms from head to boots. They were tired and their blood-shot eyes stared out of slack-jawed faces. Helen Blair eased the car off the road and into the courtyard, stopped the engine. She got down and took the baskets from the back of the car and began to move through the crowd. "Would you like some chocolate? A smoke, signore?"

She held up the baskets, smiled into their faces and spoke to them. At first they just stood and watched her pass, stared disbelievingly at this vision of a slender, fresh-faced girl in a pale blue silken dress as they crammed the chocolate into their mouths, or sucked deep on the cigarettes, answering her in monosyllables if at all. But after a time they moved to group around her, careful not to touch her with their mud and filth. They talked more freely, though still slowly, having to think about it. They were survivors of a battalion and there were only two hundred of them. They had lost many killed and wounded but some others – they looked away, embarrassed. Helen Blair realised they were talking of deserters. She asked if the other units in the line were suffering as badly. They answered that many had fared worse; whole regiments had vanished, swallowed up by the enemy advance. As they crowded about her the sour stench of them closed her in, a smell compounded of stale sweat and foul bodies, dirt, smoke and cordite. Her stomach rebelled as it always did and as always she controlled it, did not allow her smile to flicker or her body to flinch away from them. It was the smell of war that revolted her, not these men. They were war's victims.

One wild-eyed soldier said, "They have firing squads now."

The others did not say anything and Helen Blair asked, "Firing squads?"

"For deserters and spies. The firing squads are using more ammunition than the rest of the army."

"That's enough of that!" An officer, a captain, shoved his way through them. "Fall in! We march! Fall in!"

The men shifted away, formed stiffly into ranks, slung their rifles over their shoulders. The captain looked exhausted, rocked on his feet. Helen Blair asked him, "Where are they going?"

"South. To the Livenza. Into reserve. Regroup. Dig in." His voice was slurred. He walked over to stand before his men. Helen Blair could see no other officers. He croaked a husky command and they shuffled forward, picked up the step, followed him as he marched unsteadily out of the courtyard and on to the road.

Helen returned to her car and dropped the half-empty baskets in the back. There was another car pulled in at the side of the road now across from the courtyard. The driver, a corporal, stood beside it, eating bread and sausage, drinking from a bottle of wine. His officer sat in the rear seat of the car, his meal beside him on the seat on a spread white napkin. He ate it one-handed while he pored over his map. The car was mud-splashed.

The officer looked up and saw Helen Blair, shouted, "Contessa!"

She recognised him. He was a major of engineers, on a General's staff. She had met him several times, always immaculately uniformed, boots and buttons gleaming. Now the uniform was coated in dust, the boots filthy, and the man looked dead-tired as he climbed down from the car and came to her, the map fluttering in one hand as he saluted with the other. "Contessa! Where are you going?"

He spoke in Italian and she answered him in that language, easily. "To Portogruaro and then to the front."

He shook his head. "That is not possible. The front is – fluid. The army is falling back from the Tagliamento. We are going to try – we are going to hold a line along the Livenza river."

Helen said, "I passed some *bersaglieri*. They were going forward."

"For one or two kilometres only. I think they will be used to fight a delaying action."

They had to raise their voices above the rumble of the guns. They could not be far distant, certainly not on the line of the Tagliamento river that was ten or twelve miles to the north.

"Here, I'll show you." He spread out his map on the empty seat beside her. "The Third Army is here, the Second here, the Fourth here." She stared down at the map, taking in the dispositions as he pointed them out, marked in coloured pencil on his map. He went on, "The intention is that they will retire along these routes and take up a line along the river, thus."

She said slowly, "I see." He had said before that they would 'try' – then corrected himself. Now he spoke of 'the intention'.

He folded the map. "So, you see, it is no place for you, nor is this. When the front stabilises it will be different. But now you must go home and wait there."

"When will that be?"

"Oh, soon! Soon!" But he did not sound confident, was haggard with worry.

Helen Blair drove back down the road and gave the remaining contents of the baskets to the *bersaglieri* who still waited, it seemed for orders. She smiled and joked with them and afterwards got back into the car. She could do no more here but there was work for her elsewhere. She drove back to the Livenza seeing again the signs of the retreat, and on to Mestre.

The three MAS boats came alongside the drifter *Hercules* at noon, their crews rested after the night action. For once it was a fine day. The wind coming down out of the mountains was cold but the sky held only scattered clouds and the sun shone, albeit a pale November sun. The island of San Elena was a wasteland of marsh and tall grass rippling like a sea under the wind. The tower of the church of San Elena, the only stone building, lifted stark in the clear air three hundred yards away. Smith was pacing the deck of *Hercules* but halted in that pacing to sniff at the breeze and watch the boats tuck themselves neatly in beside the drifter.

He greeted the captains as they came aboard. A snatch of song accompanied them, coming from the workshop along the shore of the island. Pagani laughed. "That mad Balestra!"

It seemed the captains were hopeful he would have plans for them. They had an air of anticipation, but he did not. The letter from Winter and his orders were in his pocket because he had to go to Devereux and somehow persuade him to support Smith in an attempt on Trieste. He would need those orders to bolster his argument. But also he would need a plan, and a good one, to coax anything out of Devereux and he did not have a plan, had no idea how to get at *Salzburg*. His mind had churned away at the problem but come up with nothing. He looked at the captains' faces, cheerful after the night's success and ready for more action. He told himself he should be cheerful on a day like this and with men like these ready for him to lead. But he was bad-tempered, did not want to be bothered with people. Buckley knew that, knowing Smith, and had carefully kept out of his way and warned the crew of the drifter. Smith was aware now he had to make the effort and force himself at least to politeness.

He talked with the captains, but stiffly. When Pietro Zacco mentioned the hole in his boat and Smith went to the rail to look down at it, the captains exchanged glances and shrugs behind his back.

The shell from the Austrian torpedo-boat had smashed a

ragged hole in through the curved foredeck and another in the port side, well above the water-line, on its way out. Smith turned to Zacco, "Dockyard?"

Zacco shook his head. "No, sir. I think we repair ourselves. I think the dockyard are very busy. I have a carpenter. Lombardo, you know. We will go to the SVAN yard and get some timber. Lombardo will do it."

Smith raised his eyebrows. "He's a useful man."

Zacco grinned. "He does not like the dockyard men trampling about his boat."

"Very good. Carry on."

There was a cough and Smith turned to find Davies, the gunner. "Beggin' your pardon, sir." Only with the fierce Davies it came out like a challenge. "Couldn't help hearing you mention the dockyard. Reckon maybe I should find out about that there gun of ours."

"You speak Italian?"

"A bit, sir. I've been here near a year now."

Smith had no use at the moment for 'that there gun' but it was a part of his little force. He nodded, looked at Zacco. "Will you put him ashore to go to the dockyard?"

"Of course." Zacco hesitated, then: "The shears – we do not need them now."

Smith shook his head. "No. I'm sorry. It was a good idea but Voss was a jump ahead of us. Shears won't cut through those booms."

Zacco and Davies went off. The other two captains returned to their boats and Smith to his pacing. He was foul-tempered from frustration, beating his head against a wall, and cursing himself for that foul temper. He needed something to do and there was nothing for him aboard *Hercules*. Fred Archbold had been running this little ship efficiently for the past twenty years and did not need Smith. Nor did he need Menzies, standing stiffly in the stern. Smith growled at him, "Come on." Together they went down to the MAS boats.

The Italian captains and their crews were carrying out routine maintenance. The gunners stripped down, cleaned and re-assembled the Colt machine-guns. The torpedomen and the seamen hauled on the tackles and swung out the torpedoes, swung them in again, checked the working of the release gear, cleaned and oiled. The *motoristi* and *meccanici* worked below on the engine. Smith and Menzies moved about the boats, lending a hand when they could, but learning all the time.

While this was going on Zacco's boat returned and Davies came with it, reported to Smith, "She's still lying hauled up on a slip where we left her. They're full up wi' work in there, sir. It's a dog's life bein' a dockyard matey just now. They're working around the clock. *Harrier*'s in there now but she's ready for sea."

"Very good," Smith answered. A pontoon gun would not blast him into the harbour of Trieste. He thought that *Harrier*'s captain would be in a hurry to return to his own duty in the Mediterranean under Braddock's command. Smith did not blame him. Bennett was a good man and *Harrier* a good ship. They could not get him into Trieste, either.

Lombardo sawed and chiselled away at the holes, measured. He went aboard *Hercules* where Fred Archbold rigged a bench for him and Lombardo got some help from one of the drifter's crew who was a fair hand as a carpenter. Together they sawed and planed, the patches were fitted and sanded down, and Lombardo went to work on them with a brush and a pot of paint.

Smith stood with Zacco in the bow of his boat and inspected the work. Lombardo had done a good job. When the painting was finished the boat would hardly show a mark. Lombardo whistled as he wielded the brush, pleased with the work of his hands and in good humour as a result.

Smith envied him. Lombardo's job was done and he would sleep easy at the end of the day. And there was another man happy at his work: Smith turned as the singing came down on the wind. He stared at the long shed a cable's length away along the shore. "What is he doing in there?"

Zacco shrugged. "I don't know. Nobody sees him for days. I think he lives in there."

Lombardo said, "He's a nut." He caught Zacco's hard eye on him and added, "– sir. But everyone knows it. I was in a bar a coupla nights ago and this guy Enzo – he's an engineer, works for this Balestra – was in there. So somebody asked him what Balestra's doing and this guy laughs and says he's building a jumping-boat. A jumping-boat for Chrissakes! Who needs it?

This bastard jumps enough for anybody as it is."

Zacco laughed and shook his head.

Smith smiled, but – the hands were cleaning the boats now, sluicing down and scrubbing. He said, "I think I'll walk along and see this Balestra." He hesitated. He did not want the presence of an interpreter, but ... He asked, "Does he speak any English?"

It was Gallina who answered that, passing close as he walked from bow to stern of his own boat moored beside Zacco's, "He speaks very good."

"Thank you." The boats were moored bows-on to the shore now. Smith walked across the narrow plank and away through the tall grass.

Zacco and Lombardo watched him go and Lombardo said, switching easily back to Italian, "They might get along." And when Zacco looked at him. "That Smith, I think he's a nut as well – sir."

Zacco said harshly, "That is enough!"

Lombardo smacked the lid on the paint-pot, started carefully cleaning his brush. "All right, sir. But last night, did he have to go swimming around that harbour? He could have sent me and I could have told him all he wanted to know. But no. He had to see for himself. And when he turned back it was only because he'd seen all he wanted. I reckon if he hadn't he'd have kept on swimming round that harbour till he had! Another thing. I had a talk with that big gorilla of his – that Buckley. And he said Commander Smith is always pulling that kind of stunt and worse, and it's likely to drive Buckley crazy just riding shot-gun on him."

As Smith approached the shed the singing grew louder and now he could also hear sounds of movement inside and a low rhythmic throbbing that came from beyond it. The shed stretched back some fifty feet from the water's edge and was about twenty feet wide. It was low, flat-roofed and looked to have been knocked together in a hurry. The timbers were raw and unpainted. There were windows set in the walls of it but they were badly in need of cleaning and lights burned yellow inside. He found a door at the back of the shed and the rhythmic throbbing was explained. A rubber-covered cable looped away from the far corner of the shed, supported on poles and following a path trampled through the grass. The path wound away in the direction of the far side of the island, but the cable looped down about twenty yards away to a building hardly larger than a dog kennel. The throbbing came from this and it obviously housed a generator to supply electric current to the big shed.

And the singing?

Smith pushed open the door. It squeaked on its hinges and the singing stopped abruptly. The singer faced him, mouth open. He stood just inside the door, his hand outstretched to a spanner lying on the bench and now as he stared at Smith he picked up the spanner and held it like a weapon. He wore a navy boiler-suit and was a young man in his middle twenties, a little taller than Smith, very thin though with the deep chest of a singer. His face was clean-shaven, his dark hair curled and stood wildly on end. The dark eyes were large and fixed suspiciously on Smith.

Smith said, "I'm looking for –" He tried to see past the young officer, looking round the shed "– Tenente Balestra." He could see little because the man stood carefully in his way. Close to Smith's right hand a torpedo rested on trestles. It looked an old model. To his left was a little office, a plywood box built into the corner of the shed. He could just see a drawing-board in there. And over the tenente's shoulder he caught a glimpse down the length of the shed of a craft and men working aboard but now halted in that work and peering his way under the yellow light of the lamps that swung, just dangling bulbs, from the roof.

Then the young man moved fractionally so he stood directly before Smith. "I am Guido Balestra." The eyes were still suspicious as they flicked over Smith. "You are an officer of the British Navy?"

"David Smith. Commander." He held out his hand. "At present commanding the three MAS boats you see out there. I heard you singing and I was curious about what you were doing here."

Balestra held out his own hand, realised he still gripped the spanner and dropped it on the bench. "I regret." He gripped Smith's hand. "But no one comes here. I thought – an intruder."

Smith grinned. "That's all right. I bet I'm your first visitor for a while. You're well out of the way here."

"Yes."

Smith moved past him, or rather round him; Balestra did not make way. Now Smith could see all of the inside of the shed, the benches set along the walls and here and there piles of discarded machinery, engines, propellers, shafts, a broken rudder, a length of chain with odd steel teeth projecting from it. Smith patted the torpedo. The top of it had been cut away from the nose back along half its length. "Modifications?"

Balestra was at his shoulder. "I have done some work on it."

That told Smith nothing, as he suspected it was meant to. The wooden floor of the shed was no more than a platform at the rear that extended narrow arms about four feet wide along each wall. Between them a slip had been constructed, a simple affair of baulks of timber laid on the marshy shore, sloping gently down into the water. A winch was mounted on the platform at the head of the slip for the purpose of hauling craft up from the water and now on the slip there rested – Smith halted and stared for a long time. It was almost rectangular, about fifty feet long and ten in the beam. At first sight it looked like one of the barges seen working around the lagoon, but . . . He asked, "What the hell is that?"

Balestra did not answer. Smith moved on to see the – 'thing' – better, but Balestra moved quicker to stand in his way. The young lieutenant's face was without expression, but now the dark eyes gleamed hard and hostile. "Your questions – you should ask Admiral Winter."

"Winter?" Smith stared at him, startled.

"You come from Captain Devereux, Captain Pickett?"

Smith snapped, "No, I don't. What's this about Winter?"

Balestra said stiffly, "This is an affair of Admiral Winter. He arranged for the workshop here, for the men from the dockyard and the engineer petty officer, Enzo, to help me. My orders came from Admiral Winter. He wrote to me that he would come here again soon. You should ask him, sir."

Smith said quietly, "Winter is dead." Balestra flinched and his head moved slowly in denial, not wanting to believe. Smith said, "He was killed in action two days ago."

Balestra seemed stunned. Smith was thinking quickly. He said, "I'm here in Venice because of Winter. He had the Admiralty send me here, with orders to seek out the battlecruiser *Salzburg* and sink her at her moorings. I have heard that you are building a jumping-boat. You said just now that you were building it for Winter. I think in fact that you are building it for me." He pulled from his pocket his orders and the letter from Winter, handed them to Balestra, who read them and returned them. Smith said, "Well? How does it operate?"

Balestra hesitated, still reluctant, but said, "I will show you the plans." He led the way back to the tiny, box-like office. It was almost filled by the drawing-board but Smith saw a camp bed tucked in against one wall. So Balestra lived with his work. Now he pointed to the drawing-board and Smith stooped over it. He was no engineer but to him the plan was beautifully drawn. Balestra began to explain, hesitantly at first: "I got the idea from the tanks your army use in France ..." As he went on he became absorbed, spoke more quickly and was no longer on his guard. Only when he finished did his wary look return.

Smith felt excitement taking light inside him as he watched and listened. Now he looked up from the plans. "They told me you were building a jumping-boat."

Balestra shrugged. "I told my men to say that if anyone asked. I thought it would sound like the Mad Professor. They call me that."

"You don't mind?"

For once Balestra laughed and it was honest not bitter. "No. I suppose I'm a bit unconventional. It helps because it makes people leave me alone."

Smith said seriously. "I don't think you are mad."

The Italian's brief moment of good humour vanished. "Devereux does. And Pickett."

"Admiral Winter did not."

Balestra was silent a moment, staring down abstractedly at the plan, then: "He was a great man. I was in the dockyard one day, having an argument with some other officers –"

"What about?"

"Oh, I was saying if the enemy would not come out then we should go in after him, that if conventional methods would not work we should try unconventional ones. To them it was a joke – the Mad Professor, you know? But Winter appeared out of nowhere like a ghost. So gaunt. A head like a skull and that awful cough. He said very little, just listened and watched. Only now and again he would ask a question and it was always good. To the point, you know?" A corner of Balestra's mouth lifted in a one-sided grin. "Like you."

Smith said nothing to that. Braddock had said Winter was in poor health but according to Balestra that was an understatement. Smith nodded at the torpedo outside in the workshop and asked, "Is that to do with this jumping-boat?"

Balestra shook his head. "No – that was a different idea. But I ran into problems with it so I concentrated on this boat instead. Admiral Winter said it was urgent." He pointed at the torpedo's dull-gleaming skin. "I think, maybe, I have the answers to that now. But the boat is almost ready."

"Almost?"

"I had to make an adjustment to the drive, but now –"

Smith pressed him, "Has she had a trial?"

"Yes, but –"

"I want to see a trial. Now."

Balestra hedged. "We need more adjustments. You understand, a boat like this, so new, so different, you –"

"I know. I want to see it work. Now."

Smith knew Balestra was reluctant to put his brainchild through its paces before this strange British officer, wanted to get it exactly right first, tested again and again. But there wasn't time, Smith was certain of that. He repeated, "Now."

Balestra cast one final glance at the plan then turned his back on it. "Very well, sir."

Helen Blair left the car at Mestre with Luigi, who was relieved to see her back safe and sound, and took the train across the causeway to Venice. At the house on the Riva Ca' di Dio she found her housekeeper and a note awaiting her. It had been left by some young Air Force officers who had been wounded and were on convalescent leave but now were recalled to their squadron. They invited her to join them for dinner that evening.

She smiled. She would just have time to bath and dress but first she took a towel from the bathroom and hung it on the rail of the balcony outside her room. From there she could see her yacht, *Sybil*, and her two-man crew would see the towel. It was a simple signal and saved her from taking the launch out across the lagoon to the yacht, just to tell them to be ready to sail.

The trials ran through the afternoon and they found defects, several, one after the other. But Balestra, his tubby brown-faced engineer petty officer Enzo, and their men laboured with furious haste to set them right, and succeeded. For every problem Balestra found a working solution. Working. That was the word.

At the end of it Smith stood again in the shed and stripped off the boiler-suit he had borrowed from Balestra, washed at the sink by the wall. There were makeshift curtains covering the window now, a blackout, for it was dusk. The lamps only made more harsh the utilitarian interior of the workshop. Smith thought that Balestra had lived like a prisoner in this place for weeks and wondered how he still managed to sing. Now the young Italian stood wiping his hands on a piece of cotton waste; he was filthy. He ran his fingers through the dark, curly hair as he had done a hundred times during the trials, that was why it always stood on end.

Smith said, "It works. Be ready to go at an hour's notice – or less."

Balestra's eyes lit up. He said delightedly, "Thank you, sir!" Then he remembered practicalities, "But we will need orders, and an authority for torpedoes."

"I'll see to that," answered Smith. He smiled at Balestra's relief and exuberance. "It's an unusual craft, to say the least. Congratulations, Guido. What do you call her?"

Balestra shrugged, "She has no name as yet. Just a jumping-boat. And that isn't accurate."

Smith said, "We'll call her the *Flying-Fish*."

"That isn't accurate, either."

"Maybe not. But I wanted a flying-fish and that's what I'm going to have painted on." Smith straightened his cap and left the shed. As he walked rapidly back through the long grass towards *Hercules* and the MAS boats he heard a voice break into joyful song behind him.

Pietro Zacco's boat took him round to the dockyard and Naval Headquarters. It was night now, the surface of the lagoon like black glass. As Smith stepped ashore he said, "I may be some time."

Zacco asked, trying to sound casual, "Action, sir?" But the entire crew of the boat were watching, sensing that something was afoot. Lombardo's head poked scowling but curious out of the engine-room and his *meccanico* showed behind him.

Smith nodded. "If all goes well, tomorrow." And grinned to himself as Zacco passed the word on and a ripple of excitement ran through the crew.

He walked along by the side of the canal towards the pillared entrance of Naval Headquarters, the winged lion of Venice above it. He thought of Balestra, thin, intense, eager – and brilliant, Smith was certain. They smiled and called him the Mad Professor. With luck he and Balestra would wipe those smiles away.

The sentry at the head of the short flight of steps saluted and passed him through, but in Devereux's office he found only a solitary clerk tidying it and putting away files. He stood to attention as Smith entered.

Smith asked, "Where is Captain Devereux?"

"Gone, sir. He won't be back tonight, nor for a few days, either. A signal came from Captain Pickett today. There's some sort of conference on in Brindisi an' he wants Captain Devereux there. He's got a passage on *Harrier* sailing at midnight."

"Where is he now?"

The clerk glanced up at the clock. "He'll be at the Aurora now, having his dinner. That's a hotel on the Schiavoni, sir. But if there is anything I can do, sir? I'll be here all night. I'm on duty till the morning."

"No, thank you. I have to see Captain Devereux. Good night."

"Good night, sir."

The clerk watched Smith go then muttered, "And the best o' luck if you want any favours from that bastard."

Smith walked quickly through the narrow, winding, unlit streets. He emerged on the Riva di Schiavoni and there found the Aurora Hotel. A machine-gun was mounted on a timber platform on the roof and its crew of two Italian soldiers stood searching the sky with binoculars, keeping look-out for another sneak raid by Austrian bombers. Smith entered and took off his cap, walked through the foyer to the dim, lamplit dining-room and paused at the entrance a moment, seeking Devereux. But first he saw La Contessa. Helen Blair sat at a large central table with half-a-dozen young officers of the Italian Air Force, smiling and laughing at their jokes. Her silken dress was cut low over her breasts and her shoulders were bare. Her piled hair shone in the lamplight. She stood out in that room, but then, Smith thought, she would stand out anywhere. Her eyes met his for a second, then returned to the men about her.

Smith saw Devereux sitting alone at a table by the wall and started towards him. Devereux was also watching Helen Blair and clearly was not pleased to see Smith. He asked testily, "Is it important? Urgent?"

"Yes, sir, it is."

"Oh, very well," Devereux said grudgingly. "You'd better sit down."

"Thank you, sir." Smith took the empty chair across from Devereux.

A waiter served Devereux with soup and looked at Smith. "Signore?"

Smith shook his head. "No, thanks." And when they were alone again: "I went to Trieste with the boats, sir. This is my report."

He held out the envelope to Devereux who glanced at it without interest. "Leave it there." His eyes were not on Smith but on some point in the room behind him. A girl laughed – Helen Blair – and Devereux smiled.

Smith said, "Anyway, sir, they've strengthened the defences. There are now two lines of booms and newer, far stronger ones. There's no way a ship could break through them."

That regained Devereux's attention. "Ah?" He smiled complacently. "Common sense reasserting itself, I see. Good."

"If possible, sir, I would like the latest intelligence on Trieste, anything the Italians have obtained in the last day or two."

"Just ask the duty Writer in my office," Devereux answered easily. "I think some stuff came in just as I left."

Devereux was amiable, believing he had been proved right. Smith thought that was the easy part over. Now – "I know a way to get in and sink *Salzburg*, sir." And when Devereux frowned: "Today I paid a call on a Tenente Balestra. He has a –"

"Balestra!" Devereux's frown vanished and he laughed.

"You know about him?"

"That I do!" Devereux chuckled.

Smith said, "He told me that Admiral Winter started him on this project." And then asked softly, "Why didn't you tell me about him, sir?"

But Devereux was not put out, shook his head and sighed. "He was a sick man."

"Sick? Balestra?"

"No, Winter. A dying man would be a more accurate description. Consumption. Coughing his lungs out and near the end of the road. If *Salzburg* hadn't killed him he would have collapsed soon anyway. He had the mark of death on him, and the Fleet Surgeon will bear that out." Smith remembered Balestra's description of Winter: like a ghost. But Devereux was continuing, "When he was seized by this obsession with *Salzburg* and got involved with Balestra, well, Pickett and I took the charitable view that his illness had warped his judgment." Devereux shook his head over it.

Smith believed him. The man was sincere. But – "You could have told me, sir, and –"

Devereux broke in impatiently, "There'd been enough time wasted on that scheme. Do you know what they call him? The –"

"The Mad Professor." Smith nodded and added crisply, "I know. And it's a slander. The man is a brilliant engineer."

"Rubbish!" Devereux was losing patience.

"Sir?"

"Gatecrashing! Boom-jumping! What next, for God's sake? We're fighting a war and that demented young organ-grinder is playing with toy boats in a bath!"

The injustice of it stung Smith, temper already fraying. "He's an engineer, sir. And it's *not* a toy! I was aboard her and we put her through a trial and she *works*!"

"Puttering around the lagoon! Playing on that imitation boom he's got there!" Devereux's voice held contempt. "Oh, I know it. Pickett and I went down with Winter a couple of weeks ago when they were building the thing. A few old buoys, timbers and hawsers that he strings out in four to five feet of water! Call that a boom? Whatever kind of weird contraption he's dreamed up, it might work *there* on *that* boom – but on real defences, in the currents at a harbour's mouth . . .?"

84

There was an unpleasant smack of truth there, Smith could not deny it, and Balestra said they should have more trials. But time was against them. Couldn't Devereux see that? Smith said, "It worked. And it will work at Trieste."

"No, it won't!"

"Balestra is prepared to make the attempt, sir, and so am I. We don't want authority, just permission."

"You won't get it." That was flat denial.

But Smith kept trying. "Sir, *Salzburg* –"

"*Salzburg!*" Devereux exploded the word. "You've got that damned ship on the brain! You'll have us all looking under our beds for her and this feller Voss! This is exactly why we didn't tell you about Balestra and his tomfool ideas, in case you were bitten by the same bug as Winter. It seems you were, but you don't have his excuse."

Smith played his last card, "I have my orders, sir, and –"

"And an independent command. I know. We've discussed this already and Pickett made your position plain. Let me make this plain: you will not get authority or permission to embark on this mad attack on Trieste because at worst it would end in tragedy and at best make laughing-stocks of the Royal Italian Navy and ourselves. Balestra! You spent the afternoon with him and his contraption while the Italians are trying to hold a line on the Tagliamento river and losing men in their tens of thousands. Talk about the devil finding work for idle hands!"

Still Smith tried, doggedly, desperately, "Sir –"

But: "That," said Devereux icily, "will be all, Commander. Good night to you."

Smith pushed back the chair and stood up. He was not finished, had plenty more still to say but knew nothing would shake Devereux from his entrenched beliefs. If Smith opened his mouth now it would be to speak his mind and that would bring him nothing but a charge of insubordination. So he turned his back and strode steadily, unhurriedly from the room, this time unaware of Helen Blair.

She saw the barely-controlled anger in his set face and wondered.

Devereux did not wonder. He watched Smith go then returned to his dinner, still angry but with the satisfaction of triumph. He had put an end to that nonsense.

It was raining now and Smith's boots splashed in puddles on the quay as he strode rapidly back to the dockyard. Zacco's boat waited for him there in the canal. As he came on her out of the darkness he heard the expectant rustle among the crew, Zacco's low order and then the engines growled. Smith stepped aboard and said, "*Hercules.*"

"Sir." Zacco did not ask questions but glanced at Smith's face and saw the set of it, guessed that something had gone wrong. He took the MAS astern out of the canal and turned her head to run back to the drifter.

Smith stood in the cockpit, silent. He had prepared these men for action again tomorrow. Now he would have to retract that. Cancelling orders, changing plans, was bad for morale. He put off the moment. Besides, he was not finished. His orders stood. If Balestra and his *Flying-Fish* were denied him then he must seek another way.

He was back where he had been in the morning, beating his head against a wall. Now he knew why Winter had demanded an independent command for Smith: he had known he was a dying man, suspected that when he died then Pickett and Devereux would never support his plans for an attack on *Salzburg*. That was no comfort to Smith. He had his independent command but he was shackled by Devereux and Pickett.

When he climbed aboard *Hercules* he returned to his pacing, up and down the dark deck under the rain, up and down. Searchlights swept the sky over Venice and their light reflected on the still waters of the lagoon that washed against the drifter's side. Anger and frustration simmered inside him and he was worried by Devereux's news of the German advance and the Italian losses.

He did not know how long he paced the deck but he was aware of a boat coming alongside, the hail. Then Menzies appeared, stopping his restless striding. "From HQ, sir, Captain Devereux."

So it had been Devereux's boat. Another envelope but slimmer this time. The later intelligence of Trieste he had asked for? It was not. He read the orders. They originated from the Italian Headquarters but were endorsed by Devereux. Ammunition was needed at the front and Devereux had volunteered the services of *Hercules*. She was to tow a barge loaded with ammunition to Porto San Margherita, close to the front, and land it under cover of darkness. The barge lay waiting at the island of Certosa.

Smith stared at the orders. Certosa. Zaccó had said the ammunition dumps were there. He remembered Devereux complaining, "The devil finds work for idle hands." So Devereux, on his way to *Harrier* and Brindisi, had gone back to his office and arranged this. Smith and his little command were to be used like errand boys, given any odd job that would keep them occupied.

He climbed to the wheelhouse and looked at the chart. Porto San Margherita lay on the coast about 45 miles north-east of Venice, at the mouth of the Livenza river. It was no more than a fishing village. He laid off his course then stood scowling at the chart. There beyond the Livenza river lay Trieste, and *Salzburg*. She must still be there – no sightings had been reported – but Voss would not lie there idle much longer. Smith and *Hercules* were ordered to tow a barge up to Porto San Margherita while on a night like this with the *Flying-Fish* ... He saw the craft in his mind's eye, looking not unlike –

All along he had known that time was against them and they must take a risk.

He swung away from the chart and bellowed, "Mr Menzies! Mr Archbold!" Menzies came running from aft but Smith was out of the wheelhouse and slid down the ladder to the deck before the panting midshipman skidded around the superstructure and halted before him. Smith stepped past him to the side and called, "Mr Zacco!"

"Signore!"

"I want Lombardo!"

"Yes, signore!"

"Mr Pagani!"

"Signore!"

"Come alongside and take me to Devereux's office in the dockyard!"

"Yes, signore!"

Smith turned and saw Fred Archbold's grizzled head coming up out of the companion forward. "Mr Archbold!"

"Sir!"

"You have a carpenter?"

87

"That's what he calls hisself."

"You've got canvas, timber and black paint aboard?"

"We've got all o' that –"

"Very good. Now listen to me. Mr Menzies, you will take Lombardo and the carpenter from *Hercules*, Buckley, Davies and the crew of the six-inch gun –" He told them what he wanted done and finished, "We've got to smuggle her past the guard-boat. Understood?"

"Aye, aye, sir!" That was Menzies.

"Aye." Fred Archbold pushed back his cap and scratched his head. "I reckon we've got what'll do the job, sir."

"You have two hours! Here!" Smith scribbled a brief note to Balestra on a page torn from his note-book and slapped it into Menzies' hand. Pagani's boat was sliding alongside at the foot of the ladder and Smith went down into it, called, "Mr Archbold! Raise steam and be ready to put to sea!"

"Sir!"

"Mr Gallina! Take Mr Menzies and his party ashore!"

"Yes, signore!"

"Mr Menzies! Get a *move on!*"

"Aye, aye, sir! Leading Seaman Buckley!"

Pagani eased the wheel over as Smith dropped into the cockpit beside him. The boat pulled smoothly away from the side of the drifter, slipped around her stem and headed back to the dockyard.

At Devereux's office he found only the night clerk on duty and obtained from him the latest intelligence on Trieste. There were a number of photographs taken from an aircraft that had flown a reconnaissance that morning. There was also an up-dated map of the harbour. The photographs were sharp and clear, they and the map showed the new boom defences – and *Salzburg*. She was unmistakable. There was no ship to match her in Trieste, or elsewhere in the Adriatic for that matter. Smith smiled wryly as he wondered what Devereux would say when he learned Smith had taken up the proffered intelligence. He returned to *Hercules*.

As Pagani's boat closed the drifter he saw smoke rising in a thick black column from her funnel as Geordie Hogg got up steam. Smith climbed aboard to see Fred Archbold in the wheelhouse, head already poked out of the open window, pipe stuck in his mouth and smoke wisping as he hastily sucked on it. The anchor party stood ready on the fo'c'sle and Smith ordered, "Weigh!" As he climbed the ladder to the wheelhouse on top of the superstructure the steam capstan hammered and the cable clanked in.

When he entered the wheelhouse the last of the tobacco smoke was blowing away, drawn out of the open window by the breeze. Fred Archbold's pipe was still between his teeth but now innocently tamped with a plug of newspaper. The hail came up from the fo'c'sle, a voice lifted high above the capstan's clammer: "Anchor's aweigh!"

Smith said, "Half ahead! Port ten!"

Fred Archbold reached out to the engine-room telegraph and rang down 'Half ahead'. He said, "Port ten, sir." And put the wheel over as the screw turned and *Hercules* gained steerage way. The drifter headed for the island of Certosa just over a quarter-mile away. There Smith inspected and signed for a barge loaded with shells and charges, saw its tarpaulin securely lashed down and the tow passed to it from *Hercules*. They headed away from Certosa on a course for the Porto di Lido and the open sea but once the night hid them from watching eyes on Certosa, *Hercules* turned at Smith's order and headed for San Elena.

As they approached the point of the island they could see the little huddle of craft lying there. Smith ordered, "Stop her!" As the way came off the drifter the MAS boats ahead of her moved, one of them hauling clear of the others and towing a barge similar to that already astern of *Hercules*, but narrower and a little lower in the water. Zacco's boat was doing the towing and Smith watched as its barge was made fast astern of the first. Meanwhile Gallina's boat slid alongside and the men that crowded her deck swarmed aboard *Hercules*, Menzies, Buckley, Davies and the rest.

Menzies reported breathlessly to the wheelhouse, "Look's jolly good, doesn't she, sir?"

Smith grunted, eyes on the tow and Zacco's tall figure in the cockpit of the MAS.

Menzies went on, "Lombardo deserves most of the credit, sir. He's very quick with tools and full of ideas for saving time. Quick on the uptake, too." He paused a moment, thoughtful.

"He seemed a bit bad-tempered at first. But after he'd been working with Buckley and Davies a bit I heard him laugh and from then on he worked like a demon."

Smith grinned to himself. He could imagine the exchanges between Buckley and Lombardo; the two of them 'got along' as Lombardo would put it. That was why Smith sent Buckley with the working party; it was asking a lot for the diminutive Menzies, junior officer or no, to impress his authority on Lombardo and also fire his zeal.

Now Zacco's hand was lifted and his MAS eased away from the barges, left them drifting astern of *Hercules*, the tow slack. Smith ordered, "Half ahead." *Hercules* got under way and the tow straightened, the two barges jerked forward then followed obediently one behind the other after the drifter. "Port ten . . ."

Hercules headed for the Porto di Lido, the gateway to the sea. Zacco's MAS surged past to take station ahead of her and the other two boats fell into line following the barges.

Balestra appeared in the wheelhouse. Like Menzies he was breathless. He was also apprehensive. He had discarded the boiler-suit and now wore his naval uniform as a tenente. He took off his cap and ran his fingers through his hair. "This" – he jerked his head at the barges astern – "it means you did not get orders, sir?"

"I have orders," Smith answered absently, "but not through Devereux or from your people."

"I see." Balestra swallowed. "If the guard-boat sees what we've done she will stop us and send us back under guard –"

But Smith was peering out to starboard as the look-out called, "Yacht on the starboard bow!" It was the *Sybil*, no canvas hoisted but headed seaward under the power of her auxiliary engine.

Smith poked his head out of the wheelhouse and as the drifter hauled up to pass *Sybil* he saw Helen Blair standing in the well of the yacht, her cape hanging down to her ankles but its hood thrown back. He could not make out her face in the darkness but knew the straight, slender figure.

One of the seamen was at the tiller. Smith hailed the yacht, "Where are you bound?"

The girl's voice came clear, "North up the coast to the rear of the line."

90

"I'm taking ammunition to a battery at Porto Margherita. You can come along with us."

"Very well. Thank you."

Smith did not think it a good idea for this girl to go to Porto Margherita with the Italians still retreating but he could not stop her and suspected he would get a dusty answer if he tried. So he might as well wring what advantage from it that he could. "Take station on the starboard beam of the smaller barge until we're outside, then fall in astern of her!"

"Understood."

Smith watched the yacht drop back until level with the second and smaller barge. There *Sybil* stayed, keeping easy station. With *Hercules* at half ahead they were only making four knots, little faster than a walking pace. He stepped back into the wheelhouse.

Zacco's boat was now entering the narrow neck between the two arms of the Porto di Lido and *Hercules* followed close astern of her. Ahead of them and to starboard was anchored the guard-boat, an old torpedo-boat. A few muffled figures stood on the wing of her bridge and Smith heard faintly the hails exchanged between the guard-boat and Zacco in the MAS. He could not make out the words and would not have understood them if he did, but he knew Zacco was answering that *Hercules* was bound for Porto Margherita with ammunition.

The MAS was past. Now the guard-boat lay abeam of the drifter and Smith was aware of the scrutiny *Hercules* was receiving from the guard-boat. That was all right. But now for it –

He pushed out of the door at the back of the wheelhouse and peered astern past the funnel. He saw the first barge, loaded with ammunition, pass the torpedo-boat. Then almost lost in the darkness, the second barge, with the yacht alongside it and partly screening it. On the guard-boat they were waving; recognising the Contessa, and he saw her lift a hand. Then yacht and barge were past and he felt *Hercules* lift to the open sea. That sea would make short work of the flimsy timber and canvas Lombardo and the others had erected around the sides of Balestra's *Flying-Fish* to make her look a little more like a barge, but that did not matter now. The disguise had worked for long enough.

He ordered, "Port five ... Steer six-oh degrees."

Balestra let out a sigh and shot at Smith a glance that held awed respect and more than a tinge of worry. There would be hell to pay over this.

Davies sat at the mess table in the cramped quarters he shared with the rest of the crew of *Hercules'* six-inch gun. The mess was sixteen feet long by fourteen, narrowing towards the stern to eight feet. The deck trembled with the steady beat of the propeller shaft turning right below them. Ten of them lived in that crowded mess, littered with seaboots and festooned with oilskins, and now Buckley had come to join them. A leather-cushioned bench ran like a horseshoe around the table and below the bunks set one above the other. Buckley would sleep on the bench. Now he sat by Davies and they sipped from mugs of stewed tea turned from black to khaki by a glutinous spoonful of condensed milk.

Davies said thoughtfully, "This feller Smith – does he do this sort of thing a lot?"

"What sort o' thing?"

"Taking a boat without orders and smuggling her past the guard-boat."

"He doesn't make a habit of it, no." Buckley sipped tea. "But he pinched a monitor not long ago."

"Gerraway! Where?"

"Out o' Dunkerque Roads. Part of the Dover Patrol. Supposed to be laid up in the dockyard, she was."

Davies peered at him. "Is that a fact?" And when Buckley nodded: "What happened?"

"The monitor got shot to hell. Smith should ha' been decorated but he wasn't."*

"Ah!" Now Davies remembered. "*That* monitor." And that Smith. "He'll bear watching."

Buckley said cheerfully, "I do it all the time. The bastard's putting years on me."

"Good bloke?"

"The best."

Davies asked, "How do you reckon this lot'll finish up?"

Buckley wasn't cheerful now. "God knows." He jerked his head at the stern and the barges out there in the night. "Whether

* *Ship of Force*: Hodder and Stoughton, 1979.

that contraption works or not, there'll be skin an' hair flying. *Getting in* will be bad enough. But *getting out?*"

They sat in thoughtful silence as *Hercules* plodded northward.

7 The Marines

It was midnight when they closed the shore in pitch darkness, flurries of rain driving in on the wind. By dead reckoning they were off Porto San Margherita and Pietro Zacco confirmed this when he brought his MAS alongside. *Hercules* anchored because there was little more than a fathom of water at Porto San Margherita and she would have taken the ground if she tried to enter. The barges were hauled up alongside the drifter and Davies and his men, Balestra and his engineer, Enzo, climbed aboard the *Flying-Fish*, then the tow was shifted to Zacco's MAS and he turned his boat's head towards the shore. Smith and Buckley went with him.

Smith looked over his shoulder and saw the yacht *Sybil* coming in astern of the barges, then he faced forward. The mouth of the Livenza river was opening ahead of them and Porto San Margherita was a scattering of houses along its banks. South of it was marsh while a mile or so north lay the town of Caorle. And further to the north was the front line, marked by flashes of gunfire. The sound that had been a murmur when they left Venice was now a steady rumbling – and it was close here. Smith thought uneasily that it was closer than it should be. The Tagliamento river where the Italians were thought to be holding a line was ten miles north of here but the nearest guns he could see firing were not ten miles distant. Their flashes split the black sky little more than a mile away beyond the town. And they were not heavy artillery with a deep solid *thump!* of discharge: the reports that came back to him were more like the *crack!* of a field battery. Those guns would not be engaging a distant target. The enemy they fired on would only be five or six thousand yards away at the most.

The MAS was entering the mouth of the river. Here it was a hundred yards wide between rocky banks but ahead of them it narrowed. About three hundred yards inland they made out a jetty on the southern shore, a torch blinked at them and Zacco turned the boat's head towards it. The jetty was a ramshackle timber affair with the smell of fish hanging about it. A crowd of

94

men waited there, soldiers. One of them shone the torch on himself and Smith saw it lighting the insignia of a lieutenant on a black and yellow border. Zacco said, "The collar – he is artillery. He is our man."

He ran the MAS in alongside the jetty and the seaman standing on the counter slipped the tow and tossed it up to the waiting soldiers. They tailed on to it, hauled the first barge in alongside the jetty and jumped down into it. The crew of Helen Blair's yacht were making fast expertly on the far side of the jetty.

The MAS was secured, and Zacco climbed ashore. The gunner subaltern was plastered with mud to above his knees and when he shifted position on the creaking boards of the jetty his boots squelched wetly. Zacco spoke to him, listened to his rapid answer, then turned to Smith. "He is in charge of the unloading. The rest of the party are coming now. He says all must be done before the light comes."

Smith said, "Tell him that's what we want, to be out of here before dawn."

Zacco interpreted and the subaltern nodded. More soldiers were clumping out along the jetty and an ammunition wagon was backing on to it, the drivers at the horses' heads, urging them. The subaltern shouted hoarsely and more of his men jumped down into the barge, hauled back the tarpaulin cover and the unloading started.

Smith and Zacco went back along the jetty and found the second 'barge', the *Flying-Fish*, secured there, Davies and his men already at work stripping off the battered canvas and timber of its disguise. Balestra and Enzo, his engineer, were moving about the boat together, inspecting it closely in the light of a torch. Balestra came to stand below Smith and reported happily, "Not a scratch! Fine! But – the torpedo mountings are ready, but where are the torpedoes?"

Smith, "Take them from Zacco's boat. That is why I brought you in. You'll find it easier to take those torpedoes aboard here than outside in a seaway."

Balestra nodded vigorously. "Good!" he laughed out of relief that the *Flying-Fish* was all right, out of tension at the thought of what lay ahead. "Trieste, here we come!" Then: "Ah! Contessa!"

95

Smith turned to find Helen Blair at his side in the rain, staring open-mouthed at the *Flying-Fish*. She asked, incredulously, "Isn't it a barge? What is it?"

Balestra laughed again. "A grasshopper! Or a flying-fish!"

Helen Blair shook her head, bewildered. "I've never seen anything like it."

Smith answered, "Very few people have."

She shook her head again, then looked at him. "Anyway, I came to ask if you'd like a cup of coffee."

Smith hesitated, but only for a moment. He could do nothing until the barge was unloaded and that would be a matter of hours. "Please."

He followed her slim figure along the jetty past the men labouring at humping the boxes of charges out of the lighter and into the wagon. It was a different wagon from five minutes before: the drivers holding the horses' heads, soothing, were different. So one wagon load had gone already – but there would need to be many more. That was the advantage of supply by sea: this one barge's cargo, carried overland, would have taken a small convoy of wagons many hours to haul laboriously up to this position.

The men turned to greet Helen Blair as she passed. "Hey! Contessa!" But it was said with affection and respect and she smiled at them.

They came to the yacht and Smith climbed down after the girl into the well where the two Swiss stood up to greet her – and him – cordially, "Kapitän!"

They looked hefty, tough, open-faced sailormen, he could see that despite the darkness as they stood close in the well, saw them smile a welcome. He answered. "Good evening." The courtesies sounded incongruous to him with the men above stumbling in the darkness as they transferred the cargo of death from barge to wagon, taking it one stage nearer its killing mission, where the guns fired to the north and lit the sky.

Helen Blair stooped and entered the cabin and he followed her, stood close behind her, his body touching hers in the darkness. Then he closed the door and she switched the light on. The cabin was tiny, even for such a small vessel as this; he had thought it stretched farther forward. There was a small stove by the door with a huge kettle hissing on top of it, a table

96

let down on chains from the forward bulkhead, benches with leather cushions either side of it. He and the girl were standing crouched under the low deckhead. Now she slipped around the table to sit on one of the benches and indicated the opposite one. "Please. Make yourself as comfortable as you can. I think I warned you that it was cramped aboard."

Two white enamel mugs stood on the table with an iron coffee-pot and she poured the coffee, steaming, added milk from a punctured tin, spooned in sugar. Smith watched her and thought that she looked at home. That surprised him. Although Zacco had told him how this girl employed herself he had not been able to visualise the elegant beauty in these surroundings, but she fitted in. He saw now that she wore the cloak over a fashionable dress and the cloak itself looked expensive, was lined with a rose-coloured silk. The hood of it was thrown back and the piled hair was neat and shining in the light from the lamp above. Her face had a flush to it. He realised that the flush was rising because he was staring at her.

He looked down and muttered, "Thank you," picked up the mug and sipped at the coffee, eyes on the table but he could still see her hands, slender fingers clasped round her coffee.

She said into the silence, "I'll make a big pot of coffee soon and take it to the men working up there."

"Good idea." He raised his eyes and saw that she was looking down now. He thought it would be good to sail this yacht with her, just the two of them. But in the silence of the cabin he could hear the clumping of boots on the jetty and the distant slamming of guns.

He wished to God this war was over.

Trieste. *Salzburg*. The booms and the dark coldness of the night hiding the waiting enemy . . .

He asked her, "Why do you do this?"

Helen Blair shrugged, then explained simply, dispassionately at first, then with growing emotion. "Because I can and I want to. I can because I am fairly well-off. I was left some property and investments in Argentina. Before the war I spent several long holidays with an aunt in the south of Italy and that's how I learnt my Italian. I was there when the war started but then I went back to England. Early in 1915 I became engaged to a second-lieutenant in an infantry battalion and soon afterwards he was sent to the Dardanelles. I came out to Italy again thinking he might be able to get a few days of leave, that we might see each other. It was a silly idea, I was very young, but anyway . . .

She paused then and Smith guessed what was coming. She went on, no longer dispassionate but bitter, "Edward was killed. I never saw him again. He was twenty-two and knew nothing of war but he rushed to volunteer like all the others."

Smith said, "I'm sorry." He was, though he had said it and written it too many times.

Her fingers tightened around the mug. "That's what the letter said, or something like it. 'It is with deep regret –' She stopped and sighed, said, "Anyway that's why I bought the yacht and the car and rented the house in Venice; because of Edward. I wanted to do something for the ordinary soldiers and sailors, the men who actually do the fighting, something to ease their hardships. The Italians have done practically nothing for their fighting men, there are no canteens such as the British Army has. So in *Sybil* I cruise up and down the coast to the men dug in there and I have a car on the mainland at Mestre that I drive up to the front line inland. Wherever I go I take chocolate and cigarettes and hand them out. It's not much but I think – I hope – it helps." She smiled, self-mocking. "That's why they call me an angel of mercy, and I think the soldiers gave me the title of Contessa because I always dress up a bit. It would probably be more sensible to wear old clothes and boots. Silly, isn't it?"

Smith looked at her. "No. I think you are probably worshipped, and the name they have given you goes to show it." Contessa? She would be a vision of beauty to a man coming weary, filthy and shocked from the line, a sign that another, better world still existed outside the trenches.

Something of that must have shown in his face. There was an awkward silence. Then Helen Blair said quietly, "That strange boat – it's to do with your orders, whatever they are?"

"Yes."

"You aren't going back to Venice."

"No."

"What about returning the ammunition barge there?"

"I don't know." He had not thought about it. He was surprised that she was alert to such details. With a shrug he said, "I'll have to leave it."

"We'll tow it back."

"You think you can?"

The girl said with forced lightness, "We've an engine because I'm a lazy sailor; we never use the sails. And my crew are – experienced. We can tow it."

"Well – thank you." At least they would not be able to charge him with the loss of the barge. He grinned at himself for worrying about one empty barge with what lay ahead of them.

The girl asked, "When – when will you be back?"

"In about thirty-six hours." Their heads were very close, leaning over the table. He told himself that tonight she was just showing ordinary courtesy towards him, that she was really as distant from him as ever. Just the same, he felt –

Helen Blair sat back from the table and said quickly, "I must make some coffee for the men."

Smith was reluctant to leave her but that was an obvious hint. He rose to his feet, bent again under the deckhead. "I'll go and see how Balestra is getting on."

She smiled at him and he left the warmth of the cabin, climbed back on to the jetty and went to the *Flying-Fish*. He found Zacco and Balestra had transferred one of the torpedoes from Zacco's MAS and now were working on the other. There was nothing Smith could do.

He became aware again of the flashes tearing at the night sky, the vicious cracking of the field battery just north of the river. And there was a light above the river – that would be at the end of the bridge. He could just see the bridge and movement on it. Curious, he walked back along the jetty through the swarming ammunition party. It was raining still, a light rain but very cold on his face. It made the timbers of the wharf greasy so the men handling the heavy shells and charges from the barge to the waiting wagons slipped and skidded and swore. A loaded wagon rumbled over the boards of the jetty and he followed it as it bounced on to the dirt track at the end of it. The track wound between the houses, silent and dark, then came out on a narrow road where a wooden bridge crossed the river. The wagon turned left, forcing a way into the crowd that shuffled along the road, heading south. Smith stared after it, wondering because the front was to the north.

99

Close by Smith at the end of the bridge a lamp hung and beneath it stood a group of *carabinieri*, military police with rifles slung over their shoulders, their cocked hats worn across their heads and gleaming wetly in the lamplight. They looked suspiciously at Smith. The light spilled across the road and washed yellow over the crowd passing over the bridge, a river of people flowing slowly to the south under the rain. He stared, suddenly sick at heart.

Here and there was a donkey-drawn cart piled high with furniture and bundles, women and children perched on top. Some were pushing or pulling barrows loaded with their belongings but most trudged along under huge loads slung on their backs or over their shoulders. Old men, women, children, their backs turned to the guns that hammered in the north, their faces set to the south and blank with misery.

Smith realised he was seeing refugees; this was the people of a countryside in flight. He had heard the word but never witnessed the reality. There were soldiers among the slow flood washing past him, soldiers tramping weary-legged and plastered with mud, heads down and thumbs hooked in the shoulder straps of the packs and the slings of the rifles.

He stood there a long time watching the stumbling procession, silent but for the occasional weeping of an old woman, the fractious crying of a weary child. And this was just one road. The scene must be repeated at this moment on every road across the fifty or more miles of front stretching from the sea into the mountains.

He forced himself to turn away and walk back to the jetty. There was nothing he could do for these people. Their fate was just one more of the curses of war.

When he walked out along the jetty he found Helen Blair among the men at work there. A group of them clustered around her, passing their mugs for the girl to fill from the big coffee-pot she carried. One of the two Swiss stood by, beaming, holding a basket filled with chocolate bars and packets of cigarettes. Helen Blair saw Smith and called, "Is there a road up there? Any soldiers in position?"

"Not in position but there are soldiers and – and refugees." Even the word was strange to him.

Helen Blair nodded briskly. "I'll go there later."

Smith said, "Remember we've got to be clear of this place before it's light." He passed on, thinking that the Contessa might bring some cheer to the people he had seen on the road. Buckley appeared before him and Smith halted.

"Beggin' your pardon, sir, but I've got you a blanket and there's some o' that canvas in the corner o' the cockpit. You can get your head down for a bit."

Buckley was talking sense. Beyond the MAS lay the *Flying-Fish* and Balestra and his men were still busy aboard her. She was not ready for sea yet. If you had any sense you slept when you could. He said, "Thank you," climbed down into the cockpit of the MAS, and settled himself in a corner on the pile of canvas that had been part of the disguise of the *Flying-Fish*. It smelt of salt and petrol. He pulled the rough blanket around him, said, "Call me half an hour before it's light," and closed his eyes.

For a time the sounds of the night around him kept him awake, the boots trampling and squeaking on the wharf, hoarse voices, the field battery still firing. But then they became submerged in the lapping of the river against the hull of the MAS and he thought about Helen Blair and then he slept.

Buckley woke him, crouching over him, a huge looming shadow. "Light in half an hour, sir. An' they've shifted all that ammo an' Mr Balestra reports he's ready for sea."

Smith rubbed at his eyes with one hand, propped himself up with the other and grumbled, "Well, you move back a bit. I can't see a damn thing."

Buckley edged back. "Fetched you a drop o' summat."

Smith took the mug and gulped hot coffee laced with –? "What's in this?"

"Brandy, sir. Compliments o' Mr Balestra." Buckley paused and Smith heard a voice lifted in song further along the jetty. Buckley said, "He's a cheerful young feller, sir."

"Tell him to tone it down a bit. This isn't the bloody opera house." Smith handed back the empty mug.

"Aye, aye, sir." Buckley disappeared and moments later the volume of the singing dropped.

Smith got to his feet, laughed quietly as he rubbed his unshaven chin, and climbed on to the jetty. Darkness still covered everything. The jetty itself was empty now, deserted, not a soldier to be seen. He realised suddenly that the field-guns so close to the north had ceased firing and the gunfire now rumbled distantly inland. He shifted uneasily. It was time they were out of this, before dawn came and the Austrian artillery found both them and *Hercules* still lying off with the other two MAS boats.

He strode quickly along to where the yacht, *Sybil*, was moored. One of the Swiss was in the well but the other had just climbed on to the jetty and stood peering upstream. Smith asked, "Is Miss Blair ready to sail?"

The Swiss nodded. "Ready, ja. But she –" He pointed at the bridge. "The peoples."

So she had gone to the road as she said she would. Smith had hoped she would take one of the Swiss with her. Now he swore anxiously under his breath, then said, "I'll get her."

He hurried along the jetty. On the shore he passed an abandoned, empty ammunition wagon, the axle broken and the traces cut. He hastened up between the dark houses and came out on the road. The flood of refugees was now a trickle of old people moving slowly up the side of the road. Down the centre of the road marched soldiers, infantry, but in no orderly formation or step. They slogged along wearily under the weight of packs and rifles.

He saw Helen Blair standing close by the *carabinieri* under the lamp, went to her and took her arm. The basket still hung from it, but empty now. She looked at him. He saw she was crying and he started to say gently, "We've got to get out of this place before –"

He stopped as the whips cracked like pistol-shots up the road and there came the sound of shouting, a rumble of wheels. Then the first team appeared out of the darkness, the soldiers on the road scattering to the sides to let it pass, the driver mounted on the lead horse cracking his whip and bawling huskily for them to get out of his way. Behind the team came the limber and the field-gun, the iron-shod wheels cutting deeply into the rutted road. It passed, to be followed by another and another, eight guns in all.

The last of the battery disappeared into the darkness. Smith glanced over his shoulder towards the sea and the east, saw the first lightening in the sky there. He turned back to the girl.

"The guns have pulled out and it'll be light soon. We must be gone by then." She nodded. He looked beyond her to the infantry still plodding down the road. They remained in no sort of order, but they were not a rabble; they still carried their equipment and weapons, he saw none thrown aside nor any man fall out. They were still a fighting force but the faces he saw showed them bone-weary, dead on their feet.

All at once a body of men came into sight, marching steadily down the road. They carried full packs and equipment, rifles slung from their shoulders, bandoliers of ammunition across their chests. They wore flat, round caps and they held up their heads and looked forward. They were sailors. At the head marched two officers, one of them a tenente but the other wore the insignia of a capitano di fregato. He carried full pack, equipment and rifle like his men. When he saw Smith and the girl he stared for a moment then swung out of his place at the head of the column and halted before them.

The capitano said, "La Contessa! Miss Blair!" His voice was hoarse and deep. He saluted and gave a little bow. "It is time you went, Contessa." He glanced at Smith, his equal in rank but some years younger. The capitano looked possibly forty. He also looked broad and strong and in surprisingly good humour. He said in that gravelly voice, "Royal Navy?"

"Yes. David Smith. Commander."

"Bruno Garizzo. Capitano, Regimento Marina! Marines!" That was spoken with pride and he gestured with one big hand at the marching column, then said, "You do not talk Italian."

Smith shook his head. "No."

Garizzo grinned wryly. "The English expect the rest of the world to understand them! But I am a year in London with the Naval Attaché. I talk English good. I learned it in the Ritz bar and the pubs and the music halls. Also from English girls. Very good way to learn."

Smith smiled. "The best."

But all the time the capitano was eyeing Smith shrewdly, sizing him up. He asked, "What ship? Why is the Royal Navy here?"

Smith answered, "We brought ammunition. The ship is a drifter, a fishing-boat. Ninety tons."

The capitano's brows lifted. He took off his cap and ran his fingers through short, stubbly hair. "A fishing-boat?" He looked down at his legs, the trousers bound with puttees from the knee down and covering the tops of the boots that were shapeless with mud. He grinned at Smith. "It is a bad time for naval officers!" He roared with laughter then looked around at his men, pointed a thick finger at one small sailor burdened down with pack and rifle and bawled furiously, incomprehensibly. Laughter crackled along the marching column and the little man grinned and lifted a hand.

The capitano turned back to Smith. "I told him he should get promoted so he could talk with pretty girls while everybody else walked their legs off."

Helen Blair smiled at the compliment. "Thank you."

Smith said, "Their morale is good."

"It must be." The capitano nodded. "That is important."

"And the war?"

"Because of the war. The news is bad. We come from the Tagliamento. The army has fallen back from there. Now we are ordered to hold a line along the river Livenza."

So that was why the ammunition wagons had headed south. This was the army in retreat.

There was a shifting among the *carabinieri* under the lamp. Garizzo glowered at them and said something rapidly and loudly. They looked away. He growled under his breath and then grinned at Smith. "They look for deserters. I told them there were no deserters from the Regimento Marina."

Smith asked, "Are there deserters?"

"Deserters! Disasters! Lines broken and flanks turned and companies, whole regiments surrounded!" Garizzo glared his exasperation. "I think maybe the defences were not lined back deep enough, not enough reserves in support and in strong positions. We were caught not ready. And that German Fourteenth Army, it swung the balance against us." Then came the quick grin. "Never mind, English. It is always the last battle that counts and this isn't the last, not for me, not for the Regimento Marina."

He looked over his shoulder at the marching column then out to the eastward where the light was growing. He said quietly, "You should get away now. There's only the rearguard behind us and not very far." Smith nodded and the capitano saluted the

Contessa then turned on his heel and strode away quickly, moving faster than the marching men and working his way up towards the head of the column.

Smith turned the girl around and led her back to the jetty and the yacht. She said only, "Those poor people."

He saw her aboard the yacht and into the cabin where she sat at the table and laid her head on her arms. He turned to the two Swiss in the well. They looked grim and he told them, "Take that barge in tow and get out of here. Quick! Schnell! Understand?"

They nodded. "Tow. Ja. Schnell."

Smith returned to the MAS and Zacco took the *Flying-Fish* in tow and headed out to sea. The *Sybil* followed close astern, towing the barge, but as *Hercules* came in sight from the cockpit of the MAS the yacht turned southwards. Smith went aboard the drifter and while the anchor was weighed he watched the yacht quickly disappear from sight. The day had come now and she was barely a mile away but the mist that came every morning lay thick on the surface of the sea and hid her. It hid them too, mercifully, from the Austrian guns.

He had learnt a little more of the girl, Helen Blair. He had seen a warmer side to her character – pity and compassion. He remembered the grief in her face as she watched the refugees, how she had laughed and joked with the working-party on the jetty.

His mind went back to the weary column of marching men. The line on the Tagliamento river had been broken and now they were retreating to the Livenza. Could such exhausted men ever make a stand? If they failed it would be disaster, for Italy and the Allies.

He turned away. He had to think of the night and Trieste. He glanced astern at the *Flying-Fish*, now towed by the drifter – as were the three MAS boats, to conserve their fuel – and said, "Pass the word for Mr Balestra." They had to make a plan of attack.

Later in the morning the mist cleared and disclosed to him the north-eastward horizon. A line of black cloud hung along it, dark and foreboding. Behind it lay Trieste, *Salzburg* and Voss, and there lay his objective.

8 Assault on Trieste

Smith stood in the wheelhouse of the drifter *Hercules* and stared out into the weeping darkness. The sky was heavily overcast with lowering cloud that shed a steady downpour of rain. This was the weather and the night they needed. Old Fred Archbold was at the wheel, his cold pipe clamped between his teeth. The boy Menzies stood beside him, the glow from the compass binnacle lighting their faces.

Smith said, "Stop her!"

Ginger Gates worked the handles of the engine-room telegraph. *Hercules* slid on, slowing as the screw ceased to turn, then stopped and lay barely rolling in a near calm sea. Now the engine's thumping had ceased Smith could hear Balestra singing sotto voce where he stood in a corner of the wheelhouse. The singing ceased and he smiled at Smith, said softly, "Luck is with us. A calm sea and very dark and rain."

Smith could feel the excitement that always came before action gripping him now. He thought that although they would need more than luck to sink *Salzburg* they'd get nowhere at all without it. He only said, "Dead reckoning puts us a mile from the booms." He turned on Archbold. "*Hercules* is yours till I get back. You know what to do?"

"Patrol with the two MAS boats, a mile west then back again." Fred Archbold spoke around the pipe, unworried, and that came not from ignorance; Fred knew the danger he would be in.

Smith said, "You might not always see the boats but they'll see you. Lieutenant Gallina is in command as the senior but you'll take orders from him or Pagani. And try to keep out of trouble."

"Aye, aye, sir."

If trouble came the two MAS boats could make a run for it, but it would be God help Archbold and Menzies. *Hercules* wouldn't outrun an Austrian patrol-boat and she couldn't do much fighting with that single six-pounder pop-gun. Suppose an Austrian torpedo-boat, like the one the boats engaged two nights ago, turned up? The Austrians would take their revenge at leisure, steam circles around the drifter and shoot her to fragments.

Menzies added anxiously, "Good luck, sir!"

"Thank you." Smith left the wheelhouse and climbed down to the deck. He forced those worries from his mind. There was nothing more he could do for *Hercules*.

He made his way aft and found a party in the stern hauling in on the tow and stood beside them and watched Balestra's *Flying-Fish* brought alongside.

Back on San Elena when Smith had first seen it Balestra said he had got the idea from the tanks used by the army in Flanders. It was built of timber an inch thick on a timber frame and was a simple rectangular box fifty feet long by ten across, like a barge except for the upward slope of the square bow. That made it look a bit like a tank and the tracks that ran around the hull on either side completed the resemblance. It was completely decked over save for two cockpits, one aft and to port of the centre line and one amidships and starboard. The two torpedoes were mounted in the waist, either side of the forward cockpit, in the same type of clamp-launching apparatus as used in the MAS boats.

Balestra glanced at Smith who asked, "Ready?"

The young engineer nodded, "Yes." He was not excitable or nervy now, but quiet. He had worked a long time to prepare for this moment. Now he was no longer the abstracted inventor wary of strangers and wryly grinning at the jibes levelled at the Mad Professor. The drive that had kept him working around the clock and the toughness that had helped him shrug off the jeers, these were now welded into a singleminded determination. He told Smith quietly, "Tonight I will sink *Salzburg*."

He did not say, "– or die." But he meant it.

Buckley and the rest of the crew of the *Flying-Fish* climbed down to her deck. The torpedoman, Udina, was from Pietro Zacco's boat because the torpedoes came from her. He was a middle-sized man with thick legs and heavy shoulders. The seaman, Marani, came from Pagani's boat and was lean and wiry, quick on his feet about the deck. A heavy moustache laid a black bar across his face. Then there was the tubby, round-faced Enzo, Balestra's *motorista*. Marani was talking with Buckley and Smith could see the flash of Buckley's teeth as he grinned at the seaman's pidgin English. But Buckley could understand it and Marani understood Buckley very well.

Buckley and Marani stayed on deck. Enzo and Udina climbed into the forward cockpit and Enzo descended to his engines in the bowels of the boat. There were two electric motors under the flush deck, one to drive the twin screws, the other to drive the tracks. Smith and Balestra squeezed into the after cockpit, Balestra at the wheel. Zacco's boat slipped by, stopped. Its screws thrashed and then it went astern, sidled stern first up to the bow of the *Flying-Fish*. A line was thrown from the MAS to Marani and he made it fast to a hook in the square bow. He and Buckley cast off from *Hercules*, Zacco's boat eased forward, the tow straightened and *Flying-Fish* followed. Smith caught a glimpse of Menzies in the wheelhouse of *Hercules*, his face only a pale blur in the darkness but Smith remembered that worried, "Good luck, sir!" He understood Menzies' anxiety. Then a squall whipped rain and spray between and *Hercules* was lost astern with the other MAS boats. There were only Zacco's boat and *Flying-Fish*, alone on the black sea.

Flying-Fish wasn't living up to her name. She towed as might be expected of a rectangular box. She was a bitch. She pitched, rolled and yawed. Smith clung to the coaming of the cockpit beside Balestra, cursed *Flying-Fish* for the cow she was and gave thanks that the journey would not be long. Balestra beside him, face only inches away, gave Smith a quick grin. His hands rested lightly on the wheel and he stared ahead. If he was nervous now he showed no signs of it. The deck was empty but Smith could see the heads of Buckley, Udina and Marani poking up from the forward cockpit, packed close together.

Zacco was towing them in as far as he dared so as to save the power in the batteries of *Flying-Fish*. Already they must be close. The growl of Zacco's engines had stopped, he was now running very slowly, towing with his electric motors. There was no chance of hearing them because of the wind, the slap of the sea on the side and the drum of the rain on the deck of *Flying-Fish*.

Smith rested his eyes briefly from peering ahead and looked about him. The port-side track was only inches from him. It was like a huge bicycle-chain with steel teeth at three foot intervals, projecting six inches or so. Like the starboard track it was endless and ran along the side of the hull on pulley wheels mounted right forward in the bow, on the stern and aft on the bottom. The tracks ran in wooden channels from the bow along the bottom to the stern. Behind Smith were the drive sprockets, mounted on a shaft across the stern. This in turn was driven via worm-gearing by a shaft coming up through the deck from the engine-room below. The engine turned the worm-drive which turned the cog which turned the wheels that drove the chains. Smith grinned tightly. It sounded like some childhood song, but it was simple and effective.

In rehearsal.

They had yet to try it in action.

The tow slackened and Marani trotted lightly forward across the deck, cast off and the MAS came slipping back along the port side of the *Flying-Fish*. Zacco stood tall in the cockpit of his boat pointing out on the starboard bow. He called softly, "The mole!"

Smith saw it, picking out first the phosphoresence where the sea broke against it and then its black length. This was the southernmost mole, longest of the three. He pointed it out to Balestra who nodded and called down the voice-pipe: "Avanti mezzo!"

The motor of *Flying-Fish* purred and Zacco's boat was left astern. Smith saw the wave of his hand then his figure blurred, became one with the receding MAS. Smith turned to look forward again. *Flying-Fish* was creeping in towards the mole at half-speed, a slow walking pace. Her twin screws were driving her now, seated with the rudder in a tunnel under the stern so they did not project outside the line of the hull and thus would not catch on any underwater obstacle. Balestra was steering to port because the boom at that northern end of the mole was furthest from land. His low speed was to conserve the batteries. It would be a long night and he did not know how much power he would need.

They knew where *Salzburg* lay from the aerial photographs, not deep inside the harbour as might have been expected but anchored little more than a quarter-mile the other side of this mole. In daylight Smith could have seen the towering super-structure of the battlecruiser, but that was looking in a straight line. *Flying-Fish* had to go a roundabout route, up to the booms to force her way into the harbour and then southward into an attacking position. Smith realised the confidence Voss must have in the harbour's defences – and why shouldn't he? They would stop anything – except *Flying-Fish?* There was still that question mark. When Smith came to Venice his task had seemed impossible. It was still hazardous in the extreme but there was a fighting chance of success.

Salzburg was a scant half-mile away now.

They passed the end of the mole, a hundred yards out from it. Balestra eased the wheel over and *Flying-Fish* turned in. She handled far better under her own power, little though it was, than at the end of a tow. The boom, like the mole, was marked by a white line of breaking water but this was thinner, like a thread stretched across the sea between the breakwaters. Balestra headed *Flying-Fish* for the centre of the boom because that was not only the point furthest from the moles – and any sentries– on either hand, but also where the chains and timbers might be marginally lower in the water.

Smith licked salt from his lips. They had not been seen, not challenged. On a night like this a watcher on the mole would have hell's own job seeing anything with the rain driving into his face from off the sea, and any guard-boat would be sheltering inside, tucked under the lee of the breakwater.

Balestra had surprise on his side and that was essential. *Flying-Fish* was only a marine tank in so far as she was fitted with toothed driving chains that worked like tracks. Otherwise she was desperately vulnerable. She was not armoured at all, her timbers were only an inch thick and would not even keep out a rifle bullet, let alone a shell. Her top speed was only four knots, there were two torpedoes mounted atop of her, and below the after cockpit, right under Smith, was a scuttling charge that could blow her to pieces if capture seemed likely.

They sat, in fact, on a fragile, floating bomb.

They were close, the boom coming up at them and stretching out on either hand into the darkness. Smith could see the massive baulks of timber near-awash, the sea breaking over them and the huge connecting chains. As these slid under the bow Balestra shouted down to Enzo at the engines. The hum of

110

the motors rose to a whine as the second motor started, the worm-drive close to the after cockpit turned and the chains *clank-clanked* along the deck. *Flying-Fish* drove on into the boom.

Smith saw the bow rise and gripped Balestra's shoulder.

Balestra shouted again, "Avanti tutti!"

With the engines full ahead the sea boiled under the stern as the screws thrashed, driving the boat forward. The teeth on the slow-clanking chains hooked on to the timbers and chains of the boom and hauled her up. She lurched and wallowed, slipped and slid as she rode the boom that sagged under her weight and sank below the surface. She staggered like a drunken man trying to walk across a suspended net, but she moved forward, the screws threshing, the chains steadily clanking, sometimes slipping but then gripping and dragging her onward. She lurched and wallowed again but this time her bow went down, she slid forward and briefly the bow plunged under so the sea washed back against the coaming of the forward cockpit. Then she was over and rose, riding easily in this more sheltered water.

Flying-Fish had crossed the first boom. Balestra's bizarre device worked, even in the currents at the harbour mouth, and they were going to make it!

Enzo stopped the drive to the chains on Balestra's order and with the cessation of their clanking there was only the hum of the motors and the beat of the screws as *Flying-Fish* plodded across the open water at her best speed of four knots. Balestra shot a triumphant glance at Smith. "Only one to go!"

Only one more. Then *Salzburg*. In five minutes she would be in sight and in range of the torpedoes of *Flying-Fish*. Smith said, "Better warn them to swing out the torpedoes as soon as we are over." Not while *Flying-Fish* was crossing the boom because then her crazily tip-tilting deck would make even standing nearly impossible, let alone hauling on the tackles to swing out the torpedoes.

Balestra called softly and in the forward cockpit Udina lifted a hand in acknowledgment.

Less than five minutes. Soon Smith would see *Salzburg*. He strained his eyes to try to make out the bulk of her but she was still too far away and would have the black background of the land behind her. The night was very dark with the rain that drummed on the deck of the *Flying-Fish*, and very quiet. Only the hum of the motor below, the drum of the rain and the slap of the sea against the bows.

Very quiet.

That stillness was shattered as the second and final boom showed right ahead and the long sheer of the bow rode on to it. Balestra called down to Enzo and the worm-drive turned, the chains jerked and clanked across the deck again and the teeth bit on the timber of the boom. *Flying-Fish* staggered up on to it. And it was then, without warning, that the searchlights flicked on, one on either shore. The sweeping beams found her in seconds. Aboard *Flying-Fish* they squinted against the glare. Tracers curved out towards them but fell short. The first shells ripped overhead. Then there was a slamming blow near the bow that vibrated through the hull. Smith saw the heads in the forward cockpit duck down and then, after a moment, reappear. He made a funnel of his hands and shouted at Buckley, "Where were we hit?"

"In the bow just below deck an' went out the port side, sir! Well above the water-line – at the moment!"

But they would probably make water when they wallowed over the obstruction. They were hit again and a bellow from Buckley said it was low and they were now making water. The tracers spattered the sea and tack-tacked along the side. The chains kept up their slow clanking, Smith felt the grate of their biting shudder through the hull and the bow lifted. *Flying-Fish* staggered and lurched, always edging forward, but trapped in a circle of light. They were hit again. So far they were under fire only from small-calibre guns but still the blast threw Smith back against the cockpit coaming and he recovered to see a hole punched in the deck forward. Balestra still held the wheel, his arms straight, legs braced, face set and his eyes fixed ahead.

Clank!-Clank! of the chains.

They were hit yet again and this time the slam of it shook the bow. It was so low that Smith saw water spouting. The port-side chain collapsed, cut under the bow, and became a growing pile of useless steel sliding across the deck as the cogwheel still turned and wound it in. *Flying-Fish* swerved to port. Buckley shouted, "The bow's near shot away, sir! We're awash down here!" Tracers whipped up the deck around the forward cockpit and Buckley ducked. *Flying-Fish* was slowly turning on her axis, Balestra still struggling with the wheel, but his efforts were hopeless with only one track.

Smith knew it.

They were caught on the boom like a fish in a net and the guns would blast them to pieces.

A shell burst in the sea, sent spray lashing across them and it stank of explosive. Smith shouted, "It's no good! We'll have to swim for it!"

"No!" Balestra still wrestled with the controls and shouted at Smith, "No! Almost there! We keep on! We *must*!"

"It's too *late*!" It was. *Flying-Fish* would not move forward, only thrashed around pivoting on the boom, and the essential element of surprise was lost. Smith heaved himself up on to the deck, and bawled at the men forward. They clambered out of the cockpit, came stumbling aft, staggering as *Flying-Fish* was hit again. The motors stopped, and with them the chain's clanking and the thrashing of the screws. *Flying-Fish* lay still on the boom like a stranded whale.

Enzo appeared in the forward cockpit, started to climb out then collapsed over the coaming. Smith and the others were throwing away their oilskins, dragging off their boots. Smith panted, "Get him!" Marani and Udina ran forward.

Balestra beat his fists on the wheel then hauled himself out of the cockpit and on to the deck. He leaned back down and snapped the cover away from the housing of the time switch to the scuttling charge, threw the lever. Marani and Udina returned. Enzo hung limply between them and Balestra went with them over the side into the sea.

Smith shouted at Buckley, "Go on!" Buckley ran and dived over the stern and Smith fell as *Flying-Fish* was hit again. He lurched to his feet, looking over the lifted bow at the light-washed water of the harbour and in that instant a signal flare burst above the boom, drifted brightly down – and the shelling ceased. A big motor pinnace slipped into the lake of light and curved in towards the boom, turned her side to it. The machine-gun mounted in her bow was manned, its barrel swinging around to point at *Flying-Fish*, at Smith. He ran for it, dived clumsily over the stern and into the sea. He came up into the light, gasping as the cold of the water took his breath, and struck

113

out. A score of fast, floundering strokes carried him out of the light and into sheltering darkness. Then he slowed. He knew he had to pace himself if he was to reach the first boom. But then what?

Another flare burst and burned above him. He caught only a camera-blink impression of the near-wrecked *Flying-Fish* hung up on the boom, alone under the lights, then she was hidden by the rain and spray thrown up in his face. He laboured on. So the pinnace had taken a look, suspected a charge aboard *Flying-Fish* and cleared out. He wondered how far he was from the first boom and how quickly the Austrians would send out more pinnaces, this time to search for him and the rest of the crew of *Flying-Fish*. It would be a simple piece of work for the hunting boats and then a prison camp for him. If he didn't drown first. He was tiring and could not see the boom.

"Sir!" Something black thrashed towards him then Buckley turned to swim alongside. "All right, sir?"

"Fine!" Smith choked on seawater as he spoke, spat it out.

"Hang on to me if you like, sir!"

Smith did not answer this time, plugged wearily on with Buckley keeping anxious station a yard away. Until at last the boom showed. He found the others clinging to its seaward side, Balestra holding the face of the unconscious Enzo out of the water. Smith climbed over the boom and slipped down to hang from it beside Balestra. They felt the blast of the explosion, saw it whipping spray from the sea. Then came the *slam* of it in their ears. In that second of brilliance they watched the pieces of *Flying-Fish* hurled skyward – and Smith saw the misery on Balestra's face.

Darkness rushed in once more but there were lights moving in the harbour and they would be the boats coming to take them prisoner. Zacco was lying off, somewhere out there in the darkness covering the sea. Smith could swim out seeking Zacco's boat, like seeking a needle in a haystack and if he did not find it he would die. The beams of the searchlights fingered out again, searching over the boom, lighting them where they hung dripping and cold. It was a bitter ending to the assault on Trieste.

A hand shook at Smith's arm and he turned and found Buckley, who pointed seaward. Smith followed the direction of the outstretched arm and saw the white flicker of bow-wave and wake, the low, cigar-shaped silhouette, then the MAS dashed into the light, the lifted bow sinking as the way came off her and the engine's snarl fell to a muttering grumble. She hove to only feet away and they all left the boom and swam out to her, grabbed her side, Marani and Balestra with Enzo between them. A shell moaned overhead and burst beyond the MAS. Smith hauled himself over the low side of the boat, an Italian seaman grabbing at his arms as if to drag them from their sockets. He saw Enzo pulled in, the others clawing aboard, the big figure of Pietro Zacco standing over the wheel with his face turned towards them, counting.

Smith had also counted and croaked at Zacco, "Right! All aboard!"

The engine note became a bellow as the MAS swung away from the boom and headed out to sea. Shells burst on the boom and in the sea from which Zacco had plucked them. They lay shuddering in the well, frozen by shock and the cold sea, a huddled pile of dispirited men in the bottom of the boat. The lights and the gunfire fell away astern and there was only the bellow of the engine and the rip of the air as they tore away from Trieste. There was no pursuit. Doubtless the Austrians saw no profit in a hunt in the dark when more MAS might be lying in ambush.

In the light of a torch Smith and Balestra examined Enzo while seawater swilled under and across the gratings. They found two wounds in his back they thought were only from splinters but they could do nothing but dress them, then wrap him in blankets. Their teeth chattered with the cold, so they wrapped more blankets around themselves and huddled down, close to Enzo. They were brought a thermos filled with hot coffee laced thickly with grappa. Packed together as they were, and with the coffee and grappa coiling in their bellies, some warmth returned.

Smith saw the signal-lamp flash in the bow of the MAS and a moment later an answering blink came from starboard. Zacco swung their bow towards it and another MAS lifted out of the darkness. As Zacco reduced speed and slipped past her stern they saw Gallina's face turned towards them. The MAS rumbled on at around ten knots and now *Hercules* showed, the little drifter seeming to stand high out of the sea from their low-lying vantage point.

Fred Archbold was at the side with a party waiting to take the survivors aboard. They clambered up or were lifted to the drifter's deck. Enzo was carried below and tucked into the engineer Geordie Hogg's bunk. The cook came to look at him and gave Enzo the benefit of his meagre medical knowledge while the rest went to the crew's quarters forward. Fred Archbold said Balestra could use his bunk: "Looks as if you need it, sir."

Balestra, silent and bitter, leaned in the doorway of Smith's cabin while the latter pulled on dry clothes. Smith said, trying to cheer him, "It was bad luck them spotting us on a night like this. That's all. Just bad luck."

Balestra said fiercely, "It worked! Didn't it? *Flying-Fish* worked!"

Smith nodded. "Like a charm."

"We were so *close*!" Balestra's clenched fist pounded softly on the edge of the door.

Only minutes away. And now? Smith asked, "How long will it take to build another *Flying-Fish*?"

Balestra said morosely, "A month at least. But there is no point. Now the Austrians know about her they will stop her. Maybe they will mount spikes on the booms."

That was true. Smith buttoned his jacket and reached for the bridge-coat hanging by the door. "What about that – torpedo? What was the idea behind that? How is it supposed to work?"

Balestra told him, his eyes coming alive again. If anything, this new idea sounded even madder than *Flying-Fish*. But *Flying-Fish* had worked, would have been a triumphant success if granted another five minutes, and now Smith had no other way of striking at *Salzburg*, of carrying out his orders, save with the help of Balestra's second brainchild.

He jammed his cap on his head, stepped to the door then paused to say wryly, "I'm certain we've got Voss to thank for the strengthened booms and the Austrians being so quick to react."

Balestra scowled. "He won this time."

Smith thought, again. Aloud he said, "Get some sleep. As

soon as we return to Venice you start work on that torpedo idea. How long will it take?"

Balestra shifted uneasily, not wanting to be pinned down. "I don't know. I only *think* I have solved the problems. Maybe a month – maybe never. And now I am without Enzo". He paused a moment, lost in gloomy thought, then: "I do not think I can ask for another engineer to take his place."

Smith saw his point. *Flying-Fish* had gone to sea, and the whole desperate assault on Trieste mounted, without authority or orders. There was a storm waiting in Venice to burst around Smith's head and Balestra would get nothing from the dockyard now. He said, "I want it tomorrow."

Balestra's head jerked up. "Tomorrow!"

Smith grinned. "I know. Impossible. But we can't waste an hour, remember that. We're not finished with Voss and *Salzburg*, not by a long way."

He mounted the companion and walked aft, climbed the ladder to the wheelhouse of the drifter to resume command of her. Menzies could have the cabin to snatch a few hours' sleep. He thought uneasily that Voss and *Salzburg* had not finished with *them*. But his orders remained: Seek out and destroy.

9 "I need guns!"

Menzies had the watch when they raised Venice but Smith slept in the wheelhouse in the old easy chair from his cabin. Menzies called him and Buckley came with a cup of coffee. Smith stood up and stretched stiffly then leaned at the back of the wheelhouse, sipping the coffee. He let Menzies con the drifter in as the three MAS boats curved away across the lagoon to their berth by the Church of the Redentore on the Island of the Giudecca. The city lifted ghostly out of the mist lying on the lagoon and the marshes beyond. There was a damp chill to the air and Smith was weary. Davies the gunner was at the wheel, obeying Menzies' helm orders but, Smith suspected, perfectly ready to disobey them if the boy made a mistake.

Menzies did not. They were signalled to a berth against the Riva degli Schiavoni and Menzies slid the drifter neatly in bows-on to the quay. Men waiting there caught the lines thrown and secured her. There was no welcoming crowd, of course, *Hercules* returning as quietly as she had gone, but there was a scattering of people on the quay, gazing incuriously at the drifter.

Helen Blair stood among them on the quay, her eyes searching the deck of *Hercules*. Smith saw her speak to Buckley who saluted and grinned at her, pointed up at the wheelhouse. Helen Blair's face turned towards Smith and he thought he saw relief there. She smiled, but only for a moment, then lifted a hand to wave.

He climbed down to the deck and crossed the brow to the quay. "Good morning." He thought she looked pale and tired, as if she had not slept.

She glanced around at the mist and the cold grey surface of the lagoon. "Not very." She turned her gaze on him, shyly. "You look tired. Was it bad?"

Smith shrugged. "It could have been worse. We only had one man wounded though that was one too many." He rubbed at the stubble on his jaw and said wearily, "I won't go into details but it went wrong."

The girl looked away, then said, "I was watching and I saw your ship come in. I came down to see –" She stopped, hesitated a moment then went on quickly, "I think you are crowded aboard."

Smith said drily, "That's an understatement. Menzies, that's the midshipman up in the wheelhouse there, only has a bunk when I'm not aboard."

Helen Blair nodded. "Then why don't you stay in my house while the ship is lying here? It's just along the quay."

The invitation was casual, take-it-or-leave-it. Smith hesitated but only for a moment. There was no need for him to sleep aboard. The depressing fact was there was nothing for him to do until he thought of a way to get at *Salzburg*. He said, "Thank you. I have some duties to attend to first but meanwhile I'll send my kit along, if that's all right?"

Helen Blair said hurriedly, "Of course. I have to go to the mainland so I may not see you until tomorrow but my house-keeper will look after you. Just send your servant along with your baggage."

"I haven't got a servant. Buckley will bring it."

Smith pointed him out and Helen Blair nodded. "Very well. Goodbye, Commander." She seemed anxious to get away now.

"Good morning, Miss Blair." Smith saluted and the girl walked back to her house.

Smith returned to *Hercules* and told Buckley to collect his kit and take it to the house. A launch came alongside then to take Enzo to the hospital, and Smith and Balestra shook his hand and saw him off. The engineer was grey with pain, weak and ill, still in shock, but the young doctor who came with the launch examined him quickly before moving him and said there was no cause for worry. "A few weeks' rest and he will be over it."

Balestra left for his workshop then, rowed away in *Hercules'* dinghy by two of her crew. Smith went down to the cabin and wrote his report. It did not take long. He said that he had taken *Flying-Fish* in pursuance of his orders but on his own respon-sibility. That cleared Balestra. He went on to describe the assault on the defences of Trieste, stressed Balestra's courage and determination in pressing home the attack until his craft was trapped and immobile on the boom, stressed also that *Flying-Fish* had worked and only their premature discovery by the searchlights prevented success. He read it through, aware that in the hands of Pickett and Devereux it might end as evidence at his own court-martial. As soon, that is, as Devereux returned from Brindisi. The Italians were another matter. He could expect to be summoned by them at any time.

He was still convinced he had acted correctly and he signed the report, tucked it in an envelope and addressed it to Devereux. Out on deck he found Menzies and handed the report to him. "See that goes to Captain Devereux's office and that you get a receipt for it."

"Aye, aye, sir."

"The cabin is all yours for the time being. I'll be sleeping ashore." Smith told him where.

Menzies ventured, "Good idea, sir, if you don't mind me saying so."

Smith grunted. He went around the ship with Menzies and found there was nothing for him to do. Fred Archbold and Davies the gunner made it plain the men would be well looked after, and now Buckley returned. "I hung up your uniform an' put the rest o' your kit away in your room, sir. You should be all right there."

Smith glanced at him sharply. "What do you mean?"

Buckley returned his gaze with blank innocence. "Nice comfortable room, sir. Very pleasant young lady an' I'll swear by the food. She gave me a meal while I was there." The housekeeper had served it but Helen Blair had been in the kitchen – and asked some casual questions about Smith which Buckley had answered politely, grinning to himself the while.

Smith eyed him suspiciously for a moment, but did not press him.

He walked along the quay to the house and was admitted by the old woman, the housekeeper. Helen Blair had gone to the mainland but had left a note saying he could use the white launch which lay at the steps outside the house.

It was a polite, formal note, signed with the initials H.B. The housekeeper was grey-haired, smiling but worried. She had few words of English but only said something about the war, and was obviously distressed by it. Smith found a hot bath was available so he shaved and soaked, dozed off in the heat, woke and dressed. The old woman called him to a meal set on a table on the first floor looking out over the lagoon and he almost fell asleep again while he ate. So when he had done he dragged himself upstairs to his bed. In the few hazy seconds before sleep struck him down he thought that Voss had won again and it was incredibly bad luck for *Flying-Fish* to have been spotted on such a night.

He must see Balestra.

He wished Helen Blair had not gone away ...

He woke in the late afternoon, the room in shadow. He heard a dull rumble that might have been distant thunder but he recognised it as gunfire. The Germans and Austrians had continued their advance. How close must they now be to Venice if their gunfire could be heard?

He went down and talked with the housekeeper, then out to the launch and so to Balestra's workshop on San Elena. He found the lights burning in his little box of an office and the engineer stooped over his drawing-board. He glanced up vaguely as Smith entered then bent again to his work. Smith set down the basket of food he had obtained from Helen Blair's housekeeper and asked, "Have you slept?"

Balestra did not look up. "I will sleep tonight."

"Eaten?"

"I had breakfast."

Breakfast aboard *Hercules* would have been a bacon sandwich at most, eaten at the crack of dawn. Smith said, "You eat now. Here." He shoved the basket in front of Balestra. "There's — oh! Lasagne and a lot of other stuff. Plus a bottle of wine." Balestra smiled and gave in. While he ate Smith looked at the drawing-board and he was again impressed by the quality of the drawing. He asked questions and Balestra answered. Finally: "What are you going to call it?"

Balestra shrugged and sipped at his wine. "I don't know. I build it, you give it a name."

Smith grinned. "I wouldn't fancy it the other way around." He thought a moment, then: "What about *Seahorse*?"

"All right." Balestra stood up, ready to go back to work.

Smith said, "I suppose I'd be wasting my time ordering you to sleep."

Balestra smiled. "I will sleep. I am almost done."

121

"Is there anything you want?"

Balestra nodded. "I told you I need a good engineer, a man of his hands but with a head. And I can't go to the dockyard to get one."

"Has anything been said about last night?"

"No." Balestra shrugged. "I do not think they know at Headquarters that *Flying-Fish* has gone. I told my workmen to keep silent. But they will learn some time because Enzo was wounded and the circumstances have been reported to the surgeon. But I do not go to the dockyard too soon."

Smith agreed. Devereux was still in Brindisi. No doubt when he returned and read Smith's report he would immediately inform the Italians of the loss of *Flying-Fish* but meanwhile – let sleeping dogs lie. He said, "So what about this engineer?"

Balestra said, "There is the *motorista*, Lombardo. When we disguised *Flying-Fish* he was very clever, very quick. They say he is a good swimmer. If he is as good an engineer –"

He stopped and looked enquiringly at Smith who answered, "Zacco says he's first-class. I'll get him for you tomorrow."

"Good." That settled, Balestra turned back to his drawing-board.

Smith shook his head, retrieved the basket and left him to it. Night had fallen and he steered the little white launch across the dark waters of the lagoon. Back at the house on the Ca' di Dio he found Helen Blair just rising from the table, her meal completed. He was glad to see her and asked quickly, wanting to talk, "Successful trip?"

"Yes." She did not seem happy about it though, looked pale in the light of the lamp.

He asked, "Where did you go?"

"Up beyond Zenson. They are digging trenches on this side of the river and talking of holding a line along the Piave." Then she went on hurriedly, "Please, if you will excuse me, I am tired. Good night, Commander."

"Good night, Miss Blair."

There was tension between them. He watched her climb the stairs but she did not look back. He returned to the table and the old woman served his meal. Afterwards when she had cleared the table and he sat over his coffee she came to the door dressed for the street. She said something and gestured and he understood she would see him in the morning. He said, "Good night," and moments later heard the front door close behind her.

He had not expected that, had assumed the old woman would be sleeping in the house. Now he was alone with the girl.

He finished his coffee and went to his room which was next to hers, lay in bed and stared up into the darkness. Helen Blair's talk of a line on the Piave river worried him. When he heard the gunfire he had wondered how close the enemy was. Now he knew. There had been attempts to make a stand on the Tagliamento, then the Livenza, now it was the Piave. Each river was deeper inside Italy. The Piave ran barely twenty miles from this house.

He was no nearer carrying out his orders than the day he had stepped ashore in Venice. In fact he was further away because *Flying-Fish* and the chance it offered were gone. Now he had to wait for Balestra to make *Seahorse* work but even if he succeeded it would still be a bigger gamble than *Flying-Fish* had been.

If Devereux and Pickett let him try.

If he did not face a court-martial.

The water of the lagoon lapped against the stone at the foot of the house and the wind brought down to him the sound of the guns in the north.

He was always conscious of the girl in the next room.

It was a long time before he slept.

Then he slept badly and woke early, shaved and dressed, went quietly down through the silent house and out to the launch. He steered the little craft across the lagoon and through the mist he had come to expect. On the Giudecca he found the three MAS boats nestling among a dozen other craft alongside the quay near the Church of the Redentore and a sentry on the quay directed him to the quarters of the crews. The building was just along the quay and he met the three captains as they came out on to the steps. They seemed pleased to see him and he shook hands all round. Pietro Zacco grinned and said, "Welcome to our prison."

They explained the joke. Over the door was a sign that had read, '*Casa di Pena per Maschi*', or: 'Prison for males'. When the Royal Italian Navy took it over as quarters for the crews of the MAS boats some wag had covered over the *chi* so now the sign read: '*Casa di Pena per Mas*'. – 'Prison for MAS'.

The crews were streaming out of the prison now and heading down to the boats. Zacco said, "We are needed for patrols for two, maybe three days. Some boats have been damaged and gone back to the yard for repairs. We are needed till they return."

Smith nodded. "I have to wait for Balestra. But I want to talk to you and your engineer, Lombardo."

They went down to the boats. Already engines were starting up one by one, roaring briefly then throttling back to a low rumble. Smith and Zacco dropped down into the cockpit of his boat and Zacco called, "Lombardo!"

He came stooping out of the engine-room and straightened in the cockpit. He wore a blue boiler-suit that was tight across his broad chest and as he looked from one to the other his eyes narrowed with suspicion.

Smith said drily, "Smell a rat?"

Lombardo scowled. "From a mile off." He caught Zacco's eye then and added, "– sir."

Smith said, "It's simple enough. I want a good engineer. You."

"Yeah? What's the job?"

"Assistant to Mr Balestra."

"Balestra? That nut? I don't want –"

"That's enough!" Smith snapped, cutting him off. "Just listen. I could order you to do it but I won't because he doesn't want somebody just to tighten a nut when he's told. He wants a man who can think, plan, devise and improvise, somebody interested and willing."

Lombardo said obstinately, "That last bit lets me out."

Smith ignored that and went on, "So I am only ordering you to come and talk to him. He might decide you're not the man he wants after all."

Lombardo shrugged. "OK – sir." He glanced at Zacco. "You're going out soon. What about the engines?"

Zacco said, "Faccini's a good man and his boat is in dock. I'll borrow him for a day or two."

Lombardo nodded, ducked into the engine-room and emerged with a tool-box swinging from one big hand. He saw Smith glance at that and growled, "I ain't changed my mind, but these go where I go." He followed Smith back to the white launch.

Smith ran her gently in to nose at the platform surrounding the slip in Balestra's shed. He could see the light glowing yellow at the rear and the sound of singing came to them as the launch stopped.

Lombardo muttered, "Is this a workshop or a vaudeville theatre?"

Smith's lips twitched and he told Lombardo, "You'll find him in the office." Lombardo climbed out of the launch and made her painter fast. Smith stopped the engine then and watched him walk back through the half-light of the shed.

They spoke in Italian. Lombardo stood in the doorway of the little cubicle, his wide shoulders filling it. "Signore. The English captain said you wanted to see me."

Balestra straightened from the drawing-board and ran his fingers through his hair. He had been up and at work since first light but he had slept and felt good. He did not like the look of Lombardo glowering about the office, but said, "We haven't time to waste so I'll speak frankly. The captain brought you here because I asked for you. I want a good engineer and a good swimmer. Lieutenant Zacco says you are the best at both and I think you might be. I'm building something new. The idea behind it isn't new but the way I propose to do it is. The point is that once we move away from the drawing-board and start building we'll run into problems that we'll have to solve as we go along. Another thing: this whole affair is not official, you understand. A lot of people are against it. I've got this workshop and that's all I'm going to get. There won't be any glory, no promotion, no medals, just a hell of a lot of work. But I believe this –" he tapped the plan on the drawing-board "– could help to save Italy and finish the war a little sooner." He paused to let Lombardo think about it.

Lombardo said disinterestedly, "What is this thing, anyway?"

Balestra told him and Lombardo's scowl and lack of interest vanished. He said huskily, "Jesus Christ!" Then: "You've got a crew for this?"

Balestra nodded. "I've chosen the man."

"You're going yourself?"

125

Balestra blinked in surprise at the question. "Of course."

Lombardo looked at the slender young man with the mop of dark curls and large, dark, dreamer's eyes. He said ironically, "Can I speak frankly, Tenente?"

When Balestra nodded, he went on: "I saw that – that thing you tried to sail into Trieste and I know what happened, that they practically had to drag you off it. I think you're a screwball –" he used the Italian – *svitato* – "who's going to get himself killed but that's your affair. I'll build this thing for you and make it work if it's possible, if only to see if it *is* possible."

Balestra said, "Just two things we'd better clear up."

"Huh?" Lombardo looked at Balestra who was pale now and the dark eyes no longer dreaming.

Balestra said, "First, this is my baby. I want an assistant, a partner if you like but I'm senior partner. Don't forget. Second: You can think what you like so long as you help me build this but if you call me a – screwball – again I'll break your head with a spanner. Is that understood?"

Lombardo studied him, thought that if this man was mad it was a fighting madness, tightly controlled. He realised that this was no cushy job he was taking on with office hours and an easy routine but he was curious about the man and the machine and his own fighting spirit rose to the challenge. He said, "All right, I'll remember."

"And you'll call me Signore!"

"Signore." Lombardo lifted his box of tools. "When do we start?"

"We've already started. It's wanted tomorrow."

"Tomorrow! What nut asked that?"

"Captain Smith." Balestra smiled. "He was only half-joking. He wants it in a hurry."

Lombardo set down his tools on a bench. "Smith!" He walked back down the length of the shed but he muttered as he went, "Smith! No point in arguing with him, either. Tomorrow!" To Smith himself, when he reached him, he growled, "I'm staying, sir."

Smith only said, "I thought you would." He started the engine and as Lombardo cast off, turned the launch and headed away, leaving the burly *motorista* staring after him.

126

Smith went to *Hercules* and talked with Menzies and Archbold, made a brief tour of inspection and satisfied himself that she was ready for sea. Geordie Hogg, the fat and sweating engineer said, "I put out the fires and cleaned them, sir. I'm ready to get steam up whenever you like. What notice, sir?"

Smith thought for a moment. He had no orders for sea and there was no sense in keeping steam up and burning coal unnecessarily. At the same time this port was near the front line now and if orders came he must be ready to sail without undue delay. He compromised: "Four hours."

"Aye, aye, sir."

Now Davies: "That pontoon gun o' mine sir. Can I go to the dockyard and see how it's coming on?"

Smith sent him away in the dinghy from *Hercules* then asked, "Not bored yet, Mr Menzies?"

The midshipman smiled sheepishly. "No, sir. Mr Archbold's been explaining some of the working of the ship an' Davies an' Jenkinson have been telling me about the pontoon gun."

Smith asked, "Jenkinson?"

"He's the rating who works out the range, bearing and time of flight from a book of maths tables because most of the time they've been shooting from a map and couldn't see the target from the gun. It sounds jolly interesting actually, sir."

Smith said absently, "Very good. You never know when these bits of knowledge might prove useful." But he was thinking of Helen Blair.

He returned in the launch to the house on the Ca' di Dio. It was midday and the mist had lifted a little but now a fine rain was falling again. He found the old housekeeper ready to serve his lunch and that Helen Blair had already eaten and left. So he ate alone, wondering if she was deliberately avoiding him. But why should she do so after inviting him into her house?

Afterwards he walked along the Riva degli Schiavoni, the long, broad stretch of quay leading to the Doge's Palace. He brooded on *Salzburg* and Voss, wondered about their next move, chafed at his own inability to at least attempt to carry out his orders. Twice he had encountered Voss and *Salzburg* and come off the worse. The rain was cold on his face. As he walked he sensed a heightened tension in the city. Statues and buildings were protected by walls of sandbags, timbers and splinter mattresses. In the Piazza San Marco he found the entire front of the church covered by a timber framework that held a wall of sandbags.

Helen Blair was walking slowly across the square, head down under the rain and he fell into step alongside her. She greeted him without a smile. "Commander."

"My name is David."

She hesitated, then, "I'll remember."

"You like walking in the rain?"

She shrugged. "I hadn't noticed it. I wanted to get out of the house and think."

He paced beside her. He saw that a gang of workmen had erected sheer-legs before the church and were using ropes, pulleys and slings to lower the four golden horses down, one by one, from over the great entrance.

Helen Blair said quietly, "They are taking down such monuments all over the city for safety, in case of fire from the Austrian guns."

Smith halted. "Are they so close?"

"Almost."

If this crowded city came under fire from the Austrian batteries the destruction would be immense. The thought was appalling and he could do nothing.

Helen Blair walked on and he went with her. He felt that he owed this girl a lot and that was why he had sought her out. It was time he came to the point and he said awkwardly, "I want to thank you for taking me into your house."

She smiled at him, "You were welcome." Was there hesitation again?

He said, "I'd like to take you to dinner." He remembered his sight of her with the young Air Force officers around a table in the Aurora Hotel. "At a restaurant." He took her arm and halted so she faced him. They were back on the quay now. He saw her cheeks were flushed and thought it was the cold wind cutting in from the Adriatic and bringing the blood to them. She did not answer and he said, "Is that possible?"

She was looking down, avoiding his gaze. "No."

He stared down at the top of her head, put out. With an edge of anger now at the distance she always kept between them he said, "I only asked you to a meal!"

She answered quietly: "And then? Tomorrow?"

"Nothing. A meal and that's all, that's the end."

Was it?

Now she looked up at him and he stared back defiantly. She smiled. "Don't be angry, David, but – you're not married, not engaged?"

So that was it. He grinned, "No."

"You belong to nobody."

"That's right."

She nodded seriously, "That's right."

"So?" He was puzzled now.

"I'm not the first woman."

His grin became lop-sided. "Well –"

"How many of them do you remember?"

The cool question angered him. "What the hell!"

Helen Blair said quietly, "Some you'll remember. Only a little, but kindly. Serve them right."

Smith stared at her and she explained. "A woman would be a fool to love a man like you, here today and gone tomorrow. I'm sorry, David, but it's true. And there are other reasons." She bit her lip.

He growled at her, "That'll do to be going on with!" He released her arm.

"David, please!" She reached out to him.

"Hey, English!"

The voice was harsh and deep, like gravel pouring out of a chute. Smith remembered the voice and turned, saw the capitano di fregato he had met at the mouth of the Livenza river, Bruno Garizzo. The captain strode across the quay. Now his uniform was immaculate, fitted beautifully and his boots glittered but the voice was the same and the high good humour. "And La Contessa!" He saluted her with a flourish and added a little bow. "As beautiful as ever." He cocked an eye at Smith. "A bit of all right, eh? That is so? A bit of all right!"

Smith nodded. "Yes."

Garizzo turned back to Helen Blair. "This is better than the Livenza, better than the front. It is good you stay away from the front now. It is bad there."

The girl smiled at him. "Thank you, but I will visit the front again soon." Garizzo shook his head with a frown but Helen

Blair said firmly, "You do your duty, sir, and I do mine." Her voice was not so firm when she turned to Smith. "It's for the best, David, I'm sure." He did not answer and she said to Garizzo, "Please excuse me. I must go. Arrivederci."

"Arrivederci." Garizzo saluted again and watched her walk away. He turned to Smith, puzzled, "I said wrong?"

Smith shook his head. "No. I did. Before you came."

"Ah." Garizzo shrugged. "Your business, eh?" He gripped Smith's hand, slapped his shoulder. "I came to Headquarters for orders. They have plate full. That's right? Plate full. They have to defend Venice. The army hold a line on the Piave river. I come for orders and guns. I got orders but no guns! They say the main attack will come inland and all the guns must be there. Maybe in two – three days there will be guns but not now. I hold a line from the coast two miles south-west of Porto di Cortellazzo inland to the Cavetta canal and I have eight hundred and thirty men and twenty officers! I need guns!" For a moment there was anger behind the grin, the black eyes hard. Then he laughed. "But that is my affair! And you? What do you do with your fishing-boat?"

What indeed? Smith was still obsessed by the threat from *Salzburg* and Voss but it was a threat only he believed in: Devereux and Pickett would not listen. And now all of them here in Venice were faced with a greater, more immediate danger. He wondered what he should do, what he could do. If Venice fell there was no other naval base north of Brindisi. If Venice fell the line on the Piave would be turned, the retreat would go on. He remembered the atmosphere of tension in the city, born of the threat hanging over them all. He said, "I might see you south-west of Porto Cortellazzo."

"With your fishing-boat?"

"That's right."

Garizzo looked at Smith thoughtfully, then said, "Good. I think you would be welcome to me with or without your fishing-boat. The challenge is 'Venezia' and the answer 'San Marco'. Do not forget. We cannot take chances up there." He gripped Smith's hand. "But I must return. My men dig trenches while I talk. Goodbye, English."

"Arrivederci, Capitano."

Garizzo guffawed. "You learn, English!" He strode off along

130

the quay, roaring with laughter.

Smith watched him go, thinking of that long line stretched thinly across the marshes between the coast and the Cavetta canal and of the capitano's men he had seen at the mouth of the Livenza. It was the capitano's affair but he had said Smith was welcome.

He hurried back along the Riva degli Schiavoni to where *Hercules* was moored bows-on to the quay. Davies had the watch on deck and saluted as Smith came aboard. Smith asked, "The pontoon gun?"

"Ready for sea, sir."

"What about ammunition for it?"

"We draws that at La Certosa, sir. We just turns up wi' the gun, say what we want an' sign for it."

"Good. Call Mr Archbold and the engineer."

Davies bawled down the hatch and seconds later Fred Archbold and Geordie Hogg appeared, both blinking: obviously they had been catching up on their sleep. Menzies, disturbed by the commotion, came tumbling up after them. Smith said, "Mr Hogg, I want steam in one hour."

Geordie complained, "You said we were at fower hours' notice, sir."

"Well, now you are at one hour's notice. Can you do it?"

Geordie opened his mouth to protest then caught Smith's eye and changed his mind. "Aye, aye, sir." He trotted away to the stern and shouted down the after companionway for the stoker.

Smith glanced at Menzies and Fred Archbold, who was still buttoning his jacket. Fred nodded unhurriedly. "Aye, aye, sir. One hour."

Smith told Menzies, "Come with me." He went down to his cabin. The bunk was rumpled; Menzies had also been catching up on his sleep. As Smith sat down at the desk Menzies tried surreptitiously to twitch the blankets smooth. Smith said impatiently, "Belay that! You did right to get all the sleep you could. You may not get much for some time."

"Sir?" There was enquiry in Menzies' voice but Smith was not listening, had already started to write. He had no orders for *Hercules* or the pontoon gun so he wrote briefly to Naval Headquarters that at the request of Capitano di Fregato Garizzo he was sailing to give support to that officer's battalion.

He handed the signal to Menzies. "Read it. Then take it to HQ and hand it in to Captain Devereux's office to be passed on immediately."

He went on deck with Menzies and saw him hurry aft to where the dinghy lay alongside, its crew standing by. Smith turned and found Buckley waiting. "Come on."

He led the way along the quay to the house on the Ca' di Dio. Helen Blair opened the door to them and Smith said, "I've come for my kit." The girl looked past him and saw the big seaman. Smith said, "You know Leading-Seaman Buckley."

She nodded and smiled. "Of course. How are you, Mr Buckley?"

Buckley saluted smartly and smiled back at her. "I'm fine, Miss. Thanks."

"You'll find the commander's valise where you left it, in the room on the right, up two floors."

"Thank ye, Miss." Buckley edged past them, cap in hand, and climbed the stairs two at a time.

Helen Blair looked at Smith. "I'm sorry about today – the row. You don't have to go to a hotel. We can still be friends."

"I'm going to sea."

"Oh." That came flat and the corners of her mouth went down. "Far? For long?"

"I don't know. I'm going to join Garizzo. He's holding a line from the Cavetta canal to the sea."

She frowned, "But how can your ship help there?"

"We have a pontoon gun. Six-inch."

"I see." And then she added, "He will need a forward observation officer. Is that you?"

Smith blinked at her knowledge then remembered that this girl had been talking with soldiers for two years now. He said, "That's right."

They stood in awkward silence for some time. The girl seemed unhappy and Smith was eager to get away now.

Helen Blair said suddenly, "David –" Then stopped.

"Yes?"

She hesitated, but then said only, "You needn't take all your kit, only what you need."

"There's just the one valise anyway."

They heard Buckley's tread on the stairs and he appeared lugging Smith's valise. "Thank ye, Miss. All the best to you."

"And to you, Mr Buckley. Take care of –" She checked, then finished: "Take care."

Buckley grinned at her. "I know what you mean and I'll do my best, Miss."

He passed through the doorway and Helen Blair turned to Smith. "You too, David. Be careful."

"I always am." He held out his hand to her and she gripped it, let go. He saluted her and turned away, walked off along the quay with Buckley.

At nightfall *Hercules* sailed out between the arms of the Porto di Lido. She towed astern of her the pontoon, a wooden coal barge fifty feet long, decked over and strengthened to take the gun. It was stacked with ammunition from the dump on La Certosa. Menzies stood on the deck forward of the wheelhouse where was gathered the crew of the six-inch gun.

Davies turned to him. "Permission to carry on, sir?"

Menzies nodded. "Please."

Davies faced the gunners in the twilight and held them with his fierce glare. "Now listen you lot because we haven't much time and this looks as if it'll be dodgy. First, we're running the pontoon aground and we've got to get camouflage up because by morning we might be under observation. We haven't much in the way of netting so we'll use whatever we find on the ground, bushes and so on. That gun's got to look like just one more bump on the coast.

"Second. Billings –" The scrawny little runt of a signalman looked up from where he knelt on the deck with Buckley, a field telephone between them. Davies said, "Probably a mile o' telephone wire to be laid before morning." Billings nodded and Davies' glare switched back to the gunners. "Third –"

As he went on with his briefing so Billings proceeded softly with his, talking out of the corner of his mouth: "See, Buckley, mate, soon as you're ready to connect up you tie back the wire to summat solid like a gatepost or a rock, because it's a certainty some big-footed, awkward bugger's gonna come along an' trip over your wire and if you haven't got it tied back he'll yank the telephone away and maybe bust it. Now, connecting: You bares

133

the wire like this, unscrew your terminals —"

Menzies tried to listen to both Davies and Billings, tried to remember all he had learned in the last day or two, wished to God he had learnt more. He was terrified that he would make a stupid mistake. He knew now that Smith would not blast him but that was all the more reason for not making a mistake. He could not let Smith down.

Smith conned his ship but was aware of the little group on the deck just forward of the wheelhouse and Menzies standing very stiff in the back, guessed a little of how he was feeling. Smith thought that Menzies would do his part; he was quick and eager. He just hoped the youngster would survive.

Fred Archbold had the wheel. Smith told him quietly, "Once we're ashore you are to come back down the coast and lie off Piave Vecchia. You'll be able to anchor close in to the shore. Keep a watch round the clock and steam up. If you see a red flare and a green one that will be the gun in trouble. Come and pick them up and you'll have to be quick."

Archbold sucked at the cold pipe stuck in one corner of his mouth. "What about you, sir?"

"I'll be with the marines. You just carry out your orders."

Fred Archbold thought, 'An' where will the marines be if Fritz runs over them like a steamroller?' He answered, "Aye, aye, sir."

They were at sea and the night closed around them.

10 Battleground

HM Drifter *Hercules* steamed north-eastward along the coast, so close inshore that Smith kept a man in the chains heaving the lead. They passed Porto di Piave Vecchia at the old mouth of the Piave river shortly before midnight and made good another two miles before Smith ordered quietly, "Port five. Steady. Steer that." *Hercules* crept in towards the shore, marked by a thin silver line of breaking surf, the land beyond it so low-lying as to seem a continuation of the sea beyond a reef.

Menzies was in the wheelhouse now, and nervous. Smith said, "Tell Davies to be ready to work the pontoon in."

"Aye, aye, sir." Menzies scurried away. Davies was doubtless ready with his gunners but the errand gave Menzies something to do instead of worrying.

The seaman casting the lead chanted, "By the mark two!"

That was close enough for *Hercules*, drawing near ten feet. Smith ordered, "Stop engines."

The anchor plummeted down, the cable roaring out and *Hercules* lay to it. Now in the quiet they could hear the rumble of gunfire inland, and closer but faintly the crackle of rifle-fire, the brief stutter of a machine-gun. The pontoon was hauled in to the port side and Menzies, Davies and his gunners boarded it, slipped the tow. With splashing of sweeps and muttered cursing they edged it away towards the shore. Meanwhile Smith had gone down to the boat now lowered and lying alongside to starboard. He wore a pistol belted about his waist. Buckley crouched in the bow and a seaman from the drifter's crew pulled them to the shore, sliding past the unwieldy pontoon and leaving it astern. Buckley had a Lee-Enfield rifle slung across his back, a bandolier of cartridges across his chest. As they ran into the shallows he jumped over the bow and hauled the boat in.

A voice shouted the challenge at them from the darkness: "*Venezia!*"

Smith answered quickly with the other half of the password given him by Garizzo: "*San Marco!*" He jumped down from the bow and splashed ashore. An Italian marine appeared out of the night, still suspicious, rifle trained on Smith and Buckley. Obviously he was wary of an enemy attack from the sea. Though a risky business for the attacker, that was always a possibility.

Smith shone his torch on himself and said, "Inglese." He pointed out to sea and said, "Ship." The marine nodded and Smith asked, "Capitano Garizzo?"

The marine shouted rapidly over his shoulder, there was movement in the darkness and a petty officer came down with another marine. The PO eyed Smith and said, "English!" He slapped one marine on the shoulder. "Capitano Garizzo! Ca' Gamba!" Smith thought that if Garizzo had warned his sentries to look out for him then he'd been pretty sure Smith would come. He had seen Ca' Gamba marked on the map, 'Casa Gamba', a tiny village a thousand yards inland. If Ca' di Dio meant a house of God then this meant house of Gamba. But now he again pointed out to sea because the pontoon and gun bulked there, inching in towards the shore. "Gun. Cannone." He stamped his foot on the beach. "Here."

The petty officer nodded vigorously. "Si! Cannone! Buono!" His teeth showed white as he grinned approval.

Smith remembered with relief that Davies could speak some Italian. It would be needed. The marine, his guide, beckoned. Smith told the seaman in the boat, "Go back to *Hercules* and bring ashore the rations for the gun-crew." He turned and, Buckley at his heels, followed the marine up the beach. They came on a dirt road running along the line of the shore and their guide led them towards the front line. The rain still fell in a steady drizzle. The crackle of rifle-fire grew louder as they advanced and a flare burnt to the north, its light reflected palely on the waterlogged fields. The road ran above the fields like a low causeway and bore to the left away from the coast and inland, rutted with a succession of water-filled holes that soaked them to the knees as they trudged through.

They walked for fifteen minutes and Smith reckoned they had covered close on a mile when the marine said, "Ca' Gamba." There lifted out of the darkness a scattering of little low houses with tiled roofs and shuttered windows, strung along the road. They passed four of them and came on a fifth that stood no higher but rambled longer and larger. Two marines stood sentry at the door, waterproof capes bulging over the ammunition pouches beneath, rain dripping from their caps.

The guide spoke quickly to them while Smith and Buckley waited. Then one of the sentries opened the door behind him, shouted something and Smith caught the word, "Inglese!" There came an answering bellow from within and the sentry beckoned Smith. He pushed through the doorway, felt the door drawn shut behind him as he passed aside the blackout curtain, took off his cap and entered the room. It was narrow but ran from front to back of the house and was lit by a paraffin lamp hanging from a nail in a beam. To the right lay a wide fireplace, the ashes of a dead fire there, and a marine crouched over a kettle hissing on a primus stove. Smith saw through an open door to another room where two marines sat before a battery of field telephones set up on a trestle table, signal pads in front of them. One of the telephones tinkled and a marine snatched it up, put pencil to pad.

Smith's gaze returned to the centre of the room where a table stood under the lamp. Two officers sat at the table, one a lieutenant, sharp-faced and sharp-eyed as he watched Smith – but the other was Garizzo. His cap lay on the table alongside the map spread there and his stubbly hair showed thick and black but flecked with grey under the light.

He stood up. "English! You have come with your fishing-boat!"

Smith nodded. "And a gun. Six-inch."

"Ha!" His wide mouth curved in a grin. He said softly, "A gun!" His hand slapped down on the lieutenant's shoulder. "You hear that, Achille! We have a gun!" He flapped the hand in introduction: "Tenente Achille Sevastano, my second-in-command. Capitano Smith."

Sevastano rose, bowed, smiled and Garizzo bawled at the marine crouched over the primus, "Caffè!" Then he dragged another chair up to the table and motioned to Smith to join him.

Smith said, "My signaller is outside. With your permission?" He shouted, "Buckley!" Garizzo echoed the shout with a bellow to the sentries in Italian and Buckley came in through the curtain. Smith told him, "Stand behind me and listen."

Once seated Garizzo pointed at the map with a thick finger.

"My position. Here. We hold a line from the Cavetta canal – here – to the sea –" Smith followed the line marked in pencil on the map as the finger traced it, took out his own map and copied the details as Garizzo briefed him rapidly on the dispositions of his force.

Garizzo sat back in the chair as the coffee came, black and bitter, and scolding hot. "So. Questions?"

Smith said slowly, apprehensive, "The line seems – thinly held."

Garizzo grinned without humour. "I noticed that also."

"Reserves?"

"No reserves. Tomorrow, maybe. But for now – no reserves."

"You expect an attack?"

"The Austrians are out there now, probing. I think they will attack at first light and try to run over us. Where is your gun?"

"It's mounted on a pontoon – here." Smith marked its position on the map with his pencil.

Garizzo stared a moment, then nodded. "And you?"

"I'll be upstairs in one of the houses here, observing for the gun."

Garizzo frowned. "Not good. They will be shelled. But you will not find a better place. With your feet on the ground you will see nothing. It is very flat here."

Smith looked at his watch and stood up. "I have a lot to do. I'll report to you here when I'm ready."

"Before the light." It was not a question. Garizzo said, "Because when the light comes we will be out of here and in the trench." He jerked his thumb over his shoulder. "About three hundred metres forward." He held out his hand. "Good luck, English."

Smith shook the hand and left the house with Buckley. As they walked quickly back along the road Smith asked, "Have you ever been a signaller for a forward observation officer?"

"No, sir. But Billings gave me a few tips."

That had been done on Smith's orders. Billings was the only real signaller they had and Smith wanted him with Menzies. He had told Billings the procedure must be simple, yet it had to work. Now he thought it would not only be simple but rough and ready. "You'll have to learn damn quick."

Buckley was resigned to that. He had found that with Smith

he must learn a number of things very quickly as each different situation demanded. "Aye, aye, sir."

Back on the shore Buckley sought out Billings and together they set out with the reels of telephone wire, laying the line forward to Ca' Gamba and the house there. The pontoon with its gun was already aground in the shallows and moored close to where a stunted copse ran down to the water's edge. Davies had split his gunners into two parties. One of them was stringing up camouflage nets forward of the gun and lacing them with branches hacked from the copse, the intention being to hide the gun from any raised observation post in the Austrian lines by disguising both gun and pontoon as an extension of the copse. The other party splashed back and forth between pontoon and copse humping the ammunition ashore and arranging it in small well-separated dumps under the withered little trees, the charges stacked carefully with groundsheets below and above.

A map was set up on a board at the edge of the copse, a field telephone close at hand. That would eventually be the link with Smith in the house at Ca' Gamba. He huddled over the map with Menzies and by the light of a shaded torch marked on it the house from where he would be observing and pencilled in the position of the Italian trenches. When it was all done he asked Menzies, "Any questions?"

Menzies took off his cap and scratched his head, thinking, then said, "No, sir. I think I've got it all."

"You're in command here," Smith told him, "but if you've got any sense you'll take heed of suggestions from Davies. He's done this before, and many times."

"Aye, aye, sir."

The boat from *Hercules* had returned loaded with rations for the men ashore. Smith ordered the seaman in the boat, "Get back to the ship now and tell Mr Archbold to return to Piave Vecchia." He made one last, quick tour of the position and told Davies, "Be ready at first light."

"Aye, aye, sir."

Smith looked at his watch. It was time he was gone. He set out once more for the front carrying the pack with the rations for himself and Buckley, following the looping, trailing telephone wire. Sporadic rifle-fire winked and rattled distantly ahead of him. He met Billings hurrying back to the shore, the signaller coming panting out of the darkness. He paused only to say, "We tested the line a minute ago, sir. Mr Menzies came through clear as a bell."

"Very good."

Billings trotted away.

It was still dark when Smith came once more to the straggling row of houses, deserted now, the sentries gone, but Garizzo and Buckley stood on the road by the biggest house. Garizzo said deeply, "You're in time, English. Are they ready back there?"

"They'll be ready."

Garizzo nodded towards the darkness in the north. "So will they. There have been patrols out in no-man's land, looking for us. They found us. They know where we are." He shot a glance at Smith, stubborn and angry. "There is an estimate that our army has lost four hundred thousand men in dead, wounded and prisoners. There is talk that only a miracle can stop the Austrian and German advance now. We'll see." He paused, brooding, then: "I'm going forward. I have left the primus" – he grinned –"so you English can make tea. And there is a telephone. I'll be on the other end in a dug-out up there. So. You're welcome, English. My house is yours." He laughed bleakly and strode away into the darkness.

Smith watched him go, thinking that it did not seem so dark, he could make out the other houses scattered along the side of the road. He glanced at his watch; it would soon be light. He entered the house with Buckley and found Garizzo's telephone on the table inside. Blankets still screened the door and windows and Smith used his torch, sweeping its beam across the ceiling.

Buckley said, "Over there, sir." He pointed to the right-hand wall where a trap was set in the ceiling. They lifted the table over and Smith climbed on to it and shoved the trap up into the loft above. He poked his head through and used the torch again cautiously, saw a bare, dusty wooden floor under the sloping roof, a pile of sacks in one corner and in another an old tin trunk on its side, open and empty. The owners had taken everything they could.

He climbed into the loft, Buckley passed up the two telephones and then came up himself. Smith said, "Let's have a hole there." He pointed and Buckley lifted his foot and booted

140

the tiles so a few of them cracked and slithered away leaving a gap a foot square. Smith went down on one knee to peer out through it. Buckley sat down a few feet away with his back against the end wall of the house and a telephone set up either side of him. He quickly tied back their wires to a beam as Billings the signaller had told him.

Smith ordered, "Test those lines."

Buckley wound on the handle of one of the field telephones, sending the tiny current from the batteries down the wire to ring the bell at the other end, heard a voice in reply, answered it and repeated the action with the other telephone. "Both working fine, sir."

Then they waited as the night slipped away and the day came greyly. There was mist gathering, of course. The light opened around them until Smith thought visibility to be about a half-mile. Unless the mist closed in it would let him see the zig-zag line of the marines' front line trenches three hundred yards in front of his position, the communication trench running back from them to emerge at the houses to his left. The land was low-lying and flat. To his right and about twenty yards away another track ran between the houses and forward through the trenches towards the enemy lines now hidden by the mist. Like all the tracks in this flat countryside it was more of a causeway, raised feet above the marshes. The marshland was coarse grass interspersed with sheets of dully glinting surface water.

Smith was using his binoculars now, his map on its board resting on his knee. He ordered quietly, "Target!"

Buckley twirled the handle on the telephone, heard Billings answer and said, "Target!"

Billings' voice squawked, "Target!"

Buckley reported to Smith, "Through, sir!"

They would be taking post at the gun now.

Smith watched grey figures come out of the mist, moving slowly as they advanced in a long line stretched across the marsh. He took a bearing with his compass, used his protractor to draw a line on the map, measured the distance along it and marked his estimate of the advancing troops' position. "Target-troops advancing. Co-ordinates" – he read them off from the map, finished – "fire!"

Buckley repeated each phrase into the telephone as Smith

said it and at the end reported, "Through, sir."

Back at the gun Jenkinson would be plotting the target on his map, working out the range and bearing gun-to-target and then the various corrections for wind, temperature, etc – and finally producing a range and bearing for the gun to fire at the target that was out of sight of the gunners.

Buckley, telephone at his ear, reported, "Shot! Time of flight eight seconds!"

Smith used his glasses to watch for the fall of the shell, counting ... There was another line of men behind the first, another, and another. Garizzo had said the Austrians would try to run over his marines and there looked to be three thousand men out there already and more still emerging from the mist. Machine-guns were stuttering and all along the line of trenches the rifle-fire crackled ... *Now!*

He saw the burst, just, away beyond the leading troops and just a flash of yellow in the mist. How far? He hadn't enough experience of this kind of observation but he thought it was about a quarter-mile too far. "Five hundred yards! Two o'clock!" They were using the artillery clock code, the centre of the imaginary clock face being the target and twelve o'clock due north. So he had reported the burst as over by five hundred yards. Jenkinson at the gun could now correct.

Buckley reported, "Shot! Time of flight eight seconds!" Smith watched the tiny figures of men labouring forward through the mud and waited, counting, for the burst – seven, eight – The shell burst just ahead of the advancing troops. He licked his lips, dry now. That was luck. He might have ranged for several rounds but now – "Five rounds gunfire! Sweep two degrees!"

He waited, rubbing his eyes until Buckley reported, "Shot, sir!" Then he lifted the glasses again. The first round fell among the tiny, creeping figures out there in the open. So did the second but further to the right as the gun obeyed his order to sweep through two degrees. The machine-guns and rifles were still firing and men were falling, little moving figures stopping to become still grey dots on the marsh. It was terrible country to cross under fire, the mud and water making their advance more wading than walking.

His glasses shifted across the front and settled on the track that ran up to the house alongside him. Troops were swarming on it now, some falling but the others hurrying on, able to move fast on its drier surface. He snatched at the map, used compass and protractor, marked the position of the men on the track. "Target! Troops advancing! Co-ordinates. . . !"

This time it took him four ranging rounds before he bracketed the track with a shell close on either side. "Five rounds gunfire!"

One after the other the shells howled overhead to burst on or near the track and the troops running on it. The advance halted as the men left at the head sought cover and Smith corrected the fire, lifting it to search back along the track. "Five rounds gunfire! . . . Five rounds gunfire!"

And all the time the rifles and machine-guns of Garizzo's marines swept the marshland before their trenches. Until suddenly all along the front the grey lines were ebbing away, back into the mist.

Smith ordered huskily, "Stand easy." And: "Good shooting."

He heard that passed by Buckley as he stared out through the hole in the roof at the open ground. Nothing moved there now. The mist had lifted in the course of the action and now he could see the line that marked the Cavetta canal. The rain began to fall. The ground before him and the surface of the track were pocked with shell-holes. They had done well at the gun but he was not so sure about himself. That first shoot was lucky, the second he just managed well enough. He was weary after the exertions of the night and the nervous tension – and thirsty, his mouth dry.

The second telephone rang and Buckley answered it then passed the receiver to Smith. "The capitano, sir."

Garizzo's voice crackled down the wire: "English! Good! You like some coffee? So come down. All quiet just for now."

"Right." Smith passed the telephone back to Buckley. "I'm going down to the line. Can you keep a look-out and cook yourself some breakfast at the same time? Fetch the primus up here."

"I'll do that, sir. You look out down there. You should have a tin hat. Maybe they can find one for you, sir."

"I won't be long," Smith reassured him, then dropped down through the trap to the table beneath and so to the floor. He

143

passed up the primus to Buckley and then left the house, smiling to himself at the leading hand's concern for him.

The entrance to the communication trench was at the left end of the row of houses and sheltered from enemy gunfire by them. Then it turned to lead forward towards the front line, zig-zagging so it could not be enfiladed by enemy machine-guns. It was shallow and he had to stoop so his head did not show above its lip. It had not been revetted – there had been not enough time or timber to shore up its sides – and its floor was liquid mud that came up over his ankles. He passed little parties of marines digging out the trench in places where it had fallen in, working crouched, hurling shovelfuls of mud over the parapet. They looked tired. He had to squeeze past them, muttering an apology, but they seemed cheerful and pleased to see him. The explanation came when one of them pointed a finger and said, "Boom! Boom! Buono!" So it was the work of the gun that had pleased them.

The front line trench was deeper and partly revetted but here the water and mud was knee-deep. He had to wade through it. A long firing step had been cut into the front wall of the trench and was carpeted with bodies of marines sleeping wrapped in blankets and groundsheets under the rain. The trench twisted and turned and at each bend a sentry crouched on the firing step keeping watch through a periscope. Smith waded along, thinking that too much of this and Garizzo would have cases of trench-foot among his men. It sounded innocuous, like corns, but in fact it meant men's feet rotted because of the continual immersion so they lost toes and holes were eaten through from sole to arch.

He found Garizzo in a hole in the back wall of the trench, his dug-out. Smith had to bend almost double to enter it and Garizzo sat on an ammunition box with his knees up to his chin. He pushed another box at Smith. "English! The gun was good! *Caffè!*" That last was bellowed and was answered by a distant yell. Garizzo said, "It went as I thought. They threw in three, four battalions without preparation – no bombardment. To try to catch us before we were ready, run over us with many men. But we were ready. And they did not expect the gun, I think."

An orderly came splashing down the trench with coffee. Smith asked, "What about reserves? Reinforcements?" Garizzo sipped at the bitter black coffee and smacked his lips. "No.

There has been heavy fighting around Jésolo and up river." That was a village two miles inland. Garizzo scowled. "The generals think that is where the main attacks will be, to drive on Mestre and Venice. So any reinforcements go there."

Smith asked, "You don't agree with them?"

Garizzo thought a moment, then shook his head. "Maybe now they are right, but if the Austrians are held there? Suppose they broke through here? They walk straight down the road to the Porto di Lido. Then Venice falls."

Because from the Porto di Lido the Austrian guns would command the city. Smith saw in his mind's eye the long, low littoral and the road flat and straight, pointing like an arrow at the Porto di Lido, the gateway to the lagoon – and Venice. There was only this thin line of Garizzo's battalion of marines to bar the way.

Garizzo got out his map. "Their lines are the other side of the canal. I think they must wait until the night, and then bring over many men to wait below the bank of the canal and in the morning they will attack again. This time it will be planned. It will be bad."

Smith put down his empty mug. "I have work to do."

He walked back along the trench through the rain. At the house he ate breakfast of bacon that Buckley cooked over the primus, then made a careful little sketch of the country he could see before the house, to the canal beyond. He marked and labelled a number of salient features spread across the landscape. A low mound in the middle distance, some two hundred yards forward of the front-line trench, he labelled 'Ridge'. He marked two points on the track along which the Austrians had advanced: a clump of bushes 'Bush', and a solitary tree as 'Tree'. He marked a point on the canal as 'Canal'. There were a dozen points in all.

He twirled the handle on the telephone and heard an excited voice, "Gun!"

"Smith. Mr Menzies?"

"Yes, sir."

"Target registration. Target 'Ridge'."

"Target registration. Target 'Ridge', sir."

Smith handed over the telephone to Buckley, gave his orders and watched for the fall of the shell. He ordered successive corrections after each ranging shot until a shell fell on the 'Ridge'. Then he moved on: "Target 'Canal'."

"Target 'Canal', sir."

It went on steadily through the morning. He thought again that it was like an academic exercise, the careful plotting of each target, the ranging. It was simply preparation. When the registration was done the gun had the bearing, range and angle of sight to a dozen targets spread across the open ground and could fire on them at call without preliminary ranging.

In the afternoon Smith and Buckley took it in turns to sleep. They ate as the sun went down and as night fell the quiet countryside became alive. Machine-guns chattered and tracer arced across the sky. Grenades flashed and *thumped!* Flares burst and drifted slowly down lighting the moonscape before the trenches.

Smith twirled the handle on the telephone to Garizzo and heard his hoarse growl. "English?"

Smith asked, "Orders?"

"No. No gunfire. They are just Austrian raiding parties, to stop my men from sleeping and make them nervous. I have outposts out there. You sleep."

They took it in turns, one keeping watch while the other tried to sleep despite the continual firing, wrapped in a blanket and lying close by the wall. The ghostly, reflected glow of the flares cast leaping shadows in the loft. Smith dozed briefly to be jerked awake time and again. Helen Blair's face floated into his mind. He saw her standing cool and elegant, heard her say softly, miserably, "I'm sorry, David. It's for the best. There are other reasons."

What other reasons?

He stood on watch in the cold dark before dawn, his blanket around his shoulders. The telephone jangled and he started, fumbled for it, answered thickly, "Smith."

"English! It will be light soon."

"Right." Smith put down that telephone, shook Buckley then worked the other phone, told Billings on the shore at the gun end, "Stand to."

Ten minutes later the dawn was upon them and the first Austrian shells from batteries beyond the canal burst in the marshland before the house. There was mist again but Smith could trace the communication trench and that of the front line, saw the flash and smoke of the shells bursting there. He ordered, "Target 'Canal'! Ten rounds gunfire!" The shells from the six-inch howled overhead to add to the din and burst on or about the canal. Smith saw their flaming, though mist still hid the canal itself.

Garizzo's battalion was being pounded by several Austrian batteries. Smith could not see the front-line trench now because of the smoke that drifted over it, but beyond and distantly towards the canal lines of men were visible advancing out of the mist. This time no rifle-fire came from the trench, no machine-gun rattled because the marines were pinned down by the barrage.

Smith ordered, "Target 'Tree'! Five rounds gunfire!"

"Target 'Bush'! Five rounds gunfire!"

"Target 'Ridge'! Ten rounds gunfire! Sweep one degree!"

The gunfire switched from one registered target to another across the front of the position, returned again and again to sweep the ridge and the track, but still the advancing lines reformed and closed on the Italian defences. The Austrian barrage ceased then for fear of hitting their own men and the marines crawled up from dug-outs and the depths of the trench and opened fire. Smith watched the distant figures falling before their fire.

Ten minutes later he ordered, "Stand easy."

Once again the attack was over.

His ears still rang as he went down to see Garizzo. He had to make his way down the communication trench against a tide of wounded, limping or borne on stretchers, making for the aid post behind the houses. He found the front-line trench broken down by the bombardment in several places and the marines digging it out furiously. He had to climb over the heaped mud knowing there might be men trapped beneath it. He caught up with Garizzo as he ranged along the trench like a big bear bawling at his men, roaring with laughter, slapping backs.

He grinned at Smith but he was serious when he said, "Not good, English. I lost men and I can't afford to lose one. And it will be worse. This afternoon perhaps, or tomorrow morning. When they have regrouped."

147

Smith said, "I need ammunition for the gun. We fired a lot this morning."

Garizzo nodded. "All right. Sevastano, my second-in-command, goes back to report and find out about reserves. He will see about your ammunition."

They ducked together as a shell shrieked in and exploded short of the trench, showering them with mud and earth. Garizzo cursed and said, "Get down or get out, English!"

That shell was the first of many. The Austrians were not laying down another barrage but maintaining a harassing fire. The shells fell singly at intervals of ten seconds or so. Smith worked his way back along the front line into the communication trench, past the marines huddled down for cover. He was relieved to get away from the front, to be heading back along the communication trench towards the house. He splashed quickly through the mud but he panted as if he had been running. He knew that was because of the shelling and tried to walk more slowly and breath deeply.

He was getting away but Garizzo and his marines had to stick it out. And for how long?

He asked himself that question again at nightfall. In the afternoon the guns had lifted their aim and fired on the straggling row of houses. Smith and Buckley grabbed the telephones and jumped down from the loft, ran across the road and dropped into the shallow ditch on the other side. It was flooded and they crouched with water runnning around their waists. The guns blasted the houses for minutes on end. Some of the shells went astray and fell short, or over into the marsh close to where Smith and Buckley lay and near to the aid post. The tent with the red cross was packed with wounded, though stretcher-bearers kept coming to take them further to the rear, to the barges the Italians were using to lift them across the lagoon to Venice. Many of the hotels were hospitals now.

At the end of the shelling the houses still stood, though with holes in the walls and little of the roofs left. The house they used had the front door blown out and across the road like a leaf on the wind.

The guns went back to firing at the trench and Garizzo's marines. Smith and Buckley returned to the loft. As the light ebbed Garizzo telephoned to say Sevastano had returned. "He says the line is holding, all attacks have been beaten off but there are no reinforcements for us. They will send your ammunition but they say everybody screams for ammunition. How many have you?"

"Twenty rounds." Smith thought that he could have sent *Hercules* for ammunition but he needed her close by at Piave Vecchia in case he had to pull the gun out quickly. If the Austrians broke through . . . He asked, "How is it with you?"

"Not good. The shelling all day – I think I will lose some men with shell-shock soon. You know?"

"I know." The incessant battering that deafened, shook the teeth in a man's head, that sucked the breath out of his body and blinded him with dirt, that kept on and on until he wept and trembled, crawled around aimlessly like a bewildered animal.

Garizzo said, "Rain again. Trieste weather."

"What?"

Garizzo explained, "The wind is from the north-east so it brings the weather from Trieste. It if rains there tonight then in the morning it rains here. And if it snows . . ." He laughed. "Good night, English."

The darkness came and the shelling stopped. Instead there was once again the stammering machine-guns, the flares, the grenades bursting in no-man's land where raiding parties ran into outposts.

Smith wondered, 'How long?'

'How long could they stand it?'

Despite the surge and fall of the fighting out in the night, he slept when it was his turn. Dreams disturbed him more than grenades and woke him to lie wide-eyed, staring up at the sky seen through the shattered roof. He would sleep again, weariness claiming him, but only to dream again of *Salzburg*.

11 A fine morning . . .

It rained far into the night but stopped an hour or so before the dawn. Buckley woke Smith then to take his turn on watch and about that time the firing ceased in no-man's land and it became very quiet. The sky was clear and he stood with his blanket around his shoulders staring out into the darkness of the open ground or up at the stars seen through the holes in the roof. There were more holes than roof after the shelling of the houses. He thought about Helen Blair and that he wanted to see her again.

Finally he shrugged out from under his blanket. It would be light soon and down in the trenches the marines would be standing to. Garizzo thought there would be another attack. Smith was certain of it. He squatted down inside the little tent Buckley had made out of the old sacks found in the loft to stop the glow from the primus showing through the holes in the wall and the roof. He lit the primus and held his hands close around the hissing flame until the kettle perched on it jetted steam. Then he turned off the stove, juggled the lid off the kettle and spooned in tea. He poured it into the two tin mugs, added a spoonful of condensed milk like glue to each, got stiffly to his feet and carried one cup over to Buckley where he slept cocooned in his blanket by the wall. He shook the big man's shoulder, feeling the wool damp under his hand. Buckley grumbled and pulled the blanket from over his head.

Smith said, "Stand to. Tea. And it's stopped raining."

Buckley muttered, "They must ha' run out of it." He sucked at the tea gratefully. "Thank ye, sir."

Smith wound the handle on the field telephone and lifted the receiver. Menzies' voice squeaked distantly in his ear: "Fortnum and Mason – high class provisions. Hampers a speciality. What can I send you, Mr Buckley?"

Smith glanced at Buckley now running fingers through his hair and jamming on his cap. He said, "Mr Buckley is performing his toilet."

He heard Menzies say, "Oh, Lord!" Then: "Menzies, here sir."

150

Smith said drily, "So I gathered. Stand to."

"Standing to now, sir."

"Did that ammunition come up?"

"Not yet, sir."

And they were down to twenty rounds. Smith said, "Let me know as soon as it does."

"Aye, aye, sir."

Smith replaced the receiver and Buckley cleared his throat, said, "We've been in the habit of having a bit of a joke when things was quiet, sir. Very humorous, Mr Menzies, sir."

"I'd noticed." Smith turned away and Buckley grinned.

Smith returned to stand at the front of the house, gulped at his tea and as the light grew he peered out at the churned mud, pocked with shell-holes and stretching away into the half-light. Somewhere out there, no more than a mile away from him, lay the Cavetta canal and the enemy. He knelt by the field telephone wired to Garizzo's dug-out and wound the handle. Garizzo answered and Smith said, "That ammunition didn't come up. We're down to twenty rounds. Can you send another message?"

Garizzo swore and Smith winced as the expletive crackled in his ear, then: "I will send a message to Headquarters now."

"Thank you." Smith set the instrument down and went back to staring out into no-man's land. His gun had only twenty rounds of ammunition. The attack would come soon. He watched the light grow until he could see the canal and beyond it the enemy lines sketched by the strung barbed-wire. He had expected a barrage by now but no gun fired. It was so quiet that Smith jumped, his overstretched nerves reacting, when the telephone jangled. He snatched it. "Smith."

Garizzo's voice squawked in Smith's ear. "What the hell is going on? Can you see anything?"

Smith answered, on one knee and peering out across the marshes, "Nothing. No sign of anyone."

"They're there. Last night the patrols heard them and said it sounded as if the place was full of them."

"They could be hidden along the bank of the canal. They could hide a thousand men there." The Austrians had hidden three times that many the previous day.

"What are they waiting for? There is something strange. I

151

don't like it." Garizzo sounded uneasy. He finished, "Keep watch."

Smith put down the telephone. He did not like this quiet, either. He wondered if he should order the gun to fire two or three searching rounds at the line of the canal then decided against it. Ammunition was short. He dared not waste a round in probing when there might not be a single man hidden below the canal bank.

Buckley muttered, "Fine morning like this, you could fancy walking down and having a look."

It was a fine morning, cool but clear, the mountains hidden only in the haze of distance. So according to Garizzo it would have been fine in Trieste last night. A bird sang out in the wasteland between the trench and the house and its song carried to Smith in the stillness. Nothing moved in the open marshland but far back where lay the Austrian lines there was a drift of blue smoke as someone cooked breakfast or made coffee. To seaward· the sun glinted on blue water and was so low it hurt the eye to look into its glare. Smith lifted his hand and averted his eyes from that glare – then froze with the hand uplifted, lips parting. So for a moment until Buckley said, "Sir?" – and himself turned to gaze seaward.

Then Smith's hand snapped down to grab at the telephone and whirl the handle. As Garizzo answered Smith shouted, "Enemy ship opening fire! Take cover!" He repeated the warning while Buckley stared out to sea at the ship there, lean and graceful, steaming slowly inside her destroyer screen, pushing out of the smoke made by her own firing. On that morning and in that visibility there was no mistaking *Salzburg*. Buckley stood transfixed at sight of her. Then the salvo from that beautiful ship screamed in to turn the still morning into a hell. The eleven-inch shells burst monstrously like thunderclaps and hurled tons of wet earth and mud high into the air. The open ground before the house erupted in yellow flame and jetting smoke, and hot breath from the shells nearest the house stripped the last of the tiles from it and threw Buckley, Smith and the telephones to the back wall. Smith, deafened, pushed at Buckley and mouthed at him, "Get out!" He pointed at the hole in the floor and Buckley grabbed his rifle and dropped through to the room below. Smith ripped the wires from the telephones, tossed the instruments down to the waiting Buckley then jumped. He landed on fingers and toes, Buckley seized his arm and hurried him through the hole where the door had been. Together they ran across the track and fell into the ditch there, crouched again with water up to their waists, pressed their faces into the mud and covered their heads with their arms as the ground leapt under them and bricks rained down around them.

When the earth was briefly still Smith raised his head and saw the house gone, now only existed as a heap of rubble with the timber sticking out of it like broken ribs. He could see it through the smoke that blanketed the ground before him. Somewhere behind that smoke lay the trench, Garizzo and his marines. Beyond them – Smith jammed his head down under his protective arms as the earth lifted under him again, blast punched at him and the heavens fell.

They heard that tremendous barrage all along the line past Mestre. In Venice it came to them as a rolling thunder and they saw the far-off lifting of the smoke. Helen Blair had not slept till near the dawn and now came running from her bed with a snatched robe around her shoulders, stood trembling at the window and prayed.

Smith lost track of time as he lay and shuddered, pressed deeper into the ditch. When the barrage stopped he still lay prone, eyes closed against it, waiting in the ear-ringing stillness for the hell to burst on him again. When it did not he lifted his head from his shaking arms and saw Buckley lying with face turned towards him, eyes wide in the muddied mask.

Faintly he heard Buckley say, "Lifted, sir." He nodded in reply. The barrage had lifted. Smoke drifted before him, lazily coiling on the breeze. He pushed to his knees and then stood up. Through breaks in the smoke he could see *Salzburg* turning away eastward. She had done her murderous work and was moving on before the MAS boats and destroyers came tearing out from Venice to hunt her. He spat earth from his lips and swallowed, told Buckley, "The telephone."

They traced the wires to where they ran into the smoking rubble of the house, crouched in the shelter the rubble gave and Buckley cut the wires, bared the ends and screwed the terminals

153

of the telephone down on them. He wound the handle furiously and set the receiver to his ear, listened, eyes on Smith, then shook his head. "Nothing, sir."

"Keep trying." Smith lifted cautiously to peer over the rubble. The sky was clear above him but he could only see a few score yards of blasted earth, smoke hid everything else. From beyond the smoke came the rattle and crack of rifle-fire but now there was no stutter of machine-guns and the firing sounded sporadic, scattered. He thought numbly that although the trenches the marines held and the holes they'd dug in the sides of them gave fair protection against the light field-guns and mortars, even a near-miss from *Salzburg*'s big guns could cave in a trench dug out of mud while a direct hit would obliterate it. The marines, out-numbered and out-gunned, had nevertheless held the line up to now, but this final stroke, the bombardment from the sea, would have been too much. Some of them would probably have survived, though that was hard to believe, but they would be under attack now, the waves of infantry rolling forward from their gathering place along the sheltering bank of the canal.

"Got 'em, sir!"

He spun round at Buckley's shout, grabbed the telephone and spoke into it as he stared at the smoke. "Smith."

"Menzies, sir." His voice came faintly.

Smith raised his. "What is your situation?"

"They pasted us, sir. Pontoon's holed but she was resting on the bottom anyway. The gun is all right. I've one man dead and another wounded, sir. He's pretty bad." Menzies' squeaky voice stopped.

Smith tried not to imagine him down there by the gun in the bloody chaos, tried to forget Menzies squeaking cheerfully, "Fortnum and Mason – high class provisions." The smoke was drifting away before him and he could see across the open ground to the communication trench and away to his left the end of it where it emerged in the shelter of the houses. Now the houses were rubble. Marines were stumbling up out of the trench and staggering past the piles of rubble, across the road to the ditch beyond. Garizzo stood at the head of the trench, hauling the men out, pushing them towards the ditch.

So the front-line trench was lost and Garizzo would try to hold a line along the road using the ditch as a makeshift trench. There was nowhere else and if that failed the enemy would pour through the gap, widening it as they rolled up the defences on either side. Smith could see them now, swarming across the marshland from the trench the marines had held these last two days.

The Austrians had prepared this attack and the key to it was the bombardment by *Salzburg*. She had sailed from Trieste in the night when the weather cleared there, sure that visibility off the coast would be good enough in the morning for her big guns to pour in a heavy fire that would smash a hole in the line. They were advancing to exploit it now, across the muddy waste. This was the attack in force that Garizzo had dreaded would come if the Austrians were repulsed elsewhere. Line after line rolled over the trench and across the marsh. But there was an even closer threat. They had seen how they could advance quickly along the causeway leading across no-man's land from the canal to the houses. It was horribly exposed but now, obviously, they believed the bombardment by *Salzburg* would have neutralised any defensive fire. From the scattered rifle-fire it seemed they were right. They crowded the track, pushing along it in a dense, hurrying column.

Smith spoke into the telephone, urgently, "SOS. Target One! SOS. Target One! Fire! Fire!"

Menzies answered, "SOS. Target One! Fire!"

It was an order Smith had prayed he would not have to give. The SOS targets were in rear of the front-line trench, the gun had never fired on them and the firing data had been calculated from other, registered, targets. For Target One they had worked from a shoot on the track. He crouched behind the rubble and fumbled for the pistol at his belt. Buckley sprawled a yard away, the Lee-Enfield at his shoulder, firing as fast as he could work the bolt. Rifle-fire crackled away to the left, but sparsely. There were only the few survivors crouched in the ditch firing now.

Garizzo came running, stumbling and slipping on the muddy earth and dropped down beside Smith. He carried a rifle and a bandolier of ammunition hung over his shoulder. Like all of them he was coated in mud that had dried on his face and cracked with the creases of it. His breath wheezed as he panted,

"The trench fell in! Metres and metres of it! Those shells just levelled it, filled it! Both machine-guns lost and I only brought out about twenty men. The rest of the regiment" – he jerked his thumb westward – "are still holding but if the Austrians pour through this gap –!" He glared at Smith. "What about your gun?"

"Serviceable." Smith, telephone pressed to his ear, heard the faint squawking, covered his other ear with the hand that gripped the pistol and said, "Say again!"

This time he heard Menzies: "Shot! Time of flight seven seconds!"

"Shot!" Smith looked down at his watch, counted seconds, looked up and saw the shell fall, left of the track and just ahead of the column.

"Repeat!"

"Repeat!" That was Menzies, then: "Shot!"

Counting as the smoke drifted away and he saw the column coming on. Seven. The shell burst on the head of the column.

"Repeat! ... Repeat! ... Repeat! ..." He had to hoard his ammunition on this narrow target, so instead of gunfire ordered single rounds, ready to correct if necessary. The shells fell on or close alongside the track and the column melted away, men stumbling off across the marshy open ground, seeking cover or their own lines.

He turned away, back to the main thrust of the Austrian attack.

The attacking lines that had rolled over the lost trench were pressing home the attack, bent on breaking through. The ruined houses drew them, the sole prominent feature in a nearly featureless landscape and they closed in towards it as if advancing into a funnel.

Smith called, "SOS. Target Two! SOS. Target Two! Five rounds gunfire!"

"SOS. Target Two! Five rounds gunfire!" Then: "Shot! Time of flight seven seconds!"

Smith waited, then watched as the shells came down. The zone of the gun, those tiny inequalities in charges you could never calculate for, spread the bursts about the marsh. He needed them spread like that across the horde that filled it but they fell too far in rear, on the lines still coming forward from the trench but the leading lines were closer and still advancing. A battalion? Two? A thousand, two thousand men pouring down the narrow bottleneck towards the houses, towards himself. He saw Garizzo running crouched along the rear of the thin line of his men spaced along the ditch. They were fixing bayonets.

Smith ordered, "Three hundred yards! One o'clock! Ten rounds gunfire!"

Menzies answered, "Three hundred yards! One o'clock! Ten rounds gunfire!" Then: "Only ten rounds remaining, sir!"

"Fire!"

Smith saw Buckley in the act of reloading, thumbing the rounds from the clip into the breach of the Lee-Enfield. Buckley looked up at that order, realising it would call fire down on top of them, then closed the bolt of the rifle.

Smith shouted at him, "Get out of it! Get back to the marines!"

Buckley shook his head. "Wouldn't get a yard, sir!"

That was true. The Austrians were firing as they advanced, the *whip-crack!* ripping the air overhead. Smith watched them, now so close that he could see faces, make out features, the eyes under the helmets, the mouths open, panting. They walked, breathless and worn down by the slogging trot across the heavy ground, their ranks ragged. But there was no scything machine-gun, nothing to stop their steamroller advance from grinding over Garizzo and his handful of marines.

Smith never heard the shell howl in because it fell barely fifty yards in front. He had one camera-blink impression of the havoc wrought in the leading files then his head went down as he huddled behind the rubble. His body shook again as the earth was shaken beneath him by the impact of big shells falling close before the ruined house. These shells were not from *Salzburg* but the gun commanded by Menzies and Davies. They could kill him just the same. In theory they should fall fifty yards away but once again the zone of the gun, those tiny inequalities in charges, could spread the bursts, and mean a direct hit where he lay.

He found himself counting. When the tenth shell's exploding ripped the air and brought mud, stones and splinters cracking down on the rubble of the house and the road, on Buckley and

157

himself, he cowered under it then slowly raised his head. Smoke swirled and drifted again on the wind across the battleground. Through it he saw men standing bewildered or wandering aimlessly, other figures sprawled in the wasteland of mud and pools of black water. He heard the regular *crack!* of Buckley's rifle and the marines firing away to his left. He could hear the wounded, see them.

Buckley had stopped to reload and shouted hoarsely, "They're pulling back, sir!" They were. In expectation of a further barrage the wave was receding, rolling slowly back towards the trench and then the canal. They did not know, could not know, that the defending gun had fired its last shell.

Garizzo appeared, slapped Smith's shoulder, then turned to bawl at his marines as they dragged themselves wearily from their cover in the ditch. He bawled again at Sevastano, his second-in-command, trotting up from the flank that had escaped *Salzburg*'s barrage and leading a long file of marines. Garizzo turned to Smith again. "Magnificent! Now we take back our trench and dig it out again!" He was gone, striding inexhaustibly at the head of his men as they deployed behind him and plodded through the mud towards the ruined trench. The Austrians had made no attempt to hold it, poured past it to the canal and dropped out of sight. If they regrouped there then Garizzo would be calling for fire again.

Smith reached down for the telephone and saw his hand shaking so the receiver rattled on its stand. It rang. He lifted it and said, "Smith."

Menzies answered, "There's a steam-barge coming up the coast, sir. It might be our ammunition."

"Let me know. We'll need it."

Ten minutes later Menzies confirmed the barge carried the ammunition and: "There's a relief crew for the gun, sir. The officer's coming up to take over from you. I've seen his orders and Davies read them and said they're all right. The officer's signing for everything and I've fired two flares for *Hercules* to come up."

The line crackled. Smith was certain he heard correctly but asked Menzies to repeat it all because it seemed too good to be true. Lucky skipper of the barge. Had he left Venice a half hour earlier he would have been shelled by *Salzburg* and her escort.

158

Some time later Smith saw three men trudging up the road from the coast. At that moment an Italian marine clambered out of the communication trench trailing a telephone wire as he came. He went down on one knee by Smith, unslung a telephone that hung over one shoulder and connected it, whirled the handle. He spoke into it rapidly then handed it to Smith. Garizzo's voice said, "The ammunition?"

"It's arrived. And my relief."

"*What?*"

Smith repeated it and Garizzo swore. "I'm coming."

He and Smith's relief arrived together. The officer was a lieutenant in the grey-green drab of the army with the black and yellow flashes of the artillery on his collar. He brought with him a corporal as his assistant and a signaller hung about with telephones and reels of wire. The corporal carried their rations in a huge rucksack, the long, green neck of a bottle protruding from it. The lieutenant knew his job, saluted Garizzo and immediately became involved with him in a long conversation, Garizzo pointing out over the open ground with jabbing forefinger at the enemy positions, the lieutenant nodding vigorously. Then Smith had to indicate the targets they had registered with the gun, while Garizzo interpreted. When it was over the lieutenant looked at the shell-craters and the ruins of the house then shook his head and muttered something to Garizzo. He grinned and said to Smith, "He says you're lucky to be alive, bringing down fire so close."

Smith knew that, stared out at the corpses on the battleground.

Garizzo said, "You did very well."

He had brought about the carnage and desolation that lay before him now. This was war. Not an academic exercise in gunnery. No sword-waving, posturing figure on a prancing charger but the mutilated bodies of men. This was where blood and guts were literal, the one a sick stench and the other trailing entrails. The pistol still hung in his belt, he had not fired a shot but he had murdered –

Buckley said, "Are you all right, sir?"

"Let's get out of this." Smith looked at Garizzo. "With your permission?"

Garizzo stuck out his hand, face serious now, understanding.

159

"You saved our lives. Remember that. We will not forget."

Smith shook the hand, turned away. As he walked down the road Garizzo called after him, "Good luck, English!" Smith lifted a hand but did not halt.

When he and Buckley came to the pontoon aground in the shallows they found ammunition unloaded and Italian gunners swarming about the gun. *Hercules* lay offshore in deeper water and Smith's party were aboard the steam-barge alongside the pontoon. Her skipper was impatient to get away because they were in range of the Austrian field batteries, though not in their sight. But if the Austrians sent up a balloon with an observer in its basket the shells would soon fall.

Davies, exhausted and filthy with powder-smoke, said huskily, "Good job you ran us aground, sir. If we'd been lying off we'd ha' sunk when that bloody battlecruiser shelled us. Right bowel-opener that was. Soon as the first brick come down we were off and into the nearest hole – most of us – Billings and Jenkinson weren't so lucky."

Smith looked at the craters along the shore. "Who was wounded?"

"Jenkinson, sir. We found Billings – identified him. Mr Menzies did the best he could for Jenkinson but it was hopeless. He died an hour ago."

"Then who did Jenkinson's job in that last shoot?"

"Mr Menzies, sir. Soon as the shelling stopped he sent me to look at the gun. He found the shells had cut the telephone wire so he traced the break and fixed it. Then he did Jenkinson's job, worked out the corrections, gave us the firing orders." Davies paused, then asked, "Did it go all right, sir?"

Smith answered mechanically, "Yes, it went very well." Then he turned on Davies. "Have you ever seen it?"

Davies knew what he meant and said, "You can't blame yourself, sir. It could just as easy ha' been you lying out there now."

The steam-barge carried them out to *Hercules*, and so they came to Venice.

David Smith was exhausted in body and spirit, the horror of that morning still with him as it would be for many days. Voss and *Salzburg* had wreaked destruction yet again and he had suffered at their hands. He thought that Devereux might have returned from Brindisi and now *that* storm would break. At that

160

moment he did not care. He was sick at heart.

Helen Blair saw them from the window of her house, standing on the narrow, little balcony with field-glasses to her eyes, the squat little drifter butting in from the sea. There were men on the deck of *Hercules* and in her wheelhouse and the girl was certain she recognised one of them. She dropped the glasses on a table, snatched her cloak, ran down through the house and onto the quay. As she ran it came to her that she was truly happy for the first time in two long, bitter years.

12 In the night

Smith saw Helen Blair on the quay, skirt pressed against her slender legs, a cloak thrown around her and her hair flying on the wind. He watched her, saw her lean forward to talk to Buckley working right forward in the bow, saw her smile and his grin and salute. Lucky Buckley.

Hercules was secured bows-on to the quay and Smith told Fred Archbold, "I want a minimum watch. One hand and one officer or leading hand. Everyone else can sleep."

"Aye, aye, sir!"

Smith turned on the red-eyed and weary Menzies. "Did you hear that?"

"Yes, sir. I could sleep standing here."

Smith grinned at the boy. "Boredom getting you again?"

Menzies smiled wearily back at him. "No, sir. Not so's you'd notice."

"You did a fine job and I'll say so in my report."

That brought back some of the old perkiness. "Thank you, sir."

Buckley poked his head into the wheelhouse. "Miss Blair would like a word with you when convenient, sir, if you please."

"Very good." Buckley disappeared but Smith hesitated, wasted time shifting about the wheelhouse, exchanged forcedly cheerful words with Fred Archbold and Davies. He was reluctant to go because he thought she had made her feelings towards him very clear, but in the end he climbed to the quay and went to her, saluted.

Helen Blair looked tired but the wind beating in from the sea brought a flush to her cheeks and she had a smile for him. "It's good to see you. I was afraid – the fighting – I heard the ship shelling you. Word came that it was the marines' position." She shook her head, then: "You're all right?" She knew he was not. He had a haggard look, his eyes sunken and haunted.

He grinned faintly, awkwardly. "Well, obviously" – he looked down at himself – "a bit worn round the edges."

"David –"

But he saw Buckley climbing ashore with his valise and asked, "Where are you going with that?"

"Miss Blair said to take it up to the house, sir." Buckley's tone suggested he was simply obeying orders, and that Smith knew about it.

Helen Blair said, "That's right. Thank you."

Smith realised they had conspired against him, and that he didn't care.

Helen Blair said, "Shall we go up?"

He fell in beside her and they followed Buckley. Menzies and the crew of *Hercules* watched them go.

Again he dozed in his bath, later nodded over his meal and fell into his bed and exhausted sleep.

In the evening she came to him.

It was dark in the room and they lay twined together close under the covers. The window was open and the wind out of the north-east ruffled the curtains. The long rectangle of the window was only a lightening of the darkness for the night was starless, the sky overcast. The room was cold but they were warm and close under the covers. The water of the lagoon lapped and sucked below the window. She slept, her arm around him, her breath on his cheek. He was tired and sleepy and happy. He watched a searchlight's beam sweep distantly over the sky like a warning finger across the window, then it was gone. He heard the low mutter of gunfire.

She had asked, "What happened to you?"

"Nothing. Not a scratch on me." He meant he had not been hit. His body was covered in bruises and scrapes but there would be no new scars.

She pressed him, "Some awful thing happened." He did not answer. He would never forget that morning on the Piave line.

His eyes closed, flicked open again briefly as he remembered their quarrel of two – or was it three? – days ago. But that was past. She had told him then he was a philanderer but she was mistaken. He was sure of that.

His thoughts drifted as he lay between sleeping and waking. Menzies was shaping well, the MAS crews were fine and so was *Hercules* and her men, but how was he to sink *Salzburg*?

He looked to Balestra but with little hope that the young

engineer might have the answer. Tomorrow ... He dozed, to jerk awake imagining the bursting of huge shells lifting the ground under him. *Salzburg*, Voss, their threat continual and growing. Smith was certain time was running out for him.

He shifted restlessly and Helen Blair came half-awake, kissed him, and so sleep finally claimed him.

It was close to noon when they breakfasted and afterwards Smith said he wanted to see Balestra. Helen told him to take the launch and he asked her to go with him but she refused. "I – don't want to know what you are doing, David."

So he went alone.

Helen walked along the quay to *Hercules*, saw Davies on deck and asked if she could speak to Buckley. Davies called him and he came ashore. She asked him directly, "What happened?"

"Happened, Miss?"

"In the fighting. He won't tell me and I want to know. Please!"

Buckley told her and finished, "It was bloody horrible. And the look on his face – he's not like some o' them, callous bastards – excuse my language, Miss. And it wasn't his fault! He had to do it! It was them or us. He did it for me and them poor bloody marines."

Helen Blair bit her lip, then said hesitantly, "It was not ... for revenge?"

"Revenge? Never!" Buckley shook his head. "Duty, maybe, because duty put him there – but at a time like that you don't think much about duty. You stick by your own."

The girl stood lost in thought for a moment, troubled, then smiled at Buckley. "Well, thank you for telling me."

"That's all right, Miss. An' – I think it's right you should know."

She left him then and walked away along the quay towards San Marco. She was almost at the church when the two men of the yacht's crew came hurrying to fall into step alongside her. One of them said in Italian, "You have not been to the front for three days now."

"No."

"They will be wondering. When do you go again?"

"I don't know."

"Is it the English captain?"

"No." She shook her head but knew she was lying. He was not callous; he had been deeply distressed. That hurt her. But the men were watching. She asked, "Are you two all right?"

"We're fine. Eating and sleeping, nice and peaceful and quiet. It is you we worry about." That was sincere and concern showed on their faces. In two years a close bond had grown up between the three of them.

Helen Blair halted and smiled. "I'll be all right. I just – have to think. I'll be in touch."

She turned and walked into the church between the towering walls of sandbags and the two seamen watched her go, worried.

Smith received little encouragement from Balestra in the workshop on San Elena. He and Lombardo were working on the engine of *Seahorse*, the torpedo gleaming dully under the yellow lights of the workshop and odd-looking now because of the modifications they had already made. Balestra was singing softly while Lombardo's muttering was a bass, bad-tempered growl. But they seemed to be working amicably together.

Despite his absorption Balestra was pleased to see Smith and paused to shake his hand delightedly but talked with one eye and his mind on *Seahorse*. He thought they might be ready for a trial in a week. Lombardo grumbled, head down, "Like hell!" But Balestra only smiled at that.

Smith had to hide his frustration, and left them. He went in the launch to Naval Headquarters. Zacco's MAS was in the canal outside the gates and as Smith passed on the quay he lifted a hand in greeting. Zacco was not aboard but the crewmen on deck waved and called cheerfully, "Capitano! Signore!"

Then, at the foot of the steps of Headquarters, he met the three captains. They gathered round him, grinning, and the big Zacco explained their presence. "We saw the drifter. Some of the boats are out of the dockyard and back in service so we asked Ciano" – Ciano commanded all the MAS boats based on Venice, – "and he said we could be spared for special duties again. We went to the drifter and then to the house of La Contessa but the old woman there did not know where you were so we came here."

165

Smith said drily, "I came to see Captain Devereux." And to get an unpleasant interview over. At least that Ciano had not demanded to see him was a good sign.

Zacco shook his head. "Devereux is not back from Brindisi."

Smith heard that with relief. He said, "And I want to ask about *Salzburg*."

"*Salzburg* is at Pola."

"Pola!"

Zacco nodded. "I have the photographs – and the chart of Pola. I went to the office of Devereux to look for you and I thought you would want them so I asked. Also, in Headquarters they are pleased with you. There is a report from a Capitano Garizzo – very good."

Pagani, the piratical, laughed and slapped Smith's shoulder. "Now you are hero maybe."

Zacco hauled a big manilla envelope out from under his oilskin jacket and Smith glanced at its contents, the photographs, the chart with the ships and defences neatly marked, the typed sheets of the brief. He used the magnifying glass that the square and solid Gallina produced. The photographs the Italian fliers had taken were again excellent. The Austrian fleet lay at Pola, half a dozen battleships including three dreadnoughts, *Salzburg* lying apart as always, this time close inside the mouth of the harbour. The photographs also showed the defences ... He asked absently, "Any other news?"

Zacco said, "There are more reports of some unrest in the Austrian navy. Nobody knows what that might mean."

Smith remembered Devereux mentioning that when they first met. He knew the Austro-Hungarian Empire was made up of several races and that there was a movement among the Slavs for a country of their own, the Yugoslavs he thought they were called or something like that. They wanted independence. That was nothing new, but now –

Zacco was going on, "Their army still fights well enough, but our line holds all along the Piave river. There has been heavy fighting in many places but the line holds."

It had held for two days now. There was a glimmer of hope that they might see the miracle Garizzo had spoken of.

Smith spent the afternoon aboard *Hercules* with the three captains and Menzies, all of them crowded again into the little cabin with the photographs, chart and typed intelligence brief on Pola spread about the desk. Right at the beginning Smith said, "I want to reconnoitre the defences of Pola. Tonight." Because he needed to see for himself, and tonight because the weather was still fine and they might soon get a week or more of foul weather when such reconnaissance would be impossible. "I will have to get official Italian authority for the operation. I'm supposed to submit a request through Captain Devereux but he isn't here." He looked anxiously at Zacco. "Will you do that?"

Zacco nodded and later, after the conference broke up, he took Smith's written orders for the operation. When he returned Buckley brought him down to the cabin where Smith still pored over the chart and photographs.

Smith asked, "Any trouble?"

Zacco shook his head. "No. They asked why you did not go and I said you were busy with duties, that time was short."

Smith was relieved, but also puzzled. Devereux's attitude had led him to expect anything from a flat refusal to the command that he appear at Headquarters and plead his case in detail. But right from the start of this affair the Italians had stuck to their word given to Winter. They had given him the MAS boats and Balestra – and independent command. They had not interfered.

He shook his head. He had got his orders and that was the main thing now.

No. It was not. He looked up at Zacco and asked, "How is the morale among the crews?" Because they had been dumped under his command, a stranger and a foreigner who could not speak their tongue, taken from him and then returned again. That was unsettling, and the morale of these men was essential if he was to hope for success.

Zacco was surprised at his question, then answered it by holding his hands high above his head. "There!" He elaborated: "Things go well. After the action off Trieste you are trusted, and since you have come we learn that you were captain of *Dauntless*, and of other actions."

Somebody had been talking. Smith looked across the cabin at Buckley standing in the doorway but the big seaman did not meet that glance, stared fixedly at the chart.

Smith muttered, "Hum. Well. Fine."

He left *Hercules* at nightfall and walked back to the house on the Ca' di Dio. In the dusk the three MAS boats ghosted across the lagoon with a low rumble of throttled-back engines. They came alongside the quay and Smith paused briefly to greet the captains and their crews. He sensed in them the tension building in himself.

He ate dinner with Helen Blair, an affair of only minutes. He had little appetite and she ate nothing. Afterwards he went up to his room and changed his uniform for two thick sweaters, old trousers and a pair of canvas shoes. Buckley would bring his seaboots to the boat and Zacco had oilskins for him. He was pulling the second sweater over his head as he descended the stairs and heard the rap at the outside door. His head emerged from the sweater as Helen Blair opened the door.

Buckley stood there, cap in hand. "Good evening, Miss. I've got –" He broke off as he saw Smith appear behind the girl, then went on: "I've got your seaboots, sir. Anything else you want carried down?"

"No, thanks." They were waiting for him. "I'll be with you in a minute."

Helen Blair said, "Good luck, Mr Buckley. Thank you."

He grinned at her. "Thank you, Miss. God bless you." He strode away.

Helen Blair said, "You shouldn't go so soon, David. You should rest." He had lost that haggard, distant look but in his sleep he was restless.

"The weather won't wait." Nor would *Salzburg*. He said lightly, "It's just a reconnaissance, nip over for a look-see and back for breakfast."

She did not believe it was as simple as that but only said, "I'll be watching for you."

He could find nothing to say now, took her in his arms and kissed her, then left her and went down to the waiting boats.

13 "Like the divil was after him!"

Pola lay some eighty miles south-east across the Adriatic from Venice and at midnight the three MAS boats sighted the black loom of the Brioni Islands, two miles offshore from Cristo Point at the northern end of the entrance to Pola. The harbour was L-shaped, ran inland for three miles and its mouth was a mile across. From the southern shore at Cape Compare a massive mole, a concrete breakwater, extended northwards nearly halfway across the harbour mouth. Then came a gap sixty yards wide and inside it lay the gate to the harbour, a boom anchored at one end, with a tug at the other end to open and close it. The other side of the gate was another mole, some three hundred yards long. A boom closed the gap between the northern end of this mole and the northern shore at Cristo Point. Another boom stretched outside the entire length of the southern mole.

All this the aerial photographs showed – and that there were two more boom defences inside the harbour itself, the first some three hundred yards inside, the second two hundred yards further on. The latter ran from the northern shore, the former from close to the southern. They overlapped at the centre but two hundred yards apart, so a vessel entering the harbour through the gate would swing northabout to pass around the first boom then steam south through the gap between them to round the southern end of the second boom. Because there was this gap between them Smith would not try to reach them; he knew they could be passed. But the other booms he had to see to gauge their strength.

The night was dark and again it rained. The reconnaissance was a repeat of that carried out at Trieste. Zacco laid his boat alongside the short northern mole that lifted ten feet out of the sea and waited, every man aboard tensed for discovery and the burst of fire from out of the night, while Smith and Buckley swam inside the harbour mouth and inspected with frozen, fumbling fingers the nature of the boom that closed the gate. It was of huge timbers and chains but unlike Trieste because

169

Flying-Fish would not have climbed it. The performance was repeated with the northern and southern booms and they were of big steel cylinders linked by massive chains and again proof against *Flying-Fish*. Voss learned quickly. It was gruelling work and dangerous. The sea was bitterly cold and there were sentries stationed on the moles – twice they saw the figure of a man, slow-pacing and head bent under the rain, pass above their heads where they hung with faces pressed against the concrete. But the sentries were nowhere near the gateway. Possibly because two guard-boats lay just inside and they were considered watch enough. Smith tucked that away in his memory, tried to still his shuddering.

Afterwards he and Buckley stood in the well of the boat, shivered and dried themselves, drank coffee laced with grappa from a mug. His teeth chattered against it and he gasped as the coffee burnt his tongue and the grappa his stomach.

He dressed, thinking that he could see no way of penetrating the boom defences. *Seahorse*? If it worked, then possibly, but Smith had little faith in it. God help Balestra; he had more guts than Smith.

He wondered, suppose they set charges on the booms and tried to blast their way in? No. That had even less chance than *Seahorse*: as soon as the charges blew the defences would be alerted. The boom might or might not be broken but the defensive fire would be certain – and devastating. It would be Trieste and *Flying-Fish* all over again. But they might have to try it. He swore softly, savagely out of frustration.

They approached Venice with the light of a pale rising sun at their backs that could not dispel the mist lying on the city and the marshes, though the top of the campanile of St Mark's stood high and clear above it. Venice had not suffered another air raid since that on Smith's first day there. He thought that might have been due to the weather, though the Italians continued to fly daily reconnaissances. It was more likely that the Austrian squadrons had work enough attacking the Piave river line.

The three boats entered the lagoon between the long arms of the Porto di Lido and followed the channel until the long quay of the Riva degli Schiavoni came in sight. Smith lifted his glasses and there was the front of Helen Blair's house where it overlooked the canal Ca' di Dio, and close by *Hercules*, but the balcony was empty. Was she on the quay? But that was crowded, a sea of faces pressed close together and soldiers lined the edge of the quay. He wondered at that, turned the glasses on *Hercules* and wondered again because she had steam up, smoke rising from her funnel. But then he saw Devereux pacing the deck of the drifter. There was no mistaking his strutting walk, the swing of his stick and tilt of his chin as he looked down his nose at the world. So he was back from Brindisi.

Smith lowered the glasses. Devereux would have read his report of the assault on Trieste and the loss of *Flying-Fish*. So there would be a row but Smith was ready for that. At least now, after the shelling off Piave Vecchia, Devereux must see the threat that *Salzburg* posed. Smith and the *Gatecrashers* were not finished yet, by a long chalk.

The MAS boats slipped in alongside *Hercules* and Smith climbed aboard followed by Menzies and Buckley. Smith saluted and Devereux shifted the walking-stick to his left hand, returned the salute. His face was solemn but Smith felt it was an act, that Devereux was not as ill-pleased as he looked.

Smith said, "I'll let you have a report of last night's reconnaissance as soon as it's written, but –"

Devereux waved a hand. "You'll have time enough for that. A word in private." He strutted across the deck and Smith followed. When they stood right aft, out of earshot of the others in the waist, Devereux said, "I have bad news for you."

Helen Blair? Smith had still not seen her. Had there been a raid in the night after all?

Devereux said, "I arrived last night and went immediately to my office, of course. I read your report and learned you had sailed an hour before. I sent *my* full report to Pickett by wireless and his answer came at midnight. He takes a most serious view of the way you took that assault craft of Balestra's to sea and rashly attempted to force the defences of Trieste. It was done without authorisation and in face of my refusal to grant such authorisation. The Italians will be furious when I tell them and I'm not looking forward to *that*! Of course, I'll make out what case I can for you – I've heard of your actions on the Piave river with the gun and that will count in your favour. But I doubt if it will wipe out the memory of your flagrant breach of discipline, virtual piracy!''

Devereux was speaking without hesitation to pick his words, reciting a prepared speech, eyes watching Smith and walking-stick tapping the deck to emphasise each point. He went on: "I may be able to persuade them not to demand your court-martial. I can't say the same about Pickett. His view is that you acted recklessly and irresponsibly. It's clear that he will want a court-martial.''

Smith could hear Devereux but no one else could. He saw the three MAS boats slipping across the lagoon to their berth off the Giudecca, and Menzies in the waist of *Hercules* watching covertly, curiously, the pair of them talking in the stern. Except that so far it was Devereux who had done all the talking.

Smith broke in on the lecture: "Sir! You are aware of my orders. Admiral Winter believed that Voss would lead the Austrian fleet in a break-out, and now he and *Salzburg* are at Pola! If we don't act against him soon it will be too late and the fleet will be raising hell all up and down the Adriatic! Lieutenant Balestra is building an entirely new type of craft to break into Pola though it won't be ready for some days. But there has to be a way of breaking through the booms and attacking *Salzburg* and we've got to find it —''

"*No!*" Devereux hammered on the deck with his stick. "You don't seem to understand, Commander! Pickett sent a signal to Admiralty requesting your immediate recall. You no longer have a command! Captain Pickett is the senior officer here and has acted quite properly in my opinion in setting aside the Admiralty's instructions. I have no doubt they will confirm his decision.''

Nor did Smith. He had expected a row but now he faced professional ruin. He could imagine the signal Pickett had sent, stressing the failure at Trieste and Smith's high-handed taking of *Flying-Fish*. But then he thought of the gallantry of the MAS crews and Balestra's determination in the assault on Trieste, his singleminded dedication to his work. All that could not be cast aside now. There was still *Salzburg* and Voss and if Devereux was blind to their threat, then — "Sir, I want to speak to Captain Pickett.''

"You'll see him soon enough. His orders are that you sail

Hercules to Brindisi and report to him there." Devereux said deliberately, "You are not under open arrest – yet – but no one leaves this ship. The guard on the quay will see that order is obeyed. *Hercules* raised steam at my order and will sail as soon as I set foot ashore." Smith could see past Devereux to the guard of Italian soldiers lining the quay. They had attracted the curious crowd massed behind them. Devereux said, "The three MAS will return to their flotillas and the Italians will deal with Balestra."

Smith said doggedly, "He acted under my orders."

"No doubt that will be taken into account. It seems unfair for him to suffer severely because of your actions, but I think he is mentally unfitted for the Service, anyway." Devereux glanced at his watch. "I'm going ashore and will send a signal to Pickett stating your time of sailing." He touched a hand to the peak of his cap. Smith and Menzies saluted as he crossed the brow to the quay and passed through the guard there.

Smith said, "We're sailing, Mr Menzies. Inform Mr Archbold."

"Now, sir?" Menzies blinked. They had been only minutes aboard *Hercules* after returning from Pola.

"Now." Smith went forward to the wheelhouse. He had thought as they entered the harbour that they were not finished but it seemed Devereux and Pickett had changed all that. He faced a court-martial, was without a command save this little wooden drifter and he was a virtual prisoner aboard her.

They were mistaken. He was still sure that Winter had been right and they were wrong. All Voss had done so far had served to emphasise the fact. Italy was fighting for her life now on the line of the Piave river, Smith had seen the young men dying there. Voss had been sent to turn the Austrian navy from the passive threat of a fleet-in-being to an active one. What if the Austrians came out and struck at that long coastline stretching down the length of the Adriatic? What if Italy was forced to make peace, and the hold of the Allies on the Mediterranean imperilled?

Voss had to be stopped.

As *Hercules* headed for the Porto di Lido and the sea, the white launch came curving out from the shore and took station a dozen yards abeam. Fred Archbold was in the drifter's wheel-

173

house and Smith told him, "She's yours, Mr Archbold."

He left the wheelhouse, dropped down the ladder to the deck and stood at the rail. Helen was at the wheel of the launch, her face turned towards him anxiously but she smiled. He grinned back and waved, saw Balestra was with her in the launch. She called across the narrow neck of water, "I saw your boat go to *Hercules* and went to the quay. I met Mr Balestra there. He was trying to go aboard but the sentries wouldn't let him through. Their officer said no one was allowed to board or leave her and his orders came from Devereux." She paused, then asked, "Is it bad trouble, David?"

"Pretty bad." That was a large understatement but he would not worry her with details. "We're bound for Brindisi. I think I can clear things up there." How?

Balestra called, "An officer came from Headquarters. He said I had two days to clear out my workshop and then I report for a sea appointment. But we are so close now! A week or maybe less. That is all we need!"

Smith answered, "I hope to get those orders countermanded and be back with new orders for you to go on and make *Seahorse* ready."

"How much time do we have?"

"I believe very little. *Salzburg* is at Pola. I think she is there because Voss intends to lead the Austrians in an attack on the coast of Italy, to strike another blow while the army is still trying to re-form."

Balestra was silent, ran his fingers through his black curls and stared tight-lipped at Smith. *Hercules* was closing the guard-boat. Smith lifted a hand in salute and shouted with forced cheer, "Don't worry!"

Helen Blair waved and smiled again. He thought how beautiful she was, and hungered for her. She called, "Good luck, David!"

The launch curved away and headed back towards Venice. He watched until the mist furred it, hid it, then he sent for Geordie Hogg, the engineer.

Hercules headed south, black smoke belching from her funnel as the stoker laboured and cursed below. Geordie Hogg shouted at him above the thumping of the engines, "No good using that language wi' me! He says he wants a record run to Brindisi so there it is!"

"What's the flaming rush, then?"

"God knows, but he acts like the divil was after him." Geordie paused, then said thoughtfully, "Or t'other way round."

14 "It'll be bloody murder!"

This was their second night at sea and the morning would see them off Brindisi. The little wheelhouse of *Hercules* was comfortably full. Young Ginger Gates was at the wheel and Menzies had the watch with Davies keeping look-out to starboard and Buckley to port. Smith dozed in the worn, old easy chair brought up from below, cap tipped forward over his eyes and booted feet outstretched. The thoughts that obsessed his waking hours mingled with his dreams. Pickett's determination to rid himself of this young commander with wild ideas, and Devereux, smooth and bland, deaf to Smith's arguments. *Salzburg* roaring up over the horizon to hurl her huge broadsides at Garizzo's marines. And always Helen's face, smiling and eager, loving.

He woke at the touch on his arm, pushed back the cap and saw Menzies stooped over him, face shadowed and its expression hidden, the only light coming from the glow in the compass binnacle. "Smoke astern of us, sir. Don't know how far. Could be ten miles or so."

Smith shoved to his feet and crossed to the starboard side of the wheelhouse because the smoke from *Hercules'* funnel was rolling down astern and to port so he would see nothing there. He peered out into the night that was still and dark, an occasional star winking between scattered clouds, what wind there was coming out of the west. From here he could see aft along the deck of *Hercules* and beyond to the horizon – wherever it was. Darkness hid it now.

Menzies explained, "Can't see it now, sir. Davies just caught a glimpse because there's a searchlight to the north sweeping every few minutes."

Smith nodded. Searchlights were set up all down the coast. One of them could be too far over that hidden horizon to reach any ships out there but still light it with an effect like pale moonlight. At that instant light glowed to starboard and Menzies muttered, "There's another one." It was distant, on the coast beyond the western horizon, a faint wash of light that showed the line where sea ended and sky began, a ghostly light.

Davies said, "There it is. Right astern."

Smith snatched his glasses from the hook beside the wheel and searched along the northern horizon, the line of it now also lit by a pale, spectral glow, saw the low, black smudge on it. Smoke.

Menzies said, "Italian patrol, I suppose."

Smith lowered the glasses and nodded. "Keep a sharp lookout, though. We don't want them running us down."

"Aye, aye, sir."

Smith returned to his chair and tipped his cap over his eyes but sleep did not come at once. He thought Menzies was a funny little chap with his ears sticking out under his cap, snub nose and wide grin, but he was eager to please and quick to learn, had done well in command of the gun on the Piave river line. The men liked him, regarded him as something of a mascot, but they obeyed him smartly and without question; he handled them well. Smith opened one eye and peeped out under the peak of his cap. Menzies strode restlessly about the wheelhouse, hands clasped behind him. That was in imitation of Smith but this time done unconsciously. If imitation was the sincerest form of flattery then was this hero-worship? Smith shifted uneasily. Menzies could find better models than Smith if he wanted to pursue a career in the navy, if only for the remainder of the war.

What of Smith's own career? He had left Venice determined to persuade Pickett to reverse his orders and instead support Smith in his mission. But if he failed in that then he would go over Pickett's head and send a signal directly to Admiralty, officially if he could but unofficially if necessary, and by whatever underhand method presented itself. He could send a cable. If they put him under guard then Buckley would do it. A cable like that, sent to Admiralty in plain language, would create one hell of a row. When the mud flew he would get his share and his record was far from spotless now. But if he failed with Pickett he was destined for a court-martial anyway, so he might as well be hung for a sheep as a lamb and if it meant that action would be taken –

Davies said, "There it is again, and closer. I can't see ships but there looks to be three lots of smoke, maybe more. They must be coming down on us fast." He turned his head to look at Smith. "Gone now, sir."

Smith grunted acknowledgment. The high speed of the ships could be because their orders demanded it, or ... He said, "They might have had a warning of U-boats in the area, so keep a look-out for those, too."

"Aye, aye, sir."

Fast steaming was one way of eluding a waiting U-boat. *Hercules* had not received any such warning simply because she had no wireless. The lack of it was a curse. And there was no question of her running away from a U-boat: she was steaming full ahead now, as she had been since leaving Venice, and still only making nine knots or less. Geordie Hogg claimed ten knots were possible, but then only for a limited period. Smith climbed to his feet again, slung his glasses around his neck so they hung on his chest from their strap and stepped to the front of the wheelhouse. If there was a U-boat out there then another pair of eyes might help. He slowly swept the darkness with the glasses but saw nothing and lowered them to rest his eyes before sweeping again. The two men at the six-pounder in the bow were bulky, black outlines in the night, shifting as they moved to keep warm. He asked, "Has the gun's crew had anything since coming on watch?"

"Cocoa about an hour ago, sir," answered Menzies.

"They're due for another. It's damn cold in the bow."

"Aye, aye, sir."

Smith remembered the 'Contessa' handing out cups of coffee to the ammunition detail at Porto Margherita. Helen Blair ...

Davies said, "Looks like destroyers – more than one, maybe two or three in line ahead but I can see the leader. An' there's more smoke to port of them but our own smoke keeps coming atween – blast!"

Smith shifted to stand beside him but was too late: the search-light to the north had gone out and he could see nothing but *Hercules*' funnel smoke drifting down like a curtain astern and to port. He asked, "What's our position?"

Menzies answered, "About twenty miles north-east of Brindisi, sir."

A flotilla of destroyers returning to their base at Brindisi, then, but fast overhauling *Hercules*. "Have that signal-lamp ready."

"Aye, aye, sir." Davies lifted it from the shelf under the screen, one–handed, held the binoculars to his eyes with the other.

What about the other smoke astern? Smith held his own glasses ready. *Hercules* plugged along, the *thump-thump* of her engines a gentle shiver of the deck under Smith's feet. Davies said, "Here we go! And there's another!"

Smith set the glasses to his eyes. The searchlight far to the north was sweeping again, defining once more the line of the horizon and Smith saw a ship against it, a dark silhouette under the banner of smoke from her funnels, the white water of bow-wave and wash. She was a mile or more away and fine on the starboard quarter so she was near bows-on to him, but – He asked, "How many funnels?"

Davies muttered under his breath, then: "Can't rightly see, the way she lies. Looks like one – two ...."

Smith shifted his glasses from the ship, sweeping quickly astern, intending to return and try again, tension gripping him now. Davies had reported three separate plumes of smoke. One of them was the destroyers to starboard. That left another ship or ships right astern and more to port. He checked his sweep as the drifter's smoke swirled briefly away to port and gave him a glimpse astern but only of the loom of another ship, and further away. He swung the glasses back to the destroyer: she was still foreshortened but now –

Davies said, "Four funnels an' two more boats astern of her." He swore as the searchlight's beam was snuffed out and darkness covered the destroyers.

Smith said, "They're Austrian!" And: "Action stations! But *no klaxons*! Keep it quiet!" There was always the million-to-one chance the destroyers might pass *Hercules* and not see her if she was silent. Davies shoved the signal-lamp at Buckley and started out of the wheelhouse. Smith called after him, "I want Mr Archbold at the wheel! And no firing till I order!"

"Aye, aye, sir!" Davies went on the run.

The destroyers were Austrian because of their four funnels. The Italians had no destroyers with four funnels but the Austrians did, big, new boats that could make thirty-odd knots. These looked to be coming on at speed, better than twenty knots, and there was no escape for *Hercules*. In five minutes they would be up with her. What were they doing here? Three big, fast destroyers like the flotilla that escorted –

Smith shouldered his way across to the port side of the wheelhouse, seeing their faces pale in the gloom, eyes staring at him. He fetched up by Buckley. "What d'you see?" He lifted his glasses.

Buckley grumbled, "Damn all but smoke, sir."

Smith ordered, "Hard aport!" *Hercules'* bow swung, the deck tilting gently in the turn. She steered through sixteen points until the white water of her wake showed stretching northward. "Meet her . . . Steady . . . Steer that." He lifted the glasses. Now *Hercules* was headed north, running back along her wake. The smoke she made now and piled astern was not masking his view while that she made when running southward was dispersing, drifting away on the wind to the east and he could see through it.

Menzies said, "Ship fine on the starboard bow, sir! A big 'un! No destroyer!"

She was not. Smith stared at her.

Buckley reported, "I can see them destroyers we've been watching all along, off the port bow an' the leader's less than a mile away."

Menzies, searching: "A destroyer on the starboard bow! About a mile! Four funnels!"

Smith's glasses found her, held her a second then swept back to the big ship. He could not be certain but it must be . . . He let the glasses fall to hang on their strap against his chest. "It's *Salzburg*."

She was steaming almost straight down on him inside her screening destroyers, three either side of her and about a half-mile from her.

Buckley muttered, "Jesus wept!" He was rapidly sliding down the wheelhouse windows so the night air rushed in on them. At least their shattered, flying fragments would not add to the chaos when the action started. But one direct hit from *Salzburg* would obliterate the wheelhouse.

Fred Archbold came puffing up to take over the wheel from Ginger Gates, who ran aft to man the Vickers machine-gun mounted there. Smith briefly told the mate what was going on and he echoed Buckley: "Jesus wept!"

Smith asked, "What time is sunrise?"

180

Menzies answered, "Six oh five, sir."

Good mark for Menzies. Smith realised that *Salzburg* was only sixty miles north of the Otranto barrage and closing the gap with every second. 'Barrage' was in this case just another term for a massive boom. This one was a fifty mile long line of buoyed and mined anti-submarine nets strung across the Straits of Otranto and intended to halt or limit the passage of U-boats from their bases in Pola and Cattaro to the Mediterranean. Sunrise was in less than three hours so before first light *Salzburg* would be safely past Brindisi and have the barrage in range of her guns and those of her six escorts. He said, "She's going to shell the barrage."

The Otranto barrage was patrolled by motor-launches armed to deal with submarines, and drifters to handle the nets, drifters like *Hercules*, slow wooden craft, each with a six-pounder popgun in the bow. *Salzburg* and the destroyers would make target practice with them and the launches while sweeping along the barrage from west to east. Voss would wreck that as well, holing the buoys so the whole ponderous mass sank to the bottom of the sea. There might be doubt about the effectiveness of the barrage in stopping U-boats, Smith had some, but its destruction would nevertheless make life undeniably easier for the submarines and would be a triumph for Voss.

Menzies groaned, "It'll be bloody murder!"

It would. Smith said, "Get the Chief on the pipe."

Davies was working on the gun in the bow, others pouring up from below and scurrying across the deck to their action stations. Smith stooped over the engine-room voice-pipe. "Chief! Give me all she's got!"

Geordie Hogg's protest made the pipe vibrate in its fastenings. "She's running full ahead now! Ye'll shake the bottom out of her! Ye can't ask her to perform like one o' them Austrian destroyers."

"If you want to see an Austrian destroyer there are half-a-dozen closing us, and *Salzburg*'s in the middle of them."

Geordie's voice came strangled up the pipe: "God save us!"

Smith straightened. There was an Italian squadron at Brindisi and Pickett with his cruisers. They would be quick to come out when *Salzburg* opened fire on the barrage but by the time they raised steam, got to sea, and steamed down to Otranto

Salzburg would have finished her destructive mission. She would be over near the eastern shore and turning northward again to run for home. They would never catch her. He thought she had probably slipped southwards the previous night, stealing along the eastern shore of the Adriatic in the cover of the island chain that stretched down that coast. Then she had laid up in Cattaro during the day and set out to cross the sea this night so as to strike at the western, Italian end of the barrage. That way, as she destroyed she would be steaming away from the pursuit coming out from Brindisi. It was daring and effective. It bore the stamp of Voss.

Buckley said hoarsely, "I can see them destroyers clear. And *Salzburg*'s as big as a house!"

One destroyer leader was a bare half-mile away, broad on the port bow, the other to starboard. The rest followed their leaders in line ahead, screening *Salzburg* where she steamed between the lines. They would see *Hercules* at any second. And then? They would not open fire unless they had to, Smith was sure of that, because Voss would not want to give the game away by shooting-up one little drifter. But he dared not pass her by in case, just possibly, she was a naval patrol with wireless and could give the alarm. So – detach one destroyer to board this fishing-boat and make sure she had no wireless. That would be Voss's solution, a bad one for Smith and *Hercules* because when the destroyer came alongside and saw *Hercules* was an armed drifter she would be scuttled and her crew taken prisoner.

He could not face that, and somehow he had to alert them in Brindisi and aboard the craft patrolling the barrage.

There was one way. He ordered Menzies, "Tell Davies that when I order him to fire he's to aim for *Salzburg*'s bridge. Then you nip aft and take command of the Vickers, same target."

"Aye, aye, sir!" Menzies dashed away.

Smith thought that Ginger Gates on the Vickers was well able to pick his target without Menzies pointing it out, but there was no sense in Smith, Archbold and Menzies all being in the wheelhouse. If it was hit then Menzies would survive to take command. Poor little bugger.

The destroyer leaders were now abeam to port and starboard, those second in the lines were broad on the bow. A light blinked aboard *Salzburg* and Buckley muttered, "She's signalling, sir."

Smith nodded, guessed who she was signalling to. His gaze shifted to port, to the line of destroyers there. A moment later came an answering wink of light from the ship at the tail of the line. So she had been ordered to swing out of the line when she came up with *Hercules* and deal with her. Smith was certain he was right, would bet his life on it. Then he remembered he was already betting the lives of all aboard the drifter.

The battlecruiser bulked huge off the starboard bow, majestic, sweeping down on them. She would pass less than a cable's length away, charge past with little more than a hundred yards between them. Buckley shoved a handful of cotton wool at Smith who thrust plugs of it into his ears. Wisps of it stuck out of Fred Archbold's ears but he heard Smith's order, "Starboard ten." The wheel went over and the stubby bow of *Hercules* swung to point at the oncoming giant. "Steady ... steer that."

Davies crouched over the six-pounder. One of his crew had turned to stare back at the wheelhouse, Smith saw his face a pale smudge above the dark blue of his jersey. Smith made a funnel of his hands and roared, "Fire!" The six-pounder spat flame and barked, jetted smoke and a second later there came the flash of the burst high on the bridge superstructure of *Salzburg*, the tall tower built around and forward of the fore-mast.

Smith shouted, "Hard aport!" The six-pounder fired again, and again as the wheel went over and *Hercules* heeled in the turn, brass cartridge cases bouncing and clanging across the deck, smoke swirling back into the wheelhouse, stinking of cordite, acrid. Then the heavens burst open as *Salzburg* fired her secondary armament. The six-inch and four-inch guns licked out long tongues of flame over the sea and the blast shook *Hercules*, whipped Smith's cap from his head and staggered Fred Archbold at the wheel. Smith saw the sea lift in huge fountains to port as he clung to the screen and bellowed in Archbold's ear, "Meet her! Steer that!" He pointed to make his meaning clear and *Hercules* straightened to an even keel but bucking as she steamed down *Salzburg*'s starboard side and rode the big bow-wave rolling out from the battlecruiser's stem.

Salzburg was rushing past only yards away; she was making better than twenty knots and *Hercules* nearly ten so they were passing at their combined speed of thirty knots. The battlecruiser loomed enormous, a floating steel fortress lit by the flashes of her guns so that the big gun turrets of her silent main armament were cut sharp in black silhouette high overhead. Tracers wove lazy, criss-cross patterns and the six-pounder was still firing, Davies and his crew shifting and leaping about the deck as they trained and laid the gun, fired, loaded, trained and laid.

They were past her, *Salzburg*'s stern sliding away and *Hercules* pitching and rolling in the churned white water of the battlecruiser's wake. "Hard astarboard!" Smith sent the drifter plunging across that wake and *Salzburg*'s funnel smoke rolled over them. It cleared and there ahead of them was the last destroyer of the port side screen. "Hard aport!" Fred Archbold hauled on the wheel. The six-pounder barked and gun-flashes sparked along the destroyer's hull. *Hercules* was turning but a shell splashed into the sea close off the starboard bow and hurled water inboard that fell on the six-pounder's crew; Smith saw one of them felled by the force of it. Spray drove into the wheelhouse and into his face. It stank evilly. He felt the slam and shudder as *Hercules* was hit and ordered, "Hard astarboard! Check firing!" The destroyer was blurring, merging into the darkness, a black shadow under her smoke with only her white wash to mark where she had gone, racing on southward.

The guns had ceased firing but Smith's ears still rang. *Hercules* was tossed about like a cork in a sea made turbulent by the passing of the squadron, but now she was alone. And invisible. Smith swallowed and looked at the compass. They were steaming north-east. Far off the port beam the horizon was aglow where a searchlight was sweeping again. The men operating it would have heard and seen the gunfire. The alarm had been given and the Italians and Pickett's cruisers would be raising steam to put to sea. Voss would know it and that his chance of a surprise attack had gone. He would be cursing the drifter but would go on to wreak what havoc he could in the brief space of time now left to him. Smith was certain of that.

"Starboard ten!" Smith brought *Hercules* around and back on her course for Brindisi. His voice was husky and his throat raw as if he had bellowed orders for hours but the action had lasted only minutes.

Menzies came into the wheelhouse, short of breath and trying

184

to control the excitement in his voice as he reported, "We were hit twice, sir. One shell went clear through the fo'c'sle, in one side and out t'other without bursting. Another took a lump out of the stern. Only one casualty: young Gates had his arm laid open, by a splinter I think, but he kept firing the Vickers. The cook is seeing to him."

'Young' Gates was only nineteen, true, but he was still two years older than Menzies.

He continued, "One destroyer, the last in the line to port, she turned towards us just before we opened fire but she swung away quick when *Salzburg* fired."

She would. Some of those shells from *Salzburg* that had hurtled over Smith's head must have smashed into the sea uncomfortably close to the destroyer screen. And of course the firing effectively countermanded any order to stop and board *Hercules*; that had become pointless. Smith said, "Very good."

Fred Archbold muttered, "Bloody miracle, if you ask me."

Smith remembered the bulk of *Salzburg* rushing at them out of the darkness, the stupefying shock as her guns split the night seemingly right over the drifter. He supposed their escape could seem like a miracle to Archbold but once you accepted that *Salzburg* must be provoked into firing then it was clear *Hercules* had to be brought so close to her as to be under the trajectory of her guns, or almost so. The gunners aboard her would have been briefly dazzled by the flash of the six-pounder and *Hercules* was small, passing swiftly across in front of them. It was simple enough and they had been lucky.

There was no reason for Menzies to be staring at him like that. Smith growled, "What the hell are you gawping at? Tell Davies to secure that gun!"

"Aye, aye, sir!" Menzies scurried away from Smith's glare and out of the wheelhouse.

Reaction gripped Smith now as always when the fighting was done. He did not want congratulations nor hero-worship because he knew he was no hero. This was the time when he looked coldly at the risks he had run and tried to swallow his fear. He shifted to a corner of the wheelhouse, his back to the others and scowled out at the night and the dark sea.

Hercules made good fifteen miles before the light and in that dawning Pickett's squadron came tearing out from Brindisi, the four cruisers in line ahead, screening destroyers out on either flank, all of them streaming thick, black funnel smoke. They made an impressive sight in that first pale light, grim and urgent. Smith said, "Make: *Hercules* to Flag. *Salzburg* and six destroyers sighted 3.35 a.m. Course south-east, speed twenty-five knots. My position – get that from Mr Menzies."

He waited as the signal-lamp clattered, saw the acknowledging flicker from the leading cruiser. Then the lamp on her bridge flashed again and Buckley read: "Identify ships engaged."

Smith said, "Make: *Hercules* opened fire on *Salzburg* at 3.43. *Salzburg* broke off the action at 3.48." He saw Menzies' monkey-grin but Buckley's face was as straight as Smith's as he worked the lamp, flashing the signal across the swiftly narrowing gap between the ships. Smith added, "Ask: What report from barrage?"

That acknowledging flicker again. A pause. Smith wondered how soon he could talk to Pickett and try to persuade him to reverse the orders he had given. The lamp was blinking again, the leading cruiser abeam now, her funnel smoke rolling down over the sea towards them. Smith could make out figures on her bridge. One of them would be Pickett. The reply came: "Patrols alerted by gunfire took evasive action. Two drifters sunk. Small damage one short section of barrage only." So *Hercules'* action had saved the barrage and nearly all the craft patrolling it. Voss, knowing the alarm had been given and the cruisers would be coming out sooner than he'd expected, had not risked steaming the fifty miles' length of the barrage. He had struck one swift blow and then run. But – two drifters and a score of men caught by *Salzburg*. The big shells bursting in their wooden hulls, blasting the life out of ships and men, leaving them as flotsam on the sea. Smith swore and saw Menzies' startled glance. It might seem fortunate that only those few men had died when so many were at risk but men were men, like these about him now. And it might also seem a meagre reward for the employment of a powerful battlecruiser and six destroyers but he had to emphasise to Pickett the implications of leaving Voss to rampage at will.

The lamp was flickering again from the cruiser's bridge and Buckley read slowly: "Signal from Admiralty. Begins. Rear Admiral Braddock appointed command Adriatic immediate.

Ends. From C-in-C Adriatic to Commander D.C.Smith. Begins. Carry out orders as instructed seek out and destroy. Ends. Return Venice and comply."

Smith had time to absorb the signal as Buckley spelled it word by word but still he was stunned for a moment at the end, staring out across the grey sea. Braddock! Taking command! Confirming Smith's orders! No longer need he plead with Pickett. No longer did the threat of court-martial hang over him. He said stiffly, "Acknowledge." He still could not believe it. How had it come about? Then he remembered Braddock saying he was pushing for a sea appointment and was as well-qualified as Winter. Braddock had demanded and got his appointment – and his first action was to back Smith. He must have sent that signal from Alexandria.

Return Venice and comply. That last was added by Pickett who would be a bitter man now. Smith ordered, "Starboard ten."

Hercules started the turn that would set her once more on a course for Venice, taking him back to Helen. And *Salzburg*.

Voss had served notice. Smith was certain this was no isolated hit-and-run raid but a demonstration of the damage that could be done by an Austrian Fleet raiding out of Cattaro. It was a demonstration for the benefit of the Austrians and a successful one at that because Voss would get clean away, could point to the damage done and claim quite rightly that he would have wrecked the entire barrage but for an unlucky encounter with a small drifter.

Winter had been right: Seek out and destroy.

15 "They're shooting deserters and spies!"

Two days after the action north of Brindisi, *Hercules* steamed between the long arms of the Porto di Lido and into the Venetian lagoon. She had plugged north all the way at her best speed of eight or nine knots. She had burned all but a sackful of her coal and her stokers were tired men. Her carpenter had clapped timber patches on the shell-holes but the paint on them was raw and new like fresh scar tissue.

Smith stood in the wheelhouse, Fred Archbold at the wheel, and reflected that Pickett might have detached a destroyer to carry him back to Venice at high speed, but he had not. Pickett was obeying orders, no more and no less, right to the end. No matter: it seemed that Smith's only hope of attacking *Salzburg* was Balestra's machine, so until that was ready he could do nothing. He did not like it, but other thoughts filled his mind now.

The drifter berthed close to the house on the Ca' di Dio and Smith went there after giving orders to Menzies and Fred Archbold to see to coaling and re-provisioning without delay. He found only the old woman and had to return to *Hercules* to fetch Davies to interpret. The gunner had some difficulty because the woman was inclined to weep and talked rapidly. She was old and upset. Finally Davies wiped at a sweating brow and explained to Smith, "I savvy the Italian a bit, sir, but she natters away that quick. Anyway, it seems Miss Blair has gone up to a place called Zenson or thereabouts but she's expected back tonight."

Smith was glad of that but sorry for the old woman, the tears running down her face. "Why is she crying?"

"Dunno, sir. She keeps on about the Germans. Probably frightened they'll come an' get her." He patted the old woman's shoulder, said gently, "Don't worry, Ma."

Smith returned to *Hercules*, ordered her boat lowered and was rowed along the shore of the lagoon past the SVAN yard where they built the MAS boats and so to the dockyard, the Arsenal

188

and Naval Headquarters. There he asked the Italian Naval Police at the gate for Devereux and was taken to his office but Devereux was not there, only the clerk he had seen before. "Cap'n Devereux left about a half-hour ago, sir. I remember it was not long after *Hercules* was reported as coming in."

Smith glanced sharply at him. Was the man suggesting the two were directly related, that Devereux had walked out rather than face Smith, now returned with orders confirmed and Braddock soon to arrive to take command?

But the clerk's face was innocent. He went on, "The cap'n usually finishes at noon these days. But he left this for you, sir."

It was a note, typed, signed with the Devereux flourish. It said that pursuant to his orders Devereux had approached the Italians. Lieutenant Balestra had been authorised to continue his work and the MAS boats were to report to *Hercules* on her arrival for orders from Smith. Intelligence reports would be available at his office.

So the rigid secrecy of Smith's operation, his isolation from the Italian command, continued. He approved of the secrecy because if the Austrians got wind of a projected attack it would end in disaster. The failure at Trieste had demonstrated that, though bad luck was to blame there because only Smith's own little force had known of the attack. The secrecy was fine. His isolation from the Italian command was not, because direct contact might have helped him. He was sure that if Winter had lived, and now when Braddock came, a different order would obtain. But at least he had his command again.

A second note was pinned beneath the first. It said that inter-rogation of Austrian deserters had produced a lot of inform-ation of minor interest. One item was that rumours were cir-culating in Pola that the entire Austrian Fleet planned to move its base. Tenders and supply ships were loading dockyard stores. Devereux said he agreed with the Italians that such a move might be to Trieste or Cattaro but pointed out the report was based only on rumour and there was no indication when, if ever, the move might be made. Meanwhile the Italians were maintaining their daily reconnaissance flights.

Smith folded the notes and put them away in his pocket. The Italians could do nothing more about it. The Austrians might sail by day or night, next day, next week or not for a month. The

Italian Fleet could not maintain a day and night blockade of Pola any more than the Royal Navy in the North Sea because any prolonged blockade rendered the blockaders targets for submarine attack. There were no such problems for the Austrians. They would send out their minesweepers and destroyers first, the one to clear a channel and the other to keep submarines down. Then the fleet could come out at speed and leave any such waiting submarine behind.

The clerk was holding out a file. "Up-to-date intelligence of Pola and Trieste, sir."

There were the photographs first and right on the top the latest of Pola. It was clear and the ships were marked in ink with their known or probable names, a question mark after each. There was no question mark after the name of *Salzburg*, no doubt that it was her. She lay alongside the line of battleships moored in the harbour, about halfway down its length and about three or four hundred yards from the line. No mistaking her and she was set apart from the others.

Smith gave silent thanks for the Italian Air Force who took these photographs. The date was at the foot of it, taken only this day. He asked, "When do these photographs come in?"

"Around now, sir, if the visibility is good enough for photographs. Sometimes they can't see a thing. But now they're flying a dawn reconnaissance every day. Those latest ones came just before the cap'n left."

All the way north he had wondered where *Salzburg* might be because that was still the first step in his orders: Seek out ... After attacking the Otranto barrage she might have run in to Cattaro, kept on north for Pola, or even come right up to Trieste at the head of the Adriatic. But she was at Pola as he had expected – or dreaded. Where the Austrian Fleet also lay. There were rumours it might sail. The days were slipping away, and so would his chance to attack *Salzburg* once the fleet moved all the way down to Cattaro as he was now certain it would. The Gulf of Cattaro twisted inland like a fjord, from a narrow mouth to a bay locked-in by the mountains. Pola was wide open by comparison. But what was his chance to attack her, even in Pola? Balestra?

He had unconsciously moved to stand at the window to examine the photographs and now he looked up. From where he stood he could see a corner of the dockyard and basin, and there on the quay stood the three MAS captains. Like *Salzburg*, as a group they were unmistakable: the squat Gallina, lean Pagani and Zacco towering over the other two. Smith had to go to Balestra's workshop but first he would see them.

He tucked the file under his arm and went down and out of the building, thinking that he had to start with Balestra. He had little faith in the device the Italian was trying to create, but it was all he had.

He was walking quickly and the captains had their backs to him, staring out over the basin. So he was almost up to them when Pagani glanced casually around then gave a startled exclamation. They spun to face Smith, snapped to attention to salute him formally and he acknowledged the compliment. But then they were smiling and gathered round him.

He returned the grins. It was good to be among friends. They had come to know each other, had become close during the days and dangers they had shared. Smith asked, "How does it go?"

Zacco pointed a long finger at the basin. "I think it goes well."

Smith looked where Zacco pointed. Out in the basin was a cutter, a dozen men aboard her and alongside – *Seahorse*.

Smith stared, astounded. "It's finished? It works?"

"It works."

He watched as the cutter was pulled into the dockyard wall by four of the men at the oars, *Seahorse* towed astern of her. Smith quickly recognised *motoristi* from the boats. Lombardo and Balestra sitting in the sternsheets of the cutter were harder to recognise because both were dressed in strange, tight-fitting, one-piece suits that looked to be made of rubber and covered them from head to foot save for an opening for the face. As the cutter ran into the steps Smith saw all of them aboard her looked red-eyed and weary. Balestra did not spare himself or anyone else. Smith could hear him singing softly but then he was climbing the steps to stand at attention before Smith, who saluted him. "Well done, Guido."

He had to leave it at that for a time as the captains crowded around Balestra shaking his hand, slapping his back. Smith looked down at *Seahorse* lying almost awash below him.

It was the old torpedo, fourteen inches in diameter and fifteen feet long, that Smith had first seen in Balestra's workshop. Balestra had ripped out the original charge and warhead, leaving only the compressed-air engine. He had fitted an eighteen-inch screw and converted the engine so that the craft, if you could call it that, now had a speed of four knots and a range of eight miles. It carried two mines foward, charges each of one hundred and seventy kilos of TNT. Smith could see magnetic 'leeches', eight inches long, recessed into the tops of them. Out of his sight and coiled under each leech was a thin line about twelve feet long. Balestra intended to steer the *Seahorse* alongside *Salzburg* where she lay moored, attach the charges by the magnetic 'leeches', set the time fuse of each charge and then make his escape with the *Seahorse*, leaving the charges dangling on the lines just under *Salzburg*'s hull.

Smith turned incredulously to Balestra. "I can't believe you've done it, after losing two or three whole days."

Balestra shook his head and tried to run his fingers through his hair but was thwarted by the black rubber cap. "We did not lose one day. Nelson was blind in one eye – yes? So I think I will be deaf in one ear, the one that got my orders to finish. I went back to the workshop and we carried on. Late on the second day I got new orders – to carry on." He spread his hands. "So. Lombardo stayed with me all the time. He is very good. The *motoristi* from the MAS boats help when they are not on patrol. Also, we have authority to carry out trials in the dockyard and we ask for anything we want. It is very good."

"And the suits?" Smith had seen nothing like them before.

"Because of the cold," Balestra explained and Smith could understand that point. "It is not hard to swim in these and we practise."

Smith said, "We go tomorrow."

"An attack tomorrow night? But we have only had one good trial! It is too soon!"

"We daren't wait. You know *Salzburg* attacked the Otranto barrage two nights ago?" When they nodded he went on, "Now she is in Pola with the Austrian Fleet. I believe the attack on the barrage was made from Cattaro to show the Austrians what could be done. Now Voss will lead them there, and soon. Once they are based at Cattaro and raiding out of there against the Italian coast ..."

He did not finish, let them draw the conclusion. The Italian fleet could not be at sea all the time. The Austrians could sit in Cattaro and choose their time, steam out and hit their target and escape back to Cattaro before the Italians could catch them.

Zacco scowled and Pagani swore. Smith went on slowly: "Tonight is out of the question. You're worn out. I want *Seahorse* armed with the charges and shipped aboard *Hercules*. Then I want you three"– he looked at the captains – "to take Guido out, feed him and put him to bed in the prison." That lightened the mood and they laughed. Smith said, "We will be ready to sail from noon tomorrow. By then the latest photographs will be available and we will know if *Salzburg* is still at Pola or has gone back to Trieste. If she is at neither then I think she will be on her way to Cattaro and we sail south at once." But on a wild goose chase, because they would never get to *Salzburg* in Cattaro.

He turned to Balestra. "You have a crew, another man to go with you?"

Balestra nodded. "I think so. You want his name? In five minutes. You will excuse me." He walked away and descended the steps to the cutter.

Smith watched him go. Balestra was right: an attack tomorrow was too soon. But it was forced on them. And the chances of Balestra's success? Smith harked back to the idea that came to him outside of Pola. He still did not like it but he had to have a second string to his bow. He told Zacco, "Be ready to try to blast a way through the booms if he fails."

Pietro Zacco glanced at him, startled. "Blast?"

It would take more than one charge and any chance of surprise would be blown away by the first but they might cut a way for one boat to get at *Salzburg*. Smith said, "Every boat to carry charges. Each charge to be in a canvas bag with a strap to secure it to the boom and a timing device to fire it with delays of five or ten minutes."

Zacco hesitated, well able to see the near-suicidal nature of the plan, then nodded. "I will go to the Arsenal."

Angelo Lombardo was a man who enjoyed life, good food, wine and women, proud of his skill as an engineer and liking his sleep. Now he was tired, hungry, thirsty, chilled in spite of the rubber suit, and uneasy. He had felt an enormous sense of triumph at the final success of *Seahorse* but that was gone.

He watched Balestra descend the steps and pick his way across the thwarts of the cutter to where he was sitting alone in the sternsheets, elbows on his knees.

Balestra sat down by him and said simply, "Thank you."

Angelo shrugged. "OK, signore. Now I go back to the boat." He was a *motorista* on a MAS boat. That's what he did. This business with *Seahorse* was only an interlude.

"Ah." Balestra tried to run his fingers through his hair and failed again because of the rubber suit. The gesture was familiar to Lombardo now; he had learned a lot about this young man they called the Mad Professor. Now Balestra said, "You remember, at the start, you asked if I had a crew and I said I had chosen a man."

"I remember." He also remembered the old hand's dictum: never volunteer.

Balestra said, "I wanted a very good *motorista* and a very good swimmer. I chose the man that day."

Lombardo shook his head. "No."

Balestra said seriously, "It will be difficult, but there *is* a chance and it has to be tried." He explained why, Voss's mission and the threat to Italy.

Lombardo was not impressed. "I don't want to be a hero. I want to see out this war. Get somebody else."

Balestra said, "Suppose you had to pick somebody to take my place. Somebody who knows as much about *Seahorse* and how to operate it. Who would it be?"

Lombardo did not answer. Suppose Balestra asked for a volunteer? Suppose he got some daredevil youngster who hadn't spent the last week working with *Seahorse*, who was maybe only a passable swimmer? What chance would the pair of them have?

The sea was so bloody cold.

He swore and Balestra stood up. "Thank you. There was never anybody else, you know. No question of it. We go tomorrow. The suit fits all right?"

Lombardo answered, "Fine. Everything is fine."

He thought he should write to his mother in America. He had not written for a long time. She believed he had a safe job in the dockyard and kept asking if he had met a nice girl. She said he should settle down.

He sat staring at the cold, steel length of *Seahorse*.

Balestra returned to the group and said, "It is arranged. Lombardo goes."

"Lombardo!" The startled exclamation came from Zacco. He said, "Lombardo *never* volunteers."

Balestra smiled. "I talk with him. He volunteers."

Zacco shook his head, still unable to believe it.

Smith wondered why Lombardo was willing to risk his life in this. But why would Balestra? Because he believed in his outlandish contraption. Smith felt guilty at thinking of *Seahorse* like that but had to be honest; that was how he felt about it. Only Balestra's confidence was persuading Smith to let him make the attempt – that and the demands of his orders, and the war.

He asked, "What news of the war?"

Zacco answered, "The line holds all along the Piave. There is heavy fighting around Zenson. There are rumours that the Germans got across the Piave there but I don't know if that is true."

"Zenson?" That had an unpleasantly familiar ring to it. "Where is that?"

"About twenty-five kilometres up river." Zacco saw Smith frown. "Something wrong?"

"Miss Blair went there today."

"I do not think that is a good place for her." Zacco was frowning now and the others shook their heads.

Smith asked, "How could I get there?"

Zacco hesitated, then: "It will be difficult. I think you will have to ask the army to take you, maybe in a supply convoy."

Balestra asked, "You can drive?"

"Yes." Smith had learned during those lazy weeks of leave in England in the summer after the fighting off Ostende. There had been a girl then ...

Balestra spread his hands. "You take my car. It is at Mestre. You have a pencil, paper?" Smith produced note-book and pencil. Balestra scribbled rapidly on a blank page and handed it back to Smith. "There is a workshop outside the station at Mestre. You ask for Emilio Ossena. He is the owner and he

195

works on cars. He is a very old man, very nice, very good with cars."

"Thank you." Smith wanted to get away now. He told himself he was taking fright at shadows, that Helen had often visited the rear areas and anyway the army would not allow her into a danger zone. If they were able to stop her. If they noticed her, just one more car in the traffic behind the lines. He said, "Then at noon tomorrow, gentlemen."

They saluted and he hurried away. The boat took him back to *Hercules* and there he shouted for Buckley and Davies. "Shift out of your working rig. You're going ashore with me." Davies because of his knowledge of Italian. Buckley because he was Buckley.

They walked to the station, Davies leading the way through narrow streets and suddenly opening piazzas, across bridges. Everywhere were the stacked sandbags protecting the city's treasures of stone against the bombing and now – maybe – the shelling. But the line still held on the Piave.

They took the train to Mestre. The lagoon was a dirty grey tinged with the rust red of the mud it carried. It was a cold, wintry lake with little islands standing bleakly out of it and in the distance the green of the marshes. Rain was falling and the clouds came down to merge with the mist. Outside the station at Mestre they found the workshop. Smith asked a boy for Emilio Ossena and he came out from the shadows at the back of the shop, walking quickly between the benches where his men worked. He was a dried up, long, thin stick of a man. When he saw Balestra's note he showed them to a car standing in a corner of the shop and dragged off the dust-sheets that covered it. The car was American, a Model T Ford, a four-seater without doors – you just stepped in. There was a leather hood folded down behind the rear seats and Emilio helped them to rig this, easing it out over the car and clipping it to the windscreen. All the time he talked, obviously curious at the arrival of the young Royal Navy commander and the two bluejackets.

Davies, scowling with concentration said, "He's asking about Mr Balestra, sir. He seems to be popular with the old feller."

Smith said, "Tell him Mr Balestra is well and happy." That was stretching the truth: with what lay ahead of Balestra, he was only happy in so far as he was doing what he wanted to.

Emilio Ossena shook hands with all of them and then they were in the Ford, Smith driving it out of the workshop. They wound through the narrow streets and turned north-eastward onto the road to San Dona di Piave. Buckley sat beside Smith with the map and Davies was in the rear seat. Whenever they came on soldiers on the road Smith halted the car, got down with Davies and asked the soldiers if they had seen La Contessa. Davies laboured the question at first in his halting Italian – "Avete vista la Contessa?" – but became more fluent with repetition. There were men who knew La Contessa but had not seen her that day. Others wore puzzled expressions as they shook their heads. "Quale Contessa?" They had obviously never heard of her.

With one of these Smith told Davies, "Ask him where he's come from?"

The man answered, "Bologna," and waved a hand to the south.

So some of these men had come up from the south and so would not know Helen Blair. As he drove on Smith thought that he should have brought a photograph, though if any man had seen Helen Blair in this rain-soaked waste she would have stuck in his memory. The country was sodden under the rain and because of the mist you could not see more than two hundred yards. There were farms in the flat fields, the now familiar green-shuttered houses and the roofs with humped red tiles. The vines in the fields were planted in rigid lines, each vine trained out on either side of its supporting pole so each looked like a crucifix. They were bare and black and dripped rain.

Davies said, "Looks like one graveyard after another."

Smith snarled, "Shut up!" He did not believe in omens and portents, but Davies made him uneasy.

Near Meolo there was a regiment resting by the road, big men in grey-green uniforms with the crimson and white flashes of grenadiers on their collars. Smith spoke with their colonel who was tall and bony-faced, black-moustached, brown as the cigar between his teeth. He said his regiment had been in reserve but had now been ordered to Zenson. He was very angry because he had heard stories of deserters and said his men would not desert or run. He had not seen Helen Blair, and did not know La

197

Contessa because he was new to this part of the line. He was sorry. He shouted an order and the non-coms passed it on, bawling it down the road. The regiment of grenadiers climbed to their feet and fell in. Smith drove on.

But at last, when the gunfire was a continuous thunder, their luck changed. They came on a dressing station by the roadside, a number of large tents emblazoned with the red cross. Outside a number of 'walking wounded' sat patiently in the rain, presumably awaiting transport to the rear. As the car halted a motor ambulance bumped down the road from the front, but only to discharge more wounded on stretchers to be carried into the tents. Then it turned around and drove back up the road towards the gunfire. Meanwhile Davies had been pacing among the wounded, asking his question, Smith at his shoulder. "Avete vista la Contessa?" . . . "Avete vista la Contessa?"

Until they came to a bearded corporal, a hooked pipe dangling from his clenched teeth. He nodded, spoke around the stem of the pipe. "Si . . . mi ha dato il tabacco . . ."

Davies listened, said, "He saw her only a few hours ago. She said she was going to a place called Fassolta di Piave. That's on the way to San Dona but off the road." He listened again, chewing at his lip, then told Smith: "He says she shouldn't have gone there. It's bad. They're shooting deserters and spies."

And it was close to the front line. San Dona was on the other side of the Piave river and in the enemy hands. Smith said, "Come on." He returned to the car and pored over the map with Davies and Buckley, marked his route. They were only a mile or so from Fassolta across country but a tank could not have crossed it. They would have to make a circle to come to it by road, something like three miles. Smith turned the car around and they set off. They had little time. Soon it would be dark and then Smith knew their search would be ten times more difficult.

As it was, dusk was closing around them as they rocked up the road to a village standing on a T-junction, just a cluster of houses. Their road led into it like the cross-piece of the T and another track, the leg of the T, came in from the left.

Buckley said, "I make it Fassolta is about a quarter-mile up the road, sir."

Towards the front line. The howl and *thump!* of falling shells were close now, the flames of them bursting and the long, licking flames from the answering Italian guns lighting the near horizon, silhouetting the ragged roofs of the houses of the village. The car had now come up with the tail of a convoy slowly creeping towards the front, mules loaded with supplies or hauling wagons under the cracking whips and hoarse yells of their drivers. This was not Fassolta but there were troops busy among the houses and two sentries with rifles, their bayonets fixed, stood outside the biggest house, which had tall windows closed with sturdy green-painted shutters. Smith turned the car off the road and stopped it, leaving the engine running. "We'll ask here."

The house stood apart from the others, a lane leading down the side of it to a big yard at the rear enclosed by a high wall.

There were shell-craters near the road and the roof and upper floor of the house were smashed in, the beams ragged against the sky. Smith did not like the look of it. This place was a junction on the supply route up to the line. It had been shelled and would be again. Soldiers were digging a trench on the other side of the house from the lane, away from the front line.

The sentries at the door lifted their rifles and peered suspiciously through the gathering gloom. One of them shouted a challenge as Smith, Davies and Buckley got down.

Davies answered, "Il capitano Inglese della marina!"

An officer appeared at the door, a lieutenant of infantry. Smith and Davies approached him and Davies asked him if the Contessa was in the village. Had he seen her?

The lieutenant shook his head. A field telephone rang in the house behind him and he turned, threw a sentence over his shoulder as he went back into the house.

Davies translated. "He says they've only got one woman here and she is a spy."

Smith pushed past him and went in after the lieutenant. An oil lamp burned on a rough deal table. It showed the tall windows had not been saved by the shutters, blast had left the glass in fragments on sill and floor. The lieutenant stood at the table, the telephone to his ear, his shadow huge against the wall. He nodded. "Si ... Si." He put down the receiver, stared at them. A small wood stove hissed and crackled in one corner. Two *carabinieri* stood before it in their wide cocked hats, rifles

199

at the ready. They watched the three Englishmen as suspiciously as had the sentries outside.

Smith said to Davies, "Ask him: This woman, is she young, pretty, smartly-dressed? Is she English?"

He waited, listened to Davies' laboured Italian, the lieutenant's rapid reply, saw the contemptuous flap of his hand. Davies said, "She's young and well-dressed and claims she is English but that is a lie. She is a spy." The lieutenant was speaking again, voice high with anger only barely held in check. His eyes stared and a muscle twitched high in his cheek, jerking one corner of his mouth as he spoke. Davies interpreted as best he could, sometimes managed to halt the tirade and have a phrase repeated impatiently.

Smith listened, fear growing in him. The woman had been caught talking with a group of Austrian prisoners. One of their guards, hidden from her by a tree, had heard her speak to the prisoners in German. This had convinced him that she was just one more of the many spies behind the lines. The lieutenant was waiting for three other officers who would form a court. They would try her and shoot her, here and now.

Buckley muttered, "It can't be Miss Blair, sir? Surely?"

"Ask her name."

Davies did. The lieutenant looked irritably in his note-book, then answered, "Elena Blair."

Smith was sweating in the chill of the shadowed room where rain dripped through the ceiling into puddles on the floor. He said, "Ask if we can see her. This woman might be an impostor." She might. He could not believe it but surely it was possible. He prayed that it was.

The lieutenant scowled, then shrugged. He spoke to the *carabinieri* and they followed with their rifles as he led Smith, Buckley and Davies through a door at the back of the room. It gave on to a narrow passage and another door at the end of it, heavy and solid. The lieutenant took his pistol from its holster with one hand, a key from his pocket with the other. He unlocked the door and swung it wide but stood in the opening between Smith and the girl inside.

The room was a lean-to built of timber against the back wall of the house, a store-room with an earth floor on which lay a pile of old grain sacks. The only light came from a narrow window that only a cat could have slipped through, outside it the yard at the rear of the house. There was a small stool set under the window. On it sat Helen Blair.

She rose when she saw Smith and started forward but the lieutenant barked at her, swung the pistol menacingly and she halted. Her silk dress and the cape over it were splashed with mud, her fragile shoes now shapeless lumps. The once-piled hair now hung loose to her shoulders. Her face was pale, the eyes wide and frightened. She whispered, "David? Oh, David!"

Smith took a pace towards her but came up against the pistol. The lieutenant spat angry words at him, the muscle jumping and pulling at the corner of his mouth. From the corner of his eye Smith saw the *carabinieri* training their rifles on him and he stood still. He asked the girl, "What happened?"

"They won't listen to me! You tell them, David!" Her voice shook as she pleaded.

"What happened?"

She lifted a hand to push the hair from her face. "I was – on the road. I saw the soldiers. Gave them some cigarettes, chocolate – I don't remember. There was a crowd of prisoners, Austrians, and I gave some to them, tried to tell them I was English, that now their war was over, they were safe. Then some guard jumped out of nowhere and shouted at me, dragged me here. They said I was talking German. I told them I was English but they wouldn't listen. The *carabinieri* came and said I was a spy. They put me in here. David – what are they going to do?"

He tried to sound confident. "It's all a mistake. I think they've had a bad time." He was certain they had: the lieutenant looked near breaking point. "I'll explain."

The lieutenant was glancing sharply from one to the other, obviously distrustful of these exchanges he could not understand. He snapped at Davies, who said, "He wants to know if this is the woman you were looking for."

Smith nodded at the lieutenant. "Yes! Si!" And to Davies: "Tell him he's making a terrible mistake. Tell him –"

But Davies barely got out the first phrase when the lieutenant shook his head angrily and slammed the door in the girl's face, turning the key in the lock. He threw a comment at the two *carabinieri* and their manner changed from suspicion to open hostility. Davies muttered, "He told them we're friends of hers, sir. They don't like it."

The *carabinieri* escorted them back to the other room. Smith said, "Tell them they can check our credentials with Captain Devereux, the liaison officer at Naval Headquarters, or with Capitano Bruno Garizzo of the regimento marina."

The lieutenant and the *carabinieri* listened but remained hostile until Garizzo's name was mentioned. Then there was a laboured exchange between the lieutenant and Davies, the tension eased and the latter told Smith, "I said the lady spoke English to the prisoners, not German. He asked how long we'd known her, I said a few weeks an' he said that was no time at all and she's fooled us. He asked about the battle we were in with Captain Garizzo. I told him and he knew about it already so at least they believe *we're* genuine. But not Miss Blair."

The lieutenant shouted at the sentries outside the door and they bawled in their turn, calling a name. He turned on Davies and launched into another tirade, finger jabbing towards the front line then at the store-room, hand curling into a fist to pound the table. He broke off as the telephone jingled again, snatched at it.

Davies was sweating now, concentration furrowing his brow. "Doin' the best I can, sir. Near as I can make out they were rushed up from the south an' they'd not been long in the line when Jerry crossed the river at Zenson and got a foothold. He says he lost a lot of men and the Germans knew just where to hit them. He says it's been like that all the time, that it has to be the spies doing it. There's a lot more I missed but I think that's the story."

The lieutenant put down the telephone as a soldier came in at the door. He was a private, short and stocky, sullen. He looked at Smith and the bluejackets without interest, then at the lieutenant who rattled a question at him. He nodded. Another question brought a shake of the head, a slow answer, contemptuous, with a twist of the mouth. Davies muttered, "This is the feller that heard Miss Blair. He says she spoke German and not English. He's certain."

Smith stared at the soldier, who returned the stare stubbornly. He was wrong but he would not admit it. Smith was sure of that – the man's mind was made up, and so was the lieutenant's. Smith said, "Tell him I'm going to find a senior officer, that he must do nothing till I return."

But the lieutenant turned his back on that, threw his answer over his shoulder as the telephone rang again and he reached for it. Davies interpreted, "He says the war won't wait. They are fighting for their lives here."

Smith hurried out of the house to where the car stood with the engine still running. It was pitch dark now but the firing of an Italian field battery in the field close by the village lit the road with a flickering light. There was a nightmarish quality to the whole situation – the wild, wide-eyed, twitching stare of the lieutenant, the menacing background of gunfire, the stilted, rambling explanations and misunderstandings . . . Smith felt as if he were groping round a dark cell from which there was no escape.

But the cell was real, no dream, and Helen was in it.

As he swung into the Ford another car skidded off the road, spraying mud from its wheels, and halted before the house. The driver jumped out, opened the door and three officers got down and splashed across to the house, filed in at the door: the members of the court.

The war would not wait.

They would try her, find her guilty, pass sentence and shoot her within the hour. Smith had heard rumours of this and now he was to be a witness. He did not know where to find a senior officer or whether such an officer would listen to him. He had to stop this himself. Now. At once. But how?

The three of them in the Ford hadn't a weapon between them and even if they had, could they use it? Certainly the threat alone would not be enough to subdue the Italians: they would fight.

He stared at the house through the rain running down the windscreen of the car, remembered now Helen had looked at him with hope and trust, standing in the ramshackle little shed . . .

He tightened his grip on the wheel, warned Davies and Buckley, "There's going to be shooting. If you have any sense you'll get out of this now."

Buckley glanced at Davies then said, "We'll stick with you, sir." Davies nodded.

Smith engaged gear. "Whatever happens, you were acting under my orders. Remember that. *Under my orders!*"

The car moved forward ... They had not heard the salvo coming, but shook to its impact as the shells hurled up mud and rocks from the road, blasting the roof from one house and the corner from another. The sentries ran for the trench and after them went the officers and *carabinieri* streaming from the house. Then the Ford was into the lane running down the side of the house.

As they entered the yard at the rear Smith braked and shouted at the other two, "Tell her to get away from that back wall!" They jumped down and ran to the lean-to while Smith drove the car to the end of the yard and turned it. Another salvo fell, one shell bursting on what was left of the roof above them so that tiles rained down in the yard. In the flash of that burst he glimpsed Buckley by the window of the lean-to. Darkness descended again and he rammed his foot down on the accelerator. The wheels of the Ford spun in the mud then gripped and it shot forward. The lean-to rushed up at him as the car charged across the yard and he braked only feet away so it skidded on with the wheels locked and crashed into the wall.

He held the wheel but he was thrown forward and slammed his chest against it. The breath whooped out of him and his eyes watered but he blinked them clear and pushed himself back. The wall had collapsed inwards and the front of the Ford was inside the lean-to. The engine had stalled. Davies and Buckley appeared at either side of the car and set their shoulders to it, shoving. Smith knocked it out of gear and climbed down to shove with them so the car rolled back into the middle of the yard. He straightened and gasped at them, "Get her!"

They ran to the lean-to, hauled wreckage aside and Buckley climbed in. Smith cranked the Ford, the engine fired and he ran round to the driver's seat. The glare lit the yard as a third salvo exploded. He thought again that it was inevitable this village, at a road junction on the way up to the line, should be shelled. In that blink of light he saw Buckley coming out of the lean-to.

He was blind again, did not see them till they fetched up at the car, Davies, Buckley – and between them Helen's stumbling figure. They pushed her in beside Smith, he tugging at her arm, then they jumped into the back. Smith turned the car, the off-side wheels bumping over the littered timber of the lean-to. A man appeared in the wreckage and Smith was close enough to see the Italian lieutenant had braved the gunfire to come and look for his prisoner, perhaps to save her. But the Ford lurched on, turned into the lane along the side of the house and accelerated towards the road. Shots cracked out behind as the lieutenant emptied his pistol after them. Smith shouted, "Anybody hit?"

"No, sir!" That was Davies.

They were out on the road, mud spurting up from the tyres and Smith hauled at the wheel to send them slipping and sliding around a shell-crater. One of the houses erupted in a tongue of flame as the junction was hit again, dirt and rocks showered down on the car's leather hood, the windscreen shattered and collapsed in fragments and the rain drove in on the wind of their passage. They raced away from the village, bouncing and swaying on the rutted road.

After a quarter-mile of wild progress Smith slowed the Ford to a more sedate pace. He did not think they were followed and the turnoff to Venice was close. He braked as they came to the road crossing theirs and swung left on to it, heading eastward, away from the front. Davies in the back let out a long breath. "Bloody 'ell! We do see life!"

Buckley answered in his deep Geordie, "Told you, didn't I? Still, if you can't take a joke you shouldn't ha' joined."

Smith managed a smile as the tension eased out of him. Without them he would have failed. They had helped him all the way through and saved Helen's life, of that he was certain. They were the salt of the earth and he owed them more than he could say. "Thanks, both of you."

And Helen added shakily, "Bless you. All of you." She clung to his arm, her face against his shoulder as the Ford ground on down the narrow road through the rain-filled darkness.

205

16 "For God's sake! Why?"

They lay close in the darkened room in the house on the Ca' di Dio and she whispered, her breath on his face, "We've had so little time."

He answered, "We'll have time."

She knew that wasn't true but at this moment she was happy and let it be.

He said, "Tomorrow we must go to Devereux's office and clear up this mess. Those soldiers and *carabinieri* have your name and they'll follow it up."

She was silent, then: "All right." And: "Don't leave me." And: "You see, I didn't want to love a man in the war."

His answer was wry. "You made that very clear."

She laughed softly despite the lurking fear, or because of it, rolled on to him. "But I'm making it up to you. Aren't I? Aren't I?" And finally, sleepily, "Don't leave me."

"I won't." He knew he lied because he would have to leave her. But he would return to her, somehow. He lay in a drifting dream between sleeping and waking, quietly happy. He recalled that first day he met her and all the other meetings. He could remember every word. Every word ... He chilled suddenly, felt her warmth against him. He was wide awake. Christ, would he ever sleep again? Tiredness dragged at him. The night was long and finally he slept.

He woke in the first light of the day. His thoughts dragged him from the bed to stand naked at the window, staring out across the lagoon that was wreathed in mist. Until he looked at his watch and saw it was after seven thirty. He shivered and, moving quietly, washed and dressed, went down through the house. On the ground floor he heard the old woman moving about in the kitchen, then the knock came at the front door and he opened it to Pietro Zacco.

The tall lieutenant said, "The photographs. Trieste and Pola."

Smith took them from the envelope and looked at them.

Helen called from above, "Who is it?"

206

He answered, "Zacco. Come for me."

She appeared at the head of the stairs, a robe thrown around her. "Another operation?"

"Trieste. Tonight."

"No!" She ran down the stairs and held him, argued and pleaded: He could get out of it somehow, say the operation was not possible, the weather was wrong, they were not ready. Or he could send a junior officer, ask to be relieved. He could tell them he had seen enough of war and that was true. He had come back from the Piave looking like a ghost. "It's true, isn't it? Isn't it?"

He nodded agreement to that, but: "I have to go. It's my command, my orders."

"Orders!" She wept then, at his stupidity and hers.

All the time Zacco stood in the background, shifting from one foot to the other, embarrassed.

She pushed away and wiped at her eyes with her hands, calm now. "I have to – go to Captain Devereux."

"And I have to go to the ship."

"Don't worry about me." She kissed him, and he turned away, left her.

He went down to *Hercules* and told Buckley, "Get my glasses from the cabin." Then gave him his orders.

Buckley was puzzled but answered, "Aye, aye, sir."

Smith called for the three MAS captains, and Balestra, Archbold and Menzies, and when they were gathered on the deck of *Hercules* he said, "We attack tonight. But we're sailing very soon." He looked around at them. "Ready?"

They nodded, all watching him uneasily. He appeared to be waiting for something.

Finally Buckley called from up on the superstructure where he stood with the glasses, "Weighed now, sir, an' puttin' to sea."

"Very good. That's all." Smith turned on the officers. "We will sail in thirty minutes, gentlemen. Mr Zacco, I will come with you."

Buckley dropped down the ladder from the wheelhouse and met Fred Archbold, who asked, "What the hell happened to him? D'ye see the look on his face?"

Buckley shook his head worriedly. "I'm goin' with him."

The *Gatecrashers* were clear of the harbour and running slowly northward up the coast in line abreast, *Hercules* making eight knots and the engines of the MAS boats throttled back to a mutter to conform. Smith stood in the after cockpit of Zacco's boat. To port he could just make out the drifter through the mist that patched the sea. Somewhere beyond her was Gallina's boat while to starboard and just in sight was Pagani. Smith balanced to the pitch and roll of the boat with the glasses to his eyes, searching. Buckley stood behind him, eyes on Smith, bewildered and uneasy like the rest of them. On Smith's order small-arms had been issued. He wore a pistol himself and so did Buckley. The Colt machine-guns were manned, Smith had given the orders, curtly, but no explanation, and now stood with face set and haggard, his mouth a thin line. Now he lowered the glasses, wiped spray from the lenses, lifted them again to his eyes. It was as if the boats were playing hide-and-seek in the mist: sometimes he could barely make out the craft on either side but again and again they broke out into a patch of clear water. They did so now and he said flatly, "There she is. Fine on the port bow. Full ahead."

The engine note climbed and the stern sank deeper with the surge of power and bite of the screws. Zacco eased the wheel over and the bow slid around to point at the yacht *Sybil*. She was a quarter-mile ahead and under way, no sails set but leaving a foaming wake from her screw. Even so her auxiliary engine made barely five knots. Buckley thought there was something different about her rigging and identified the wireless aerial strung from her main mast just as muzzle-flashes flamed from her well aft.

Smith shouted harshly, "Open fire!" The machine-gunners looked doubtfully over their shoulders, appealing to Zacco, who hesitated then nodded as a bullet ripped splinters from the fore-deck of the boat and Smith shouted again, "*Open fire damn you!*"

The machine-guns chattered in short bursts. Again. Again. All the time they were closing the yacht, working up to twenty knots or more. The machine-guns hammered away, the bursts longer, and finally the rifle-fire from the yacht ceased.

Smith said, "Lay us alongside." He drew the pistol from its holster and Buckley copied him. The MAS slid in to the yacht, ran alongside, edged in to rub against her and Smith jumped. He landed on his feet in the well but stumbled and fell to hands and knees. Buckley landed cat-like beside him and pulled him to his feet as the MAS sheered away, the machine-gun still trained on the yacht. Smith reached out a hand to the engine control and stopped it. The two Swiss lay in the well with their rifles. Blood spattered the deck and the tiller, the engine-housing. The hull of the yacht was splintered and holed where machine-gun bursts had ripped through the timber. Smith lurched forward and into the cabin. Its former surprising smallness was now explained. The table was now hung up on chains at one side and a door had been opened in the forward bulkhead. The space beyond held a wireless and a wide shelf and a stool bolted to the deck. Helen Blair sat on the stool, slim hand still resting on the morse key. She stared white-faced at Smith as he stood with the pistol dangling in his hand at his side.

He whispered, "For God's sake! *Why?*"

She did not answer him but said, "You're too late. I've sent my message and they've acknowledged it in Trieste. And when we passed the guard-boat I gave them a letter for the Ammiraglio at Naval Headquarters telling him exactly what I was going to do. He will have it soon. So you cannot go on to Trieste because he knows that the Austrians will be waiting for you. It's all out in the open now, and you dare not take the chance." She was very calm but as she took her hand from the morse key he saw her fingers tremble.

He asked again, "Why?"

"Don't look at me like that, David!" She shook her head. "You've no right. I act for the same reasons as yourself: orders. I'm Austrian, and I serve my country. My family lived in England for many years and I was brought up there, went to school, but when the war came we returned to Austria and then to Trieste because my father was given a diplomatic post there. In the summer of 1915 the Italians bombed the port. They killed my father and mother – and Edward. I told you Edward was my fiancé and killed in the Dardanelles. The truth is that he was my brother. He was fourteen years old."

Smith heard the MAS slip in alongside again with a low rumble of engines that then cut out. The yacht heeled gently as the MAS rubbed against her.

The girl said, "I wanted the Italians to pay. There was a major in the army, a friend of my dead father – he was in intelligence and told me how I could help. I had learned Italian on holidays as I told you. I speak it well, but with an accent, so they gave me a British passport. The real Helen Blair lived in Taranto. She was the mistress of an Austrian consular official and she's living with him now in Vienna. Her passport needed some doctoring, a new photograph, but it was good. I burned it this morning after you left."

Smith was conscious of Buckley standing behind him in the well, listening to all this. Buckley would be a witness when . . . He rubbed at his face.

She went on, "My money came from Argentina, from German funds there. The yacht I bought as I told you." She stopped, then: "That's all I can tell you. Except that you were right about revenge. It's meaningless . . . When I saw those poor people walking in the rain with only what they could carry, everything else gone, their homes . . . And you came . . ." She looked up at him. "How did you find out?"

Smith remembered the moment, when he lay close beside her and his dreams became a nightmare. He said savagely, "Out of your own mouth. You'd told me you learned Italian in a few weeks or months. Yet you were with two seamen who spoke German and you said you didn't know a word of it. And that was after *two years*. It didn't make sense. So, suppose you knew German and were hiding it? Why? I started remembering things, looking at them in a different light." Lying cold by her side. "How you saw us set out for Trieste with the *Flying-Fish* and it was as if the Austrians were waiting for us."

Her eyes still held his. "That was my last transmission, David. My men knew, so I had to send it. They would have if I hadn't and at that time you were still an enemy – I thought. But that was the end for me. I didn't sleep that night, thinking about you. After that I was just – going up to the line out of habit."

Smith went on as if he had not listened to her: "And that soldier at Fassolta, I thought he was a stupid oaf prejudiced by the rumours of spies and treachery, but he was right. You spoke German to those prisoners. I should have suspected a long time ago but I didn't. Until this morning." He had been blind and knew the reason.

Perhaps that showed in his face. Helen Blair said softly, "I didn't lie about loving you, David. I didn't use you." She tried to read belief in his face, then sighed. "You can't believe that a woman could love you, really love you, not just for a night."

He stepped back from her and called harshly, "Leading-Seaman Buckley!"

"Sir!"

Smith turned and faced the big man stooped at the door of the cabin. "Guard her!"

"Sir?" Buckley peered past him at the girl, the wireless.

"You've got eyes and ears! You've seen and heard! She's a spy!" Smith thrust him aside and blundered out into the well, stood holding on to the cabin's coaming. The two seamen lay where they had fallen in pools of their own blood, their bodies shifting slackly to the slow roll of the yacht. They were probably Austrians rather than Swiss, with forged or stolen papers, but it hardly mattered now. He saw Pietro Zacco watching him, puzzled and anxious, and turned away. The other two MAS boats lay off a cable's length on either beam. *Hercules* was bustling up astern, men on her deck, Davies at the six-pounder in the bow. Smith threw over his shoulder at Zacco, "Tell *Hercules* and the other boats to come alongside. I want to talk to all captains." They had to be told.

He heard the clicking of the signal-lamp, saw the answering flicker from *Hercules*, watched her come on but with his thoughts still on the woman below. Had the Austrians put her and the 'Swiss' ashore in the south of Italy one dark night? Or sent them by a roundabout route as passengers on a neutral ship, maybe out of Holland? And the yacht – had she and the two men sailed it across to Cattaro or Pola to have the wireless fitted? It was more likely they had picked up the equipment. from a submarine and the two men had done the work while the yacht lay in some quiet cove and the girl sunned herself on deck, an Englishwoman of leisure. It did not matter how it had been done – the Italians would dig it all up now they were on to her. They would interrogate her before . . . but his mind shied away from that.

Hercules slipped in alongside and men climbed down from

her to make fast. Balestra was on her deck with Menzies, both staring incredulously at the shot-riddled hull of the yacht and the dead men in the well. Smith shouted, "Buckley! Bring her aboard *Hercules*!"

"Aye, aye, sir!"

Smith climbed up to Menzies and Balestra and was immediately followed by the three MAS captains. He returned their salutes, looked up at the wheelhouse and saw Fred Archbold there, well within earshot. He turned at Balestra's startled exclamation. Helen had appeared in the well of the yacht, Buckley at her back, his pistol trained on her. For the first time Smith realised she was stylishly dressed as always, the dark hair piled, an expensive dress showing off the slim legs and feet in small shoes. She was playing out her part to the end. He wondered how many men had died because of her devotion to her duty as she saw it. Then he remembered the corpses littering the marshes on the banks of the Cavetta canal, laid there by the gunfire he called down as he himself did his duty.

He lifted his voice so all aboard could hear but it was devoid of expression, the formal laying of a charge. "This woman is an Austrian spy. Her trips up to the line were to gather information. She passed it on by wireless from the yacht as she sailed up or down the coast, probably at night, making only short transmissions so they would be impossible to pinpoint."

The girl was climbing the Jacob's ladder to the drifter. Balestra started forward to help her but Smith snapped, "Leave her!" Balestra glared at him and everybody else scowled or looked sullen.

Smith went on: "She warned them in Trieste we were on our way with *Flying-Fish*. They were waiting for us, remember?" She stood on the deck with no man near her but Buckley, her guard. Smith said, "And today she sent word to Trieste that we attack it tonight."

Zacco swore. Pagani snatched off his cap and hurled it to the deck in frustrated rage. Balestra said bitterly, "Then the attack is cancelled!"

Smith said, "No!" The girl's head turned sharply and she stared at him, lips parted. He said, "I told her we were bound for Trieste. The photographs show *Salzburg* still at Pola. That's where we'll get her." He saw the stricken look on the

212

girl's face and said, "Take her below and lock her away!"

He turned his back on her and walked aft, stared unseeingly out over the stern at the cold grey sea. She had sent a letter to the Italian Admiral, confessing, with the sole objective of stopping the attack and thus saving Smith's life.

But she had warned Trieste also, doing her duty as she saw it. As he did his.

That duty would not let him be. "Signore?" That was Zacco's voice. Smith turned to face him. "We return to Venice, sir?" It was more a statement than question.

"No. If we set course for Pola immediately we'll close it by nightfall. Before then I'll call all captains aboard for final orders."

Zacco cleared his throat. "Will one boat take the prisoner to Venice and then rejoin?"

Zacco was only tactfully reminding Smith of his duty, but it got him hard looks from the others. Smith realised they must all have guessed that he was the girl's lover.

And – the prisoner? He had to think of her as such now, but he still could not bear to send her back, alone and so soon, to Venice and to the firing-squad that awaited her there. "No." Then he gave his excuse: "If one of us returns to Venice we may be ordered to cancel the attack, so we stay clear."

He did not believe it and neither, clearly, did the others. But Zacco said quietly, "That is understood."

The MAS captains returned to their boats, *Hercules* cast off from *Sybil* and eased away from the yacht, took the boats in tow to conserve their fuel and turned on to a course for Pola. Smith stood by the wheelhouse alone and tormented. The yacht was left to drift with the dead men aboard her.

Hercules churned sedately across a grey sea patched with fog, under a grey sky, the MAS towed in a bobbing line astern of her like so many ducklings following their mother. Squalls of rain swept in to rattle on the deck, then were gone.

Balestra and Lombardo worked over *Seahorse* where she lay aft on the deck of *Hercules*, checking her over thoroughly for one last time, practising unclamping the two big charges. Smith paced the deck forward, his face expressionless. The crew of *Hercules* left the weather-side clear for him and kept out of his way. Menzies watched him anxiously from the wheelhouse, Buckley from tasks he found for himself about the deck or with Davies on the six-pounder right in the bow.

Once Davies said, "He looks like he's got a lot on his mind."

Buckley answered shortly, "He has. Tonight's going to be a right bloody caper."

Davies nodded, "Aye. And on top o' that, there's the lass."

Buckley grunted agreement, said bitterly, "I still can't believe it. But I saw the wireless . . . heard her telling him."

"So he's going through it." Davies was silent a moment, then: "He should ha' sent her back. Why didn't he?"

Buckley answered angrily, worry goading him, "I know he should. How the hell do I know why he didn't?" He paused, thinking.

Davies said, "If she got away somehow, they'd murder him."

Buckley spun round, startled, "Don't be bloody daft! How could she get away?" Davies stared at him wooden-faced. Buckley muttered, "No. He never would. She's a spy." He swore in frustrated bewilderment. Then: "You know summat? I still feel the same about her."

Davies said drily, "If she was a spy for *us* you'd think she was a heroine. Nobody knows we've got her but us." He waved a hand at *Hercules* and the three MAS boats.

"Somebody would talk."

"Who?"

Buckley hesitated, then shook his head decisively, "No. He still wouldn't do it."

Smith called a conference of the three MAS captains, Balestra and Lombardo. The captains came aboard and he met them cheerfully. They all looked relieved. He never mentioned Helen Blair but briefed them on the coming operation with the chart, the aerial photographs of Pola and the notes of his own reconnaissance.

"As you see, they've made a hell of a good job of the defences. At the harbour mouth, between the southern mole and the northern mole is an opening sixty yards wide. That is the way in and out." His finger moved down the chart to the centre of the harbour mouth. "At the entrance here and just inside, the photographs show two guard-boats and we saw them when we reconnoitred the booms. The one inside the northern mole is an old torpedo-boat. That inside the southern mole is a tug. Barring the entrance is a boom of timbers and chains, and the tug is there to open a section of that boom like a gate to let ships in and out. She tows it aside and then tows it back into position." He looked around at them. "Clear so far?"

They nodded and Pagani muttered, "Too clear."

Smith went on, "The aerial photos show they didn't stop there. About three hundred yards inside the gate are two further booms, running out from the northern and southern shores and overlapping in the middle. Therefore any vessel entering the harbour has to pass through the gate, steam north to round the first of these booms then south to swing around the second. There are what appear to be two guard-boats inside the northern boom below Cristo Point, and two more at the southern end of the first boom inside the harbour."

His finger stopped in its tracing. Balestra's eyes moved intently from chart to photographs. Smith took a breath, said grimly, "Now the ships. The aerial photographs are fine as you can see. Full marks to your Air Force. They show six battle-ships moored or anchored in a line two thousand yards long and stretching from just inside the second boom to the island of San Andrea. And beyond them, anchored off the arsenal, is *Salzburg*. There's no mistaking her. She is four thousand yards from the gate at the entrance." Voss had moored *Salzburg* deeper inside the harbour. Some instinct warning him?

There was a moment of silence while they all stared at the photographs. Then Zacco blew out a breath in a whistling sigh. "Four kilometres!"

Smith looked at Balestra. This was the man facing the task. Balestra showed only frowning concentration. He said, "Well, to start with –" And he went on to sketch out his plan, simply, boldly.

Smith listened and at the end nodded slow approval, not because he liked the plan but because he could not improve on it. He said, "I think a start time of 10 pm, no earlier." Balestra nodded agreement. Smith went on, "Dawn is at 5.35. And remember you'll have a stiff current against you."

Balestra nodded again, gave a small apologetic smile. "I am not over-confident. Just determined. I believe we can do it."

Smith was not over-confident either. Theoretically, at her maximum speed of four knots *Seahorse* should cover the two miles between the gate and *Salzburg* inside an hour. But not only would the current be against her, but she must also some how work around an intricate succession of obstructions, with Balestra navigating in darkness, aided only be a small compass. There were the guard-boats and God only knew what else they might encounter. Smith said to all of them, "I would have liked to have spent more time on trials. That isn't possible. I'm convinced that now *Salzburg* has moved to Pola the entire Austrian Fleet will soon move to Cattaro to mount operations from there. And once *Salzburg* is inside that harbour our mission becomes impossible."

They muttered agreement; the land-locked harbour of Cattaro would be an impregnable base for *Salzburg*.

Smith went on, "Our orders are to seek out and destroy her. We have to do it now, while we can." He stretched and relaxed, grinned at Balestra and Lombardo. "I've got some details to discuss with the captains but they don't concern your plan. I suggest you get what sleep you can."

So Balestra and Lombardo went away, the thin lieutenant talking eagerly, the chunky *motorista* scowling unco-operatively.

Smith looked at the captains. "You have the explosive charges and men instructed in their use?"

Zacco answered, "Yes, sir. The torpedomen." Then: "You don't think Balestra can do it?"

"He has surprise on his side. But that's all. Nobody has done anything like this before or even dreamed of it. You know what he's up against. What odds do you give him?" They exchanged glances. Smith said, "I give him one chance in a thousand. But because Balestra himself believes he can do it, I'm sending him. Questions?"

Zacco looked as if he was glad the responsibility was Smith's and not his. He checked with the others. "No questions."

"Very well, gentlemen." Smith turned again to the chart and the aerial photographs and they got down to detailed planning.

Night was falling as the captains returned to their boats. Zacco was last to go down the ladder and Smith said, "When you collected the photographs from Headquarters, what was the news of the war?" At that time his thoughts had been full of

Helen Blair: he must not think of her now.

Zacco paused at the head of the ladder. "The line on the Piave holds and there is hope at Headquarters, but most of the talk was about a German *Leutenant* involved in the Austrian attack on the heights of Caporetto. The prisoners taken recently, some of them talked of him. They said on the first day of Caporetto he took prisoner a whole regiment with only a dozen men. Later he captured the height of the Matajur with just one company of mountain troops and when the town of Longarone fell he led the first German troops into it. They say his name is Erwin Rommel."

Smith shook his head. "Never heard of him." He shrugged. "But it is good that the line holds." He watched Zacco's MAS slip into station astern in the dusk. The line had to hold. And his boats had to get *Salzburg*.

17 *The Gatecrashers*

Smith stood in the wheelhouse of *Hercules*, staring out at the night, Menzies on one side of him, Balestra on the other. Guido Balestra wore his one-piece waterproof suit, closed tightly at wrists and ankles, rope-soled shoes on his feet. The suit had an air pouch on chest and back to give extra buoyancy. A line was wound around his waist and his belt held a knife. Fred Archbold had the watch and Ginger Gates was at the wheel.

Smith stepped over to the port side of the wheelhouse to stand by the look-out. From there he could see aft, and the three MAS boats in line astern of *Hercules*.

The look-out reported quietly, "Land off the port bow, sir, 'bout a mile or more."

Smith set the glasses to his eyes. Balestra said, "Brioni Islands?"

Smith lowered the glasses, nodded. "Time?"

Menzies said, "Nine-fifty, sir."

They were on time. Smith ordered, "Stop her."

Balestra left the wheelhouse and Smith turned on Archbold. "She's all yours. Fred. You know your orders?"

They were virtually the same as those given him off Trieste and Archbold repeated them around his cold pipe: "Patrol off the islands. Keep a sharp look-out and steer clear from trouble – run if we have to and come back if we can. If there's no sign of you by first light we return to Venice."

"And no lights. That includes your pipe, Fred."

"Aye, Skipper." Then as Smith turned to leave Archbold added, "Best o' luck, sir."

"Thank you. The same to you." Smith grinned at him and at Menzies, being left aboard the drifter because Smith would not take any unnecessary man in the boats on this operation. "Cheer up, Mid! Mr Archbold'll see you don't get bored."

Menzies raised a smile. "Bet he will, sir. Good luck."

Smith left the wheelhouse and walked aft. *Seahorse* lay there on the deck and now Balestra was with Lombardo, supervising the work of a party hoisting the craft out. They used the

218

drifter's derrick but not the steam winch because they dared not let its clamour betray them. *Seahorse* was hoisted out by man-power, lowered gently down to the sea. Zacco's boat was already alongside *Hercules* where she lay stopped while the other boats lay off. Balestra and Lombardo went down into Zacco's boat, cast off the strops from *Seahorse* and attached the towing-line from the MAS. Buckley went down and Smith followed him. He glanced just once towards *Hercules'* forward companion leading to the cabin where Helen Blair was held prisoner, then he stepped down into the crowded cockpit.

Besides Zacco at the wheel there were now Balestra, Lombardo, Buckley and Smith in the cockpit. They shuffled a moment or two, sorting themselves out, finding room. Then the electric motors hummed and the boat stole away from the drifter, the other two falling into line astern. Smith saw beyond them *Hercules* getting under way, heard faintly the soft *thump-thump!* of her engines. Archbold had a nerve-racking night ahead of him. His orders were simple but not easy. "Steer clear of trouble . . . run away." Any patrolling Austrian boat that saw her would out-pace and out-gun her. Smith knew that and so did Archbold.

Smith faced forward. The boat pitched and rolled gently, the motors hummed. *Seahorse* slipped along obediently at the end of the tow, the long, slender length of her awash, like a following shark. Smith hoped no one else would make a comparison. It was an old superstition that a following shark meant a death soon. Mere superstition – but they could do without that kind of ill omen.

Zacco said, "We're on station."

Smith answered, "Very good."

The motors stopped and the other two boats crept up to lie one on either beam, only yards away. Smith could see the lift of the land and a faint, thin sprinkling of lights. They were little more than half a mile from the entrance to the harbour of Pola.

Lombardo was dressed like Balestra in a one-piece waterproof suit. The air pouches on chest and back made huge his stocky, barrel-chested figure. He bent over to haul *Seahorse* alongside and Buckley went down on his knees in the cockpit and leant over the side to hold her there.

Smith thought that war was often dignified by calling it a

science. It wasn't. It was a haphazard, bloody business when only too often men were forced into taking huge risks for the sake of some imperfectly-perceived advantage. He shook Lombardo's hand, then Balestra's. Lombardo lowered himself over the side into the sea and took hold of *Seahorse* forward. Guido Balestra's thin face was smiling, his eyes bright. He said softly, "Do I get a last request?"

Smith said awkwardly, "Don't be damn silly."

Balestra was deadly serious, despite the smile. "I'll succeed or die."

Smith saw he meant it and asked, "What do you want?"

"The Contessa. Ask for her word that she will keep silent, and neutral, for the rest of the war. Then give her a boat."

Balestra wanted nothing for himself. Smith stared at him, then shook his head. "I can't do that."

Balestra sighed. "That's what I thought. May God help you, sir."

He slipped over the side into the sea and took hold of *Seahorse* at her after end where the engine controls were positioned. He started the engine. It throbbed faintly, the screw turned and *Seahorse* moved away into the night, only her black back and the heads of the men showing. There was left just the thin line of phosphoresence of her wake, then that too was gone.

Zacco said quietly, "Now we wait."

Balestra trailed his body in the water, his right arm resting on the back of *Seahorse*. He could feel as well as hear the slow throb of the compressed air engine and the steady beat of the screw. Lombardo's head showed as a black football forward and on the other side of the narrow, fifteen-foot length of *Seahorse*. Rain was falling now, a slow pattering of drops to begin with and then a downpour that struck hissing into the sea around them. The sea was bitterly cold, and their eyes were so close to its surface they could see nothing ahead of them, only the wrinkling of the waves and darkness. So they plugged on and Balestra began to wonder if Zacco's navigation had been at fault and he had dropped them too far from the harbour mouth.

Then he heard Lombardo calling softly, "Something right ahead! Rocks or a boom!" A moment, then: "A boom!"

Balestra stopped the engine. *Seahorse* slid on a few feet,

slowing, then bumped gently, stopped. Balestra could see the obstruction now and paddled forward along the length of *Seahorse* until he was at the round nose of her and opposite Lombardo. The boom was made of huge metal cylinders, each ten feet long and linked by thick steel hawsers. That he had expected. But which boom was this – the one outside the southern mole or that spanning the gap between the northern mole and Cristo Point? He had to find out: they had to know where they were starting from or they would blunder about in the darkness all night. He took a chance. "We'll go north."

They edged northwards along the boom, not using the engine because a guard-boat might be only yards away from them, the watch standing ready at a searchlight. So they moved slowly, eyes blinking against the wash of rain, striving to pierce the darkness. A light showed behind them. Balestra turned his head and saw a searchlight's beam sweeping the sea. It was on Cape Compare and far to the south.

He gasped, "Too far north! Turn around!"

Paddling with their feet and one free hand they hauled *Seahorse* around and started back the way they had come. More dragging minutes passed and then a rectangular black shape slowly formed out of the darkness. It had to be the northern mole because there was no boom outside it, and that which they followed ended at the mole, was secured there. That was better, Balestra told himself. Now they knew where they were, but – he peered at his watch. They were already behind time.

So they rested beside the mole for only a minute, feeling safe in the blackness at the foot of the concrete cliff which towered above them. Even if there was a sentry up there he wouldn't hear them.

They moved on along the mole for two hundred yards and came to the southern end of it. Here was the entrance to the harbour, a gap sixty yards between this northern mole and that further south. Inside but still unseen was the gate, one section of which could be swung aside to let ships enter or leave, then closed again. They must pass through the gate. They pushed past the end of the mole, started to turn *Seahorse* into the current running out of the harbour mouth. Both of them swam desperately, trying in vain to shove *Seahorse* forward towards the gate. The current was carrying them relentlessly out to sea.

Balestra gasped, "Hang on! I'm starting the engine!"

Lombardo's face turned towards him. "What if there's a sentry?"

But Balestra remembered Smith had not seen sentries near the gate on his reconnaissance. Besides – "We've got to take a chance or we'll never get in."

He eased over the lever and the engine throbbed, the screw turned slowly then faster. Paddling with their feet they pointed the head of *Seahorse* at the gap between the north and south moles and now they were closing. They were passing between the moles, making slow headway against the current. Balestra heard the hiss from Lombardo, saw his finger point, looked where it pointed and saw the two guard-boats, the twin funnels of the old torpedo-boat where she lay inside the northern mole and the stubby outline of the tug lying inside the southern. Both ships showed drifts of smoke from their funnels. The tug was much the closer of the two but he could see no one on her deck. Probably whoever was on watch had taken shelter from the rain in her wheelhouse; there was a light in there. The torpedo-boat was too far away to see *Seahorse*.

He turned his head forward only just in time. Lombardo's hand flapped. "Stop!" The whisper came back to Balestra but he was already cutting the engine. A moment later *Seahorse* bumped against the gate and Lombardo grabbed hold, held her there.

The gate was a double line of long floating timbers linked by chains, with other beams connecting the lines at regular intervals. From these connecting beams projected steel spikes each three feet long, their points turned seaward. Balestra wiped at his face, caught his breath and thought that *Flying-Fish* would never have crawled over this, would have stuck on the spikes. Who had thought of them? Voss? But *Seahorse* was another matter, only fourteen inches wide and there was room and plenty for her to pass between the connecting beams with their spikes. He paddled forward again until he was opposite Lombardo at the nose and they worked *Seahorse* along the gate until they reached a submerged connecting chain then hauled *Seahorse* over it an inch at a time. Keeping very close to her they pushed her on between the spiked timbers to the second line, shoved her again over the chain then held on to her with one hand, to a timber with the other. They had passed through the gate.

They rested there again; they had to. The continual exertion had to some extent countered the bitter cold, but it had exhausted them. Balestra looked at his watch and swore softly with frustration. He whispered to Lombardo, "That current lost us more time, far too much time. We're a long way behind schedule. Are you ready?" Balestra himself was not, would have rested longer, but *Salzburg* lay far up the harbour. They had to move.

"Ready when you are, Tenente." Lombardo's voice came easily. If he was weary or nervous he did not show it.

Balestra thought, 'Thank God for Angelo Lombardo!' Aloud he said, "Good man."

They started the motor and headed slowly into the harbour. The rain had stopped now and Balestra could see the land to the north and pick out the bay of Val Maggiore but it was impossible to judge distance. They had only been moving a minute or two when he found his compass had filled with water and was useless. Somewhere ahead of them were two more booms, one overlapping the other, the gap between them somewhere to the north. He thought the set of the current would still be towards the gate but at the same time it could be edging them sideways. Were they making headway against it? He could not tell. But it was a long time before Lombardo near the nose held up his hand again.

Balestra stopped the engine. Lombardo was holding on to another boom formed of three lines of buoys all joined together by steel nets hanging down below the surface with only the top strands of them visible. With time it might be possible to climb over them, but they did not have time and the nets could be wired to an alarm system and even mined. He said, "We'll move north."

He started the engine again and they worked *Seahorse* northwards along the line of the boom. The current thrust them continually away from the boom so they were continually shoving and hauling *Seahorse* back on course. Balestra could see the loom of Cristo Point to the north. He knew there were two guard-boats there but could not see them. They laboured on, came at last to the end of the boom, rounded the big buoys there and headed once more into the darkness of the harbour.

223

Only to run into another, similar boom of nets. This one, according to the aerial photographs, overlapped that just left behind so this time they worked south, struggling wearily with *Seahorse*, mouths gaping wide as they gasped for breath and spat out seawater. Balestra wanted to rest, knew they should, that they were both on the point of collapse, but they were already very late. Another delay might mean –

The rest was forced on them. A spark of light came close ahead. Balestra stopped the engine and they each hung on to *Seahorse* with one hand, gripping the boom with the other. Now they could see the ship. They would have seen her before but for their preoccupation with wrestling with *Seahorse* and the current. She was an old sailing ship, moored to a buoy at the end of the boom; a guard-boat. The spark of light had been a match. They saw the man who had struck it, leaning on the rail of the ship, saw the glow of the cigarette as he drew on it.

They hung there, breathing shallowly through open mouths. Balestra thought the ship and the man were only twenty or thirty yards away. It was incredible that he had not seen them: he must have just come up from below and his eyes were not fully adjusted to the darkness.

If they moved now he would see them and give the alarm. They stayed still as death.

He too stayed, lit another cigarette from the stub of the first. Balestra heard Lombardo groan softly; himself he would have killed the man if he could. To have come so far only to be stopped by one man, one piece of ill luck ...

Pietro Zacco, scowling with worry, looked again at his watch. "It is late."

Smith nodded. The operation was far behind schedule: the night had dragged by and soon the day would be on them. He had waited as long as he dared but now he faced the unavoidable truth. Balestra was dead. He remembered the lieutenant's determination aboard the *Flying-Fish* at the assault on Trieste; he would succeed or die. Voss had learned from that attempt and Smith was certain he was responsible for the network of booms defending Pola, and that Balestra and Lombardo had been caught on one of them. Both men were dead, drowned somewhere out there in the bitter darkness.

He told himself again, for the hundredth time, that he should not have sent them; the whole idea was too wild, impossible of achievement. There had to be another way to get at *Salzburg* but so far he had failed to find it and his failure would mean disaster in the Adriatic.

"Sir?"

Smith realised Zacco had spoken to him and lost in his brooding he had not heard. "What did you say?"

"The torpedomen are ready with the charges, sir."

Now he had only the MAS boats. He looked across at the other two where they drifted close abeam, lying a mile or so out from the harbour entrance. He had moved his tiny force there to wait for some sign that Balestra's mission had been successful. They had all run their electric motors for brief periods during the long hours of the night to keep station but now they were silent, still waiting. They looked very small, fragile, lying low in the sea. He said, "No." He would not order these men into a hopeless attack, to certain death. They deserved a fighting chance.

Zacco hesitated, then: "Sir, we are ready. You said we must not delay because *Salzburg* might escape. This could be our last chance —"

There came a low call from the seaman in the bow and Zacco turned to peer forward, said quickly, "Ship coming out!"

Smith saw her, growing out of the darkness, steaming slowly, quietly. A destroyer – no, she was an old twin-funnelled torpedo-boat like the one they had met outside Trieste. This would be the guard-boat that had been lying outside the entrance gate, just inside the mole. Should he fight her? No. The MAS boats' torpedoes were not swung out and they would be out-gunned. Starting the engines would give them away and there was a chance, just a chance, that she might not see them. The boats lay low and black, still on the sea and no movement aboard them except for the slowly training barrels of the machine-guns as they followed the torpedo-boat. But she was going to pass close . . .

A light winked aboard her and Smith heard the catch of Zacco's breath. Smith whispered, "*Still!*" If the Austrian was signalling them he might have taken the MAS for fishing-boats and be planning to steam on. Zacco was muttering softly as he read the stuttering flashes. They came from a very small lamp, possibly a shielded torch, and Smith wondered why they used –

Zacco said, "Amico." The light had stopped and so had the torpedo-boat, she now lay as still as the three MAS boats. He went on, puzzled and suspicious, "She sent just that: 'Amico' – friend."

Not a challenge. Just the one word, in Italian: friend. Smith stared across the sea at the ship. A trap? But why? If she wanted to sink them she could have cracked on speed and blown the MAS out of the water. He could see her guns trained fore and aft, no threat to the boats, and then remembered something Zacco had told him back in Venice – He ordered, "Close her." But added quietly to Gallina and Pagani, "You two wait." There was no sense in leading all three boats into what was possibly a trap, though now he doubted it.

The motors hummed and Zacco's MAS slid in towards the torpedo-boat until Smith could see a group of men on her deck forward of her bridge, their hands held high. Zacco took the boat sidling in alongside and stopped her at Smith's order so she lay six feet away from the men lining the rail. One of them called nervously across the gap, voice high and quick, breathless.

Zacco burst out incredulously, "He wants to surrender!"

Smith asked, "Who is he?" He listened, put questions to Zacco as the lieutenant drew the story from the man. He was a petty officer. He said most of the crew were Slavs, sick of fighting for an Austrian Empire they held scanty allegiance to – Zacco had mentioned this unrest in the Austrian navy and so had Devereux in his first meeting with Smith. When the Slavs had learned that the fleet was to sail for Cattaro and a more active role in the war, it had been the last straw.

"*What?*" Smith broke in there. "He's certain? When?"

Zacco put the questions, said, "They had orders. The fleet sails at first light."

"Go on." So the rumours had been correct. Smith listened, mind racing, as Zacco got out of the PO the rest of his story. The crew had mutinied, locked their officers below and were now bound for Italy to surrender the ship. Despite the darkness they had recognised the cigar shapes of the MAS boats, all too familiar to them. Zacco winked at Smith. "He says some friends were badly shot-up off Trieste by a madman in a MAS a week or

226

so ago." And: "He asks if you'll take the ship to Italy?"

Smith shook his head. "Tell him to make his own way, fly plenty of white flags when it's light and steer south-west." That last to take the Austrian well clear of *Hercules*.

Zacco interpreted and the PO, hands lowered now, lifted one again but this time in acceptance. Zacco said, "He's agreed but he says we should get away, that soon the fleet will sail. In less than half an hour there will be many destroyers."

Smith nodded; he would bet on it. "Haul clear."

The group aboard the torpedo-boat broke up, chattering among themselves. The MAS slid back to the others and Smith watched the torpedo-boat get under way and turn onto a course of south-west. He turned back to look across at the other boats and heard Zacco giving a rapid explanation to Gallina and Pagani. They were watching Smith. The fleet was coming out. There was no radio either on the MAS boats or out on *Hercules* to call for support, and no time anyway for Pickett's cruisers and the Italian fleet to cross the Adriatic and intercept before the Austrians reached Cattaro. The screening destroyers would be first out and would sweep the MAS boats from the sea. The three captains knew all this. There seemed nothing they could do but run with their tails between their legs. Gallina growled angrily and Pagani swore.

Then Smith gave his orders, heard the low mutter of excitement and finished, "Keep those charges ready. Half ahead on the motors." Now suddenly they had a fighting chance.

The motors hummed and the screws turned slowly, silently, as they approached Pola. Smith used his glasses and picked out the long line of white phosphorescence where the sea broke against the southern mole, the shorter line against the northern mole. Between them was a black gap, the entrance to the harbour. He quietly ordered, "Port five." The stem of the boat edged around to point at the gap. They closed it slowly, then more slowly still, even though the electric motors were set full ahead, as they stemmed the current running out of the harbour. Smith's eyes lifted from the moles to the far-off mountains behind Pola and saw the first pale edging of light there.

The moles loomed above them and now they saw lights inside barely a cable's length ahead. The lights were moving aboard the stumpy outline of a tug, smoke streaming black from her funnel. Her bow pointed at the gap as if headed out to sea and water foamed at her stern, churned up by her screws, but she was hardly moving.

Zacco hissed, "*She's opening the gate!*"

As Smith had told them when he gave his orders: "They'll open the gate for the fleet – and for us!" The tug was towing one end of a section of the boom a hundred yards long, pivoting it on its other end, anchored to the sea-bed. It was moving, though painfully slowly, like a door opening towards them. He saw the boarding party crouched ready on the foredeck of the MAS. All the time they were sliding quietly down on the tug. Her foredeck was deserted but figures were moving in the stern of her. They were men using the torches, the lights Smith had seen, watching the tow. They were close on the tug now and surely the boats must be seen. Buckley shoved a pistol into Smith's hand. At that moment there was a muffled shout aboard the tug. From the skipper in her wheelhouse? But the MAS bumped against the tug's port side and two Italian seamen leaped quietly up onto her deck with lines and held the boat alongside as the motors cut out.

Smith, Buckley and Azzara, the after machine-gunner, scrambled aboard the tug together. Smith ran on his toes for the ladder to the wheelhouse, took it in leaping strides and pushed in at the door. There were two men inside, blue-jerseyed, one at the wheel and the other fumbling at a rifle standing with others in a rack. He stopped as Smith's pistol menaced him, stood gaping. Buckley crowded in behind Smith, who reached for the handles of the engine-room telegraph and rang them to 'Stop engines'. The thunderous beat of the twin screws ceased.

Azzara appeared and Smith told him softly, "Watch them!" He pointed at the men and Azzara lifted his rifle to cover them. Smith shoved out of the wheelhouse, closely followed by Buckley, dropped down the ladder to the deck and ran aft. A group of men, the tug's deck crew, huddled together in the stern with the forward machine-gun of the MAS trained on them. Smith smelt the engine-room smell of coal and oil on a further party of men as they were hustled to join the others by a man from Gallina's boat. The men hurrying about the deck were all Italians and Smith saw Gallina's boat secured now to the starboard side of the tug. Zacco's torpedoman Udina was there and so was Gallina's, both of them carrying the explosive charges that had been intended to blast a way through the booms. He told them, "Below!" He pointed down at the deck then lifted his hands, spread the fingers. "Cinque minuti!"

"Si." They nodded and padded away.

He turned on the tug's crew and pointed at the boat slung aft on the starboard side. "Go!" They stared at him, nervous and bewildered by the sudden attack out of the night, eyes sliding to the machine-gun. Then Zacco hissed at them and they understood. They set to work hauling out the boat and Smith told Buckley, "Fetch those other two up in the wheelhouse."

"Aye, aye, sir!" And: "Engine-room's cleared now, sir."

Smith looked at his watch and then around him. Five minutes. Pagani's boat lay off to starboard of Zacco's. Beyond it he could see the gap in the boom opened by the tug, only a few yards across, but widening slowly as the current took them towards the harbour mouth. They had in tow a hundred yard length of the boom and the huge deadweight of it acted like a sea anchor.

He went to the rail and told Zacco. "Pagani is to go in!" Zacco called softly across the narrow neck of water to Pagani and a moment later his boat edged forward and slipped through the gap into the harbour. Smith crossed to the other side and Buckley came aft, herding before him the two men from the wheelhouse. Smith gripped the skipper's arm and waved his pistol at the crew now lowering the boat to smack into the sea. "All? Alles?"

The skipper looked them over and Smith saw his lips moving as he counted. Then he nodded; "Ja!"

Smith pushed him towards his men, already climbing down into the boat. "Auf wiedersehen!"

He turned to see the two torpedomen, now empty-handed. Udina held up one hand with the fingers spread, but then folded down the thumb. "Quattro!" Four minutes.

Smith smiled at them. "Buono!" He leaned over the rail and saw the tug's boat pulling away from her side with her crew aboard, the skipper in the sternsheets. Gallina's face, square, calm, looked up at him from the after cockpit of the MAS. Smith said, "Into the harbour." He sketched in the air the

229

course Gallina should take around the tug and through the gate.

The MAS skipper nodded: "Si, signore!" His boat cast off, went astern then turned, moved ahead, slid across the bow of the tug and turned again towards the open gate.

Buckley said, "All gone. Just us left, sir. I reckon no more'n three minutes."

They climbed down into the cockpit of Zacco's boat, bow and stern cast off and the boat moved ahead, still running on the electric motors. Smith said, "Start the main engines! Half ahead!" There was no point in further stealth: the charges had only two minutes to detonation. As if to emphasise his order a searchlight's beam poked out from the northern shore, fingered along the mole then shifted jerkily across the harbour mouth and the gate, came on the tug and halted there some seconds. The engines of the MAS fired and it surged forward under their power as the searchlight's beam shifted on from the tug and traversed the gap in the gate they had just left.

"Port ten! Steady!" The boat turned to run northward round the end of the next boom, about two hundred yards inside the gate. They passed Pagani and then Gallina, their boats lying with idling engines, waiting for Zacco to take the lead. As he passed they swung into line astern.

There was a muffled *thump!* from the port quarter, then another. Smith spun round and made out the tug against the lighter darkness of the gap between the moles, saw her lie over in the water, settling. With two holes blasted in her bottom she would sink in minutes. The gate was wedged open just enough. There was room for an MAS boat to pass but nothing larger.

They were through. The wolves were loose in the fold.

Balestra watched as the seaman aboard the old sailing ship straightened and took one last drag at his cigarette. The glow lit his face, the nose and eyes, the fringing beard, then he flicked the stub over the side into the sea and walked away aft.

At last they could move. Not daring to use the engine, they shoved away from the boom. The cold had got into their bones as they waited and now they had to fight not only the current but stiffness and lassitude, a numbness they knew was a creeping death. They fought it and swam around the sailing ship, pushing *Seahorse* between them. It took them long minutes. As they rounded her stern they saw a rowing-boat lying there, tugging gently at the line that secured it against the pull of the current. Then Lombardo pointed and Balestra saw a ship ahead of them and little more than a cable's length away. She was bows-on to them, big: a dreadnought battleship, smoke streaming from her funnels. A boat was rowing out from her towards the buoy to which she was moored. Balestra looked beyond her. The sky was paling above the mountains that ringed the bay and against that first distant light he could see smoke rising all the way up the harbour from the ships lying there but still hidden by the night.

He remembered what Smith had told him, that he believed the fleet would soon sail to Cattaro.

The fleet had steam up now and the ship ahead of them looked to be preparing to slip and get under way. He had to make a decision and quickly. It was a bitter decision but he faced it. They could not reach *Salzburg* where she lay far up the harbour before it was broad day and in the light they could not escape detection. And if the fleet were putting to sea then his task would be hopeless. *Seahorse* with her speed of four knots could not get near a ship under way, let alone lie alongside her and attach the limpet mines.

He said, "I'm starting the engine. We'll take this one."

Lombardo nodded and Balestra reached out over the back of *Seahorse*. Lombardo gripped his outstretched hand, grinned and released it.

The engine throbbed softly and *Seahorse* moved forward. They guided her, circling, away from the boat that was heading towards the buoy, then turned and made for the ship's starboard side. Now they saw she was moored fore and aft, there was another shadow of a boat astern of her, hooking on to the buoy there. As they crept in the black bulk of her grew and Lombardo could see men moving about her deck, the anchor party on the foc's'le, figures high on the bridge of her. Then *Seahorse* was right under the black wall of her side, Balestra stopped the engine and *Seahorse* bumped gently against her target.

Together they unclamped the two charges. Each weighed 170 kilograms but because of air compartments they had buoyancy and were easy enough to handle in the water. They set the charges against the hull, working with stiff, fumbling fingers. There was no time to swim below the ship and plant them on her bottom. They felt the magnetic 'leeches' bite on the steel and Balestra set the time fuses. Ten minutes. They edged *Seahorse* away and saw the charges sink slowly to hang at the ends of their lines – 340 kilograms of TNT.

Ten minutes, and the seconds already ticking away.

There was movement all over the mooring, shouted commands, engines rumbling, the clash of steel hawsers. Balestra started the engine and they guided *Seahorse* away from the ship's side. His original plan had been to head for the shore once the mission was accomplished and then try to escape across country. But the shore was half a mile away and across the current; they would not reach it before daylight. Nor could they reach the open sea. He turned *Seahorse* back the way they had come.

As the old sailing ship lifted out of the night again, a squat minesweeper steamed past the battleship they had just left and turned to follow the channel through the booms. She was followed by six more in quick succession and then by a destroyer that was the leader of a flotilla in line ahead.

At that instant a searchlight beam swept out from the northern shore and along the mole, halted there. The rowing-boat bobbing at the stern of the sailing ship was close. Balestra stopped the engine of *Seahorse*, ran a caressing hand along her back, then opened the valve underneath her. Lombardo patted her. They swam away towards the boat, leaving *Seahorse* sinking as the sea flooded in through the open valve.

They climbed in clumsily over the stern of the boat and Lombardo used his knife to cut her mooring. The boat drifted away from the ship and as they got out the oars there came the *thump-thump* of double muffled explosions. Balestra muttered, "Not ours. What the hell ... that was towards the gate!"

Lombardo growled. "How long now before they blow?"

Balestra chewed his lip. "Too long already." They bent and pulled at the oars with what strength they had left, weak, splashing strokes, and stared back at the dreadnought bulking black against the faint dawn light under her funnel smoke.

Lombardo ground out, "Those Goddam' charges –"

The flash seared their eyes and the blast shoved at them. The explosion was a thunderclap.

Smith turned away from the sinking tug and the wandering beam of the searchlight, and faced forward. Suddenly a flash lit the sky. Then the deep roar of the explosion came rolling out at them from somewhere ahead in the harbour.

Zacco shouted, "Balestra!"

Smith nodded. Zacco was laughing and Smith grinned at him. It was incredible, but – "He's done it! Not *Salzburg*, though – I think that was too close."

Zacco nodded reluctant agreement. That flash and explosion were a bare half-mile away and *Salzburg* lay far up the harbour, a mile or more further inside.

They were steering due north and working up speed, the spray beginning to fly from the bow. Their eyes were still blinded by the flash so that when the other ships appeared they were already close off the starboard bow. They were mine-sweepers, a line of them, and headed for the gate.

The three MAS boats swept safely by them and on. Smith's eyes were regaining their night vision and he used his glasses. Fine on the port bow was the hump of Cristo Point and off the starboard bow the deep indentation of the bay of Val Maggiore. Smith shouted above the engine's rumble, "Boom should be to starboard! Look out for it!"

But Buckley yelled, "Ship! Starboard bow!"

Smith's head jerked round. She was a quarter-mile away and looked like a destroyer, her head coming round to point at the MAS even while he watched.

Another destroyer astern of her was still headed north. The tug had started to open the gate to let these ships out, the mine-sweepers going ahead of them to sweep up any mines laid in the night. The leading destroyer was turning around the northern end of the first boom, the other still coming up the channel between the first and second booms. "Full ahead!" No need now to feel his way into harbour, watching out for the booms. The destroyers were showing him the way.

The rumble of the engines became a roar and the stern dug in deeper, the spray flew higher from the bow. Now destroyer and MAS were on a course to meet head-on, the gap of sea between

233

them shrinking with every second. The destroyer's bow lifted above them but Zacco's touch on the wheel sent the MAS tearing down past the destroyer's starboard side, leaping and bucking as they rode her bow wave. Smith snatched a glance astern and saw the other two boats, Gallina's close astern and Pagani's close on him. He turned forward. They were past the destroyer and bouncing through her wake, her smoke rolling down and around them. There was the second coming up and astern of her a third, a fourth – a flotilla in a long line and coming up the channel between the first and second booms. Smith pointed and Zacco was expecting it and turned the MAS to starboard to run down that channel and past the flotilla.

Smith shouted at Buckley, "Look out for a boom to port!"

"– Sir!"

A fire was blazing inside the harbour but Smith had no time for that. The three boats went racing down the starboard side of the flotilla, close enough for them to see men on the decks of the destroyers, the pale smudges of their faces. Too close to be fired on by the destroyers' main armaments, below their lowest angle of depression, but machine-guns were flaming above them and tracer sliding in flat arcs through the night. None came near them. Ship after ship lifted up at them, lurched by as they bucketed past on the churned and turbulent sea, and was left astern. Zacco twisted the wheel and the MAS swerved to starboard then straightened. They shot past a boat, two men at the oars, black shapes in the darkness. Buckley, startled, burst out incredulously, "What the hell are they doin' here? Fishing?"

Smith shook his head, dismissing them, and stared into the darkness over the bow. One more destroyer ahead and fine on the starboard bow but leaping up at them, the MAS boats running at their full speed of twenty-five knots now. Off to port was another vessel, masts and spars standing out against the glare of the fire beyond.

Buckley shouted, "Ship! Port bow! – An' I think I see the boom out there, sir!"

So did Smith and that was an old sailing ship anchored on guard at the end of it. The gap between her and the destroyer was barely fifty yards. The boats tore through it and Smith shouted, "Hard aport! ... Meet her! ... Steer that!"

They were through, the last of the booms left astern and the harbour open before them for all its long length. Wolves might be loose in the fold, but the sheep were very big, very dangerous. There was one ahead of them now. Smith and Zacco shouted together: "Balestra!" No doubt this was his work. The ship was a dreadnought battleship, a monster of twenty thousand tons of armour plate and huge 14-inch guns, lying steeply over on her starboard side, wreathed in smoke. A fire burned amidships, lighting her up, and there was an irregular thumping as ammunition exploded aboard her. There were boats in the water, clustered around her side, but she could lower no more because she lay too far over. Men were sliding down her side and leaping into the sea, tiny figures that became a scattering of black dots on the surface of the water under the yellow light of the flames. Balestra had more than proved his point – two brave men and one tiny craft had accomplished all this.

They were leaving the dreadnought behind but another was anchored astern of her. Smoke poured from the funnels of this one also. Smith, straining his eyes against the darkness, made out a third ship further ahead of him and she too had steam up.

The mutineers' information had been correct. The entire fleet was preparing to put to sea. He had been justified in not delaying. If he had waited just one more day his chance would have been gone forever.

He saw the white faces of the torpedoman and his assistant in the forward cockpit. He shouted, "Torpedoes!" Zacco's bass bellow translated the order. Udina and the seaman climbed out of the forward cockpit onto the deck between the two torpedoes where they lay in their clamps. The men stood wide-legged, bracing themselves against the pitching of the boat and hauled on the tackles. The starboard torpedo lifted from the deck, swung over and lowered to hang in its three pincer-like clamps outside the hull and above the foaming sea. Seconds later the port torpedo had been swung out. Smith peered astern, saw through the spray that Gallina and Pagani had copied the evolution and their torpedoes were out and ready.

The line of battleships at anchor or moored stretched for a mile, deep into the harbour. The MAS boats passed them one by one, six of them, each first appearing as a vague black mass that then sharpened rapidly and grew into a floating fortress, with big guns, its towering superstructure crowned by the control-top. The boats were coming under fire now from the secondary armament of the dreadnoughts, five-inch guns or smaller, long tongues of flame seeming to lick out right overhead, but they were passing too close and too fast. The shells burst over or astern.

The sixth and last battleship slid up and past like a great black shadow. Smith picked up the signal-lamp. The harbour before him was bounded by the circling mountains and the light behind them was growing. Already there was a greyness to the night. Off the starboard bow stood Fort Max on its hill. To port lay the island of San Andrea while fine on the port bow and a mile away was the dockyard.

If the reconnaissance photographs were correct, he knew they must be close to *Salzburg*. His head turned, searching for her, his hand gripping the signal-lamp. Buckley shouted, "Forty on the starboard bow!"

Smith stared, picked out the ship, big and vague in the last of the night half a mile away. He pointed her out to Zacco then turned and blinked the lamp once at the boats astern, the signal for a turn to starboard. He saw the answering lights wink from them and shouted at Zacco, "Now!" He blinked the light again, the executive signal, as Zacco spun the wheel and the three boats skidded around as one and headed for the ship.

The range closed rapidly as they went into the torpedo attack at full speed. Smith glanced across and made out the solid, square figure of Gallina rock steady at the wheel of his boat. Beyond him was Pagani but hidden by the spray hurled up by Gallina's boat. Smith faced forward again. Gallina gave a man confidence. He'd follow you to hell and bring you back. He stared at the ship, saw the wink of flame on her, a pinpoint that became a rash along her hull. Seconds later the shells shrieked overhead or burst far ahead of them hurling up a tower of water. Smith stared at the ship, eyes narrowed against the bursting spray, she was a big cruiser, but – "*It's not her!*" And: "Hard aport!"

He blinked the signal-lamp twice at the other boats, the signal to turn to port, blinked it again then screwed his eyes shut as a shell burst on Gallina's boat. He opened them as the MAS heeled under his feet in the tight turn but he was blinded for some seconds and when his night sight returned they were tearing on through the darkness, deeper into the harbour and it was Pagani's boat that followed in their wake.

He shouted at Pietro Zacco, "Gallina?"

The lieutenant shook his head, "All gone!"

Buckley said, "When I looked round there was just bits of her falling into the sea."

This was where the aerial photographs had shown *Salzburg* to be lying but she was gone now, as if spirited away.

The girl still lay on the bunk in the tiny cabin of *Hercules* as she had passed the night, wide-eyed and listening, afraid. She thought that this had been his cabin when he had slept aboard. Now it was her cell, a lock on the door and a sentry outside it. She had no lamp, had refused it, and so they'd agreed not to screw the deadlight down over the scuttle. She wanted to see the night outside.

The flicker of gunfire jerked her from the bunk to stand peering out of the scuttle. She could not hear the guns because of the steady beat of the drifter's engines but she could see the distant flashes.

He would be out there, in the midst of them.

She hammered on the door and the sentry shouted for Menzies. He told her unhappily, "No news, I'm afraid. Still, no news is —"

She asked, "Are they late?"

"Well, they can't run these things like a train timetable, you know." He was trying to cheer her but she turned from him and he said awkwardly, "As soon as I have any news – I'll do anything I can ..."

"Thank you."

Menzies climbed to the wheelhouse. Gunfire lit the horizon and he heard the distant rumble of it as he ran up the ladder. In the wheelhouse he said, "She wanted news."

Fred Archbold muttered, "Who doesn't?" Then he added, "I think we ought to give her a breath of fresh air when it gets light."

"She's worried." Menzies stared at Archbold. "Not about herself, though she should be." He did not want to think about what lay ahead for the girl locked below. He looked towards the lightening on the horizon. "Something's gone wrong. They're under fire." He and Archbold had their orders, to patrol and wait for the return of the boats but to leave at first light, without them if necessary. Tamely wait for dawn and then run for home? The boats were in trouble but what could *Hercules* do? She was not a fighting ship, could do nothing against the fleet in Pola or its defences. And the orders were given by Smith, who was not a man to be disobeyed.

But they had to do something. Menzies turned on Archbold but Fred, cold pipe clamped between his teeth, forestalled him. "I know what you're thinking, Mister," he said.

18 *Salzburg*

The sky was growing lighter and Smith could make out the loom of the shore to starboard. His head turned, seeking *Salzburg*. She had to be here, *had* to be! Gallina, the solid and dependable, was gone and all his crew. Now there were only the two boats. Seek out and destroy ...

Where was *Salzburg*?

Off the starboard bow appeared what looked like a tender, low in the water and butting slowly in towards the inner harbour, on a parallel course but the MAS was rapidly overtaking her. She was a quarter mile to starboard, they were passing her –

Smith shouted, "*Salzburg! Starboard bow!*" He pointed. There was no mistaking her this time. For some reason Voss had shifted her even deeper inside the harbour. Had he suspected an attack? More likely she had gone into the dockyard for some minor repair. But the move had almost saved her and now she was under way and heading for the sea, going to pass close to and inshore of the tender. Smith's head turned and he flashed the lamp once at Pagani in the boat astern, shouted at Zacco, "*Now!*"

He blinked the lamp again and the boats heeled over together then straightened to race side by side, thirty yards between them, their lifted bows trained on *Salzburg*. The tender was on the starboard bow now. They were seen. *Salzburg*'s side erupted in flame and smoke as she opened fire. A shell fell astern and another alongside. The sea between the boats and *Salzburg* lifted in a long ragged line of water-spouts and the *slam!* of a bursting shell came from starboard. Smith spun on his heel, afraid for Pagani but his boat was still in station on the beam, bow lifted high and seen through her curtain of spray. The shell had burst on the tender, her bow had slewed towards *Salzburg* and flames roared high out of her waist.

Smith faced forward as the boats lurched and leapt through the broken water left by the salvo. *Salzburg*'s bow lay right ahead, the long length of her filling the eye, the bridge and control top towering as she steamed to pass across the course of the boats. Voss would be up there on the bridge. Smith swallowed at the size of *Salzburg* as they closed her ...

A flash lit them all, boats and *Salzburg*, leaping up to starboard with a sullen roar. Smith ignored it, his eyes fixed on the battlecruiser. Now. "*Fire!*" The torpedoman yanked the handle of the starboard torpedo and the gunner heaved on that to port. The connecting rods slid and clicked, the clamps opened like claws and the torpedoes dropped from them. They ploughed into the sea at the speed of the boat, instantly their engines burst into life and they were away.

Zacco swung the stem in a tight turn to starboard and Pagani, copying the manoeuvre, was ahead of them now. Beyond him was the tender and the flash and roars were explained; she had burst open along her length and was afire from stem to stern. Whatever she carried, petrol or oil or both had been blasted out of her so that she burned in the centre of a spreading lake of flame. The boats ran into the glare, an easy target for *Salzburg*'s guns, and Smith knew they had to get out, and quickly. "Starboard!"

Zacco nodded and held the MAS in the heeling turn through three-quarters of a circle then spun the wheel to bring it back to an even keel, heading out of the light and towards the inner harbour. Smith saw Pagani turn to follow. His boat was astern of them when the salvo howled in from *Salzburg* but when the spray fell she was gone.

Smith tore his eyes away and looked for *Salzburg*. That was when the torpedoes hit her, two hammer-blows almost simultaneously then, seconds later, a third. He saw her heel and sag. Hoarse cheering around him rose thinly above the roaring of the engines but he did not join in it. He saw Zacco's curious glance and said harshly, "Pagani was hit! Finish!"

Zacco winced, bellowed the news to his crew and the cheering stopped. Smith rubbed at his face. It felt numb and his eyes were sore. They were heading deeper into the harbour but now they had to get out. Daylight was not far off. If they tried to return the way they had come then the battleships would be ready for them this time and they would have to run a gauntlet of fire for a mile or more.

The tender was still afloat and burning in its ring of flame, a huge ring now. Smoke billowed from it, black and oily, and drifted over the surface of the harbour towards the sea. Smith thought salvation might lie that way and pointed it out to Zacco. He turned the boat again through 180 degrees to starboard and the MAS slipped down to run between the tender and *Salzburg*. The battlecruiser was down by the head and listed heavily to starboard. Smoke and steam roared from her leaning funnels, her deck was awash and the sea was full of swimming men, rafts and boats. The MAS passed them by, her crew silent; they could do nothing to help the men struggling in the sea, only pray for them.

Smith stared at *Salzburg*'s crazily tilted bridge: Voss would be up there, at his post to the bitter end. Only at the last would Voss leave his ship. He was finished here. He had come to lead the Austrians to victory but instead had lost the pride of their navy – and that inside their base. Voss would go back to Germany and the High Seas Fleet. He would live to fight another day.

Smith turned away from the sinking ship. His solitary MAS was leaving the circle of light cast by the blazing tender, and the smoke from its fire and *Salzburg* rolled down ahead of her. The smoke wisped around them, coiled, then they were into the thick of it and coughing as it got into their lungs. The machine-gunners stood ready with the Colts, one in the forward cockpit and the other close by Smith, balancing on the port side of the after cockpit at the gun on its tall mounting. Two look-outs crouched right forward in the bow. The compass said the MAS was steering parallel to the shore and heading towards the sea, but the compass might be inaccurate after the way the boat had been thrown about. She could be a quarter-mile from the shore or only a few yards. Besides, there were many other craft in this harbour, two guard-boats ahead for certain, anchored at the shoreward end of the first boom inside the moles.

They cruised steadily at fifteen knots through the smoke as it drifted and eddied. Once they emerged briefly and found themselves in the first light of day, the shore two hundred yards away to port in a thin veiling of mist, while twice that distance to starboard lay the long line of capital ships and off the starboard bow the old sailing ship. Beyond her, seen vaguely, was a destroyer lying still in the water and seemingly at anchor. Then Zacco spun the wheel and the MAS scurried back into the smoke.

Smith said, "There'll be guard-boats right ahead – and look out for the boom." Zacco called an order and the two in the bow lifted acknowledging hands. Smith thought the destroyer must be at the tail of the flotilla they had passed as they tore into the harbour, the other destroyers and the minesweepers all anchored, ahead of her, crowded up close to the sunken tug that locked them in. The MAS would have to run past them to escape. She would need all her speed, no matter what. "Full ahead!"

The note of the engines deepened, working up to twenty-five knots again as Zacco leaned forward over the wheel, coughing in the smoke, peering out of streaming eyes as he strove to pierce it. If they came on another vessel at this speed and in this visibility there would only be a second in which to react before the collision. The smoke was thinning, they burst into a pocket of open water, streaked across it and into the smoke again but it was dispersing on the wind. Only that saved them from disaster.

The rowing-boat appeared dead ahead and barely a score of yards away. Udina up in the bow yelled but Zacco had seen it, twitched the wheel to starboard and as the MAS swerved past the boat's stern Buckley shouted: "Lombardo!" Zacco spun the wheel to port and the MAS skidded around in a circle, the engine note dropping from a roar to a grumble as she straightened out and ran down again on the boat with the way coming off her.

Smith saw Balestra and Lombardo waving, then lifted his eyes to search about him. He saw the other ship as Udina in the bow called again but now softly, urgently. She was a tug at anchor, a mere couple of hundred yards away astern but visible only intermittently through the drifting smoke. She had a gun mounted forward and it was manned. Then the smoke drifted between. They had passed her unseen in the smoke but that was thinning now. Had she seen them?

Buckley said, "End o' the boom, sir." So they had almost run the gauntlet. He pointed at the boat while a seaman helped Balestra and Lombardo climb aboard the MAS. They swayed, their legs almost useless, their faces grey and drawn with exhaustion. They collapsed in the cockpit, shuffled backwards on their arms into the entrance to the engine-room so as to be out of the way and sat there, eyes lowered, glad simply to be alive.

Smith saw the boom ahead, the triple line of buoys and the connecting hawsers from which hung the nets. He waited for a ranging shot from the tug now invisible astern, but none came. They had not been seen. Then Balestra reached out to tug weakly at Smith's leg. "I heard torpedoes. Did you get her?"

Smith looked down at him and said softly, "We got her, Guido. And *Seahorse* was terrific. We saw the one you got. Congratulations."

Balestra sighed and leaned back, pillowed his head on Lombardo's shoulder and closed his eyes. Lombardo was already unconscious.

They got under way and turned towards the sea once more, passing the end of the boom and swinging to starboard now to head for the gate. They were out of the smoke and working up to full speed again. There was a thin, wisping mist that hid the gate from them still but visibility was close on half a mile. The southern mole stood clear on the port beam and there was the other guard-boat! The last of the smoke had hidden her but now they were swiftly closing her. She was another tug at anchor, her gun in the bow training around towards the MAS. They would pass at a hundred yards or less, point-blank range.

The Colt machine-guns opened up and Smith clapped his hands to his ears as the weapon hammered beside him, spent cases raining around him and clattering down into the cockpit. He saw the windows of the tug's wheelhouse punched away, splinters flying from her side. One of the men at her gun fell back and the others threw themselves down. Then the MAS was past, the machine-gunner shouldering Smith aside as he swung the gun around to train it over the stern and loose off long bursts at the receding guard-boat.

The end of the mole was in sight and there, where Smith had sunk her, were the masts of the tug poking out of the sea at the centre of the gate. Clustered inside the boom were the mine-sweepers at anchor, and beyond them, also at anchor, was the first of the destroyers with the rest of the flotilla lined out astern of her. They had either been ordered to stop there when chaos erupted in the harbour, or had anchored on their own initiative when they found the tug sunk and the gateway to the sea blocked.

Smith swallowed. One way or another it would all be over in a

243

minute. It depended on how ready the leading destroyer would be, whether she was waiting for them, how her crew handled their guns. But the MAS was a small leaping target and tearing through the sea now. He croaked at Zacco, his throat raw from shouting and the smoke, "Steer close outside the tug!" She marked the gap in the boom. The tall lieutenant nodded, his eyes fixed on the opening between the moles. He did not spare a glance for the minesweepers or the destroyer.

The MAS was exposed now in the grey light of dawn. The roar of the boat's engines signalled their presence while the spray bursting over the bow and the churned white wash astern marked their position like banners. The machine-guns had trained around, were ready. The masts of the tug were only a cable's length away and the MAS was racing towards them and the gate. North of the masts and another two hundred yards lay the minesweepers and the first destroyer. She would mask the fire of those beyond her but – A muzzle-flash flared aboard her and the Colt machine-guns of the MAS hammered.

A shell burst near the mole and another fell astern, far behind in their wake. Now they were close on the gate, the masts of the sunken tug flicked by on the starboard side and ahead was the sixty yard wide gap between the moles. There was a ripping in the air all about them from the destroyer's small calibre, quick-firing guns. A hole was punched in the turtleback of the hull right forward then there was a *slam!* and the turtleback burst open. Zacco fell back on Smith who pushed aside his crumpling body to grab at the wheel. The boat's head had swung towards the breakwater but he spun the wheel and the MAS skidded around, then shot through the gap between the moles and on to the open sea.

It was gun-metal blue with a marble streaking of whitecaps, but a quiet sea, stretching out to the mist that banked a mile or so away. Then the shell burst right under the bow which slewed away from the impact and the boat seemed to falter under him. He heard shouting from forward and saw Udina and a seaman jump from the forward cockpit and scramble up to the bow to sprawl there, hanging over.

He guessed the boat was holed forward and making water, shouted down into the engine-room, "Half ahead!" He searched for the phrase, remembered: "Avanti mezzo!" Charging ahead would swamp the boat.

The note of the engines dropped and the boat's speed fell away to around ten knots. They were clear of the moles and heading out to sea. The destroyer and the minesweepers had ceased firing, the MAS hidden now by the northern mole. For a minute they laboured seawards. The seaman had torn off his oilskins and Udina had got a line over the bow and under the hull. They were trying to rig the oilskin as a patch over the hole. It seemed they succeeded; Udina shoved up with one arm from his prone position on the deck and waved triumphantly with the other. Then the two of them scrambled back. The clank of a pump came from the engine-room and a stream of dirty water gushed over the side. So it seemed the MAS might not sink.

Balestra and Lombardo had roused themselves and were peering about, moving stiffly as they squatted by Smith's legs. Also crammed in the tiny cockpit was the conscious but white-faced Zacco and Buckley who had cut away the sleeve of the lieutenant's oilskin and the jacket beneath, and was now fastening a dressing round the bloody upper arm and shoulder. Zacco struggled to rise but Smith told him, "Be still till he's finished!" Zacco subsided. The machine-gunner balanced on the strip of deck one side of the engine-room and a seaman crouched on the other. There was no room for them in the cockpit.

Another yell from the forward cockpit, but that was the instant the shell fell in the sea a hundred yards off the starboard bow. Smith spun the wheel, turning the boat's head towards the water-spout, trying to throw the gunners off their aim. He glanced astern and saw the wink of a muzzle flash at the end of the southern mole, under Cape Compare. There was a gun or guns firing there, four-inch or smaller, possibly twelve-pounders. The heavier batteries mounted ashore had not opened up, possibly because the mist obscured their view of the target, but even twelve-pounders were quite big enough to destroy the MAS. Another shell burst far astern of them.

Udina was still yelling in the bow and now Buckley was on his feet and bawling at Smith. "Look at 'er! Ah, the bonny lass!" Then discipline asserted itself and he reported, "*Hercules*! On the bow!"

She was taking shape out of the mist and waddling down on them. Smith saw the flash and heard the crack as the six-

245

pounder in her bow fired, high over his head. She was a mile away just inside the limit of visibility in this grey and misty light but the gap between was closing at the combined speeds of drifter and MAS, about twenty knots. In two or three minutes they would meet.

Smith glanced astern again. He could still see the mole though not the shore, and the orange wink of a gun firing from under Cape Compare. And now the guns on the destroyers inside had the MAS just in sight, over the top of the mole, and were firing. He altered course again. The boat felt sluggish but she seemed little lower in the sea, the engines still growled. Pump and patch between them were holding the sea at bay. A shell fell close, and seconds later another, but the boat ran on its swerving erratic course and *Hercules* was almost on them, only three or four hundred yards away.

They were hit again forward, the shock of it shaking the little craft, sending them all staggering and grabbing for handholds. Once more Udina climbed from the forward cockpit to sprawl on the deck and peer over the side but this time the face he turned to Smith showed only despair. He had expected it, had felt the boat's head fall away, the sudden change in her under his hands. The bow was going down; the hole there must be massive. He called, "Ferma la macchina!" And as the engines stopped, "Buckley! Get 'em out!"

Hercules was closing them. Her screw stopped, thrashed briefly astern to take the way off her, then stopped again. Smith saw Fred Archbold in the wheelhouse, Menzies on her deck with a crowd of men at her side. *Hercules* slid alongside the stricken MAS and lines came flying down from her.

Udina grabbed the line forward and Smith the one aft and they hauled the boat in to slam against the timbers of *Hercules*. Smith bellowed, "Abandon her!" The order was unnecessary. The MAS was sinking, down by the bow, the cockpit filling with water that washed about Smith's feet. Davies and his crew were at the drifter's six-pounder still banging away at the mole. Zacco went up, clawing one-handed with Balestra one side of him, Lombardo on the other, and Buckley's shoulder under his rump thrusting him upward.

Udina jumped across the gap as the bow of the boat swung away from *Hercules*, hung on her side spread-eagled then scrambled inboard. The engineer and stoker crawled out of the engine-room, pushed past Smith's legs. They reeked of petrol fumes. Buckley was aboard the drifter now and leaning down with hand outstretched to Smith, shouting, "Come on, sir!"

He realised he was alone aboard the sinking MAS and his arms aching from holding the line that held her stern in close to *Hercules*. He shifted his grip higher on the line, steadied and jumped, crashed against the side of the drifter and for a split second was in the sea up to his waist. Then Buckley and the others were hauling in on the line and they brought him up on the end of it like a hooked fish.

He stood with his hands on his knees and caught his breath. *Hercules* was under way and turning. The wreck of the MAS wallowed in the drifter's wake, was left further astern and sank deeper with every second, the sea washing over her. Pola was better than a mile away now and lost in the thin mist. There was no sign of pursuit. The guns were still lobbing shells after them but they were whistling high overhead to fall far off the bow. Those guns' crews could not see the drifter, and were firing at random along the line of the last bearing. It was a million to one against them dropping a shell anywhere near *Hercules*.

Smith looked instinctively to Zacco because the sinking MAS was his boat, and saw the big man watching her, grey-faced with the pain of his wound. Smith said, "Sorry, Pietro."

Zacco grimaced, then said, "We got what we came for."

Balestra nodded. He had pushed back his rubber cap and the curls were plastered damply to his brow. His face was still blue with cold. Throughout the ship there was an easing of taut nerves. The crew of the six-pounder secured the gun, unable to bear astern as *Hercules* steamed out to sea. One of them laughed, Davies grinned. They had done it.

Smith looked away, saw Menzies' face, pale but excited and smiling, as he appeared up the forward companion. He handed Helen Blair out onto the deck, then turned away to the wheelhouse. Smith walked towards her where she stood alone. She was smiling. He remembered Balestra's pleading for her life and knew what he must do.

The flash seemed to leap from the companion. He felt himself lifted and thrown backward as the deck in front of him burst upwards and smoke rolled with it. He struck the deck with one shoulder, a jarring shock and then pain all down that side. He was conscious of thinking: million to one chance or not, they had been hit. He saw men running jerkily through a fog of smoke, dragging on the hoses, the water jetting. Buckley knelt over him, relief on his face.

He tried to get up but his left leg and arm would not obey him. Buckley protested, "Just lie still a minute, sir, till we see –"

"Help me up! Help me *up*! damn you!"

Buckley shook his head in exasperation but obeyed, set Smith on his feet and steadied him there. Life was returning to the left arm and leg. They throbbed painfully, but the leg supported him and he could move the arm. The world rocked around him and it was not through the motion of the ship though *Hercules* still steamed full ahead. He could not see forward because Zacco stood before him with Balestra at one shoulder and Davies at the other, like a wall.

Smith asked automatically, "Damage?"

Davies answered, "Cabin flat's a mess, sir, but it's no worse than that. Fire's out."

Smith could see that much, glimpsed over their shoulders the charred timbers of the deck, the smoke blown away and only wisps of it shredding now. He knew the other question he wanted to ask, but he also knew the answer.

Davies was not meeting his eye.

Zacco said, "Signore, you should rest. That was an unlikely hit. We're clear away."

Davies added, "That's right, sir. Why don't you shift aft and have a sit down outa the smoke."

"Good idea, sir." That was Buckley, his hand on Smith's arm and trying to turn him. "I'll get you a cup o' coffee in two shakes."

Smith resisted the pressure of that hand. Only Balestra met Smith's eyes and only Balestra had not spoken. Smith asked him, "The Contessa?" Balestra did not answer but the misery in his face was enough. Smith said harshly, "Get out of my way!"

That was an order and they fell back reluctantly. He walked between Zacco and Balestra towards where Helen Blair lay on the deck, the cook on his knees by her side, his first aid satchel open. Smith knelt across from him on the girl's right side. To his surprise she was not dead. Her eyes were wide open, watching him, her face very pale. The deck on which she lay was soaked dark by the water they had used on the fire, her hair had come down and was spread around her head.

Smith looked at the cook, his fat face haggard now, and asked him, "What's wrong?"

"Splinters, sir." The cook's voice was hardly more than a whisper. "Her back's wide open. I had a look but I can't do nothing no more'n a doctor nor a hospital could. Can't move her, neither." A downward look. "'Ere! She's choking!"

He moved to lift the girl's head but Smith was before him, sliding his hand under her neck and raising her, her head on his arm. The choking passed. Her eyes were on his and he said, "I was going to set you ashore."

She smiled at him. Her lips moved, but no sound came.

He went on talking to her. He would not remember afterwards anything of what he had said, but he believed it had helped. The cook went away: there was nothing he could do. The life was running out of her, Smith could feel it in the loosening weight on his arm.

When it was over he gave the necessary orders and walked aft to the wheelhouse. He told Menzies and Archbold, "You did very well. I'll make that clear in my report."

Fred Archbold did not answer. Menzies said, "I'm very sorry, sir."

Smith wondered what was wrong with the boy: he looked ready to weep. Smith told him, "Go and get something to eat. And put your cap on straight."

"Aye, aye, sir!"

He stood in the wheelhouse and looked out at the broadening horizon. For once the mist was lifting, sucked up by the sun. It was going to be a beautiful day.

Venice was in sight, the low littoral of sand and marsh a smudged line on the horizon, when the destroyer ranged alongside. She flew an Admiral's flag and that flag was Braddock's. He came aboard and Smith met him at the side, took him to the wheelhouse and briefly made his report.

Braddock, broad and black-bearded, growled bad-temperedly, "Devereux is on his way home and Pickett will follow him soon.

249

There's nothing worse than men with a misguided sense of duty, who follow it to the bitter end. Even after I confirmed your orders – do you realise the Italians believed Devereux sanctioned the attack on Trieste by *Flying-Fish* and so had no complaint? Can you credit that they were ready to keep their word to Winter and give you anything you wanted for *this* attack?" Smith shook his head and Braddock went on, "Well, they were. Destroyers, more MAS, whatever they had ... but Devereux actually told them it was considered that a small force had a better chance of success. He told me straight that he saw no sense in risking more ships and men on a hopeless gamble."

If Braddock expected anger he was disappointed. Smith shrugged. "Maybe he was right. We were lucky."

Braddock grunted, puzzled, then: "You carried out your orders to the letter. With *Salzburg* sunk the Austrians will hang all the blame on Erwin Voss and send him home. Without him they'll play the waiting game as before. That may tie-up the Italian Fleet, some of our ships and the French, but it's better than having the Austrians raising hell in the Adriatic. You've done very well."

From Braddock that was praise indeed. Smith only said flatly, "Thank you, sir." He lapsed into silence.

There was a cold wind out of the north-west from the mountains where the guns still thundered and men died in holes in the ground. He wondered briefly about the other Erwin – Rommel, the young 'Leutnant'. Perhaps by now he too was one of the dead ...

They were entering the lagoon. The crew of the guard-boat cheered them and a gun fired a salute as Venice opened before them, the campanile of San Marco standing tall in the sunlight. He could see San Elena where he had met the three MAS captains. Of those only Zacco lived.

Braddock, baffled at Smith's sombreness, said with gruff cheer, "Their Lordships of the Admiralty will be pleased."

They were passing the destroyers moored off the canal that led to the Arsenal and dockyard and they were dressed overall, the bunting streaming on the wind. Beyond them was the quay that was the Riva Ca' di Dio and at the end of it a narrow little house that seemed to stand right in the sunlit water that lapped below its empty windows.

Epilogue

In December 1917 *Leutnant* Erwin Rommel was awarded the highest honour of the *Pour le Mérite* for his actions in the battle of Caporetto.

At the beginning of this book I said all the other characters are fictitious. They are not based, in any way, on the gallant officers and men who actually carried out feats very similar to those described. I say similar because in my fictional accounts I have felt obliged to tone down the action; a bald recital of what these men actually did would strain the credulity of the reader.

Lieutenant Pellegrini in *Grillo* (the jumping-boat on which *Flying-Fish* is based) attacked the boom defences of Pola and surmounted no less than three before shell-fire wrecked the boat on the fourth and last boom.

Lieutenants Rossetti and Paolucci with *Mignatta* (on which I based *Seahorse*) penetrated the harbour defences of Pola and sank the dreadnought battleship *Viribus Unitis*.

Lieutenant Rossi in MAS 9 cut through the boom defences of Trieste and once inside torpedoed and sank the old battleship *Wien*. At a later date, in MAS 15 off Premuda, he found the Austrian Fleet on passage from Pola to Cattaro. In a dawn attack he torpedoed and sank the dreadnought battleship *Svent Istvan*, upon which the Austrian Fleet – probably suspecting a trap by larger forces – made off and returned to Pola.

If you have enjoyed this book and would like to receive
details of other Walker Adventure titles,
please write to:

Adventure Editor
Walker and Company
720 Fifth Avenue
New York, NY 10019